THE
CHAMBER

Howard Gordon has been a writer and producer working in Hollywood for more than twenty years. He is the executive producer of the hit show *24* and was also a writer and executive producer of *The X-Files*. He lives with his family in California.

Also by Howard Gordon
The Obelisk

THE
CHAMBER

HOWARD
GORDON

**SIMON &
SCHUSTER**

London · New York · Sydney · Toronto · New Delhi

A CBS COMPANY

First published in the US by Touchstone, 2012
A division of Simon & Schuster, Inc.
First published in Great Britain by Simon & Schuster UK Ltd, 2012
A CBS COMPANY

1 3 5 7 9 10 8 6 4 2

Simon & Schuster UK Ltd
1st Floor, 222 Gray's Inn Road
London
WC1X 8HB

www.simonandschuster.co.uk

Simon & Schuster Australia, Sydney
Simon & Schuster India, New Delhi

A CIP catalogue record for this book is available from the British Library.

Trade paperback ISBN: 978-0-85720-095-2
Ebook ISBN: 978-0-85720-096-9

Printed and bound by CPI Group (UK) Ltd, Croydon, CR0 4YY

For my parents, Bob and Sylvia

A top FBI counterterrorism official says the bureau's "biggest concern" is "the individual who has done the training, has the capability but is disenchanted with the [right-wing extremist] group's action—or in many cases, inaction—and decides he's going to act alone." A high-ranking Department of Homeland Security official added that "it's almost impossible to find that needle in the haystack," even if the FBI has an informant in the group.

—Time magazine, October 11, 2010

THE
CHAMBER

PROLOGUE

POCATELLO, IDAHO

Amalie Kimbo had learned long ago to keep her mouth shut.

At first, she couldn't restrain herself from telling the other children about the helpful spirits and treacherous demons whose presence only she could sense. But her mother had warned her that unless she wanted to be taken for a witch and sent away, she should swallow her thoughts. So when she arrived in the place called Idaho, she shared none of her dark premonitions with the other women. They were here to work, to earn more money in a few months than they could earn in a lifetime. But the moment Amalie stepped onto the frozen ground, she realized that coming here had been a terrible mistake.

She was born in the western Congo, in the city of Kama, and for the last five of her twenty-one years she had worked for Monsieur Nzute in the cassava factory, processing the potatolike roots into meal. The job itself was not so bad, although Mr. Nzute drank too much and would often beat her and the other girls. Or worse. Christiane Shango was Amalie's best friend, and the youngest and prettiest girl in the factory. Mr. Nzute gave her more trouble than the others. One night Christiane had crawled into Amalie's bed, her body trembling uncontrollably beneath her torn dress, a smear of blood crusted on the soft inner part of her thigh. Christiane would not say what had happened—not that first time or any of the times afterward—but Amalie did not need to be told. She understood.

So when the American who called himself Monsieur Collier offered Christiane work in his cassava factory in the United States, she had begged Amalie to come with her. A slight man who spoke with a soft voice, Monsieur Collier had said he would feed and house them, and pay them each $3,000 US for three months of work. Which meant Amalie and Christiane could return home with enough money to buy a house and start their own business, perhaps a small shop that sold cloth or pots and pans. Then Christiane would be able to pass Monsieur Nzute in the street and show him with her eyes just what she thought of him.

The work in Idaho turned out to be almost exactly the same as it had been in Kama. Amalie operated a machine that stripped the dark skin from the white, grainy flesh of the cassava. Cassavas were root vegetables that were ground into a meal that was used to make bread or cakes, although they could also be cooked and eaten like potatoes. The meal could also be processed into tapioca, the small beads that were mixed with milk and made into pudding.

Amalie's job required speed and a special skill. The skinner worked by feeding the cassava roots through two large rasps that tore the skin from the meat. Sometimes the cassavas jammed the machine and you had to reach in without letting your arm get sucked into the rasp plates. That was a mistake you only made once. The rasps would either tear off your arm, or flay the skin and muscle down to the bone.

So far Amalie had been careful. And lucky. She even began to wonder if maybe her premonition had been wrong, an echo of a harder time in a harder place. But then one morning in the middle of their third month in Idaho, Christiane collapsed—her lips bubbling with foam, her eyes rolling back in her head—and Amalie knew right away that the evil spirits had finally revealed themselves.

Amalie's arms were still slick with cassava juice as she cradled Christiane's head. Guilt rose up within her like a tide; she should have warned Christiane.

Estelle Olagun shook her head and said, "Konzo."

The other women crowded around them, nodding and clucking

their tongues. Konzo was the disease that came during the droughts, when people had little to drink, and little to eat besides cassavas. Some people said there was something in the cassavas that poisoned you, but Amalie knew that Konzo, like all diseases, was only one of the many ways demons worked their evil on people.

"Monsieur Collier will have medicine," Estelle said. "I will call him."

"No," Amalie said. "I will help her. Help me carry Christiane back to her bunk."

"Help her how? Do you have medicines like Monsieur Collier?"

"I can help her fight the evil spirits."

"Evil spirits, evil spirits, you with your evil spirits," Estelle said, scowling. "You'll go to hell, talking like that." Estelle had joined a holy roller church a few years ago and was always talking about people going to hell.

"I know what I know," Amalie said. "Let me try before you call him."

Ignoring Amalie, Estelle picked up the phone. Because she was the oldest among them, Estelle had assumed a kind of maternal authority over the other women, and Amalie could find no ally in her appeal.

After a few minutes Monsieur Collier appeared, stamping his feet and brushing snow from his coat. "*Qu'est-ce qui s'est passé?*" he said in his oddly accented French. The women stepped aside like a parting curtain, revealing the prone Christiane, her small breasts rising and falling with each shallow breath.

Collier pressed his palm against the young girl's forehead, which was beaded with perspiration. "Konzo," he said sympathetically.

"But you can help her, yes?" Estelle was kneading her hands like unbaked loaves.

Monsieur Collier looked at Estelle. He seemed to be making up his mind about something before he finally nodded. "She'll be fine. But I'll need to take her to the hospital."

"No!" The word leapt from Amalie's mouth before she could stop it.

"What is wrong with you, girl?" Estelle snapped her fingers at one of the other women. "Help me get her up."

Amalie followed helplessly as two of the other women lifted Christiane and carried her out into the cold. Around them the trees creaked and groaned, their branches weighted with snow. Somewhere in the forest a limb splintered loudly, and fell to the ground.

Monsieur Collier opened the door to his pickup truck. Monsieur Nzute would never have opened a door for a woman—certainly not for one of his workers. But Amalie knew that Monsieur Collier's gesture of concern was empty. Behind his polite mask lurked the *Mbwiri,* a demon who possesses people and causes them to thrash around and spew foam. Sometimes the *Mbwiri* even forced its host to eat human flesh and perform shameful sexual acts.

Amalie felt the warmth of the truck as the women slid Christiane inside. Monsieur Collier buckled the safety belt around Christiane, taking just a little too long in straightening her clothes as they bunched around the belt. The sight of his revolting pale skin against Christiane's lovely dark flesh made her shiver. *Please, God, tell me what to do,* she prayed. But God sent no answer.

"Go back to work," Monsieur Collier said over his shoulder, his thin lips exposing a set of small, crooked teeth.

The other women started back to the factory as he drove off, but Amalie stood in the cold, watching the truck disappear, certain that she would never again see her friend Christiane. Only the leafless trees understood the truth of what was happening, their tiny green needles hissing in the wind like a thousand snakes.

Dale Wilmot still could not find the right words. Although he'd written dozens of speeches, business plans, and corporate mission statements over the years, nothing had ever been as hard for him to write as this. It was a letter to his son. Part of Wilmot's indecision came from knowing his words would eventually find a much wider audience than Evan. They would be disseminated by the media, scrutinized by law enforcement agencies, and ultimately, judged by history. Was it arrogance to compare this document to the Declaration of Independence or the Gettysburg Address? After all, it was more than just one man's attempt to explain himself to his son; it was a call to action intended to wake the American people from the stupor of complacency that had enslaved them for so many years. And for that, he was willing to give up everything, including his own life.

He sighed and turned away from the blank computer screen. On the nearest wall of his mahogany-paneled study hung photographs of himself shaking hands with presidents and prime ministers, playing golf with quarterbacks and corporate titans. The photographs showed a man of great confidence. Beneath the thick head of hair and above the square jaw, his quick grin told you this was someone who not only moved comfortably among the rich and powerful, but who could just as easily ride a horse, rewire a breaker box, and shoot a Winchester rifle. Over the years he had amassed a small fortune through timber interests, heating and air-conditioning, and trucking. He was a big man, with big hands, and the impression he left was of a man used to giving orders.

But Dale Wilmot no longer recognized the man in the photographs. The fire of optimism that once animated his eyes had dimmed over time, until it had finally been extinguished, replaced by a cold, singular determination. He had become a stranger to himself. And the photographs that once inspired feelings of patriotism now mocked him, staring down at him as a reminder never again to trust the hollow words of other men.

Anger had always fueled Wilmot, whether on the gridiron or in the boardroom. And so it was with this. Into the rich soil of his anger, the seeds of a plan had been sewn twenty-one months ago, when Evan, his first and only child, had returned from war.

He remembered walking down the echoing corridors of Walter Reed, past a room where young men with wrecked bodies sat like zombies before a droning television. He remembered being met by Major General William D. Bradshaw, who solemnly ushered him into his office. When you were Dale Wilmot, news of any kind—good or bad—was always delivered by the most important man in the building. But Wilmot preempted the general before he could get out a word. "Where's my son?"

Bradshaw put on a face intended to express regret and said, "Mr. Wilmot, we've made tremendous strides in our ability to treat our wounded warriors and help them transition—"

"Take me to my son. And don't make me ask you again."

Wilmot's hands balled into fists at his side. They reminded Bradshaw of sledgehammers. "This way, sir," Bradshaw said, leading him from his office down a short hallway to the elevator bay. They rode down together in silence to a subterranean floor, where they followed a sign directing them to the burn unit.

The shrunken grotesque patient Wilmot saw sleeping inside the transparent oxygen tent bore no resemblance to his son. His thicket of short sandy hair was gone, replaced by a motley skullcap of scar tissue. His once-handsome features were denuded, as if his lips and his nose had been melted into blunt shapes. The bandaged remains of his legs terminated just below his knees, and his right arm extended only as far as his elbow. His left arm remained intact, although a patchwork of frag wounds and burns were visible through the clear antibacterial bandage.

A ringing phone pulled Wilmot from his memory. The sharp smell of hospital disinfectant and urine lingered in his nostrils as he put down his pen and picked up the receiver.

"What is it?" Wilmot said.

Collier's soft voice answered. "We've got a problem, sir."

A few minutes later Wilmot pulled up to his horse barn in his Jeep Wrangler, parking beside Collier's F-150. After Evan enlisted in the army, Wilmot had sold all the horses, and now the barn and the adjacent hayloft stood empty.

Wilmot entered the frigid barn. The stalls had been swept clean, but inside one of them Collier was standing over one of the young women he had brought over from Africa. She was lying on a thin, rust-stained mattress atop an army cot. Her eyes were large but rheumy, and now rolled toward Wilmot, silently appealing to him for help. He found himself distracted by her beauty until Collier spoke. "Konzo," he said.

When he first presented the plan, Collier had warned Wilmot that this might happen. He'd explained that in the Congolese factories, the hydrogen cyanide contained in the cassavas presented a workplace hazard even more dangerous than the machinery itself.

Collier had said they could avoid toxic exposure among the women by limiting and rotating their shifts, but he'd clearly miscalculated. Wilmot tried keeping the irritation from his voice. "Will she die?"

Collier nodded. "Paralysis usually sets in after the initial seizures, resulting in respiratory failure." Collier hesitated a moment before he continued. "But, sir, we can't risk taking her to a doctor."

"You think I don't know that?" Of course Wilmot knew they couldn't bring the girl to a hospital or even bring a doctor to her. Because she had cyanide poisoning the doctor would be compelled by law to report the case to some public health service, not to mention the immigration authorities. Their only choice was whether to let her die a painful protracted death or to end her suffering themselves.

"I'll handle it," Collier said.

Wilmot heard in Collier's voice more than a simple willingness to carry out this unpleasant but necessary act; he was eager to do it. Collier had grown up on Wilmot's ranch, where his mother worked as a housekeeper. When he was in his early teens, a stable hand found a dog in the woods that had been dismembered and disemboweled. Six months later, a fawn was discovered hanging from a tree, suspended by a grappling hook. Even back then, Wilmot had suspected Collier of committing those atrocities. Now, the predatory darkness in the young man's eyes only confirmed Wilmot's earlier suspicions.

"*No.*"

Collier blinked, surprised by Wilmot's sharp tone.

"I'll do it myself," Wilmot said, his voice softer this time. Dale Wilmot had always prided himself on identifying what needed to be done and getting it done as efficiently and dispassionately as possible. To set an example, he had once broken the jaw of a backtalking employee who was subsequently too frightened to file a lawsuit. To save his platoon, he had killed a dozen Viet Cong. And now he would spare the young woman lying before him the unnecessary indignity of dying at the hands of a sadist.

He leaned close to the girl's face. Her warm breath smelled of bitter almonds, the telltale symptom of cyanide poisoning. "I'm sorry, darling," he said softly. "Truly, I am."

In a quick and decisive movement, he pinched her nostrils shut with his thumb and forefinger, and clamped the rest of his hand over her mouth and chin, covering the lower half of her face like a muzzle. Her eyes widened, and she began to buck and writhe. Wilmot pressed her to the mattress with his left arm. She was surprisingly strong, her body fighting through the cyanide-induced weakness in a desperate attempt to preserve itself. He pressed down harder, pinning her pubic bone to the mattress with his massive forearm.

He was not insensitive to the sexual aspect of the moment, the girl's breasts moving beneath her thin dress, her warm hips bucking beneath his strong arms. Christiane's resistance, however, soon gave way to resignation, until her eyes stared emptily at the ceiling.

Wilmot removed his hand from her face. Then, tenderly, he lowered her eyelids and straightened her wrinkled dress. "I want her given a proper burial," he said without looking at Collier. "Ground's frozen solid. You'll need a pick." And with that, he left the barn.

1

GEORGETOWN UNIVERSITY

Gideon Davis scrutinized the Windsor knot in his yellow tie in his rearview mirror as he waited for the stoplight to change. It had been eight years since he was last in front of a classroom, and tying a knot was just one of the skills he had lost. Now, as he fiddled with it in the mirror, he missed his days as a diplomat and presidential adviser, where he'd conducted his business in rolled-up shirtsleeves. At least his tuxedo had come with a clip-on bow tie.

The light turned green, and Gideon turned right off the bridge that connected Virginia to Washington, DC. The Mortara Center for International Studies was located in a tony section of Georgetown with rows of town houses and its fair share of diplomats and politicians sprinkled among the students and faculty. Gideon loved the energy of the area, the youthfulness of the residents, and the international flavor of the restaurants and shops. But it lacked the green lawns and space he wanted for the family he was planning to start with his fiancée, Kate Murphy.

Eighteen months ago he never would have imagined buying a Federal-style home in Alexandria, Virginia. But that was before a group of terrorists allegedly led by Gideon's brother, Tillman, had seized Kate's oil rig, the Obelisk, a state-of-the-art platform in the South China Sea. If not for Gideon's intervention, the terrorists would certainly have destroyed the rig and, with it, the truth of

Tillman's innocence. Coming home to the United States, however, had proved more complicated for both Gideon and Tillman. Because Tillman's long service as a covert operative had involved some rule bending, coupled with maintaining the plausible deniability of his superiors, he had worked without a net. For his efforts to keep America secure, he was prosecuted for "providing material assistance to enemies of the state" and sentenced to serve twenty years at the federal supermax prison in Florence, Colorado. As far as Gideon was concerned, his brother was taking the fall for a group of spineless bureaucrats. Gideon lobbied fiercely for his release and successfully petitioned the departing president to pardon Tillman. The pardon, however, ignited a firestorm of criticism, and the incoming president, Erik Wade, forced Gideon to resign from the State Department.

As bitter as he felt about the Obelisk affair, it was behind him now. Plus, he had come away from it with the woman who stood by his side during the ordeal and with whom he planned to spend the rest of his life. Kate Murphy was the loveliest woman Gideon had ever met, with auburn hair and hazel eyes that sometimes looked gray, sometimes green, depending on her mood. After nearly a decade of international troubleshooting, Gideon was ready to settle down. It was his good fortune that Kate agreed to have him.

When he pulled into the parking space reserved for him near the school, however, he wasn't thinking about the Obelisk. Instead he was wondering about the lime-green Impala that he had noticed in his mirror, and that was now sticking to his rear. Maybe it was just paranoia, but the car seemed to slow when he did and made every turn behind him when they came off the bridge together.

He locked the Land Rover and walked down Thirty-seventh Street. At an alley he used as a shortcut to get to the school, he turned right. In his peripheral vision he could feel someone tracking his movement. He walked calmly, without rushing, until he came to the rear door of a deli where he usually bought his lunch. He ducked into the doorway and waited.

Within twenty seconds a wiry white guy approached carrying a small paper cup. His head swiveled constantly, as if scanning the area for an ambush. He wore a khaki photographer's vest, khaki cargo pants that flapped around his emaciated legs, a black T-shirt and wraparound shades that gave him a vaguely military look. Gideon recognized the telltale signs of his addiction: methamphetamine. His gaunt face was ravaged, with a large angry sore festering on one cheekbone. As he passed, Gideon spotted the lump under his left arm. It had to be a pretty large piece—a .357 or maybe even a .44.

Gideon stepped from his hiding place and put the guy in a guillotine headlock. He regretted his actions immediately. A sour smell came off the man's body, like some kind of chemistry experiment gone wrong, and the tobacco-stained saliva in the Dixie cup spilled onto Gideon's shoe.

"What the fuck," the man spewed.

Gideon quickly disarmed the man of the gun—a .357, he noted—unloaded it, then stuffed it back in the man's shoulder holster. "What the fuck yourself," he said. "Why are you following me?"

"I just want to talk to you."

The man wriggled in Gideon's grip like a hooked fish. Gideon released him, and the man skittered backward and nearly tumbled into a passing student.

"I'm not an idiot," said the man. "I know I don't look right, but I've got information worth a lot to somebody."

Gideon looked at his watch. His class started in ten minutes. "Information about what?"

When the man didn't answer right away, Gideon shook his head and started past him.

"An attack on US soil. A high-value target."

Gideon blinked, absorbing the tweaker's claim. Then he turned around and faced the man.

"The people I'm dealing with? They're talking mass casualties and they do not fool around. But before I tell you anything else, I want a hundred thousand dollars, cash American."

"You've got the wrong guy," said Gideon. "I don't make deals in alleys with tweakers. If you've got that kind of information, talk to the FBI."

"The FBI," the man said disdainfully. "Bunch of backstabbing bureaucrats. I can't trust them."

"But you can trust me?"

"You think it's an accident I'm coming to you?" A sneer of arrogance curled his lip. "You're the Man of Peace shithead."

As special envoy to former President Alton Diggs, Gideon had sometimes been referred to in the media as the Man of Peace, a moniker he had grown to hate.

"I can't speak to the shithead part—"

"I read on the Internet you terminated twenty hostiles during that oil-rig operation. Man of Peace. There's some real irony for you, don't you think?"

Although the man's words oozed bravado, his body language betrayed fear. The trembling hands, the constant scanning of the horizon, the nervous twitch in his cheek. He was definitely a meth tweaker, and paranoia was a symptom of his addiction.

"I still don't understand why you're coming to me," Gideon said.

"Your politics may be misguided, but you seem like someone I can trust to do the right thing. After the way the government treated you, you could've gone underground, but you're here, preaching the gospel to our youth. You are a true patriot."

The way the man said it, it didn't sound like a good thing. But it was true that even though the president had abruptly dismissed him from public service, Gideon remained dedicated to his country. Maybe he was naïve, but he believed certain principles were worth fighting for: truth, justice, democracy. The country had its problems, but he was not one to sit idly by and watch them fester.

"Who are you?" he asked.

"Ervin Mixon." He cleared his throat and spat yellow phlegm on the pavement. "I like to think of myself as a freelance constitutionalist. Not some geek in an ivory tower, I mean hands-on. Second Amendment says 'the right of the people to keep and bear arms shall not be abridged.' Simple phrase. Doesn't say 'the right of the people to keep and bear revolvers shall not be abridged.' Doesn't say 'the right of the people to keep and bear guns-that-only-shoot-once-when-you-pull-the-trigger shall not be abridged.' Plain, simple English words. An individual wants to protect his home and hearth with a suppressed full-auto MP-5 submachine gun, that's his constitutional right. I back up my beliefs by supplying like-minded individuals with specialty items that you can't procure at your local gun shop.

"One of my customers is a guy named Verhoven—Colonel Jim Verhoven. Lives off the grid on a big piece of land way up in West Virginia." Gideon was somewhat familiar with the area; it was where his brother Tillman had settled since his release from prison. Mixon continued, "Verhoven's got a handful of followers in his militia, some of them bivouac on his property in trailers or campers. Most of these militia guys and Nazis and whatnot talk a lot of smack, but at the end of the day they're not interested in getting downrange in any serious capacity. But one night I was there about a month ago, and I overheard Verhoven's side of a phone conversation . . ."

He hesitated for a moment—his eyes sliding reflexively to his left. In his work as a negotiator, Gideon had become fairly expert at assessing whether people were lying to him and to one another. One of the simplest indicators or "tells" was the direction a person's eyes went after making a statement. A look to their right generally means someone is constructing an image or a sound—in other words, lying—while a look to their left generally means they are remembering something that actually happened. Of course, it wasn't foolproof, and for left-handed people, the direction was sometimes reversed. But Mixon's gun was holstered for a right-handed person, and he had looked left before he resumed his story. "I'm not talking about the usual saber-rattling bullshit. He sounded serious."

"Meaning what?" Gideon said. "What did you hear?"

"Some very specific operational details."

"Go on."

"See, we're fast approaching the juncture where I need more than just good wishes."

"Back up a minute," Gideon said. "Because there's something I don't understand. You have a long-standing and profitable relationship with this guy Verhoven. So why are you ratting him out?"

Mixon's mouth twisted bitterly. "I have some very pressing and assertive financial needs. Whatever I'm making from my business with Verhoven isn't enough to cover that."

"A hundred grand is a deep hole," Gideon said.

"Look at me. I know what I am. I've been a stone-cold crystal meth addict for ten years. Only reason I've made it this long is because I use top-grade pharmaceutical-quality crystal. You think they give that shit away? So yeah, I'm always fishing for some extra income. I knew Verhoven was up to something that wasn't just queer bashing. So I came prepared. And guess what? I caught Moby god-damn Dick."

"What's Verhoven planning to do? Set off a nuke in Dupont Circle?" Gideon was testing him, seeing if he'd overreach and make a ridiculous claim.

"Do I look like a fool? Where would a bunch of redneck militia guys get a nuke? But this is not some lone gunman trying to sneak a Glock into a campaign rally in Pittsburgh because his wife doesn't love him anymore. This is an organized conspiracy of very serious operators. And if you don't get on them double-quick, they're going to execute their mission."

"And you expect me to call some people and tell them to trust the story of a desperate tweaker?"

"No. That's why I've got proof."

"Proof?"

"A recording of Verhoven's side of the conversation. Part of it anyway."

"Let's hear it."

Mixon let out a wheezy rattling sound that was meant to be a laugh. "Not until I see some cash."

Now Gideon was going to be late. But there was something about Mixon and his story that had the ring of truth.

"How did you record it?"

"Zoom H4."

"What kind of mic?"

"Ergil 37D. Wireless."

Gideon was trying to trip him up, to get him to reveal some sign of improvisation—looking up in the air while he was think-ing, changing his story in midstream, odd facial expressions, inap-propriate smiling or anything of that nature. But if Ervin had a tell, Gideon hadn't spotted it yet. In fact, the informant didn't miss a beat as he went on to describe in great detail how he'd recorded Verhoven's conversation.

"And what did he say?"

Mixon looked around furtively, then pulled a digital recorder from his jacket pocket. "This is just a snippet, understand? If the US government wants to hear the whole tape, they're going to have to pay for that privilege." Mixon pressed a button, and the recording began to play. It was scratchy, recorded from some distant microphone, but the words were audible enough.

"Yeah." The man's voice was presumably Verhoven's. *"We have the target isolated and surveillance established . . . We'll wait for your instructions."* The recording stopped, and Mixon looked up at Gideon expectantly.

Although he didn't realize it at first, Gideon had felt that old excitement rising up inside him as he listened to the recording. But this was not his fight, and not his job anymore. His new career was waiting for him about four hundred yards away, and it wouldn't wait forever. And Gideon knew he'd gotten from Mixon all that he was willing to share.

"I can make a call," said Gideon. "Someone in the FBI I can trust."

"One person. Any more, and I'm gone."

Mixon handed Gideon a scrap of paper. "This is where I'm staying. There's a shopping mall about a mile down the road. Meet me there at six."

"I'll be there."

"Good," said the tweaker. "Your country is counting on you."

2

McLEAN, VIRGINIA

E rvin Mixon was terrified. As he steered his Impala out of the parking lot he couldn't get his right foot to stop jiggling.

Ten years ago he had been a pretty normal guy. Married, three kids, decent job as partner in a gun store down in Tennessee. Then he'd met crystal meth and it all went into the shitter.

There had been several points where he could have turned it around. Say, for instance, the day he decided to steal $41,000 from Ronnie Revis Jr., his partner at AAA Gun 'n' Pawn back in Tulla-homa. If he'd just bit the bullet and cleaned up instead, everything would have been different. Or maybe the first time he sold a bootleg full-auto SKS to David Allen Kring, the grand dragon of the Idaho KKK. Or maybe the time he sold six cases of MP5s to the Baltimore chapter of the Pagans Motorcycle Club, one case of which was real, and five cases of which were Taiwanese airsoft guns with the Day-Glo orange caps cut off the end of the barrels. That, in particular, had been a major mistake, one that had in turn forced him make certain promises to Jim Verhoven that he was not going to be able to keep.

Mixon swung onto the Jeff Davis Parkway and headed south, paralleling the Potomac, checking constantly in his rearview. Every time he saw a Harley, he about had a fucking heart attack, thinking he was about to get iced by the Outlaws or some other biker gang.

Driving through McLean, he noticed that there was nothing but colored people on the streets. Never been so glad in his life to see spooks. At least if a guy was black, you knew he wasn't some biker or some inbred militia asshole from West Virginia, ready to terminate your shit.

A 360-degree battlefield. That's what he was living in. The threats could come from anywhere.

He checked his rearview for the millionth time. What about that van? Hadn't he seen that before? A white van with a bunch of ladders on top. Christ, America was so jam-packed with vans full of Mexicans, you couldn't tell one from the next. At least he'd never fucked over the Mexican mafia. Those sumbitches played for keeps.

If he could just do this thing with Gideon Davis, get paid, he would clean up and start living right again. He'd said that after he scammed the Outlaws for fifty K, too. But then the money had all disappeared into a pipe, and before he could do anything to stop himself he was jonesing again.

This time things would be different, though. This time he'd get clean. Definitely, this time.

He looked at his watch. Davis had said he would meet him tonight. *The bastard had better come through,* Mixon thought as he steered into the parking lot of his motel, the transmission bottoming out as he bumped over a pothole and settled into a parking space between two Dumpsters.

As cautious as Mixon was, though, he failed to see the Dodge Ram pickup with heavily tinted windows parked on the shoulder of Dolley Madison Road.

Behind the wheel sat Colonel James C. Verhoven, self-appointed commanding officer of the Seventh West Virginia (True) Militia. Nestled in his lap, concealed beneath a camo-colored Snuggie given to him by his beloved wife, Lorene, was a Rock River Arms AR-15 with a collapsible stock, quad Pickatinny rail fore grip mounting a green laser, a 230 lumen flashlight, and an Aimpoint red-dot scope. On his hip he carried his pride and joy, a Les Baer 1911 with a hard chrome finish, Novak ramp sights, and mother of pearl grips, running 230 grain Hornady jacketed hollow-points. He also wore a backup gun on his ankle—the old standby, a compact titanium

J-Frame Smith .38 with Crimson Trace laser grips, loaded with 129 grain + P Federal Hydra-Shoks. Plus, of course, a little CRKT neck knife hanging by a piece of paracord under his shirt.

Verhoven's eyes narrowed as Mixon's Impala turned into the motel. He waited until Mixon had parked before easing into the far end of the Word Up Lodge parking lot. Unit two—Lorene and the Upshaw brothers—pulled up beside him in a white Ford Econoline van with CRUZ PAINTING & DRYWALL painted on the side and a bunch of ladders piled on top.

Verhoven gave the signal, then hopped out and strode across the parking lot, hands on the AR-15, followed by the Upshaw brothers. As Mixon climbed out of his car, Verhoven pointed his trigger finger at the yellow stripe peeking out from under one of the Impala's half-bald tires and said, "So I guess you never graduated from parking school, huh?"

The subject looked blankly at the yellow stripe, blinked once, then looked up at Verhoven and said, "Oh, shit."

Four seconds later, there were flex cuffs on his wrists and a sock in his mouth as he was dragged into the van, his feet kicking wildly. Verhoven saw the fear in Mixon's eyes as he slammed the door shut, and the ruckus was over.

Two black men stood on the balustrade drinking out of paper bags and looking down curiously into the parking lot.

Verhoven and his men were all wearing CamelBak load-bearing vests, black combat boots, and black BDUs with Velcro patches on the shoulders that read POLICE in bold yellow letters. The two men were not likely to question the ruse. But, still, there was no point in encouraging anyone to pay excessive attention to the colonel's team.

"Police business!" Verhoven shouted. "Get your black asses back inside your room."

The men muttered angrily to each other but didn't move.

Before Verhoven could say anything else, the driver erupted from the fake painting van. She was a very tall, fit-looking woman with bleached blond hair, wearing an AR on a single-point sling. She had a wide smile on her face as she pointed her AR at the young men on the balcony. "Please," she shouted, "just give me an excuse to shoot."

"I got it, Lorene," Verhoven said softly to his wife. He had known her to go beyond what tactical necessity strictly dictated, sometimes leaving a bloody mess in her wake like a trail of chum.

His wife's smile hardened as she continued to stare down the young men. She had one eye that was brown and another blue—a condition known as "heterochromia"—and it only added to the impression that she was a woman not playing with all her marbles. The two young men on the balcony saw the look in her eyes and quickly hustled back into their hotel room.

Lorene watched them go. The charge of the hunt left her twitchy and eager. She turned back to the van, her fingers itching, frustration giving way to anticipation of the violence she had planned for Ervin Mixon.

3

POCATELLO, IDAHO

Dale Wilmot heard a thump and a grunt of pain coming from the third floor. His heart began to race.

"Son of a bitch!" he muttered and sprinted up the flight of stairs to Evan's room.

Without knocking, he burst into his son's room, expecting the worst.

Looking through the bedroom, he saw the door to the bathroom was open. Evan lay on the tiled floor. He'd obviously been trying to maneuver himself into the shower and had fallen from his water-slick wheelchair. The shower continued to spray while water backed up on the floor. Wilmot hadn't seen his son naked in a while, and the vision was horrifying. The network of scars covered much of what was left of his body. On top of that, he'd cut himself over the eye in the fall, and a steady stream of blood ran down the side of his face.

Evan Wilmot had been blown up by an IED in Mosul and then badly burned when the troop carrier in which he was riding had burst into flame. The medic at the scene said he wouldn't be able to survive his wounds and had decided to stop pushing transfusions. But the company commander threatened to court-martial the corpsman and said, "As long as this kid's still fighting, you're putting blood into his arm." They'd called for volunteers and kept pumping blood, going straight from the veins of other soldiers into Evan's arm, a hundred boys lined up around the shed where the corpsman was treating him. It had taken fifty units before Evan's blood had started coagulating enough to stabilize him.

He'd been unconscious for a week, waking up finally at Ramstein Air Base.

Wilmot was tempted to shout at the boy for being so bullheaded and foolish as to try taking a shower unattended. But he couldn't bring himself to do it.

"It's okay, son," he said gently. "Here, let me help."

Evan's startling blue eyes rolled up toward his father. He didn't answer, just grabbed hold of the wet seat of his wheelchair with his claw of a hand and attempted to pull himself up. Wilmot ran forward to grab him, splashing through the water on the floor.

Evan waved him away, but Wilmot couldn't watch the boy do this to himself.

Wilmot had spared no expense on the bathroom. It cost over $120,000. Remote control on/off and temp controls for the huge wheelchair-accessible shower. A motorized harness hanging from tracks on the ceiling so he could be hoisted into the shower or onto the toilet. A wall-size forced-air blow-dryer so he didn't have to wrestle with a towel. Wheelchair-accessible toilet with built-in bidet, wheelchair-accessible sink, special faucets custom made at the Kohler plant in Sheboygan, Wisconsin.

And that wasn't all. There was an attendant in the house fourteen hours a day. A nurse practitioner came every morning and stayed for the day. Then in the evenings John Collier came for a few hours, helping him wash and go to the toilet, reading to him or just hanging out.

But Evan had to do it the hard way, trying to drag himself to the shower using the wheelchair for support.

Wilmot lowered his voice. "Evan. I'm here. Let me help."

Evan's jaw clamped shut and his eyes flashed at Wilmot. But he didn't say anything. The doctors said Evan hadn't lost any of his cognitive abilities. But sometimes it was hard to tell. Wilmot grabbed him under the armpits.

By the time he got his son back in the chair, he was sopping wet, and Evan's blood had spattered onto his pants. He reached over, grabbed the towel that had fallen into the bath and blocked the drain, and pulled it free. Then he found a fresh towel and dried Evan off.

"'S fine, Dad. 'S fine." Most people wouldn't have been able to make out the slurred sibilance of Evan's words. But Wilmot had gotten used to his son's speech by now.

"Let me get you something for that cut," Wilmot said, dabbing at the wound with another towel. "You really don't want another infection."

"Can I just. . . ." A helpless rage twisted the melted features of the boy's face. Moisture and blood streamed down his cheeks. He might have been crying—though it was hard for Wilmot to tell.

"I'm sorry, son," Wilmot said. "I'm so sorry."

Then the anger seemed to drain out of Evan's body. His muscles softened and the contorted expression dissolved. He relaxed into the chair and looked away from his father in resignation.

Wilmot set his phone and his watch on the sink, then pushed his son back into the spray of the shower. There was something pleasurable about stepping into the stream of water fully clothed, a little transgression against normalcy. As Wilmot poured a dollop of antibacterial soap on the washrag and began running it across his son's body—the folds of calloused skin around his amputations, the scarred mask of his face, even the crack of his ass—his mind drifted back to the first time he'd held his son. Wilmot's wife, Claire, had been very sick during the pregnancy—a sickness they didn't realize until later was the beginning of the progressive disease that eventually killed her—and Evan was born premature. But when Wilmot held the tiny red body of his only son, it had been as though the entire world had telescoped away. All that mattered to him was right there in his arms. At the time the helplessness of the boy had made Wilmot feel more hopeful and serene than anything he'd ever experienced.

By then, Wilmot was already a wealthy man, and there was nothing he didn't give to Evan. Good genes, wealth, a big house, a healthy rural environment, an endless supply of baseballs, all the food he could eat, all the books he could read. And love—the one thing Wilmot's own son of a bitch of a father had never once provided. Wilmot had given that to his son, too.

But he hadn't spoiled him either. A couple of luxuries here and there, sure. What was the point of being worth several hundred million dollars if you couldn't give your kid a horse on his eighteenth birthday? But he'd never let the boy think he rated anything just because of who his father was. If Evan wanted his three-dollar-a-week allowance, he had to do his chores, keep his bed made, pick up his room, fill the dishwasher, do his homework. You proved yourself every day. That was what Wilmot believed, and he lived by that code.

And Evan had never disappointed. Captain of the baseball team, president of the senior class, raised money for poor families at Christmas, valedictorian. Tall, handsome—Christ, what a boy he'd been!

There had been a time after Evan returned when Wilmot blamed his son for his own misfortunes. He had gone to Iraq against Wilmot's express wishes, joining the military a year before he should have graduated from Harvard. Wilmot had been so angry that they had not talked for nearly a year. He had been against the war from the beginning, seeing it as more overreaching by a government that couldn't even handle its problems at home. But Wilmot had come to realize it wasn't his son's fault. It was those bastards, those parasites, those pieces of shit in Washington, grinding up American boys—barely more than children—for some misguided principle or thinly masked greed. But soon the bastards would pay.

His mounting rage was interrupted by Collier. "Mr. Wilmot." He was standing in the doorway, looking at him with a curious expression on his face as he took in his boss's soaked clothing.

"John," Wilmot said, with every ounce of self-control he could muster, "can't you see that we have a situation here?"

"So do *we*," Collier said.

"And it can't wait until my son finishes his shower?"

Collier met Wilmot's eyes but said nothing.

"Hang on, son," Wilmot said, buckling Evan into his chair. "Will you be okay by yourself for a minute?"

Evan nodded.

Wilmot grabbed a towel and walked out of Evan's room, drying himself as he walked.

"What is it, John?" he said.

Collier frowned. "Our guy Verhoven in West Virginia. One of his people is trying to sell information to the Feds."

Wilmot swore. "How would one of his people know anything? Verhoven wasn't supposed to say shit to any of those morons of his."

"It's not one of his militia kids. It's a gun dealer who hangs out with them. I've met him a couple times. Shifty little prick. He's a meth head, half his teeth missing, smells like a chemical toilet. But he's former military and not an idiot."

"Tell Verhoven to pick the son of a bitch up and find out what he knows."

"He's already doing that."

"He better find out every goddamn scrap of information this guy's got. He needs to find out exactly what he said and who he said it to."

Collier nodded. "I'll make sure he's doing the right thing."

"We're at a point where we can't afford any loose ends. Tell Verhoven once he finds out what this guy knows, he needs to get rid of him. Make it look like an overdose."

"Understood."

After Evan finished showering, his cheerless nurse, Margie Clete, toweled him off as he lay on his bed. She was a large woman, nearly six feet, with no waist, thick forearms, and large breasts, which she controlled with a brassiere that showed through her overly tight uniform like the girders of a postmodern building. Evan's father had once said of her that she had a face like a canned ham. Margie scolded him for not calling for help in the shower. Even after nearly two years of being tended to in his most intimate bodily functions, Evan still felt a wave of shame at being forced to rely on a middle-aged woman just to get dried off.

But finally it was over and Evan was left alone in his room. He lay in his bed in his clean dry clothes and reached under the mattress for his secret bottle of pills. He popped the cap off and dumped a couple of oxycodone on the blanket next to him.

What the hell had his father been talking to John about in the hallway? They'd been having these secretive, whispered conversations for months now. Evan had turned off the shower in hopes of eavesdropping on them—but hadn't been able to pick up anything.

What few words he could hear seemed to come out of a tunnel, one word disconnected from the next. Evan knew he was in a fuzzy, stupefied state. Despite his father's watchful eye, Evan had been taking double the drugs the doctors prescribed for him. The weekend nursing assistant had a connection in Couer d'Alene who could get you anything you wanted—oxy, Nembutal, Dilaudid, whatever. But even doped to the gills, Evan knew this much: His father was not a whisperer or a conspirer by nature. He was a big man with a big voice and a big personality, the kind of guy who liked standing up in front of people and barking out commands in a loud voice.

It surprised him the first time he'd heard John Collier's voice in his home. Evan was sure at some level John hated him. They had known each other since they were kids, and had a complicated history to say the least. Now John was back in Idaho, working part-time as Evan's caretaker and spending a lot of time with his father. Something odd was going on, but Evan was damned if he knew what it was.

He stared sourly at the pills on the bedspread. *Screw it,* he thought. Maybe he'd skip the pills, see how he felt. Slowly, painstakingly, he picked up each pill with his two working fingers and dropped them back in the pill bottle. For the first time in a long time he actually felt curious about something. Curious and a little concerned. But if he was going to give the matter some thought, he'd need to be clearer in his head.

When he finally got the pills into the bottle, he lay back and watched the television on the far wall. He could feel the pain coming toward him, slowly, sinuously, like a big hungry snake. Evan smiled. *Come on, motherfucker,* he thought. *Let's see what you've got.*

4

McLEAN, VIRGINIA

He's late," said FBI agent Nancy Clement, looking at her watch. "He'll be here."

They were waiting in Nancy's car, a government-issued black GMC Tahoe, at a shopping mall about a mile from Mixon's hotel. Mixon had chosen such a public place because, he said, it would make an ambush more difficult. Given Mixon's competence tailing his car, Gideon questioned his countersurveillance abilities, but the mall was anonymous enough and would be just a short ride home in time for dinner.

Washington's horrific rush hour had crept up on them, and drivers used the parking lot as a shortcut to avoid the lights. As a result, Gideon's and Nancy's heads kept swiveling to keep watch on the passing traffic.

They had met three years earlier at a national security conference in Colorado and dated briefly for six months. Nancy was a good agent whose beauty turned out to be more of a career liability than an asset in the FBI's male-dominated culture. She navigated her way through it by cultivating a tough self-reliance that alienated her from many of her colleagues. As much as Gideon admired her independence, the sharp edges of her personality had quickly chipped away at his initial affection. Yet sitting with her in close confines in the front of her car, he couldn't help admiring her athletic legs and honey-blond hair.

"I appreciate you coming out here," he said.

"I appreciate the call."

"It's probably nothing, but I thought it was worth checking out."

"You always had good instincts."

"Did you tell Ray you were coming to meet me?" Ray Dahlgren was Nancy's boss, the deputy director of the Bureau's Counterterrorism Group. Gideon met him at the same conference where he'd met Nancy, and his impression was that the man had earned his reputation as an ambitious and arrogant bully who was smart, but not nearly as smart as he thought he was.

Nancy smiled. "What do you think?"

She was wearing a familiar perfume, something light and flowery, and its scent reminded Gideon of lying next to her in her loftlike apartment. Nancy collected medieval brass rubbings, and the apartment was decorated with expensive framed canvases. Late at night the black-and-white renderings of monks and dignitaries took on an eerie three-dimensional glow in the reflected light from the street. He had spent a good number of hours tracing their outlines in pursuit of a sleep that never came.

"Dahlgren doesn't like me," Gideon stated.

"He's got nothing against you, personally," said Nancy. "He's just loyal to President Wade."

Dahlgren was a political animal who specialized in managing up, and he had risen on the same tide that had swept Wade into the nation's highest office. Because Gideon was no friend of the new administration, Dahlgren would do him no favors.

"If this guy Mixon turns out to be the real deal, it's all his. Dahlgren can run with it."

"What makes you think he might be?"

"I told you. He knew his stuff, and the tape sounded authentic. If he turns out to be a phony, no harm done."

"Except the wasted time."

"Gives us a chance to catch up."

Nancy smiled. Her teeth were as white as Chiclets. "So you're really getting married?" Gideon had avoided the subject, but leave it to Nancy to be direct.

"Yep. Three weeks."

"Wow. Lucky girl."

"Lucky me."

Nancy nodded slowly. He couldn't tell what she was thinking. When they broke up she hadn't protested, but she was eager to take his call and quickly agreed to meet Mixon. Maybe it was just her national security concerns, but Gideon suspected there might be something else there.

Nancy looked at her watch again. It was almost seven o'clock, an hour after Mixon had agreed to meet them. "Do you have any way to reach him?"

"No, but I know where he's staying."

Gideon called the Word Up Lodge, but not surprisingly they had no record of anyone named Ervin Mixon staying there, and Gideon didn't want to raise suspicions by asking further questions.

"I don't have a good feeling about this," he said.

"We could drive over there," Nancy suggested.

"Let's do it."

They left Gideon's car at the mall and drove the short distance to Mixon's hotel. The Word Up Lodge was about as inhospitable as a hovel or a prison. The parking lot was rutted and potholed. The paint peeled off vinyl siding (*never a good idea to paint vinyl*, Gideon thought). Half the lights were out in the motel's neon sign. The balcony that ran the length of the second floor looked dangerously unstable and pitched so steeply at one point it looked like the top of a wheelchair ramp.

"There's his car." Gideon pointed to the green Impala, which was still parked between the two Dumpsters.

They got out and examined the car, which was unlocked and cold to the touch. "Been here a while," Nancy noted. She opened the door and poked around inside.

On the ground about six feet from the rear tire Gideon discovered a snap shackle that looked like it had popped off a piece of rubber or canvas, but he recognized it immediately as coming from a sling meant to hold a rifle, probably an AR-15. He fingered it and showed it to Nancy.

"I don't like this," he said. "Looks like somebody yanked it off."

"Let's check at the front desk," Nancy suggested.

The motel clerk was a stringy-haired kid with a bad case of acne. When Nancy flashed her ID he immediately stiffened. Gideon described Mixon, and the kid said he had checked in yesterday but he hadn't seen Mixon since. He gave Nancy the key for Mixon's room, and she and Gideon went upstairs to inspect it.

"Not enough time to get a search warrant," Nancy said.

"Exigent circumstances," Gideon agreed.

The room, however, was completely empty except for a toothbrush next to the bathroom sink. "Amazing. I wouldn't peg the guy for caring about oral hygiene," said Gideon.

"Where do you think he went?"

"He wouldn't leave if he was expecting a payday."

Nancy nodded. "Maybe someone else saw him."

At the other end of the balcony, where it began its dangerous downward plunge, two black men leaned over the edge, smoking cigarettes. Nancy flashed her badge again and asked if they had noticed the guy in room 25.

One of them looked down and didn't respond, and the other just shook his head and said no.

"You sure?" Nancy pressed.

But this time the second man didn't even answer, and the other man looked at his shoes. Nancy gave the men her card, but as he headed downstairs Gideon noticed the cards fluttering down from the balcony.

"Those guys aren't talking," observed Nancy. "But they know something."

"Someone scared the shit out of them."

"Verhoven?"

"Exactly."

5

ALEXANDRIA, VIRGINIA

It was nearly ten-thirty by the time Gideon arrived back at his new house in Alexandria, carrying a bottle of Oregon pinot and a bag full of English cheeses and Spanish sausages. Except for a single lamp in the living room, the house was dark.

After leaving the hotel Gideon had followed Nancy to the Bureau in the hope of speaking to Deputy Director Dahlgren, and to access the NCIC database for anything they could find on Mixon. But Dahlgren had left for the day, so they arranged to meet tomorrow. They also discovered that aside from two arrests for drug possession (later dismissed), shoplifting (Radio Shack), and one for forging a check, Mixon was clean. The database noted his connection to Verhoven, although it didn't make much of it. He was, in short, another lowlife tweaker with a penchant for electronics and petty crime.

He'd called Kate from Nancy's office and explained that something had come up. She didn't pry, although she wasn't happy, and he told her he'd explain when he got home. Then he'd stopped by the supermarket on the way home, thinking that a nice dinner might smooth the waters. Unfortunately, the stop at Whole Foods had taken a little longer than expected. Then there'd been an overturned truck on 66 that snarled traffic. When he called home again, no one answered, and he assumed Kate was punishing him for the delay.

But when he got inside, Kate was asleep on the couch, barefoot, one slim leg pulled up beneath her. She wore a simple black dress and a strand of pearls, her auburn hair pulled back, and though the only makeup she wore was some lipstick, her face glowed. A thick report from the Bureau of Ocean Energy Management had slid from her hands, fanned open on her lap.

A special commission had been convened to examine the causes of the Deepwater blowout and to provide recommendations to help prevent, or at least lessen, the impact of future spills. As the only member who had spent any real time on a rig, Kate understood better than the others the nearly impossible task of allowing the government oversight for the complex, highly technical, and deeply risky business of drilling for oil beneath the sea. Trying to balance the competing interests of environmentalists and major energy companies—and the politicians whose campaigns these opposing groups funded—only made the committee's mandate even more untenable. As much as she aspired to become an honest broker, she expected that whatever recommendations she made would become mired in the political and bureaucratic gridlock that plagued most government committees.

But she had put aside her work that night for him. She'd laid a cloth on the folding table—two place settings, nice china, wine-glasses, candles. The candles had burned down so far that wax had run onto the tablecloth.

She murmured something as he entered the room, then slithered down deeper into the couch, her hair tumbling over her face. Rather than waking her, he poured himself a glass of wine, sliced off a big hunk of sausage, and watched her sleep. Kate's tan had faded over the past few months, since she was no longer out on oil rigs standing in the sun all day, and her naturally fair complexion had reasserted itself. She breathed easily and slowly, her face free of its usual signs of worry and care.

I'm a lucky man, Gideon thought.

And yet.

Something tickled at the back of his brain. He had earned an international reputation successfully mediating crises in various conflict zones around the world. Central to his success was a deep and long-standing conviction that military intervention should be used only as a last resort, after every diplomatic effort was exhausted. But the events of eighteen months ago had prompted him to question his public commitment to nonviolence. He had demonstrated that he was more than simply capable of killing other men when necessary—he was surprisingly good at it. He found himself still haunted by images of the men he'd killed, not because he felt guilty, but because he felt no guilt at all about taking their lives.

Was it possible this wasn't what he wanted? Could it be the intellectual life was no longer the place for him, that he was no longer a "Man of Peace"? The thought made him uneasy.

Gideon's parents' marriage had been a loveless and tragic one—one that ultimately ended when Gideon's father killed his mother and then turned the gun on himself. Out in the world, Gideon knew he was a man of unusual confidence. It wasn't faked. He knew what he knew and trusted his intuition, and he had learned from long experience that he generally made sound decisions.

So marrying Kate had just felt like the right thing to do, something he knew from the first moment they were together.

And yet. After Kate had quit her job and moved to D.C. to work as a lobbyist for Trojan Energy, he had sometimes been assailed by a suspicion that maybe he wasn't cut out for civilian life. It was the feeling of unease at the end of the day when night descended and the world was quiet. It was peace, itself, that gave rise to an itchy feeling, the sense he should be out there engaged in the struggle. It was something Tillman had said to him after they left the Obelisk: A life in the shadows is not a life lived at all.

He finished the glass of wine just as the candles on the floor burned out. A waxy, sooty smell filled the air.

He put down his glass, picked Kate up, and carried her up the stairs to the bedroom. She had unpacked the rest of their moving boxes while he was gone, making the bed and hanging pictures on the walls. Unlit candles surrounded the bed. She sighed as he tucked her in but didn't protest, and her eyes shut as quickly as they had opened.

Gideon's mind kept returning to Mixon, like a train jumping off the tracks, spinning possibilities, conjectures, contingencies, questions he wanted to ask but couldn't. What had happened to him? Where did he go? Was his disappearance proof of his allegations? Or was the supposed conspiracy just a chimera dreamed up by the paranoid imagination of a delusory drug addict?

He tried to tell himself that Nancy was a big girl, that she didn't need his help to pursue Mixon's lead. He had agreed to make the contact, and now it was out of his hands. But he couldn't help thinking of ways he could contribute, things he could say to Dahlgren in the morning to get him to devote some FBI resources. As he brushed his teeth, then climbed into bed, he reviewed the events of the day, searching for moments where he could have learned more from Mixon and perhaps been more useful.

His thinking made him restless, and his restlessness made him toss and turn. Kate's eyes opened slightly and her arms went around his neck. Her skin felt hot. She smiled sleepily. "Hey, you made it," she whispered.

"I made it," he said. "I'm home."

He kissed her gently. That kiss kindled a deeper and longer kiss, and soon they were making love.

But long after Kate fell back asleep, Gideon lay back, staring at the ceiling, thinking about the missing man who claimed to have knowledge of an attack on American soil.

6

FBI TRAINING ACADEMY, QUANTICO, VIRGINIA

So let me get this straight," FBI Deputy Director of Counter-intelligence Ray Dahlgren said after Nancy had finished her explanation about the events of the previous day. "You brought a civilian to a meeting with an informant on a subject regarding national security?"

It was bright and early the next morning. Nancy Clement had brought Gideon to the FBI's Quantico training facility so that he could meet her boss and help her advocate to find Ervin Mixon. The deputy director had just given a speech to the current class at the FBI Academy and was now about to join them as guest instructor on the firing range. Nancy and Gideon were riding in a golf cart that Dahlgren was driving toward the shooting range, keeping his eyes pinned on the small track they were navigating. He had not yet looked at Gideon once.

"It was Ambassador Davis who brought the informant to our attention. I'm sure you're familiar with his work in the Diggs administration."

The deputy director was a big man who looked like a cop's cop—the sort of guy who probably grew up on a farm in Minnesota, served in the Marines before joining the FBI, and cleaned his guns to relieve stress. Every syllable he uttered seemed intended to make it clear that he was in charge and you weren't.

"We're fighting a war against terror," he said, "and you come to me with a story about a meth head looking for a payday. He gave you no specifics and disappeared before you could even talk to him."

"He claims to have information about an attack on a high-value domestic target," Nancy said. "He links it to a militia group in West Virginia."

Dahlgren cut her off with a wave of his hand. "So you've said. And so far as I'm aware, this worthless tweaker has since contributed precisely zero evidence to corroborate his claims."

Gideon interrupted. "I think he's telling the truth. He has a recording—"

Dahlgren slammed on the brakes. "We're here," he said to Nancy. "As soon as the class assembles, I'll be instructing them. So if you have some new data point to add, you need to haul it out right now." Without waiting for her to respond, he turned and for the first time looked at Gideon. "You claim to be a good judge of character, Mr. Davis? What was your impression of this informant?"

Gideon noted that the deputy director had made a pointed choice to refer to him as mister, rather than as ambassador. Not that Gideon cared a whit for titles. But it was a signal. Gideon could see that if he was going to have any chance at all with Dahlgren, it would not come by beating around the bush.

"What's my appraisal of Mixon?" Gideon said, climbing out of the golf cart. "I think he's a slippery piece of shit."

Dahlgren studied his face impassively for a moment. "And yet here you stand," he said finally.

"Because I believe the guy knows something."

"Walk with me," Dahlgren said. A group of FBI trainees wearing baseball caps and blue jackets were milling around near the firing line. Dahlgren strode quickly toward them.

When they reached the trainees, they assembled quickly in a neat line.

"All right, people, listen up," Dahlgren shouted. "I'm sure that your instructors have given you superb training in the basic operation and handling of your weapons. But I'm here to talk about some of the finer psychological aspects that come with using lethal force. A firearm is not simply a machine that goes bang when you press the trigger. If you find yourself using your weapon, it will inevitably be under some high-stress circumstance. Life or death. With that kind of sudden stress, your fine motor control deteriorates, your field of vision narrows, your hands get slick with sweat, and your body trembles. So you better be way past the point of fumbling around trying to remember how to run your gun. It's got to be dead instinctive."

He turned and pointed at Gideon. "We have a special guest with us today. I'm sure you're all familiar with Gideon Davis. Some of you may even know him as the Man of Peace. I hear, however, he's pretty good with a gun. Isn't that right, Mr. Davis?"

Gideon nodded. He knew the deputy director was toying with him. "I can shoot," he said.

Dahlgren drew a pistol from his hip, slid out the magazine, and racked the chambered round into his fist. Then he handed the pistol to Gideon. "Can you identify this pistol, sir?"

"It's a 1911. A Les Baer. Nice gun, but I was under the impression that it's not an FBI-approved firearm."

Which drew a scattering of laughter from the trainees.

"You were, huh?" He smiled coolly. "In fact, ladies and gentlemen, the 1911 *is* an FBI-approved firearm for agents who have received special clearance."

Gideon smiled. "I stand corrected." He handed the 1911 back to Dahlgren.

Dahlgren surveyed the range. "Give me two targets, seven yards," Dahlgren called to the range officer.

"Yes, sir," the RO said. He pressed a button on a small control panel located to his right, and two human-shaped targets rose from small bays in the ground.

"Mr. Davis clearly knows his firearms," Dahlgen said, holding up the weapon. "So let's stage a brief exercise to see what FBI training is all about." He motioned to the range officer. "Agent Stimson, you think you might be kind enough to lend your sidearm to Mr. Davis?"

The range officer looked intensely uncomfortable at the request. But he nevertheless dutifully unhooked his belt and handed the weapon to Gideon. Gideon recognized it as a Glock 22, the most commonly used law enforcement weapon in the United States. The gun was unloaded, with no magazine inserted in the weapon.

Gideon fumbled a little as he strapped on the belt with the weapon. His apparent unfamiliarity with the gun, though, was a pretense. He owned one himself and was quite comfortable operating it.

Dahlgren walked to the white stripe painted on the grass.

The RO laid a powerful hand on Gideon's shoulder and put his head close to Gideon's ear. "Deputy Director Dahlgren used to be on the Hostage Rescue Team, that's the FBI's elite SWAT-type unit," he said. "And he was the number-one man on the FBI pistol team. Don't try to beat him, okay? Just be safe, draw slowly and carefully and don't shoot anybody."

"Got it," Gideon said.

"Don't patronize me," the RO whispered. "I don't give a good goddamn who you were or what the deputy director says, if you do anything stupid or unsafe, I'm gonna kick your ass so far you'll need a map to find it. Clear?"

"Crystal," Gideon said.

Dahlgren motioned impatiently to Gideon. "Come on, son. Toes on the line."

Gideon felt a thrum of excitement. He had been a competitive shooter in his youth, with several national championships under his belt. But after his father killed his mother and then turned the gun on himself, he had sworn off shooting for several decades. Eighteen months ago, however, he'd been forced to use firearms again. Since then he'd spent two or three afternoons a week at the range, each time rediscovering the power that came from firing a loaded weapon.

After Gideon stepped to the line, the RO handed him a magazine.

"Make it hot," Dahlgren said.

Gideon slid the magazine into the Glock, racked the slide, and holstered it.

Dahlgren addressed the crowd again. "Now, folks, it's natural for a man to get a little nervous in a situation like this. Would you like to try out the weapon, just to see how it works?"

"If you don't mind," Gideon said.

"Five shots be enough?"

"I guess it'll have to do," Gideon said, throwing a weak smile toward the crowd. This drew scattered laughter.

"Draw and fire five," the RO said, "no time limit."

Gideon drew with exaggerated care, extended the weapon using an inefficient, old-fashioned cup-and-saucer grip, squeezed his left eye closed with a conspicuous grimace and fired five slow shots. Three shots hit the bull, one hit the nine ring, and a flier hit the seven.

"Not bad!" Dahlgren raised his palm toward Gideon. "How about a hand for our honored guest?"

The crowd of trainees applauded tepidly. Probably no more than a third of them could have shot any better. But it was nothing to write home about.

"How about a little wager," Dahlgren said softly to Gideon. "If you outshoot me, I'll give Agent Clement some rope on your informant. If not, then you drop it."

Gideon had seen this coming, seen it a mile away. He suppressed a smile. Dahlgren had no intention of giving Nancy any leeway and was using the moment only to humiliate Gideon. Well, he would play it out and go where it took him.

"Seems like a cavalier way of addressing an issue of this importance," Gideon returned, quietly enough that the trainees wouldn't hear him. "But that's just one man's opinion."

"Then I'm glad I didn't ask for it," Dahlgren whispered back. Then he raised his voice and addressed the trainees again. "What we're going to do is simulate an attack by an advancing adversary. Imagine, for a moment, that in the course of interviewing a suspect, you're surprised by an attacker at your back. You turn to find an assailant rushing toward you with a loaded weapon. What do you do?"

"Simple drill," the range officer said, taking his cue from Dahlgren. "Gentlemen, turn and face me. On my command, turn and engage the target with three shots—two to the body, one to the head. We've got synchronized shot timers built into every station, so if both shooters put all three shots on target, the fastest time wins."

"Okay," Gideon said.

They stood silently for a moment, backs to the targets, the wind whipping across the broad expanse of grass. Gideon waited for a beep or buzzer signaling the start of the string.

Suddenly the range officer shouted, "Gun! Gun! Gun!"

It caught Gideon off guard. For the briefest of moments he hesitated. But then his body kicked in. He whirled, drawing the Glock in one smooth motion, assuming a modern thumb-over-thumb grip. This time he didn't squint one eye but simply acquired the target with both eyes open and squeezed the trigger of the Glock. In his mind he registered that Dahlgren's gun had already sounded by the time he broke the first shot. His own two shots to the body, however, sounded so close that they almost appeared to be one shot. Then he slid the front sight up toward the target's head and fired another shot. Almost immediately the target flipped sideways and then slid down into a slot in the ground.

The range was completely silent.

"Holy *shit*," someone said finally.

"Unload and show clear," the RO instructed.

Gideon unloaded the Glock and holstered it.

"Time?" the range officer shouted.

A second RO stood at a small computer station on the edge of the range. "Deputy Director Dahlgren, one point zero three seconds," he called.

There were whistles and cheers from the trainees.

"Mr. Davis, uh . . ." The second RO hesitated. "I'm not sure if this is right . . ."

"Just read us the time," Dahlgren said.

"Mr. Davis—zero point nine nine one."

There were several gasps from the trainees.

"Score the targets," Dahlgren growled.

The RO hit a button, and Dahlgren's target rose from the ground, then flipped around so it was visible.

There were three holes in the target, two in the circle at the center, one right between the eyes.

"Ten, ten, and ten," called the RO. "For a total perfect score of thirty."

The RO hit another button and Gideon's target rose from the ground. A long, slow groan rose from the crowd. "Ten. Ten. Zero.

Two hits and a clean miss." The RO scribbled something on his sheet, then called out, "Well, if Mr. Davis had hit all three, he would have shot the fastest perfect Mozambique in FBI history. Sadly, his second shot was a clean miss and Deputy Director Dahlgren wins the contest thirty points to twenty."

There was a thunder of applause. Dahlgren finally calmed the crowd. "Well, Mr. Davis gave us a little surprise there. He was a better shooter than he let on. Wouldn't want to play poker with him. But point made. Your FBI training will teach you to survive . . . and to prevail." He winked at Gideon. "Sorry, Mr. Davis. Nice try, though."

He then gave the trainees some choice tips from his days with the HRT.

While the deputy director spoke, Gideon crooked his finger at the range officer. "Let me see that target," he said.

The RO shrugged and pressed a button, bringing the target back to the firing line. Gideon examined it, then pointed out the tiny circle in the middle of the target. The RO squinted at it carefully. "I'll be damned!" he said.

He waited for the deputy director to finish his pep talk and dismiss his trainees, then motioned him over.

Dahlgren looked irritated at being summoned. "What?"

"Um, sir?" the RO said softly, putting his finger next to the hole in the center of the target. "There are two grease rings here."

Dahlgren came closer and glared at the hole. "Bullshit."

"I'm just telling you how I see it, sir. Two shots in one hole. Mr. Davis hit him three times. It's a thirty. Perfect score. Mr. Davis won."

"You sure of that?" Dahlgren said. "*Absolutely* sure?" His question was etched with an unspoken threat.

The RO looked carefully at the target. It was a close call, no doubt. He swallowed, met Dahlgren's eye for a moment, then said, "No, sir. I guess I'm wrong."

"Excellent," Dahlgren said. "Glad you see it my way. One hit, one clean miss. Right?"

The RO looked at Gideon apologetically, then shrugged in agreement.

Gideon shook his head in disgust.

"Give us a minute, Agent Stimson," Dahlgren said. The RO quickly disappeared. Dahlgren put his meaty hand on Gideon's neck. Gideon fought the urge to break the small bones in Dahlgren's wrist with a quick upward jerk, but he restrained himself. Dahlgren continued, "The Counterterrorism section of the FBI gets twelve thousand tips each day from wackos just like your informant. If we had to follow every one, I could waste my entire career each day on the job. Now if Agent Clement had come to me with tangible evidence, I'd follow up on it. But right now we've got the word of a tweaker, and the hunch of a college professor who used to be somebody." He smiled coldly. "We can't go chasing every rabbit down every hole, Mr. Davis. Bottom line, I'm not wasting FBI resources to satisfy your appetite for relevance."

Nancy Clement stepped closer. "Sir, witnesses at the scene strongly implied that he'd been kidnapped. Why would he have been kidnapped unless—"

"Strongly implied," Dahlgren interrupted sharply. "What does that even mean?"

The usually outspoken Nancy fell quiet, so Gideon spoke up. "I don't have a dog in this fight, but I think you're making a mistake. I spoke to this guy, heard his recording, and I think there's a strong possibility that he's telling the truth."

Dahlgren stepped back and raised his voice a little as he extended his hand toward Gideon. "Well, sir, I sincerely thank you for taking an interest. It's always a pleasure to meet a public-minded citizen. You take care now, Mr. Davis. My assistant will see you back to the gatehouse."

7

What is it?" Kate asked.

They'd been unpacking for an hour and Gideon hadn't said much.

"I just can't get this thing out of my head," he said, pulling a stack of books out of a box and putting them on a shelf.

"You're talking about this Mixon person."

Gideon nodded. He had given Kate the details of his encounter with Mixon and his frustrating visit to the FBI with his old girl-friend, Nancy Clement, which she had taken surprisingly well. "If this guy is right, we could be looking at a major attack. He used the phrase 'mass casualties.' For all I know, he could be talking about another 9/11."

"What does Nancy think about it?"

Gideon had a long conversation with her after they left Quantico. He couldn't convince her to go around Dahlgren to pursue Mixon. "At the end of the day, she's a loyal public servant. Her boss ordered her to let it go. So unless something surfaces, she needs to follow orders."

Kate nodded, watching Gideon as he slid another book on the shelf.

"But I did a little poking around online," he continued. "The militia group Mixon talked about live in a pretty remote part of West

Virginia that's filled with fringe types who live off the grid—militia guys, survivalists, end-timers, bikers, people trying to get away from everything and everybody."

"Isn't your brother up in West Virginia somewhere?"

Gideon hesitated. A thought had been growing in his mind since yesterday, a thought that had sunk its talons deep in his head. "Funny you should mention that . . ." he said finally.

Kate looked at him for a moment. "Seriously? Tillman lives in the same area as these people?"

"Their compound's not far from him." He paused. "My guess is, they're holding Mixon there. Assuming he's still alive, they'll question him hard until he tells them what he told the FBI."

His voice trailed off. He knew what he wanted to do. *What he needed to do.* He needed to go to West Virginia, hook up with his brother, Tillman, and find out precisely what the hell was going on with Ervin Mixon.

But it was only a matter of weeks until he and Kate got married. All the books on how to be a sensitive caring male in the twenty-first century told him the right thing to do at this moment was to let it go and lovingly unpack the crystal together.

"Are you looking for permission from me to help out on this?" Kate said.

Gideon didn't answer. He wasn't asking for permission. Not exactly. He knew the consequences of what he was considering—not only the potential danger, but the legal mess that would inevitably follow—and he didn't want to take it any further without Kate's blessing.

"How did she look?"

"Who?"

"Don't give me that hand-in-the-cookie-jar look. You know who. Nancy."

Gideon shrugged. "Good, I guess."

"Did she let you hold her gun?"

"Stop it. You're not jealous, are you?"

"Should I be?"

"No," Gideon said. "But the truth is, I think this guy had something."

"And you think you can help?"

Instead of answering, Gideon reached into an open box and pulled out a book. "*A Diplomatic History of Yugoslavia*," he read.

"You're changing the subject."

"Bear with me." Gideon leafed through the book for a few seconds. Then he turned the book around and showed Kate an old black-and-white photograph of a nerdy-looking young man with a thin mustache and a sad expression on his face.

"Recognize this guy?"

"Looks very much like Gavrilo Princip," Kate said.

"You read the caption."

Kate smiled. "Busted."

"Gavrilo Princip was a Serbian anarchist. One day he snuck up on Archduke Franz Ferdinand, heir to the Austro-Hungarian throne, and shot him in the neck. One bullet, one angry little man. That's all it took to start World War I. Four years later, nearly ten million people were dead."

"I sense you're making a point," Kate said.

Gideon's green eyes went serious. "What if you were the guy who said, 'Aw, we get threats against the archduke every day. I wouldn't take this one too seriously.'" He put the book on the shelf. "I mean one bullet really can change the world."

"You're saying you want to get back out there, follow this where it leads."

"It could be nothing. It's probably nothing. But what if it turns out to be something, and I could have stopped it?"

"Is that what this is really about?" Kate's hair was still damp from her morning shower. It hugged the delicate curve of her neck.

"Of course. What do you mean? What else would it be about?"

"Come on, Gideon. You think I haven't noticed how antsy you've been since we moved in together? Maybe . . ." Her voice trailed off, and she shook her head.

"Maybe what?"

After a girding moment, she turned to him. "Maybe this isn't right for you." She waved her hands at the boxes. "The house. The teaching. Me."

"Kate—"

"I'm a big girl. I can take it."

"It's not you. It isn't. But if I don't follow this up I don't know if I could sleep at night." What he didn't tell her was that some part of him had woken up on the Obelisk. And now that he was awake, he didn't want to go back to sleep. "It's just for a few days," he said. "While I run this down with Tillman."

She looked at him, and he wondered if she could read his uncertainty. Then she said, "I'll pack you a bag." She walked off toward the stairs.

Gideon watched her go, his heart thrumming with anticipation in his throat. It was a feeling—if he was totally honest about it—that he liked. No, not just liked. Loved.

As Kate disappeared from sight, he picked up his cell phone and dialed Nancy Clement. "Hey," he said. "It's me. I think I might be able to help find Mixon."

"Gideon," Nancy said, "I've been ordered off this thing."

"I know. That's why I'm going to help. If we do it right, you'll have total deniability. If I find something useful, you can run with it. If not, nothing I do can be connected to you. But I'm going to need a couple of things from you . . ."

Kate poked her head over the railing of the stairs. "Honey, do you want the Glock or the SIG?"

Gideon put his hand over the receiver for a moment. "The SIG," he called.

8

ANDERSON, WEST VIRGINIA

The big boar was nervous. The rest of the herd was busy shoving their snouts into the ground. But the boar kept surveying the area, ears twitching, the big ridge hairs on its spine sticking straight up. Tillman Davis crouched behind a stand of mountain laurel about thirty yards out from the nearest animal, his arrow nocked, the bow ready to draw, his heart beating fast. But he couldn't move. Not without the boar catching the flash of motion.

Tillman had been tracking the herd for a couple of weeks. There were eleven of them—smart, fast, and mean, with sharp eyes and noses that rivaled any animal on four feet. Like a lot of feral hogs in the area, their bloodstock ran mostly to Russian wild hog. Same thick dark hair, same little ears, same aggressive temperament, same three-inch tusks.

The biggest male probably weighed close to five hundred pounds. Hogs were considered to be nuisance animals, not wild game. No hunting season, no bag limit. Nobody cared if they lived or died. A herd over in Bledsoe County had attacked and disemboweled a child. They had been eating the kid alive before Grandma got her shotgun and started shooting. The little boy survived, but he was never the same after that.

If Tillman had been hunting the hogs with a gun, it would have been no big thing to take a couple of them. He'd figured out their feeding patterns, so he knew he could track them down easy enough. But he wanted to take the alpha boar with a bow. And to do that, he had to fool eleven snouts and twenty-two eyes. And once he'd made the shot, he needed to get away without ending up like the kid from Bledsoe County.

Thirty-two, thirty-three yards to the target. A hell of a long shot. He wasn't shooting with a high-tech compound bow like most hunters used. This was a longbow that he'd made himself from yew, the same wood used by the English longbowmen who'd won the battles at Crécy and Agincourt. It was powerful but finicky. No peep sights, no counterweights, no carbon fiber arrows—just a stick and a string and a homemade arrow.

Tillman could feel his heart beating, a sloshing noise in his ears that seemed so loud that surely the hogs could hear it.

He breathed in slowly and concentrated on becoming invisible. Not that he believed he could *actually* become invisible. But he did believe it was possible to transport your mind so far from the moment that you gave off no signal of your presence—no motion, no sound, nothing that would attract attention. And in so doing you simply blended into the vegetation. He had done it in the jungles of Mohan, guerrilla fighters walking within ten or fifteen feet of him when he stood in plain sight—*almost* in plain sight anyway—and not seeing him.

His predatory focus on the boar dissipated and his mind spread out like ripples on a pond, taking in everything around him—the sharp tang of hickory and the softer smell of oak, the patch of warmth on his cheek as a shaft of sunlight found his face, the black tangle of bare tree limbs against the pale sky, the barely audible breeze-rustle of the few tenacious dry leaves that still clung to the branches overhead. And still there was the boar: every hair visible and sharp, every twitch of ear and snout, every exhaled breath.

Tillman was not one to give much credit to joy. But this, surely, was as close to joy as he had ever come.

His was not a life that had been exactly filled with pleasure. His father had murdered his mother and then shot himself when Tillman was sixteen, leaving behind a bankruptcy that stripped Tillman and his brother Gideon of every possession they owned. Then Tillman had fought in the army, seen friends die in distant places, uncared for by the people whose interests they served. After that, he had lived thanklessly in the jungles of Southeast Asia, prosecuting a minor CIA war. The failures of that war had ultimately resulted in Tillman being made into a sacrificial goat, serving two years in prison for mistakes that were not of his own making. Never a husband, never a father, no real relationships of any consequence other than the fraught and distant relationship with his own younger brother.

Come to me. Tillman closed his eyes and concentrated on the boar. *Come to me, brother.* The boar was getting old, scars visible on the armored plate of callus across its chest, muzzle rimmed with white bristles, a big chip out of its left tusk. It might have another few years in it yet, but it had sired its offspring, had ruled its small patch of woods—and maybe now was its time to return to its source. Hunter and hunted, arrow and flesh—these were things that were meant for each other, ends of a never-ending circle.

Sometimes Tillman wished he could have said the same for himself, that he could have taken a bullet back in that fight on the oil rig, the one that had drawn a curtain on his career. But he had been spared that—if *spared* was the right word. In the midst of his greatest failure, Gideon had come to his aid, saved his life, sparing him from drawing the circle neatly closed.

Every day the shame and pointlessness of his life pressed down on Tillman like a massive weight. He cooked his stew, he grew his corn and beans and turnips and carrots on his rocky little plot of land, he trapped his rabbits and hunted deer, he read his books, he tried fitfully and with little success to teach himself how to play bluegrass banjo. But on most days, it felt like a pathetic waste of time.

But there was still this. There was still the hunt.

For a moment the hog looked down. Tillman drew in one smooth stroke. There was a feeling of rightness that told him if he released now, his arrow would find its mark.

But just as his fingers loosened on the bowstring, he heard a loud noise behind him, a car gunning its motor on the dirt road that led up to his house. He couldn't see it through the dense mountain foliage, but he could hear it.

The hog, startled at the noise, dropped to its haunches, as though prepared for an attack. As a result the once-perfectly aimed arrow caught it high, passing just above the lungs and heart, just to the left of the spine. It was still a certain kill. But not a quick one.

The car rattled on up the trail, the noise fading.

Goddamn it, Tillman thought. *Who's the asshole in the car?*

But he didn't have time to think about the question any further: The hog screamed, a primal noise of anguish and rage, then tore straight toward Tillman. There was no time for a second shot, no time to nock a second arrow, draw, fire.

The boar was running crazily. The arrow still protruded from its body, just inches from its tail. The big backstrap muscle running down the spine must have been ruined. But still, somehow, the pig found the will to attack.

No time to run, no time to climb a tree. The big boar would be on him in seconds. Tillman flung the bow to the ground, drew his knife. It was the same knife he'd carried for years, through the jungles of Southeast Asia and across the arid mountains of Afghanistan. He kept it sharp enough to shave with, and it had been with him for so long that now it felt like an extension of his hand.

The pig's tiny, red-rimmed eyes were full of malice. There was none of that brotherhood-of-ancient-warriors shit there now. It just wanted to kill him, and rip his flesh with its tusks. A thin runnel of drool ran down one of its tusks.

It struck Tillman as ironic that after having been in gunfights on three continents, he might end up getting killed by a pig.

He grinned. "All right, you old bastard," he said. "If that's how it is . . ."

It charged straight at Tillman. Because of its wound, it couldn't maintain a straight course and veered offtrack, just far enough to the left that Tillman was able to sidestep and slash with the knife. The blade sliced deeply across the pig's chest.

It was only after the blade sliced deep into the pig's hide that Tillman realized he'd made a mistake. Wild boars develop a thick plate of callus several inches thick across their chests to absorb the tusks of rival hogs. So though the blade just sliced into the chest plate, the pig seemed to barely notice the wound.

It whirled with astonishing speed. With a quick flip of its head, the massive boar tossed Tillman. He flew through the air close to ten feet before crashing down in a low mountain laurel bush. The pig rushed the bush, but it had thrown Tillman so high that he had landed three feet off the ground, only his right boot dangling near the pig.

The boar gamely slashed at Tillman's foot with one of its tusks. Tillman stomped the big pig in the face. It squealed and then thundered back around to take another swipe. Tillman tempted him with the dangling foot, then snatched it out of the way, like a toreador baiting a bull. And like a toreador, he made the animal pay for its charge, sinking his blade into the boar's back.

The boar squealed and then ran off about ten yards with the knife before it came around, glaring at Tillman with its beady little eyes. Its flanks rose and fell as it panted. Blood was now pouring from all three wounds on its body. But it showed no inclination to quit the fight.

Again it charged.

Tillman dangled his foot again, hoping to duplicate his previous trick. But the boar was too smart; it slammed instead into the base of the mountain laurel. The shock of the collision was so great that the entire bush trembled. Tillman sensed himself slipping, and he felt a burst of fear mixed with admiration.

Thud! The pig hit the tree again.

Tillman figured it was better to seize the initiative than wait to fall on his ass, so he dropped out of the bush and hit the ground. His leg buckled, and he saw blood running down his calf. Apparently the boar had tusked him when he threw Tillman—though he hadn't even felt it at the time.

He forced himself to his feet. The pain hit him for the first time. But he knew that he had to shrug it off and keep fighting.

The entire herd of pigs had filtered out from beneath the trees and were eyeing him and the boar uneasily, like a crowd gathered to watch a bar fight. They weren't menacing him, just watching, waiting for a clue from their leader as to what they should do.

But the old boar wasn't paying attention to them anymore. He only saw Tillman.

And Tillman had no weapon now. The pig screamed and screamed, eyes locked on Tillman. It was obviously losing strength quickly now. It stamped the ground with one hoof, lowered its head, and prepared to charge. Blood and drool leaked from its mouth, the lower lip working with fury or pain.

The bow.

Tillman saw the bow lying on the ground, three arrows left in the quiver. He edged toward the bow.

The pig shook its head, grunted.

Tillman knew he'd only have one chance. He dove for the bow.

The pig attacked. Everything seemed to slow down. Tillman felt the throb of his gored calf, heard the thud of the pig's hooves on the ground. There was no time to be afraid. It was survival of the fittest.

His fingers closed around the bow's leather grip, then his other hand scooped an arrow from the fallen quiver. There was another impact as the boar smashed into him. It was like being hit by the biggest football player he'd ever played against. Only worse. And without pads.

Tillman crashed to the ground and lay there, the breath momentarily knocked out of him, the bow gone, the arrow clutched in his hand. The boar came around again and faced him, grunting softly.

The herd of pigs had begun to close in around Tillman. They stank of stale urine and pig shit. The big hog lowered its head again, preparing to charge.

Instinctively Tillman brought up his last weapon, the arrow itself, interposing the razor-sharp three-pronged broadhead between himself and the pig. The arrow tip was the only part of his bow-and-arrow rig that he hadn't made himself. It was a commercially made broadhead—basically a pointed spike of hardened steel, surrounded by three razor blades, ground, honed, and stropped to surgical sharpness. There was no way to shoot it. So he was going to have to turn it into a tiny little spear. He clamped his hands around the fletching and propped the nock against a button on the bib of his camouflaged overalls, then clamped the soles of his boots around the shaft of the arrow.

For a moment all he could hear was the squealing of the pigs around him.

Then the pig made its final charge. There was a massive shock as the huge boar slammed into the soles of Tillman's feet. He felt himself catapulted end over end, landing facedown on the ground.

The old boar stood over him, eyeing him. The other hogs went silent.

Tillman momentarily felt the boar's rank breath on his face as it lowered its head toward him, turning its head and peering at him with one eye.

"All right, then," Tillman said. "Get it over with quick, huh?"

The boar winked. At least it seemed like a wink.

Then the hog settled down on the ground as though for a nap. It closed its eye again. And with that, it died.

The fletching of the arrow protruded no more than five inches from its chest. The arrow had gone straight through its heart.

For a moment there was no sound. Tillman struggled to his knees. Around him the circle of leaderless pigs stared at him momentarily, then whirled and were gone.

Tillman tried to get to his feet. But he was suddenly so tired that he couldn't even stand. A part of his brain recognized this as the adrenaline dump that occurs after combat, forcing the body to shut down until it regains equilibrium. When that happens, he knew, there's no fighting it.

So he rolled over and leaned against the hot, bloody flank of the old pig. The bristles prickled his flesh as he patted the dead beast on its great head.

He wanted to say something appropriate, to offer up some benediction that would sum up the old boar's life and dignify its magnificent death. But Tillman had never been a man of words particularly. His brother had gotten all the flowery-benediction genes.

"You look like shit," a voice said, interrupting his weary rumination.

He looked up and saw a man standing about twenty yards away.

"You asshole," Tillman said, closing his eyes. "You spooked my goddamn hog."

"Is that any way to greet your brother?" Gideon said.

9

ANDERSON, WEST VIRGINIA

Gideon returned from Tillman's bathroom with a military surplus first-aid kit and began cleaning and dressing the wound on his brother's leg. It was a bad gash, one that probably should have been closed with a couple dozen stitches. The blood—half-dried and caked with dirt—ran down into Tillman's boot. Gideon swabbed out the wound with alcohol while Tillman lay rigid with his eyes closed, not even making a noise. Then he spread some antibacterial cream, jury-rigged a series of butterfly bandages, and wrapped the whole oozing mess up in gauze.

When he was finished, Gideon looked around the bare little room. It was lit by two oil lamps. The walls were unpainted, decorated only by a gun rack containing four rifles and a shotgun. The kitchen consisted of a camp stove and an oven made from the top third of an oil drum. There was scarcely any evidence of personal possessions at all. It saddened him to see that Tillman's life had been boiled down to this. It was beyond mere poverty, beyond spartan. It had the look of a penitent's chamber.

Tillman himself didn't look much better. Although he was shorter and more muscular than Gideon, he looked dirty, dried out, and clearly exhausted. Gideon felt a heavy twinge of guilt. Guilt . . . and sadness. Two years earlier, his brother had been made a scapegoat for a lot of things that weren't his fault. Gideon had promised to keep him out of trouble. And had failed to keep his promise. Yet Tillman would never know just how much personal and political capital Gideon had spent for him. There were people in Washington who would have left him to rot in jail for the rest of his life. If it hadn't been for Gideon, they probably would have. Still, Gideon couldn't help feeling responsible for where Tillman had ended up.

For a moment Gideon considered driving back to D.C. Mixon wasn't Tillman's problem.

But before he had a chance to make the decision, Tillman's eyes flicked open. "Come on, Gideon," he said. "You didn't drive all the way out here to help me field dress that hog. Tell me what you want."

Gideon eyed his brother for a moment. "A while back you told me about a group of Nazi-type guys who live around here. You said you'd had some dealings with them."

Tillman grunted. "Not Nazis. Militia."

"Okay. You said these guys had contacted you several times, said they knew who you were, and that they tried to recruit you for their group. You said they figured you for a like-minded kind of guy."

Gideon explained everything that had happened until now.

When his brother finished telling him about Mixon, Nancy Clement, and the domestic terror attack he believed Verhoven might be part of, Tillman sighed and peeled himself off the bed like a piece of adhesive tape.

"Bullshit."

"Why do you say that?" Gideon said.

Tillman ran his hands wearily through his hair and leaned forward. "Will you let me get some sleep if I explain what's really going on at Verhoven's place, and why he's not trying to blow up a bunch of innocent people?"

"Fair enough."

"Let me school you here, lay a little prison knowledge on you about the far reaches of right-wing craziness in America." He extended his right arm straight out from his body and waggled the fingers of his hand. "Way out here on the far end you've got Nazis and the skinheads and Christian Identity—all the white power people. You've also got the Aryan Brotherhood, which is really a criminal gang operating out of penitentiaries but that shares the same philosophy about racial politics with the other white-power types.

"A step or two closer to the mainstream, you've got the militia people. Some of them have some cross talk with the Nazis and the racists and the Christian Identity guys. But most don't. Some of the militias are guys I can talk to. Basically they're armed libertarians, constitutional fundamentalists, Second Amendment guys, gun guys, folks who are tired of taking shit from the US government. Every few weekends they like to stomp around out in the bushes with black rifles and camo face paint. Basically harmless shit-talkers."

"Okay, so what about Verhoven?"

Tillman smiled thinly. "Supposedly he talks a good game about how America was built by Constitution-loving Protestants and how we've lost our way and this and that, how his people need to arm for some kind of big confrontation with the government, storm troopers coming out to take their guns away, whatever. But as far as I can tell, it's just window dressing. Politics is not what he's into. Not really."

"What is he into, then?"

"Pharmaceuticals. Mostly crystal meth."

"You're sure of this?"

"Everybody around here knows it. He's a large-scale manufacturer. He distributes weight, mostly through biker gangs and skinheads."

"How is it that this is common knowledge and they don't get caught?"

"From what I hear, Verhoven's grandfather was a big-time moonshiner—and, by the way, sheriff of Hertford County. It's a tradition around here. Long as you don't bother other people, nobody's gonna rat you out to the Feds."

Tillman felt a creeping unease. Had he put his money on a lame horse? What if Mixon turned out to be exactly what Ray Dahlgren claimed he was. "So you're saying—"

"Again, I'm just talking hearsay from people I've spoken to around here. But supposedly he runs the militia group as a nonprofit, which gives him tax-exempt status. The ideology gives him a pitch to use when he's recruiting muscle out of prison. He keeps all these armed guys around for security so he won't get ripped off. Does he believe any of his militia BS? Maybe. But at the end of the day, he's a businessman. He's in it for the money. So why would he want to set off a bomb in Times Square? It's bad for business."

Gideon leaned toward his brother. "Look, I may be barking up the wrong tree. But I think there may be something here." He explained about Mixon, how he believed that a plot to take out the government was being hatched at Jim Verhoven's compound.

When he was done talking, Tillman looked at him and shrugged. "And?"

"You once told me some of the guys in this militia group knew what you'd been through, and wanted you to join their group. I was hoping you could reach out to them, visit their compound, see if Mixon is there. If he is, just let me know and I'll pass the word on to the FBI."

Tillman looked disgusted. "Why should I help the federal government? So they can lock me up in jail again?" Tillman stood up, took off his shirt, and draped it over the end of his bed. "Get off my bed, man, I'm tired."

Gideon stood. Tillman lay down and grunted wearily.

"Will you do it, Tillman?"

"Sounds like a wild-goose chase."

"If it isn't, a lot of innocent people are going to get hurt."

Tillman closed his eyes and pulled up the rough woolen army blanket on his bed. "I did my bit for this country and look how they thanked me. Nope. I'm done."

"I know you don't owe the federal government anything. But you owe me."

Gideon let that sink in before he continued. "You know what I did for you. You could be dead now. Or still in prison."

Tillman had twenty pounds on Gideon, but lying in his bed he looked smaller, diminished somehow. He squinted back up at Gideon with one open eye.

"What does Kate think about this?"

"This has nothing to do with her." Gideon heard his own voice sounding a little too insistent.

"She know you're here?"

"Of course she knows. She says hello."

"If I were you, bro, I'd be back in that nice house cozied up next to my very fine woman."

"After we check this out."

"All right. Whatever. I'll go poke around in the morning. But then we're square." He turned over, face to the wall. "Now can I go to sleep?"

Gideon went to his car and came back with a duffel bag filled with mil spec communications equipment he'd cadged off Nancy Clement.

By the time he'd unpacked the equipment, Tillman was already snoring.

10

POCATELLO, IDAHO

How close are we?" Wilmot asked.

Collier stood with Wilmot on the balcony overlooking the twenty-thousand-acre Wilmot property. In the distance the Bitterroot Mountains rose out of the snowy white expanse of forest. A thin blue ribbon of river wound through the valley between them. A small plume of steam rising in the distance was the only indication of the existence of the cassava processing factory.

"Close," Collier said.

They stood silently for a while. Below them the now unused paddocks sprawled down toward the barns, which had once been full of beautiful horses. Collier sensed it was an emotional moment for Wilmot.

"I worked very hard to build this place," Wilmot said. "It's not easy to leave it behind."

"You'll be leaving a legacy that's a lot bigger than all this," Collier said.

Before Wilmot could respond, there was a noise from the treeline below. A hundred yards away, a figure burst out of the white woods, running furiously toward the house. It was one of the Congolese women. Amalie, the troublemaker, who'd been bothering him about Christiane.

"*S'il vous plaît!*" the woman yelled as she continued to charge through the snow toward the house. "*S'il vous plaît!*"

Wilmot took Collier's arm in one of his powerful paws, gave it a painful squeeze. "Go down there and handle this, John," he said. "It's time."

"Yes, sir!"

Collier walked briskly back into the house. As he did, he passed Evan wheeling himself in the opposite direction. He sprinted as soon as he got out of Evan's view. By the time he reached the ground floor of the house, he could hear banging on the front door. He ran through the kitchen, pausing at the refrigerator to pull a small red cardboard box out of the butter tray, which he stuffed in the pocket of his parka.

Then he threw open the front door, where he found Amalie standing on the front porch. Her eyes widened, as though she had expected someone other than Collier to be standing there.

"*Bonjour, ca va?*" Collier said, smiling. "My goodness, what seems to be the problem?"

Evan had rolled his motorized wheelchair as close to the railing as possible. He was feeling very sore, now that he had been off the painkillers for a while. The pain was sharp and crisp, like the air. But in an odd way it didn't feel all that objectionable.

"What the hell is going on, Dad?" he asked. "Who's that?"

Down below them John Collier was leading a thin, pretty black woman toward the stables.

Evan's father looked intently into Evan's face. "You look different today," he said. "How come?"

Evan didn't tell his father he had stopped taking his pills. He needed to focus, to see things without the haze of the drugs. If his father was involved in something, Evan didn't want to raise his suspicions.

"Seriously," he said. "Who is that woman? What are you and John doing in the woods?"

"John's an extraordinary young man," Wilmot said. "Brilliant, actually. He's been developing a new method of alternative energy production—ethanol from wood pulp. You know how much wood pulp waste we produce here. I thought I'd bring him out here, fund his little project, see where it went."

"So he's running some kind of factory out there in the woods?"

Wilmot nodded. "Labor's a little tight around here right now. A bunch of Congolese women showed up in Coeur d'Alene last year, escaping from the genocide in eastern Congo. I hired them to help John out."

"I was wondering," Evan said. "When I found John here . . . well, I found it odd that you hired him to take care of me."

"He's your friend, isn't he?" Wilmot said sharply. "You've known him since he was this high." Evan's father held his hand two feet off the ground.

Evan didn't say anything. John was pleasant enough to Evan, and was always scrupulous in his duties. But Evan understood people. He was pretty sure John Collier resented him as much as ever.

Wilmot put his arm around Evan. It felt nice. He knew his father loved him . . . but he wasn't an effusive or emotional guy. "You're going to get cold out here, son."

"I'm fine. Feels good, actually."

His father squeezed his shoulder. He seemed uncharacteristically meditative. Ordinarily he was in constant motion, always doing something, directing somebody, driving forward, pressing on.

"Let's get you back inside before you catch a cold," he said, stepping behind the wheelchair and pushing it back inside without waiting for Evan's consent.

For months there had been whispered conversations between Collier and his father, sudden changes in their demeanor when he rolled into a room. Somewhere in the back of his doped-up brain, he'd been dimly aware of their strange behavior, but now that he was feeling clearheaded, he felt like he was being whacked in the face with it. Now, as his father pushed him back into the warmth of the house, Evan felt more sure than ever that something was wrong. Why would his father hire a bunch of African women who didn't speak English to work at an experimental ethanol plant in the middle of the Idaho woods when there were plenty of local out-of-work loggers who would gladly do hard work for shit pay?

Although it had wrecked his body, Evan remained proud of his service to his country. But Evan's sacrifice had changed his father, turned him from an outspoken isolationist into someone whose quiet anger ran deeper than Evan could fathom. Now, Evan was determined to find out what he and Collier were up to.

Keeping his sudden resolve to himself, Evan pushed the joystick, steering the wheelchair away from his father. "See you later, Dad."

"Where is Christiane?" Amalie demanded. "You say everything is fine but you won't show me Christiane!"

"Okay, okay," he said. "I'll take you to her. Will you calm down if I promise to take you to her?" He shepherded Amalie down the semicircular driveway in front of the massive Wilmot house. He had been planning to deal with her in the barn. But he could see that wasn't going to work. She was still too agitated.

"Let's get in the car," he said, placing a hand on her arm.

She yanked her arm free of his hand and glared at him.

"Do you want me to take you, or not?"

After a moment, she nodded tensely and walked to Collier's F-150.

Collier sighed loudly and looked back over his shoulder. He wanted to make sure that he didn't do anything Mr. Wilmot would disapprove of.

Evan and Wilmot were still up on the balcony, looking down at him.

The sight of Wilmot with his arm around Evan's shoulder was like a knife twisting in his gut. Collier was not the sort of person to spend a lot of time reflecting on the past. But he couldn't help thinking about the time he'd left this place.

It had been an ugly thing. And only Wilmot knew the whole story.

John Collier had been born right here on the property. His mother had been Evan's babysitter and housekeeper.

It was never clear who Collier's father was. His mother wouldn't say. And she'd died before he wormed the truth out of her. As a kid, Collier had occasionally fantasized that Wilmot himself was his father. But the older he got, the less plausible that seemed. Where Dale Wilmot was big and strong and rawboned and square jawed, Collier was small and delicate and thin, with fine, almost elfin features, and red hair. Since Collier's mother was none of these things, it could only be that he'd gotten these qualities from his father.

Still, growing up fatherless on the estate, he couldn't help but look toward Wilmot as a father figure. There had been no other candidate—unless you included Arne Szellenborg, the Wilmot family butler/gardener/whatever, who was queer as a three-dollar bill and had a barely hidden drinking problem.

Wilmot had intermittently recognized Collier's talents—rewarding him with a watch or a BB gun when he won the spelling bee or the science fair. But Wilmot's attention to Collier had always been off-handed, a bone thrown to the help.

And so John Collier had grown up in the shadow of Evan.

Evan, the golden boy. Evan, the perfect son. Evan, in whom Dale Wilmot had clearly placed all his hope for the future.

And Evan, the son of a bitch, was worthy of those hopes. Where Wilmot was handsome in a slightly brutal way, Evan was downright beautiful, his features chiseled and fine boned. Where Wilmot had earned a football scholarship at U of I based on his relentlessness and competitive spirit (and possibly on his cruelty), Evan had won trophy after trophy on pure grace, on an ability to run distances without tiring, on a gift for sensing holes in the defensive line and snaking through for impossible eight- and ten- and fifteen-yard gains. Where Wilmot saw men as tools he could pluck from a box and manipulate, Evan had a genuine interest in people. He was a leader because people wanted him to like them, not because he calculated the advantage he might gain from them. It was only in school that Collier could offer Evan any competition at all. In every class, Evan Wilmot was first and John Collier was second. Except science and math, where it was the other way around.

Three weeks before Evan's eighteenth birthday, he had won the state dressage championships down in Nampa in his age range. And so, for his birthday, Wilmot had given his son a $75,000 horse.

Collier's birthday, as it happened, fell only two days later. Wilmot got him a $500 gift certificate to Radio Shack.

The disparity had chafed at Collier. Every day he'd gotten out of bed, looked out the window of the little house where he and his mom lived. He'd hear the sound of his mother hacking and coughing as she cleared her lungs with a first cigarette, and look out the window at the ring where Evan was already busy working with his horse. Rising up behind the paddock was the Wilmot house. Like everything that touched Wilmot, it was a reflection of the man himself. At first glance the house looked like any other large pseudo-rustic post-and-beam house that you might find throughout the western mountains of the United States. It was only after a certain amount of comparison between the building and its foreground that you realized just how massive it was. It had a sort of sham humility that was not supposed to fool you but to give off the message: "See, I'm just like you. Normal, no frills, salt-of-the-earth, jeans-and-work boots. Except vastly superior to you in every aspect."

Collier watched Evan canter and then gallop, practicing jump after jump. Collier was allowed to ride the horses on occasion, so he knew just how beautifully Evan rode. It was early, not yet hot, but Evan had already taken his shirt off. A thin sheen of sweat covered his perfectly proportioned torso.

After a moment Collier saw a figure appear on the balcony of the Wilmot home. It was Dale Wilmot himself, wearing a bathrobe. He stared down at his son for a long time. Evan couldn't see his face. But he didn't need to. It was evident in every motion of Wilmot's body—a sense of pride and accomplishment. This is mine. My land, my house, my timber, my view . . . my perfect son.

The rage spilled through Collier like a fountain of acid. No matter what he did, no matter what he achieved, no matter where he went in life, there would never be a father who would look at him the way Wilmot looked at Evan. Never.

Collier had a chemistry lab set up in the garage. He had started it in elementary school and over the years accumulated a decent supply of beakers and test tubes, pipettes, jars of chemicals, a small centrifuge, a Bunsen burner, and an autoclave. If he wasn't working on schoolwork, he was performing chemistry experiments. Always an unhappy child, Collier found something in the lab that approached joy. The sense of power as the chemicals coalesced and changed. The exactitude, care, and precision that was so unlike the messiness of life. All of the giggling phoniness of the girls, the cruelty of the PE coaches, the idiocy of the school administrators, the stupidity of the boys—all of them playing by rules he couldn't fathom. His childhood had been one misery after another.

But he understood the chemicals. If it was possible, he even loved them. The drip-drip of titration, the sensitivity to temperature and pressure, the dance of catalyst, reactant, and reagent, the beauty of the arrows that said this plus this yields this.

After watching Evan ride the horse for nearly an hour, Collier went into the garage and worked for six hours straight. To produce what he produced—without causing an explosion, without poisoning himself on the waste gases, without ruining the batch and producing some placid beaker of worthless sludge—required total concentration.

In the end, the chemistry worked perfectly. But everything else had fallen apart.

He concocted a poison to put in the horse's feed bag. He'd practiced on other animals over the years, but this one was specifically designed to cause the horse a maximum of pain. The dose, too, had been precisely calculated. Just enough to kill the horse. But not enough to do it quickly.

He had soaked the oats in the poison, then put the feed bag in the stall. The horse had sniffed at the bag, and for a moment Collier had thought the horse wouldn't eat it, that something about the odorless chemical would alert the sensitive nose of the horse.

But then the horse had begun eating, crunching away on the oats until they were gone. Minutes later the horse fell and began to twitch and scream.

As the horse writhed on the ground, he felt a power coursing through him and settling in his loins. He found himself standing there, mesmerized by his handiwork, thrilling with his newfound strength. The horse kicked and thrashed while Collier smiled, swelling with pride.

And then, he'd heard a noise. Turning around, he saw Wilmot standing silently in the doorway, a look of horror on his face. Collier's eyes flicked toward the beaker of colorless liquid on the gatepost, then to the horse, then to Wilmot, then to the beaker again.

Collier froze, expecting Wilmot to leap into the stall, maybe start beating the crap out of him. Instead the man spoke in a quiet, measured voice that only seemed to underscore his rage.

"Get your things," he said. "And get the hell out of here."

Collier ran as fast as he could out the barn's double-wide entrance.

His mother was sewing a torn garment when he stumbled back into the house. "What the hell did you go and do now?"

By way of answer, he had gone into the garage, locked the door, and smashed every beaker and pipette and test tube while his mother howled at him through the door. "What the hell's wrong with you, you disgraceful little snot?"

Afterward, he'd shoved past her, packed his few belongings in an old army rucksack that he'd bought the previous summer down at the Army Navy down in Coeur d'Alene. He'd saved twenty-seven hundred bucks from his job at the Pack 'n Save. Enough to set him up down in Boise for a while.

That had been six years ago. In the meantime, he found his way to West Virginia, where he met Verhoven and began using his considerable chemistry talents to cook meth for him. He hadn't seen Mr. Wilmot or Evan until the day Wilmot walked in unannounced at Verhoven's packing store where Collier worked during the day in the back office handling the ordering and accounting. Evan had been hurt, Wilmot explained, and he needed Collier back at the house. Collier's mother was dead, and his own life numb and meaningless, but Wilmot's arrival was like a second chance, a new lease on the family he'd always wished he'd had.

Poisoning the horse had been the height of stupidity. What was he thinking?

He should have poisoned Evan.

• • •

Amalie sat in the Jeep, listening to the whirring of the heater. It seemed like Mr. Collier had pinched her. But now, looking back, she realized there had been something in Mr. Collier's hand when he opened the door to the car, something that had stung her on the hip. For some reason, though, she was feeling a little confused. So she sat and waited patiently as Mr. Collier slammed the door and circled around to the driver's side.

He started the Jeep and began to drive.

As the trees passed outside, it became very warm inside. With the warmth she began to relax. *I've been so tense,* she thought to herself. *The whole time I've been here, I've been tense.*

But for all her worrying, nothing really bad had actually happened. Sure, Christiane had gotten sick. But people got the Konzo at home, too. It was one of those things that just happened. And now she was being treated by an American doctor. Back in Kama, there were no doctors at all. You had to take the boat forty kilometers downriver to see a doctor.

Soon Amalie began to feel a deep calm running through her, a sort of peace that she had only felt a few times in her life. She realized that she was very tired. She'd been working too hard, hadn't she? So tired.

She could feel the sleep coming from a great distance, like a downpour on the horizon, the first blessed rain after the long dry season. She imagined flashes of lightning amid the dark boiling clouds, great winds whipping and tearing at the trees.

And then the black storm washed over her. And with it, came peace.

11

ANDERSON, WEST VIRGINIA

I prefer to work in a chair," Lorene Verhoven said. "Maybe I'm lazy, I don't know, but I get tired feet when I stand for too long."

Ervin Mixon was himself sitting in a chair. Unlike Lorene Verhoven, he was secured at his wrists, feet, neck, and chest by black duct tape. His mouth, too, was covered by duct tape so he was unable to speak. The chair sat in a dark concrete bunker of a room. He was familiar with the room. It was the place where Jim Verhoven's people cooked their meth—a cheerless but carefully built space that had been designed by John Collier. Forty feet belowground, you could yell until your throat bled and nobody would ever hear you.

He had been here for several hours, entirely alone. Until Lorene showed up.

"Jim gave me this chair. It's made by Steelcase, and you can roll around on it." Lorene demonstrated, pushing off with her feet and propelling herself across the polished concrete floor. "Isn't this fun?"

"Fuck you," Ervin tried to say. But his mouth was covered by the same duct tape that secured him to the chair so it came out, "Mmmm-mwoooo."

"Oh, Ervin," she said. "Do you *have* to? You know, I was raised in an atmosphere of constant profanity. But Jim took me away from that. I haven't cursed in eight years. Not once. Jim showed me how much better you feel when you stop swearing. You should try it."

She rolled the chair back toward him, step by step, until finally she was sitting face-to-face with Ervin, their knees nearly touching. She was dressed, as usual, in a crisp white cotton blouse, buttoned to the neck, and a black sheath skirt that Ervin might have found sexy under other circumstances. Over the blouse, she wore an incongruous tan vest, apparently homemade, which was covered with numerous oddly shaped little pockets.

"I was always good at art," she said. "After I got together with Jim, I discovered my talent for taxidermy. My favorite thing? Squirrels. They're so small. The work requires real devotion. Precision. The face especially. The eyes. The lips. The skin is just paper thin."

Ervin felt sick, terrified. He was afraid he might vomit inside the tape and choke to death. He needed a hit. But it was more than that. As much as Jim Verhoven scared Ervin Mixon, it was his wife who truly terrified him. Although he'd never seen her do anything especially evil, there was a cruel violence in her eyes, those two different colors like a schizo-psychopath, shining too brightly as she came near.

"I made this vest myself, Ervin," she continued. "It's for my taxidermy tools. Each tool that I use has its own little pocket. It saves so much time to know exactly where each and every tool is." She began pulling out tools. "Rasp. Needle. Thread. Various little rotary grinder attachments for my Dremel. Caping knife. Smaller caping knife. Even smaller." She pulled out a tiny curved knife. "I had this one custom made by a knife maker in Arkansas. It's an eyelid knife. That's the hardest part, the eyelids of a squirrel. I love squirrels. Their little teeth?" She curled back her upper lip and mimicked a squirrel munching on a nut.

Then she rolled her chair around to his side, bringing the tiny little knife close to Ervin Mixon's face. He could smell her, a clean soapy scent. Ervin's heart began to pound with terror.

"Don't move," she said softly, pressing one finger delicately against his cheekbone. "Wouldn't want you to get cut inadvertently." Then, with a small noise like the opening of a zipper, she cut a slit in the tape from one side of his mouth to the other. The cut was so perfect that he didn't even feel the knife. He gasped with relief.

"See?" she said. "Didn't spill a single drop of blood."

"Fuck you, you fucking cunt," Ervin Mixon said.

A figure separated itself from the darkness. Mixon recognized it as Jim Verhoven. How long had he been there? Mixon hadn't even seen him enter.

"I'd ask you not to speak to my wife that way," Verhoven said.

Ervin Mixon didn't even look at him, though. He couldn't take his gaze off Lorene's face. She returned his stare with a faint smile, her eyes wide and fixed.

Verhoven put his hand on his wife's shoulder.

"Who have you told about our little operation?" Verhoven asked.

"I don't know what the fuck you're talking about." Ervin Mixon heard his own voice, high and shaky. He was trying to control his terror. But there was nothing he could do.

Verhoven held up the recording Mixon had made of his conversation. That's when Mixon knew he was truly fucked.

"Eyelids," Verhoven said mildly. "I think we'll save his eyes for later." She reached toward him with her blade.

"Wait!" Ervin Mixon tried to thrash around, but he was secured so tightly with the tape that he could barely move. "I'll tell you what you want to know—"

But before he could continue, Lorene made one quick stroke with her blade, slicing open his left eyelid. Before the searing pain had even begun, blood pooled in his eye, obscuring half his vision.

Ervin Mixon began to scream.

12

Tillman drove his fifteen-year-old Dodge pickup around the rear of Circle Seven Packing Company. With the hog tied to the hood, he backed up to the loading dock and parked with the engine idling. He honked once, and the metal door scrolled slowly open.

The man standing on the loading dock was the owner of the shop, Jim Verhoven. As usual, he was dressed in BDUs and combat boots. Circle Seven was a thinly veiled front for Verhoven's real business, a way for him to pay the minimum in taxes to avoid federal inquiry. Everyone knew his employees were busy distributing meth while Verhoven tended to the occasional slaughterhouse and meat-processing business.

"My goodness," Verhoven said as Tillman climbed out of the cab, "that is one monster hog."

His speech was excessively formal, Tillman noted, as if he were a foreigner who had learned English from a book. Tillman looked into the bed of his truck and nodded. "Yup," he said.

"What'd you take him with?"

"You wouldn't believe me if I told you," Tillman said.

Verhoven raised one eyebrow.

"I was shooting a longbow," Tillman said. "He spooked, I blew my shot, and I ended up going hand-to-hand with the sumbitch.

Lost my knife in the scuffle, finally had to stab him to death with an arrow."

There was a steel track extending out over the loading dock, with a chain and a hook attached to it. Verhoven pulled the chain down and hooked it to the rear legs of the hog. "Look at those tusks!" he said as he hoisted the carcass up by the legs. "Lucky he didn't gut you like a fish."

Tillman laughed. "Wasn't for want of trying." He pulled up his pant leg to show off the eight-inch-long bandage on his calf.

"My, my," Verhoven said. Then he turned and hauled the hog down the steel runner back into the little slaughterhouse. After a moment he came back out and said, "Normally it'd take until to-morrow around noon." Verhoven studied Tillman impassively for a moment. "Might could do it while you wait, if you was to keep me company."

Tillman looked at his watch. He knew that Verhoven was inter-ested in him—and had been for a while. Guys with Tillman's résumé didn't come around every day. Members of Verhoven's militia group had spoken to Tillman in the past, inviting him to come over for briefings or maneuvers or training now and then. But Tillman had always put them off—and not always politely.

This time he wanted an invitation he could accept. But he didn't want to press or seem overeager. He needed to let Verhoven come to him.

"Sure," Tillman said. "I guess I could stay a little."

He followed Verhoven inside, watched in silence as the "colo-nel" sharpened a long boning knife on an Arkansas stone. There was something sinister about the room. Everything was sparkling clean, and the fluorescent fixtures overhead flooded the room with pale, shadowless light. Chains and hooks and cutting implements lined the stainless steel walls, everything gleaming and sharp and purposeful.

With one swift stroke Verhoven slit the boar from pelvis to breastbone, the guts spilling out onto the floor in a glistening blue pile.

"Sorry I didn't field dress it," Tillman said. "I was pretty much whipped by the time I got the bastard home last night."

"Truth be told, I'd rather do it myself." Verhoven cut the anus out of the pig in two swift motions, then yanked the intestines free of the body. "I can't tell you how many times a day I end up spoiling a great deal of meat because some cretin poked a hole in the guts and flooded the body cavity with fecal matter."

Verhoven worked silently for almost a minute before he said, "I know who you are."

Tillman gave Verhoven a long, hard look. "The reason I moved up here was to be left alone."

"I would, too," Verhoven said, "if I'd been as wronged by the United States of America as you've been."

Tillman let the comment pass.

"I don't know if you know it," Verhoven continued, "but to people like me, people who believe in the true America, the pure and unspoiled America that our founders envisioned, the name Tillman Davis epitomizes true heroism."

"Kind of you to say," Tillman said. "But whatever I did or didn't do for the United States, it's in my past. I'm just trying to get on with my life."

This was not a pose. Tillman knew that he had become a sort of Rorschach blot during his trial. Those on the far left of the political spectrum saw him as a rogue military adventurer, while those on the far right claimed him as a kind of folk hero, a scapegoat for a failed foreign policy. For a while after he'd gotten out of prison, he'd been assailed by self-serving people who'd wanted him to speak or to write or appear on television or otherwise serve their own ends by either making him into a whipping boy, or by holding him up as the victim of a tyrannical government. Neither had been a role he was willing to play. So one day he'd simply thrown his cell phone in a ditch and driven him up here, where he could live unmolested.

"Would you be interested in mounting this fine specimen?" Verhoven asked, indicating the boar's massive head.

"Wouldn't have any use for it."

"Shame for it to go to waste. A hog like this, I'd mount it here in the shop as a conversation piece."

"It's yours for the mounting."

"Much obliged. I'll give you my services for free in exchange."

Tillman nodded. He could feel Verhoven working his way around to something. But he wasn't quite sure what it was. Maybe it was just an invitation to come up and play soldier with his militia group. But Tillman had a feeling that there was something more in the wind than just that.

Verhoven caped the boar silently, his movements slow and methodical as he cut the delicate skin of the head free from the skull. Occasionally he stopped to sharpen one of the small knives, shaving off little patches of hair on his arm to test the keenness of the edge.

"You have to be especially careful around the eyes," Verhoven said finally. "One slip, and the entire effort is wasted. I'm not bad at this, but I'm just a butcher compared to my wife. You'll have to meet her sometime. She's an extraordinary woman."

Tillman folded his arms, leaned against the concrete wall.

"Would I be prying if I inquired as to how you make a living?" Verhoven said. "I only ask because I read that you were robbed of your military pension."

Tillman didn't speak for a while. "I live pretty simple. Hunt, fish, grow a little corn, some tomatoes, some beans."

Verhoven continued scraping the skin free of the pig's eyes.

"Now and again, though," Tillman continued. "Now and again, I'll take an assignment for somebody I trust. Or maybe put one person I trust in touch with another person I trust."

Verhoven didn't look up from his work, his face a mask of concentration. "I only mention it because I've recently come into a rather pressing need for several unusual items. Items that one can't just buy off eBay."

"And, what—you think I might be the kind of guy who could help you get them?"

Verhoven pulled the cape free of the boar, covered the interior surfaces with a heavy coating of salt, then set it carefully inside a large plastic bin. He began butchering the hog in earnest now.

"There's a good deal of markup when one sells things that the federal government finds objectionable," Verhoven said. "I only mention this in the context of what seems to be the unfairness of your circumstances."

"It gets better by the day, too," Tillman said bitterly. "I recently had my right to get treated at the VA hospital taken away from me. Got a form letter in the mail. Fifteen years honorable service in the US Army, then another ten with a certain agency that shall go nameless, and the federal government just . . ." He rubbed his palms together like he was washing his hands.

Verhoven's face grew pinched and angry. "Goddamn traitorous bastards," he said. Then his face relaxed again. "I'm sorry, but it angers me."

Tillman felt briefly as though something very cold had been permitted to melt inside him. He realized how lonely it had been, how hard it had been to stand up straight every day when he'd been accused of betraying the trust of the very country he risked his life to serve. For a moment he felt terribly grateful to Verhoven.

The moment passed, though. He was here for a purpose, and he knew he needed to stay focused on that. He had promised Gideon.

"You get to where you have a hard time trusting anybody," Tillman said. "I want to trust people. I do. And yet I can't afford the luxury."

Verhoven shook his head sadly. "That is a very, very keen insight, sir," he said. "I feel much the same way myself." He sliced a long section of backstrap free of the big beast, set it on a package. "It seems to me to be the central tragedy of our nation. We need to trust each other. We need to feel a sense of brotherhood. We have such a hunger for it. And yet, we are surrounded by enemies in our midst." He chopped the ribs free with a small hatchet. When he was finished chopping, he added, "I sense a bond between us, sir. And so I'm going to take a leap and trust you. The items I spoke of . . . I need them quite soon. A gentleman promised me these items and then welshed on the deal. It's put me in a very, very uncomfortable position."

Tillman said nothing.

Verhoven took the last bones off the hook, tossed them in the garbage, and then began hosing down the concrete floor. "If I were to give you a list of items I needed, would you be able to get them for me? Would you extend me that trust?"

Tillman watched the bloody water circle the drain. "You got a list?"

Verhoven pulled a piece of butcher paper off a roll, scrawled something on it, and handed it to Tillman.

Tillman read the list.

Det cord
.50 caliber BMG—armor piercing incendiary
Blasting caps
C4 breaching charges

"Sounds like you're throwing quite a party," Tillman said drily.

"All I can say is that something historic is about to happen. If you were to help me with this, you would be contributing to an event of great importance."

"Why would I want to do that," Tillman said, "after all I've been through?"

"We all have to decide where we stand, don't we? I can't answer that question for you."

Tillman paused, put a thoughtful look on his face. He'd set the hook perfectly. Now was the time to begin reeling him in.

"I could make some phone calls," Tillman said finally.

Verhoven finished spraying off the floor. "Why don't you join me for dinner this evening and we can discuss the details?" he said as he hung the sprayer on a hook. "My wife, I know, would consider it a privilege to meet you."

"I'd like that," Tillman said. "I'd like that very much."

13

POCATELLO, IDAHO

Its over! We're going home!"

It took Amalie a moment to get her bearings. She woke feeling groggy, slightly nauseated, and with a pounding headache. The sound of the other women laughing and exclaiming was like knives piercing her head. She sat up and looked around, still feeling disoriented. She had been lying in her bed in the windowless dormitory where she and the other Congolese women had been housed.

"Sleeping beauty rises," said Estelle Olagun, the oldest woman, looking at Amalie with her lips pursed in her usual attitude of disapproval.

The other women laughed. All the women from the factory were in the dormitory, a palpable air of jubilance about them.

One of the younger girls held up a fan of money, American hundred-dollar bills. "Monsieur Collier paid us!" she shouted joyfully. "Look! He even gave us each a five-hundred-dollar bonus. We're going home rich!"

The women began to dance. "We're going home! We're going home!"

Amalie shook her head—partly to clear the cobwebs and partly in disagreement. It was coming back to her, her exchange with Collier, the pinch he'd given her. It had made her sleep—she saw that now. He'd been shutting her up. He'd lied about taking her to see Christiane at the doctor.

"No!" she shouted. "He lies!"

The women stopped dancing and stared at her accusingly. "Why must you always be so negative?" Estelle said.

"He told me he was going to take me to Christiane!" Amalie said hotly. "But he didn't. Instead he gave me a poison that made me sleep."

One of the women pointed at the little table next to her bed. A thick envelope lay on the table with Amalie's name written on it. "And I suppose the one thousand five hundred dollars he left you is poisoned, too?"

Amalie grabbed the envelope and held it over the bed. Sure enough, a thick pile of money fell out onto the blankets. She picked up one of the bills, held it against the light. Even in the Congo, you learned how to spot real American money—the watermarks, the little security stripes, the shifting colors. The rebels from Burundi and Rwanda were always printing fakes, so you had to know. It was obvious: The money was real.

For a moment, doubt infected her.

"Look at her face!" one of the other girls hooted, pointing at her. "She's been so sure that something horrible is going on, that when something *good* actually happens, it makes her angry."

The other women laughed.

The laughter continued until the loud, ominous hissing noise started in the far corner of the room. She smelled something odd, too, the faintest tinge of a sour, nutty odor.

Everyone turned to look. It was a noise unlike anything she'd heard inside the big metal building before.

"The heating is making a strange sound," Estelle said, frowning.

But Amalie knew it wasn't the heating. She didn't know what it was, but she knew something was wrong, and she didn't want to be here anymore. She ran toward the door and twisted the handle. But the door wouldn't open. She scrabbled at the lock and shouted, "*Ouvrez! Ourvrez la porte!*"

The other women had begun screaming. Then one woman fell. Then another. Two more began clawing at their throats and foaming at the mouth. Another began raking her face with her own finger-nails, slashing so hard that blood began trickling down one side of her face before she fell.

At last only Amalie was still alive.

She continued to pound on the door. "*Tu bâtard*! Monsieur Collier, *tu putain bâtard!*"

The girl's anger turned to panic. She began shrieking—a horrible inhuman noise like the grinding of some unoiled engine. Then she fell to the floor, where she began spasming, slamming her head into the door so hard it boomed.

From the other side of the one-way glass, Collier and Wilmot observed the dying women.

"According to my model, there's a little air pocket around the door," Collier said. "It creates a sort of whirlpool effect and it takes a while before the gas reaches the door. Whoever gets there is the last to die."

Wilmot watched Amalie writhing in agony.

"She's *tu-toyezing* me," Collier said. "It's very disrespectful. Frankly I'm a little hurt."

Wilmot didn't think it was funny. The glee that Collier took from poisoning and killing sickened him. But that was the cost of enlisting a sociopath. Wilmot still had enough humanity, however, to feel pained at the death of these innocent young women. But collateral damage was an inevitable part of war, he told himself, and the innocent were often sacrificed for the greater good.

"Cyanide gas liquefies at seventy degrees Fahrenheit," Collier said. "The moment that the jets come on the liquid sodium cyanide turns to gas." He looked at his watch.

Amalie was foaming at the mouth. Her body twitched with one last spasm, and then went still.

"Eighteen seconds," said Collier.

The fans continued their work, but the cyanide had already been dispersed. There was no movement behind the glass.

Collier handed Wilmot a respirator, and the two men placed gas masks over their faces. Then Collier unbolted the door, and the two men stepped inside.

The dormitory in which the women were housed had not been constructed randomly. Its dimensions were carefully chosen: 181 feet by 209 feet, with a 47-foot ceiling. The contours of the walls, the height of the ceiling, designed precisely according to plans revised and signed by the architect Thomas Walter in 1851 when he expanded the US Capitol and added its famous dome. The air volume of the room was precisely 1.777 million cubic feet.

Wilmot had secured the new heating and air contract at the Capitol last year. The idea had been Wilmot's, but the plan was Collier's. It was the only reason Wilmot had gone to West Virginia to find him. After Collier poisoned Evan's horse, Wilmot banished the boy from his home. He never expected to see him again. But in war, as in politics, you couldn't always choose your allies, and Wilmot needed someone with Collier's expertise and loyalty.

Now Collier pointed to the massive set of fans and ducts that stood behind the metal building. "This machine duplicates the real one in every single detail," he continued. "It was designed by Clauser Industries in Bettendorf, Iowa, and installed last March. The machine includes four compressor units, an eight-million BTU natural gas furnace, and a set of three-gang blowers capable of moving well over one million cubic feet per minute. An active baffling system allows zone heating so that certain portions of the building can be heated at different temperatures than others. By taking command of the controls, we can override the normal baffling system and direct all three sets of blowers into a single zone, effectively tripling throughput. Because cyanide gas is heavier than air, my air-flow models indicate it's not necessary to replace one hundred percent of the air volume in order to—"

Wilmot pushed at one of the bodies with his toe, suddenly anxious to get out of there.

"I'm sorry. I'm talking too much." Despite the frigid air inside the building, Collier's upper lip glistened with sweat and his hands shook slightly. A terrible, empty smile came and went briefly.

"Why don't you just give me the bottom line?"

Collier cleared his throat. "Bottom line? When we override the system we'll have about forty-five seconds before the ignition turns on, then another thirty seconds until the gas jets fire. By the time they realize what's happening, it will be too late."

Because cell phone and most radio transmissions were jammed, they would have to go into the belly of the beast themselves and trigger the ignition manually. There would be no coming back, but they were willing to sacrifice their lives for the greater cause.

As he surveyed the corpses—the panic of the women still reflected in their lifeless stares and in the impossible angles of their limbs—Dale Wilmot realized he had crossed a line from which he could no longer step back. Before now, their plan had been an abstraction, but for Wilmot, killing these women had made it a flesh-and-blood reality. As he watched the life draining from their bodies, he felt draining from his own body whatever residual uncertainty remained. Flashing in his mind's eye like a rapid-fire slide show, he saw the faces of the hypocrites—the politicians and the corporate titans—whose photographs hung on his wall.

"Take care of the mess," said Wilmot. "We'll leave first thing in the morning."

14

FBI HEADQUARTERS, WASHINGTON, DC

Ray Dahlgren remained seated behind his desk as Nancy Clement entered his office. The office was nondescript, with no trappings of authority, no family photos, no framed diplomas on the wall. It could have been the cell of a monk. His desk was entirely bare, except for a single piece of paper situated squarely in the middle of the desktop.

Dahlgren was typing on his computer, attacking the keyboard like a boxer trying to batter an opposing fighter into submission. He did not look up, or even turn away from the screen, nor did he invite Nancy to sit.

"Is it me?" he said.

"Pardon?"

"Is there something about me that invites disloyalty? Hm? Something that begs for insubordination?"

Nancy cleared her throat but did not answer. When Dahlgren engaged in this sort of performance, it was always a solo act. He was not inviting participation.

Dahlgren typed a few more lines. Then, with one last stab at the keyboard, he finished savaging the computer and swiveled around in his chair to face her. He made a minute adjustment in the location of the piece of paper in the middle of his desk, as though to square it perfectly with the rest of the furniture. "I trust you are aware of our computer system, VORTEX?"

Nancy was. VORTEX was a computer system designed to cull and correlate vast quantities of data to isolate potential terrorist threats. Phone records, pharmacy purchases, credit card data, flight records, computer searches—the list of databases went on and on.

"I'm a simple man," Dahlgren said. "I don't pretend to understand how VORTEX works. It's been explained to me a dozen times. But when I start hearing about third-order correlations and stochastic variates, my eyes glaze over. What I do understand is that when the computer generates a report that so-and-so is connected to such-and-such, I pay attention."

Nancy nodded. She had been tangentially involved in the development of VORTEX and found that it had been a fairly disappointing tool, given the hundred or so million dollars invested in it. But on occasion something useful popped out.

"My understanding of VORTEX, though, is that it operates by drawing connections. Vectors, I believe they're called? And then those vectors are assigned a numeric value based on the potential connection between one scumbag and another scumbag. The higher the number, the more profound the connection. Hm? That about right?"

Again Nancy nodded. Her heart was beating a little harder. Dahlgren was not one who usually beat around the bush. In the rare instance when he didn't come right to the point, it was because he wanted to beat you up and humiliate you.

"The reason I bring this up," Dahlgren said, "is I tracked your friend Gideon Davis because I didn't trust he'd leave well enough alone. And now I find here a report linking one Gideon Davis to one Jim Verhoven. I'll spare you the technical mumbo jumbo about threat nodes and assessment vectors. But look here. I drill down into the details a little and, guess what I find? Your pal Mr. Davis bought gas two and a half hours ago in Anderson, West Virginia. Last I heard, Ervin Mixon was occasionally bunking at the camp owned by Jim Verhoven in Anderson, West Virginia."

Nancy didn't speak. Nothing she could say at this point would do her any good.

"You might have noticed I was typing when you came into my

office," Dahlgren continued. "I was starting an OPR file on you." Dahlgren hesitated, relishing the moment, before he continued: "For requisitioning equipment without authorization, disobeying direct orders, various irregularities in your expense reports . . . I'm still coming up with examples of your insubordination."

OPR was the FBI's Office of Professional Responsibility—analogous to the Internal Affairs found in police departments. OPR investigated everything from corruption to sexual misconduct to treason. An OPR file, at best, was a career killer. At worst, it could result in firing, criminal charges, and even prison.

Dahlgren continued, his voice dripping with condescension. "Our office has two missions, Nancy, with respect to potential domestic terrorist organizations. One is to pursue those who violate the law. That's a simple matter. But the other is more delicate. Our other mission is to monitor, anticipate, and control those who might break the law but have not yet done so. The vast majority of militia groups, neo-Nazis, racists, and Aryan nut jobs, are just saber-rattling cretins who do not and will not ever threaten the good order of the United States of America. But there are some—and Verhoven's group is one of these—which are on the fence. They could fall either way." He took off his reading glasses and set them on the desk. "Nancy, it is critical that the FBI never, ever, be the one to push them off the fence. The Federal Bureau of Investigation is not going to create another Waco. Not on my watch."

"Sir—"

"Shut up, Nancy." Dahlgren did not raise his voice. "I'm a reasonable man. You are a valuable agent in your way. I've opened the OPR file, checked the little boxes, filled in all the forms, typed in the relevant paragraphs. But I haven't sent it yet. Whether I send it or not will depend on whether or not Gideon Davis has pushed Verhoven off the fence."

"I don't know what you're asking me."

"Did you send Gideon Davis up there to snoop around and ask questions about Mixon?"

"Send?" Nancy said. "I didn't *send* him."

Dahlgren shook his head sadly. "Jesus Christ, are you entirely incapable of giving me a straight answer to a simple question?"

Nancy was silent.

"Did you, in fact, requisition FBI property from Operational Technology Division including a Motorola model 231A single side-band radio transceiver/receiver, a Bluewater GPS tracking device, a Bushnell 2.5 by 24 night-vision spotting scope and two digitally encrypted cell phones?"

"Yes," she admitted.

"And did you not, further, transfer possession of said equipment without departmental authorization to Gideon Davis, a civilian with no formal relationship to the Federal Bureau of Investigation?"

She thought she'd covered her tracks well. Apparently, not well enough. There was only one thing left to do.

"No," she lied. "I requisitioned that material for a training op."

Dahlgren sighed loudly. "I don't believe you. And when I find out you're lying to me, I will most certainly hit the send button on your OPR file."

"But—"

"I can see this is going to require my personal intervention. That makes me extremely unhappy. I have not yet decided precisely what I will need to do to stop your friend Gideon from provoking some kind of public relations disaster. But it will most certainly involve me going down there to speak directly to Mr. Verhoven and appealing to his better nature, so that if he should happen across Mr. Davis blundering around on his property, he will not shoot him."

"But sir, what if—"

Dahlgren's glare silenced her.

Nancy Clement returned to her office, closed the door, sat down, and put her head in her hands. What was she going to do? She had to reach Gideon and warn him. Dahlgren would be there by tomorrow and would certainly find him and shut him down. Then it would be her job, and Gideon's neck. And what if he and his brother had found something? She made her decision, got up, and left the office.

15

ANDERSON, WEST VIRGINIA

It did not escape Tillman's notice that Jim Verhoven's compound shared many of the same characteristics commonly found in fortresses. Situated on the top of a tall hill, it was accessible only by a serpentine dirt road hemmed in so closely by pine trees that only one car at a time could pass along it. And then the house itself lay in the middle of a sizable pasture, which would have to be crossed before reaching the house. A well-armed defender in the house could make a lot of trouble for anybody who wanted to cross that pasture. Behind the house were a number of functional-looking metal buildings. In the distance, were two U-shaped berms that had obviously been ploughed up to function as shooting ranges.

When Tillman's pickup rattled up to the house, Verhoven was in the yard, marching up and down on a parade ground with about twenty young men wearing camouflage uniforms. As Tillman parked, Verhoven barked, "Dismissed!" and the young men drifted off toward a collection of rattletrap cars over near a barnlike structure behind the house.

They shook hands, and Verhoven said, "On paper my unit is company strength, but those fine young men are the core of my militia."

This was Verhoven's way of saying that—despite its grandiose name—the Seventh West Virginia (True) Militia Regiment amounted to roughly one understrength infantry squad. Tillman, however, simply nodded approvingly.

"The purpose of the regiment is to protect the constitutional and God-given freedoms of the people in this region," Verhoven continued. "As I'm sure you'd agree, our freedoms are under unprecedented attack. If the international capitalists and Jews have their way, pretty soon we'll all just be a pathetic mob of slaves, reduced to penury and servitude while the fat cats in New York City and Washington, DC, drive around in limousines drinking champagne."

Tillman smiled mildly, neither agreeing nor disagreeing with the increasingly passionate Verhoven.

"If the storm troopers ever come here trying to take our guns, though, they'll very quickly find out that West Virginians don't cotton to having their rights trampled on." It sounded like Verhoven was quoting something he'd written in a pamphlet—the kind of thing that he and his crew probably dropped off in truck stop bathrooms throughout the state.

Several cars full of young men rolled by. A couple of them bore bumper stickers on the rear that read DON'T TREAD ON ME. Verhoven tossed a crisp salute to each car as it passed.

"Did you serve in the military, Colonel?" Tillman said.

"I did not have that privilege," Verhoven said. "I did, however, serve in the sheriff's office for ten years. Ultimately I became deputy commander of the Hertford County Sheriff's Tactical Unit. I was offered command of the STU, but by that time I was so sickened by government service I was forced to decline and return to private life."

Tillman had heard around town that Verhoven's departure from law enforcement was connected to busting other meth dealers and stealing their clients and product. But he figured that splitting hairs on that point was not going to help his cause.

"My wife, Lorene," Verhoven said, indicating an unusually tall woman with straight, unnaturally blond hair.

Something about Lorene made Tillman nervous the moment he saw her. She dressed with the sort of ostentatious plainness that Tillman associated with Nazi propaganda posters from the 1930s: sheath skirt, starched white cotton blouse, no jewelry other than her wedding ring. Everything about her seemed demure except for her eyes—one brown, one blue—which had an intent staring quality that he'd seen occasionally in a certain variety of battlefield maniac, the kind of guy who liked charging into machine-gun nests.

"I'm so pleased to finally meet you, Mr. Davis," she said, fixing him with her freakish eyes. "We've heard a great deal about your tribulations."

Tillman nodded soberly. She had the same excessively formal manner of speaking as her husband.

"I hope I've cooked the boar to your liking," she said.

"I can't begin to tell you how fine that sounds," Tillman said.

Fifteen minutes later they were seated at a heavy wood table in a room decorated with paintings of eagles, racks of vintage firearms, and a faded reproduction of the US Constitution.

Tillman noticed that Lorene Verhoven was observing him whenever she thought he wasn't looking. He'd turn to try to catch her eye, but at that moment she would look away and busy herself with the dinner. It added to Tillman's feeling of unsettledness.

Verhoven, meanwhile, had begun a monologue—the conversational form to which he seemed best suited. He talked about the dietary shortcomings of vegetarianism, the history of Persia, the calls of various upland game birds, certain subtle issues in the translation of the New Testament from Greek, the hidden reasons for the formation of the European Union, and the reasons why Jews could not enter the Kingdom of Heaven.

"I am tired of going to bank machines where I'm asked if I want to do business in a foreign language," Verhoven said between forkfuls of mashed potatoes and roasted boar. "I am tired of seeing hardworking Americans put out of their jobs by illegal foreigners. I am sick of seeing rich men profit from these people. And while I bear no personal grudge against Mexicans, I don't like seeing my friends living on welfare because nobody hires white roofers or carpenters anymore. I am tired of paying exorbitant taxes. I'm tired of liberals talking about how I'm some kind of bloodthirsty menace to society because I believe in the Second Amendment to the United States Constitution. I'm tired of being unable to turn on a television without exposing my children to a parade of filth and violence and depravity and profanity and vulgarity."

He paused, his hands shaking slightly with emotion.

This was Lorene's cue to excuse herself. "I know you have business to discuss," she said. "I've got some cleaning to do in the kitchen. I'll leave you to it."

Verhoven watched her go, his gaze both feral and adoring. Then he turned to Tillman. "Feel like stretching your legs?" He did not wait for an answer but stood and led Tillman out the back door of his house onto a small patio.

The sun had already gone down, but the clear sky still contained a few vestiges of the evening's light. He waved his hand in a long slow arc, taking in the swath of trees, the broad fields, a couple of grazing horses, the barns, the house—and perhaps the whole valley below it. "I'm proud of what I've accomplished here," he said. Normally his voice was somewhat harsh and strident, as though he were perpetually addressing an audience of people not quite as bright as he. Now, however, it softened, becoming meditative and confiding. "But I've come to realize that these little efforts probably won't change much of anything. Oh, sure, I educate the young minds that will carry the struggle forward. I protect our freedoms—at least on this parcel of ground. But ultimately the fight will be won on a larger battlefield."

Verhoven sounded saddened, maybe a little chastened, as he continued. "I did not come to this conclusion without a certain amount of struggle. You accomplish something in life, you start to get invested in it. Comfortable. Complacent. But there are other minds engaged in the struggle, some of whom are bolder and more ambitious than mine . . ." His voice drifted off.

The night was coming on rapidly. The air was cold and crisp. After a moment's silence Verhoven said, "That list I showed you in the shop earlier. Maybe we could talk about it in greater specificity in the morning?"

Perfect, Tillman thought. That would give him the opportunity to do a midnight reconnoiter. "Sure. I've already made my phone calls."

"Excellent." Verhoven scanned the horizon. "We've got maneuvers at oh dark thirty," he said. "Input from a man of your experience could be enormously valuable to my unit. Join us?"

"I'd be proud to help, sir," Tillman said.

16

Gideon had laid out all of the equipment Nancy gave him on a table in Tillman's house. He had given Tillman a radio. But it was going to be tricky to use. It went without saying that Verhoven would be more than a little suspicious if he saw Tillman chatting away into a radio transmitter. So Tillman would have to get clear of the house in order to reach Gideon.

The plan was for the brothers to join up at the Verhoven property after Tillman's dinner and try to find evidence of Mixon's presence there. The Verhoven property was situated about five miles away as the crow flies, but about fifteen by the circuitous mountain roads he'd have to drive. Although it was cold outside and growing colder by the minute, Gideon was looking forward to the challenge of spending the night in the woods.

After he had checked and rechecked the equipment, Gideon had nothing to do. Tillman didn't have a stereo or a TV. A cheap banjo hung in one corner on a peg. But Gideon had never been the slightest bit musical. A small shelf of books stood in the corner. There were a few thrillers, but most of the books were military history—everything from the Punic Wars through Afghanistan.

There was no dresser. Tillman's entire wardrobe filled two cardboard boxes. The only discordant item in the cabin was a tuxedo hanging on the wall covered in plastic wrap from the rental store.

Tillman was going to be Gideon's best man in just a matter of weeks when Gideon and Kate tied the knot.

The threadbare quality of his brother's life saddened him. Tillman seemed to have so little: neither material possessions nor someone to share his life. And yet, if Gideon were honest, there was a part of his brother's life he envied. The ruggedness; the immediacy; the visceral thrill of the hunt. Waiting for Tillman to radio him, Gideon felt the excitement he recognized from his time on the Obelisk, and from when he first met with Mixon. He had spent his entire adult life avoiding conflict, and now it seemed that part of him craved it.

As he was musing, his cell phone rang. He didn't recognize the number.

He answered the phone and a female voice returned: "Do you have any idea how hard it is to find a pay phone in America today?"

"Nancy?" he said.

"Just listen," she said. "Ray Dahlgren knows everything. I'm calling from a pay phone because for all I know he may be bugging my cell. He figured out that you're up in West Virginia. He's afraid you're going to go stomping around on Verhoven's property, get caught or shot or something, and the next thing he knows, he's going to have another Waco on his hands. I don't know exactly what he's going to do, but I think he's going to come up and warn Verhoven about you."

"What about Tillman? Does he know about Tillman?"

"No."

"When's he coming?"

"Don't know. It's a two-hour drive up to Verhoven's place. My guess is that he'll wait until the morning. But whatever you're going to do, you've got tonight to do it. Tomorrow will be too late."

"I'm waiting for Tillman to contact me."

"I think he should just clear out, Gideon. Both of you should."

Gideon thought about it. "I can't reach him right now."

"Then get him out as soon as you can. It's not worth it."

"Are you serious about Dahlgren bugging your phone?"

"He's threatening to open an OPR file on me. He wouldn't even need a warrant, not for an internal investigation. FBI agents give up their rights on that score when they sign on to the job."

"Then how can I reach you?"

"I'll contact you." Nancy's voice sounded shaky.

"But—"

The phone went dead.

Dammit, Gideon thought, gathering up the FBI surveillance package. *I better get over there.*

17

Lorene was a night owl. Tillman could hear her moving about the house after he went to bed. He could tell it was Lorene because Verhoven called out for her a couple of times. Finally, she stopped prowling and returned to the bedroom, for which Tillman was grateful. But then the bedroom gymnastics began. Lorene was a howler, and just when Tillman thought she had finished, she started up again. It seemed like several hours before all was quiet and Tillman could finally begin looking for Mixon.

He got up and slipped out of his room, then eased down the front hallway to the door.

Gideon had given him an aerial photo of the property. Verhoven owned several hundred acres, most of it in hardwood timber. But in the center was a clearing of fifteen or twenty acres surrounding Verhoven's house. Behind the house was a horse barn, a toolshed, and some other outbuildings. Another 150 yards away—toward the front of the property—lay a long shedlike barracks where the "soldiers" bivouacked. As far as Tillman could tell, there were a good twenty young men in the building, staying there in preparation for the maneuvers in the morning.

The air was cold and clear, and a thin sliver of moon gave Tillman just enough light to move around the property without using a flashlight.

He crossed the grass to the horse barn. Once he was out of ear-shot of the house, he screwed the radio Gideon had given him into his ear. It looked like a Bluetooth for a cell phone but it wasn't. According to Gideon, it ran an encrypted signal on a law enforcement frequency, with an operational range of around a mile.

"I thought you'd fallen asleep." Gideon's voice came out of the earpiece. "I'm freezing my ass off out here."

"I got detained," Tillman said. "Give me a sit-rep."

"Change of plans," said Gideon. "We have until dawn to find Mixon."

"That's not a lot of time."

"Long story, but Nancy's boss is coming down here looking for me."

"So where do we start?"

"There's a guard stationed at the gate on the gravel road coming up from the highway," Gideon said. "He's armed with an AK. The lights went off in the barracks shed about three hours ago."

"Dogs?"

"Nope. I guess Verhoven's a cat person."

"That explains a lot," Tillman said.

Gideon chuckled. "Stay on the radio."

Tillman headed into the horse barn. Three horses slept in their stalls. They didn't even stir at his entrance. He began checking the floor for trapdoors. With all the straw on the floor, it was a painstaking business. The cold was already seeping into his bones.

The brothers had agreed that Tillman would take the area closest to the house and the interior buildings while Gideon scouted the perimeter and the roads. The Verhoven property was vast. Tillman wasn't sure quite where the edges of the property were, but it was clearly well over a hundred acres. Maybe several hundred. After the stables, he searched the barn, and the hayloft. Soon, it was 3:15 A.M. The barracks shed was situated near the gate at the front of the property where upward of a dozen of Verhoven's "soldiers" were spending the night. And after his eyes had adjusted to the light, he had seen that one of the young men was actually standing post at the gate, guarding against interlopers. Which meant he not only had to be quiet, but he also had to move slowly and carefully so as not to attract attention.

Next came a low crawl to the last of the outbuildings clustered near Verhoven's house. Despite the cold, a thin sheen of perspiration covered his brow by the time he'd reached the shed. It contained a tractor, a hay baler, an aging International Harvester stake-bed truck, and a white van with ladders on the top. There was no evidence of any sort of basement, no blood, no handcuffs, no evidence anybody had been tied to a wall or chained to a floor.

He peeked out the various windows, surveying as much of the property as he could, and saw nobody. A sudden idea came to him, and he raised his radio, his voice low. "What's your twenty?"

Gideon's voice answered, "I'm up in the woods about a quarter mile west of you."

"Is there a guard at the gate?"

"Yeah, but he looks like he's sleeping. You find anything?"

"Zilch. No blood, no hidden rooms, no nothing."

"Maybe they've got him in that barracks shed with his militia guys."

"Doesn't make sense," Tillman said. "He's creating twenty potential witnesses to a federal crime if he sticks him down there. You think he trusts all twenty of his guys that much?"

"Not likely. What about the house? Maybe there's a basement."

"No, it's just a typical old farmhouse with a crawl space underneath. There's no basement. But I have an idea where Mixon might be."

"I'm listening," Gideon said.

"Verhoven cooks crystal meth, right? So where does he make it? I didn't see any evidence of chemical manufacturing, no test tubes, no beakers, no pressure vessels. Didn't even smell anything. I mean supposedly meth cooking is the most horrible-smelling thing in the world."

Gideon didn't respond for a moment. "Maybe there's another property somewhere. He might have a cabin up in some holler or something."

"What if it's underground? There's some kind of entrance up near the shooting range."

"Worth a try," Gideon said. "But I still have to scout twenty percent of my grid."

"I'll check it out." During their conversation, Tillman had been making his way toward the front gate where he saw the guard Gideon had spotted. Gideon was right: The kid was totally motionless, slumped over in his seat. Probably dead asleep.

Still, he couldn't take any chances. He dropped to his knees and high-crawled toward a pair of berms four or five hundred yards away. After he'd crawled ten feet, he flattened out, surveyed his surroundings for about a minute, then crawled another slow ten feet. Hunting boar was one thing, but this excruciatingly slow process made him realize how old he'd gotten since he'd last done this as a sniper. Five hundred yards was a hell of a long way at this pace. But it was the only way. He sighed and began to crawl again.

Gideon walked slowly through the woods, surveying the rest of the grid he was responsible for searching. He didn't like letting Tillman out of his sight, but he had no choice. Mixon could be anywhere, and time was running out. The woods were filled with trails leading from Verhoven's house. *Where did they go?* he wondered. If there was a meth factory here somewhere, one of the trails might lead to it. It was a lot of ground to cover in the few hours before dawn.

He began walking slowly up the path, one step, then another, wait, watch, then another step. Gideon's father had taught the boys to move through the forest like that when still-hunting. It was slow, but it was the only way to be relatively sure of not blundering into anybody before you saw them.

The woods were dark and frightening. Now that he was moving, he had warmed up a little. But still he was freezing. It occurred to him that he could hike right out of these woods, climb in his car, and head home. If he left right this second, he could be lying next to Kate before the sun even cracked the horizon.

But of course he wasn't going to do that. Not to Tillman. Not after dragging him here against his will.

He sighed. He couldn't tamp down the creeping feeling, though, that this might be a total waste of time. And a dangerous one at that.

• • •

Tillman reached the shooting range around 5:30 A.M. On one side was a two-hundred-yard rifle range, while the other was a smaller pistol range surrounded by a U-shaped berm. Between them was a small metal shed, chained shut and padlocked. He tried briefly to jimmy the lock. He'd taken a lock-picking course once when he was in the Special Forces. But apparently lock picking was a perishable skill, and he hadn't practiced five times since the class was over.

He finally gave up and worked his way around the building. The shed was built on a concrete pad, with a tiny gap underneath. If he shined his flashlight under the gap, he'd be able to look around inside the shed. He also might wake the sleeping guard.

It was taking a chance, but he was close to half a mile from the house by now. He lay down, probed the interior of the shed with the light. There were some steel shooting plates, some target racks, a couple of five-gallon buckets—probably filled with range brass. But no Mixon. And no sign he might have been here.

There was only one more structure in the area, a tiny concrete shed about four feet high. He was puzzled until he reached it. The far side of the minuscule structure was open. It was a trap house: inside was a small machine for throwing shotgun clays into the air. Only then did he see that the field behind it was littered with smashed bits of orange: thousands and thousands of shattered clay pigeons, barely visible in the moonlight.

He looked at his watch. He realized he needed to be getting back. He would have to get back inside Verhoven's house, and then make some excuse to leave early—before Nancy's boss showed up.

It was two hundred yards back to the shooting range, and another four hundred to the house. No way he'd have time to crawl it. He circled behind the berm at the back of the rifle range, putting himself out of view of the house, then jogged quietly to the rear of the shooting range. When he reached the far side of the berm, he spotted something that made his heart shift into high gear.

Lorene was walking swiftly up the trail toward him. And she was carrying a rifle.

He barely had enough time to remove his radio earpiece before Lorene raised the gun and pointed it at him. "Lorene?" Tillman said.

"Why are you sneaking around the property?" The carbine in her hands was still pointed at him.

"Thought I'd get up and take a look at the terrain before maneuvers started," he said.

"You shouldn't be out here," she said.

"I told you—"

"What are you *really* doing?" Lorene's crazy two-tone eyes narrowed as she stepped toward him. "And don't feed me some bullshit. My husband's a good man, but he can sometimes be a bit naïve."

Tillman held her look, but before he could answer, a sharp crack echoed in the early morning air. Tillman's practiced ear registered it as a .223—the cartridge used in M-16s and its variants: M-4s, AR-15s, and so on. His pulse was suddenly racing. Had somebody discovered Gideon back in the woods?

Lorene turned on him. "You set us up! I told Jim not to trust you!"

"Hold on," said Tillman, raising a hand in self-defense, when he saw three tiny flashes of light down at the gate on the far side of the house. Muzzle flashes. The sound reached them half a second later. *Ba-bang . . . bang.* It sounded like a heavy handgun, probably a .45.

She motioned with the gun. "You're coming with me," she said. "If something's happened to Jim, I swear I will kill you with my own hands."

He didn't give a shit about Jim Verhoven, or Lorene's threats. But if the gunfire had anything to do with Gideon . . .

With Lorene's carbine at his back, Tillman moved swiftly toward the sound of gunfire.

When Gideon heard the gunfire, he had already searched half the trails along the western portion of Verhoven's property but had found no structures or subterranean bunkers anywhere in the woods. When he heard the shot, Gideon tried to reach Tillman on the radio, but got no response. He hurried back toward the shooting range, where he knew his brother was checking. But he couldn't see Tillman anywhere. Peering through the night-vision spotting scope, however, he saw two figures in the distance. One of them was definitely Tillman. The other looked like a woman with a gun.

In his zeal to find the elusive hidden room, he had left his brother exposed. Now he heard more gunfire, and the woman was taking Tillman at gunpoint toward the main house. Gideon drew his pistol and began running through the trees.

18

ANDERSON, WEST VIRGINIA

Sixty seconds earlier Deputy Director Ray Dahlgren had been driving up the long steep gravel drive toward the Verhoven house. The rutted washboard road made the entire body of his Crown Vic vibrate so that even with the windows rolled down, it was impossible to hear anything from outside the car. He had killed the lights, hoping to approach stealthily. But with all the racket the car was making, he now knew there was no point to it.

If anybody was paying any attention at all, they'd hear him coming.

As he was thinking, a gate swam up out of the murky half-light of dawn. He slammed on his brakes—though not in time to prevent the car from thumping into the gate.

He saw movement out of the corner of his eyes, made out a figure bounding up out of a chair. It was a young man dressed in camo, an AR-15 hanging from his neck on a single-point sling.

"What the fuck!" the young man said, looking around wildly.

Dahlgren opened the door and started to climb out.

"Hey, whoa. You're in the wrong place. Get the fuck out of here."

Dahlgren continued to exit the car, hands in the air. "Easy," Dahlgren said. "Take it easy. My name is Deputy Director Raymond Dahlgren with the Federal Bureau of Investigation. I'm here to see Colonel Verhoven."

"The fuck you are!" The young man's entire body was twitching. Dahlgren could see he was scared shitless.

"Young man, pull yourself together," he barked. "I'm here to see Jim Verhoven."

"Bull*shit*," the young man said. His voice was high, and his hands were shaking as he pointed his AR-15 at Dahlgren.

"Look, I'm here to talk to Colonel Verhoven about a man named Gideon Davis." Dahlgren reached into his coat pocket to retrieve a photograph of Gideon. He didn't make it. Apparently the kid thought he was reaching for a gun. Or maybe he was simply so nervous that he pressed the trigger by accident.

Whatever the case, the AR went off with a sharp crack. Dahlgren felt a thud in his side, like he'd been hit with a baseball bat.

Ray Dahlgren had spent a great many years training with his weapon, until its use was so instinctive that he didn't have to think.

He drew and fired blindingly fast. Bang bang, two shots center mass, bang, a third shot to the face. It wasn't until he'd let off the third shot that his eyes even became aware of the three greenish white dots of his tritium sights. But by then it didn't matter. His third shot had drilled a very large third nostril in the boy's face, then tossed a torrent of red muck out the back of his head.

The boy fell in a heap.

"Shit," Dahlgren muttered.

Down the road, two cars were waiting, containing four more agents he had instructed to stay behind. His radio squawked and one of his men's voices was saying, "We heard three shots fired, sir. Please respond."

It took Dahlgren a moment to respond. "Threat neutralized. I want you to stand down and stand by."

"Copy that, sir."

Dahlgren reached into the cruiser, pulled out a bullhorn. He realized his hand was shaking as he raised it to his mouth. "Colonel Verhoven. This is Ray Dahlgren of the FBI. I have been fired upon and have returned fire. I do not, repeat, do *not* seek any further engagement." Even as he launched into his speech, though, a horrible feeling was sweeping over him. He'd come up here to defuse a potential situation, and now he realized he may have ignited one as he saw dark figures spilling out of a long low building a hundred yards away. It had the look of an old chicken coop. But the men pouring out of the building were not chickens. They were armed.

Within seconds they were firing on him.

Dahlgren tossed the bullhorn into a patch of kudzu next to the gate, emptied his magazine in the direction of the oncoming men, and then jumped into the car and threw it into reverse.

"I am under fire," he shouted into his mic as he floored the gas and steered backward down the gravel road. "Previous order countermanded. Teams One and Two, engage threats at will. Rendezvous with me on the gravel road and seal the perimeter."

Even as he steered down the road, bullets whacking into his car, all he could think about was the headlines that would follow. The nut jobs in the blogosphere would be calling this another Ruby Ridge, another Waco.

Gideon goddamn Davis. *This is all his fault,* Dahlgren thought as he retreated. He also had a dawning realization that the only way his career would survive this situation was to make sure the president understood that Gideon was responsible for everything that had happened and everything he feared would happen very soon.

19

Tillman pounded down the trail toward the house, Lorene a few steps behind him, the barrel of her rifle aimed at the center of his broad back. There had been a lull after the first few shots. Now, a full-on firefight was happening.

Near the barracks at least a dozen guns were firing at a black Crown Vic backing into the trees. A cop car.

Tillman understood there was only one possible conclusion. Gideon had warned him that Nancy's boss was coming to look for him. He must have been surprised at the gate. Tillman needed to find his brother. Then they both needed to get the hell out of here.

Within minutes, the FBI had returned in force. He could see muzzle flashes in the tree line. Slow, measured fire. Like somebody shooting a bolt gun. And if he was hearing it correctly, it was a deeper, louder thump than the higher crack of the .223s down by the barracks. Something in the .30 cal range. Probably .308s.

Sniper. There was a sniper in the tree, which meant they needed to find cover fast.

Tillman saw the muzzle flash again, this time on the near side of the woods, the side he and Lorene were running on. The sniper was about two hundred yards east of the gate, only a couple of hundred yards from the house.

"Lorene," he shouted, "we have to find cover!" He pointed at the woods.

"You stay right where I can see you!" Her eyes were glazed with adrenaline, and if the sniper didn't get him first, she might.

"No, there's a sniper in the—"

A red mist suddenly exploded from her back. Lorene screamed and fell.

Tillman knew the smart play was to haul ass for the trees. But he couldn't leave her here.

He scooped her up and began charging toward the trees, hoping that the sniper would move on to richer targets. His heart pounded from exertion. Lorene was a big woman, close to six feet, probably 150 pounds.

Tillman staggered toward the woods. He could see the sniper's hide now, a few pieces of misplaced vegetation, a dark splotch of something that didn't match the background. Another ten yards and he would reach cover—a creek bed that had eroded a cut in the earth. He picked up a black circle in the dense vegetation. A scope lens. The sniper's scope swiveled, trying to track him.

He plunged over the edge, then the black circle was gone, hidden behind the lip of the creek bed. They splashed down into the water in a heap.

"You okay?" he said.

Lorene winced. Her face was gray, and he could tell she was in danger of going into shock. "I don't know. I can't . . . I think . . . those motherfuckers. Fuck those goddamn piece-of-shit mother-fuckers."

"Let me see," he said, tearing open her shirt. The wound was pretty bad. Survivable, but bad. It had entered her side just under one rib and exited her back about an inch from the spine and a couple of inches below her bra strap. Fortunately the bullet appeared not to have deformed much, so the exit wound was clean. "Wiggle your toes," he said. "Can you wiggle your toes?"

"Eight years," she said. "I haven't cursed in eight years." She shook her head vaguely. "Feels kinda good." She smiled fiercely. "The goddamn shit-sucking motherfuckers."

"Wiggle your toes."

"My toes are fine. There's no spinal injury." She drew a Glock 17 from her hip, passed it over to him. "I'm sorry I didn't trust you. Now go find 'em. Kill those fucking motherfuckers before they kill us."

He heard a whizzing sound over their heads. Someone was firing on their position, trying to pin them down in the creek bed.

She was right. If he was going to get out of here alive, he was going to have to figure out a way to neutralize them. There'd be a sniper and a spotter. The sniper was probably still firing at the guys near the barracks.

So it must be the spotter, lying down suppressing fire, hoping to preserve their position.

He'd have to flank them. He press-checked Lorene's Glock. The chamber was loaded.

"Stay here," he said.

Then he ran along the little ridge in a crouch, looking to flank the snipers and drive them out of their hide.

Dahlgren had left two teams as backup at the head of Verhoven's driveway. The sniper was already in position. The second team took about half a minute to reach him. When they did, Dahlgren slammed on the brakes and leapt out of the car.

"Sir, are you hit?" shouted the head of the team.

"Don't worry about me," Dahlgren shouted back. He could feel blood running down inside his shirt. The .223 had penetrated his vest near his left shoulder. It hurt like a son of a bitch, but he sensed that he was okay for now. No bones smashed, no major nerves or arteries damaged.

"That's a hell of a volume of fire coming from the camp," the HRT man shouted. "All we've got up there is the sniper. If they pin him down and we can't help out, he's fucked."

"So let's reinforce him," Dahlgren said.

"Yeah. Thing is, we've got eight men, half of them armed only with shotguns or sidearms, and they've got twenty, all of them armed with military-grade weapon rifles. If we go up there now, we'll take casualties. Do you want that?"

Dahlgren scowled. If FBI guys died in this op, it would be the end of his career, no doubt. There was only one thing to do. He put his radio mic to his mouth. "Sniper team retreat to your rally point. We're falling back to consolidate our position. Repeat. Retreat to your rally point at this time. Copy?"

"Roger."

Dahlgren turned to Agent Ferris. "Secure the perimeter. Call for additional backup from Charleston. Every spare agent they've got." He pulled out a map, spread it out on the hood of the car, pretending not to notice that he dripped blood on the paper. "We're okay here on the south perimeter. But look, there's a logging road on the south perimeter. We need a unit on that road to block them or they'll retreat out the back and we'll be combing the hills for the next thirty years looking for these assholes."

"Yes, sir."

"And call DC. We need HRT up here yesterday. We need air support. We need . . . Hold on." He felt a gloomy, corrosive anger pouring over him, but he knew the boys were counting on him to stay cool, so he concentrated on keeping his voice commanding but conversational. He pulled out his cell phone and dialed a number. "Director Wilson? Yes, sir, Dahlgren here. I'm afraid things have gone sideways on us up in West Virginia. Yes, sir. Yes, sir. We're probably looking at a standoff. It's that moron Gideon Davis. He provoked this entire thing, I'm afraid."

Tillman trotted up the creek bed in a crouch, hoping to turn the sniper's flank. In about fifty yards the cut through which the creek flowed began to flatten out, decreasing the amount of cover available to him. He went to his knees, then to a low crawl, finally slithering out behind a clump of rhododendron.

It took a moment for his eyes to pierce their camouflage, but eventually he was able to make out the sniper and his spotter. They wore ghillie suits with vegetation shoved here and there to break up their outlines and make them blend into the surrounding woods. The suit was hiked up enough on one of the men that he could make out big white letters on the back of his shirt:

FBI.

So they were Feds.

Tillman considered what to do. Shooting them was out of the question. He considered simply bailing into the woods and leaving Lorene to die. But he didn't like that option for a variety of reasons. Leaving a woman to die—no matter how crazy or deadly she might be—just wasn't his style. Besides, another plan was beginning to form in his mind. Until he could bounce it off Gideon, though, he had two well-trained and well-armed men lying not thirty yards in front of them, men who wouldn't mind a bit if he was dead, but who he couldn't respond to with lethal force.

The spotter was situated behind a 20-power scope, an M-4 in his right hand, periodically spraying a barely aimed three-round burst at the area where Lorene was still concealed. It was obvious that his primary concern was not Tillman and Lorene, though. He was focused on the spotting scope, still calling whispered shots to the shooter, who was picking out targets of opportunity down near the house. The shooter lay prone behind his bolt gun, eye to the scope, oblivious to everything but the image in his scope.

Tillman pulled out the balaclava he was carrying and slid it down over his head until it covered his face and neck. As much as anything else, he needed not to be recognized by the men he was about to take on. He crept closer. Eventually the spotter exhausted the magazine on his M-4. As he rolled onto his side to feed another mag into the carbine, Tillman charged out into the opening and jumped between them.

"Don't even think about moving," he said softly, the Glock aimed at the spotter's face.

The spotter was a big, hard-looking man. Ex-military unless Tillman missed his guess. Tillman could see the spotter was deciding whether or not to make a grab for his sidearm. The shooter swiveled his head around and then froze like a deer in the headlights. Tillman knew that in sniper teams, the spotter was generally the more senior and experienced man. Whatever the spotter did, Tillman was counting on the shooter to follow his lead. Control the spotter, he'd control the team.

Before the guy could make a wrong decision Tillman planted his boot on the spotter's hand, and said softly, "Guys, I'm not here to hurt you. But I will kill you if you don't do exactly what I tell you to do." He was keeping his voice low. The plan forming in his mind required Lorene to remain ignorant of what he was up to. "Spotter, pull out your SIG with your thumb and index finger, taking great care not to get your finger near the trigger. Then drop the mag and very carefully pull the slide back and show me clear."

The spotter seemed oddly reassured by Tillman's professional manner. After only the briefest hesitation, he unloaded his SIG.

"Now the same with the M-4 . . ."

Once the spotter was disarmed, Tillman ran through the same drill with the shooter, making him unload his sidearm and the Remington 700 bolt gun. Having disarmed both men, he whispered to the spotter, "Give me your radio."

The spotter did as he was told.

Tillman screwed the radio into his ear just in time to hear a commanding voice on the other end say, "Sniper team, retreat to your rally points. We're falling back to consolidate our position. Repeat. Retreat to your rally point at this time. Copy?"

"Say 'Roger,'" Tillman said to the sniper. "Not one word more, not one word less."

The sniper didn't hesitate. He hit the send button on his radio and said, "Roger."

"You guys have been ordered back to your objective rally point," Tillman said to the spotter. "I'm gonna make a deal with you. I'm gonna let you take your weapons with you. Load 'em up when you get back to the rally point, your boss'll never know I got the drop on you."

The two men looked at each other, then nodded.

"What's your name, spotter?"

"Crane," the big man said.

"Agent Crane, you can tell your commander your radio got hit, whatever, you lost the thing. You don't mention me, nobody's ever gonna be the wiser what a shit job you did of holding your position. Hoo-ah?"

"Hoo-ah," Crane said, confirming Tillman's guess that the man had served in the military before joining the FBI.

"All right guys . . . bolt comes off the 700, upper comes off the

M-4, slides come off the SIGs, stow all the pieces in your drag bag. Then I'm gonna fire four or five shots in the air. Soon as I fire, you start running. Got it?"

The two looked confused.

"You don't need to know what my agenda is, boys," Tillman said in his best NCO voice. "Just do what I say. Clear?"

"Yes, sir."

The two Feds stowed their weapons in the sniper's camouflaged drag bag, the bag used to protect the sniper rifle while crawling into position.

"I was never here," Tillman said. "You never saw me."

Without waiting for an answer, he fired the Glock into the ground close enough to spatter dirt in their faces. Ba-bang. Ba-bang. Bang.

The men were gone within seconds.

Tillman waited until they had disappeared completely into the trees, then sprinted to the creek bed, where he found Lorene lying on her side, pale and sweating.

"What happened?" she croaked. "I heard shooting."

"They're dead," he said. "Now let's get you back to your husband."

Surprisingly the firing had ceased within a matter of minutes. Tillman was unsure what had happened, what had driven the FBI to withdraw from contact. He suspected that they had not brought enough agents to take on Verhoven's men.

Whatever the case, by the time he and the pale and bloody Lorene had reached the Verhoven house, no one was shooting.

"Thank God!" Verhoven said as Tillman brought her in the back door, supporting most of her weight. "What happened?"

"I caught one," she said, trying unsuccessfully to smile. "I'm okay, though. Tillman saved me."

"In here," Verhoven said, pointing to a guest bedroom on the first floor.

The mood inside the house was tense and chaotic. Despite all the maneuvers and range practice, this was the first time any of them had ever exchanged live fire, and several were clearly in shock. Two had thrown up, and one was pacing a tight line back and forth, muttering repeatedly, "What are we going to do? What are we going to do?"

"Sir," one of the young men said, "the guys think we should surrender."

"Get out," Verhoven snapped, slamming the door in his face.

"Worthwhile question, though, Jim," Tillman said evenly. "The FBI's not going to hunker down out there forever. What *is* your plan?"

Verhoven looked around furtively and then answered. "We're getting the hell out of here is what we're doing."

"What about your men?" Tillman said, trying to keep the contempt out of his voice.

"Keep your voice down," Verhoven flashed. "I told you yesterday that Lorene and I have a mission. The importance of that mission outweighs the lives of my men. They'll hold off the Feds long enough for us to get out of here. We've got some ATVs out back we can use."

Tillman raised one eyebrow. "Well, whatever you're planning, I don't think she's going to be in any shape to be of much help. But if you want, you've got me."

Verhoven looked out the window but didn't answer.

Lorene lifted her upper body off the bed, grimacing. "He saved my life, Jim. We were pinned down by a sniper. He killed him and his spotter and brought me back to you."

"That may be, but—"

"He could have left me to die in that fucking ditch! He didn't. You can trust him."

Verhoven's eyes met hers. Then he nodded brusquely. "Help me get her to the ATV, Tillman," he said.

Tillman nodded. "Why don't I go get them for you. You don't want your men seeing you retreat any sooner than they have to."

"You're right," he said, then tossed Tillman a ring with several keys on it.

Tillman went out the back door and jogged toward the shed where three ATVs were parked. He started the closest one, drove it quickly to the house, and left it idling.

"Let me get the other one started before you go, Jim," he said. "That way we won't get separated in the woods."

He ran back to the shed. As soon as he was out of sight of Verhoven, he pulled out the radio Gideon had given him. "It's me," Tillman said. "Do you copy?"

"Are you okay?" Tillman could hear the concern in Gideon's voice.

"Yeah. Verhoven's bailing on his men, getting out of here with his wife on some ATVs. I'm going with him."

"What are you talking about? You need to get as far away from Verhoven as you can."

"Verhoven knows something. But he's definitely not the ringleader, claims he doesn't even know the target. If I stick with him, I can follow this operation back to whoever's running it."

"Tillman—"

"You want to kill the snake, you got to chop off the head, right?"

Gideon sighed. "I didn't mean for you to get in this deep."

"Too late for that."

"You sure you're up for this?"

"It's not like I'm giving up any big plans I had. Plus, I didn't like owing you, but I think I'm gonna like you owing me."

Gideon laughed. Although their previous estrangement had been resolved, Gideon felt their bond being burnished by Tillman's solidarity. They were now not only brothers, but also brothers in arms. But whatever gratitude Gideon felt was tempered by the fear that his brother was putting his life on the line because of him.

"Fine, you stay with Verhoven but you need me to shadow you. Especially to get through the FBI perimeter," said Gideon. "I'm monitoring their comm frequency, so I can clear your escape route. Remember that game we used to play in the woods? Tracker?"

A voice called out from the house. "Tillman? What are you doing?"

"I gotta go," Tillman said.

"Head down to the logging road at the rear of the compound. I'll direct you from there."

"Copy that," Tillman said, pulling the radio from his ear and shoving it deep in his pocket. Ten seconds later he pulled up to the house with the ATV. Verhoven and Lorene were sitting on the other ATV, Verhoven's fatigues sticky with her blood.

"Sir!" someone shouted from the building. "Where are you going? What are we supposed to do?"

"I'm getting Lorene to a safe place. Whatever you do, don't let the FBI follow us."

"We need you to—"

Before the man could finish his sentence, Verhoven's ATV leapt forward, throwing up a spray of dirt. Verhoven cranked the ATV's throttle to the peg and headed toward the logging road at the perimeter of the property.

20

ANDERSON, WEST VIRGINIA

Ervin Mixon had been in the chair for a long time. Long enough that the open seam of flesh where his eyelids had been had finally stopped bleeding.

The sclera of his eyes were dry and caked with blood, and now all he could see was a soft blur. He found himself thinking about his children, about the son he had abandoned, about the daughter who once upon a time thought he hung the moon, but who now probably thought he was lower than dog shit.

And she was right.

He began to cry. Slowly, the tears spread across the dry surface of his eyes, stinging like a thousand tiny needles.

And as they did so, they slowly washed away the crusted blood. And just as slowly, the blurry surroundings began to resolve into focus around him.

Same concrete walls, same chemistry equipment, same barrels of ether and bags of chemicals.

The air was heavy and thick. After leaving him there, Verhoven and his monster of a wife had turned off the air system. It was a completely sealed space, Mixon knew, kept livable only by a quarter million dollars' worth of filtration and air circulation equipment. The minute you turned the air off, you started consuming all the oxygen in the air. Once the CO_2 concentration reached 3 or 4 percent, you began suffocating.

He sensed it was now getting close.

Wherever Verhoven was going, whatever this crazy mission he was on, he was leaving and he was never coming back. What a mistake it had been, trying to make a buck off of Verhoven, and now he would pay for that mistake with his life.

Verhoven's sick bitch wife had cut off his left thumb, his ears, and skinned his right hand so that he appeared to be wearing an oozing brown glove. After she was done, she had tossed the skin onto the floor. He could see it now, a shriveled wadded thing, like an old-fashioned kid glove.

She hadn't done the sick shit to get information. No, she had done it because she liked it.

The result was that he kept fainting from the horror of what she was doing to him. Skinning his fucking hand, especially. It wasn't the pain. It was just the invasiveness, the wrongness of it, slowly slicing away all his skin like that with the small, precise strokes of her tiny little knife.

At first he had lied and told them that he had only given up the meth operation. But after she took off his thumb, he'd given up on lying and started telling them that he knew about the terrorist operation. After that, they'd focused on exactly what he'd said and to whom. But he hadn't given up Gideon Davis's name. Not because he cared, or had any sense of honor, but because he hadn't stayed conscious long enough to tell her. And in preserving that secret, keeping that one piece of information to himself, he had accidentally preserved some small shred of dignity. It was his last comfort as the room darkened through his lidless eyes, and he fell into a permanent sleep.

21

ANDERSON, WEST VIRGINIA

Gideon was situated behind the shooting ranges, looking down on Verhoven's entire spread, trying to find a clear path for Tillman through the FBI's cordon. They had called in reinforcements, and he could see the ATVs carrying Tillman, Verhoven, and Lorene moving up the hill. He sprinted through the woods toward the road where the FBI was approaching, a chopper flying toward them, just over the treeline.

He reached the road just in time to see a black SUV barreling toward him on the rutted dirt, kicking up a cloud of dust as it pulled to a halt. He didn't have much time. He'd been monitoring the FBI's comms on the radio. One team had been assigned to the logging trail at the rear of the property. He didn't know how big a team was, though. Was it a single car? Four cars? Ten? No way to know. But he had heard a radio call for assistance to the state troopers and to the Milner County sheriff's department. They would be closing off the county road to the east. Which meant he'd need to steer Tillman to the west. There were no paved roads for several miles in that direction, and the smaller logging trails were not shown on any maps.

He ducked back into the woods, plunging through a thicket of briars that tore at his clothes. When he came to the other side, he searched until he found a trail that had clearly been formed by the wheels of ATVs. He then picked out a large oak tree and cut a double chevron into the bark with his pocketknife. He piled three rocks immediately to its left. With that he slowly worked his way back down the hill toward the logging trail.

When they were boys, he and Tillman had lived in a fairly rural part of northern Virginia, with few other children around. As a result, they had played mostly with each other, developing a number of intricate games using trees, sticks, rocks, and other things found only in the woods. One of the games was Tracker, a game inspired by James Fenimore Cooper's character Natty Bumppo, whose superhuman tracking skills had led to frustration for millions of boys over the years as they tried to duplicate impossible feats of woodcraft.

Once they had realized that they were never going to match Natty Bumppo's magical skills at reading smudges and broken twigs, Tillman and Gideon had developed a language of twisted vines, stacked rocks, and blazes on trees that they used to direct each other. It wasn't magical . . . but it worked.

The chevron that Gideon cut into the tree indicated danger ahead. The piled rocks indicated that safety lay to the west of the tree. He could hear the muted sound of a V8 engine chugging up the logging road. As long as he could identify exactly where the FBI was, he could steer Tillman and the Verhovens around them. To do that, though, he needed to get closer to the road. Doing so exposed him to possibly being caught by the FBI. But it was a risk he would have to take. He had to get Tillman out of there, and then follow him to whatever the Verhovens had planned.

Working his way down toward the road, he paused occasionally to scan the woods with his night-vision scope, which helped him pick out objects in the morning gloom. Eventually he got close enough to the road to see a couple of the agents and a black Suburban. It appeared that there was only one vehicle—which meant there were probably only four agents.

He moved quickly back up the hill and piled more rocks, indicating that Tillman should continue moving west. Eventually he came across a clear-cut—a broad patch of recently logged land. In the distance stood a ramshackle truck that looked operable. If Tillman or the Verhovens could hot-wire it, they'd be home free. He slid back into the undergrowth at the edge of the clear-cut and waited.

Tillman hit the small rise on the other side of the shooting ranges, then tore down the hill, trying to pass Verhoven. If Gideon was going to leave a sign for him, he needed to be in front.

Just as he passed Verhoven, he saw it—the old danger sign from their childhood.

He slammed on the brakes so hard that Verhoven nearly ran into him.

"What the heck are you doing?" Verhoven said.

Tillman held up one hand, then signaled to turn off the ATVs.

Verhoven shook his head. It was obvious he wanted to plunge down the hill and get the ATVs to the logging trail.

Tillman turned off his ATV, then reached over, grabbed Verhoven's key and twisted it.

"Are you out of your mind, son?" Verhoven said.

Tillman held one finger to his lips, then pointed down in the direction of the logging trail, still hidden by the trees.

"What?" Verhoven said angrily.

"I thought I heard something. If the FBI's down there, they'll hear our engines."

Verhoven scowled. "We can't move Lorene without the ATVs," he said.

"We have to."

Verhoven reached toward the key. But as his hand hit the switch, Tillman heard a muffled thump in the distance. A car door.

Verhoven slowly took his hand away.

"Look, I've hiked hundreds of miles with eighty-pound packs," Tillman said. "Put her on my back. I can make it a mile or two. We'll follow this ridge to the west. It'll skirt the road and let us get around the Feds."

"No," Verhoven said. "We should go east. That gets us to the county road."

"That's the point," Tillman said. "If they've got people on this logging road, I guarantee you they'll have somebody down there cutting off the county road to the east."

"We have to take that chance," Verhoven said.

"This is my world," Tillman said. "You need to listen to me."

"He's right," Lorene said.

"You need to get to a doctor," Verhoven said.

"I'm fine," she said. "I'll be fine."

She climbed slowly off the ATV, as if to demonstrate.

"Let me help you," Tillman said. "Give me your hands." Tillman grabbed her wrists and wrapped them around his neck, draping her behind him, piggyback style, and hefting her off the ground. "Let's go," he said.

Lorene Verhoven weighed a lot more than the standard eighty pounds of gear that he used to carry in the service. After the first few steps, Tillman realized it had been a very long time since he'd done a full ruck march through wilderness terrain.

He began moving gingerly down the hill, trying to distribute her weight evenly across his back. At each footfall she moaned slightly.

"A mile or two, that's all," he said. "You're gonna make it."

"Yeah, but can *you*?" she said.

"Piece of cake," he grunted.

It took about half an hour to get out of the woods. Tillman's back was aching and his knees felt wobbly. Verhoven had spelled him a couple of times—but he was a decade older and thirty pounds lighter than Tillman, so he wasn't able to carry his wife very far.

Finally they reached a broad clear-cut. Sitting near the edge was a rusting old pickup truck, attached to a trailer full of branches. Tillman set Lorene down and said, "Let me try something."

He jogged to the truck. It was unlocked. Among the arcane skills he'd learned in his days with the CIA was hot-wiring vehicles— a skill that he'd hung on to better than his lock picking. Within thirty seconds he had the old Ford belching blue smoke from the tailpipe. He steered it around to where Verhoven and Lorene were crouched.

"Let's get you both in the trailer," he called. "The FBI isn't looking for me, so if we get stopped I'll be fine."

He yanked some of the tangled brush off the back, creating a hollow where Lorene and Verhoven could hide. Once they were situated, he piled the brush back on top of them, then covered the brush with a tarp.

As soon as they were free, he saw a figure emerge from the woods. His heart started to race. But then he saw that it was his brother.

Gideon gave him a silent thumbs-up and a grin, then waggled his hand next to his ear, giving him the universal I'll-call-you-soon signal. Then he melted back into the thick vegetation.

Tillman smiled and put the radio back in his ear. Then he headed south toward the Virginia border.

22

Sir, I see a white flag in the window."

Ray Dahlgren turned to the sniper, who had his spotting scope trained on the house from the command post at the base of the hill leading up to Verhoven's compound.

"It might be a trick," the head of the HRT unit said. "It might be a ruse to walk our guys into an ambush."

"Or it might not," Dahlgren said. He felt the pressure of wanting to resolve this situation as quickly as possible, worried that it could turn into a Waco-type media circus. If it was humanly possible to avoid that nightmare, he was going to do it—even if he had to risk the lives of a couple of his guys. "Sniper, can you give cover from here?"

"Affirmative, sir."

"All right, have the hostage negotiator talk them out one by one. As they come out, place them under arrest and move them to the command post. If anybody fires on you, you will disengage under suppressing fire from the sniper and the HRT unit. And we'll start from scratch. Got it?"

"Yes, sir."

It was a painstaking process, talking the men out of the house. Dahlgren tried to hurry the process along, but he was too late. Well before the last man had been taken into custody, there were choppers circling the compound, long-lensed cameras trained at the ground. A CNN truck was parked on the road, too, its telescoping antennae thrusting skyward.

Still, two hours and ten minutes later, it was over. All the militia members in the house had been arrested, the house had been cleared, and all the outbuildings were secure.

The militia members were huddled in a group, cuffed at the wrists and ankles. They didn't look like scary terrorist monsters, just frightened kids with too many tattoos and too few teeth.

"That's all of them, sir," the head of the HRT unit said.

Dahlgren studied the faces in fury. "Where's Verhoven? Where's his wife?"

The HRT man shook his head. "Not here, sir."

"Goddamit," said Dahlgren. His phone rang. It was the head of the FBI.

"It's everywhere," Director Wilson said. "CNN, Fox, you name it. Tell me you have this guy Verhoven."

Dahlgren found himself struck dumb, unable to answer. Which was answer enough for Wilson.

"Dammit, Dahlgren, you better get your shit straight. Until you find that guy, this story's not going away."

"We have reason to believe Gideon Davis was here, and he may know where they've gone." Dahlgren imagined his career hanging in the balance. Everything he had worked so long and so hard to accomplish was on the line. He held his breath, waiting for a response from his boss.

Wilson finally answered with a question. "What are you saying?"

Dahlgren explained the situation with Gideon that had caused him to lead a small group of agents to Verhoven's compound. He discredited Gideon's theory of a terrorist attack as a paranoid delusion and suggested that Gideon was responsible for what was happening.

"You have no evidence he was even there, Ray! This is *your* hornet's nest."

"With all due respect, sir, my hornet's nest is your hornet's nest. I suggest you consult with legal and find a charge against Davis you can keep in your hip pocket. If we need to play that card, we'll have it. Meantime, we need a wounded FBI guy on TV looking all heroic and talking about how we're putting the full-court press on the terrorists in our midst."

The director of the FBI sighed in resignation. Dahlgren could tell that he'd bought himself some time. However grudgingly, Wilson wouldn't yet hang him out to dry. "Find Verhoven, Ray."

"I will, sir."

"You goddamn well better."

23

I want to close my presentation," Kate Murphy said, "by thanking this commission for providing a real opportunity to bridge some gaps. I don't like to accuse my fellow commission members from the oil industry of being shortsighted, but oil is a finite resource. Even if we drilled anywhere and everywhere, it wouldn't solve our energy problems in the long term. But sticking our heads in the sand and pretending we can convert the United States to solar and wind in the next five years isn't realistic either. Somewhere in the middle there's a sane course of action that will help us move from prostrate dependence on fossil fuels to a world powered by cleaner, safer renewables. That course needs to be hardheaded and practical, guided not by ideology, but by a clear and carefully considered long-term strategy. Thank you."

During the break Kate was approached by Tom Fitzgerald, the secretary of the interior, who said, "That was a heck of a speech."

Kate looked up from her papers, a flicker of paranoia in her eyes. She had already spent enough time in Washington not to trust that sort of statement.

She said, "Look, I know I probably alienated everybody. But this whole commission felt like a Kabuki drama. The guys from the oil companies stand up and stake out one ridiculous, revenue-preserving position after another, and then the guys from the environmental side spin some fantasy about how everybody in America could be driving to work next year in solar-powered cars if we just wanted it bad enough." She felt her face heating up and her voice rising defensively. "I'm sorry. As you can see, I've been a little frustrated."

The secretary smiled. He was a handsome, smooth-faced man whose background was in the electric utility business. In her experience it was a sector that tended to attract the dimmer bulbs in the energy industry, but so far she had been impressed with him.

"Two things," Tom Fitzgerald said. "First, I'm going to speak to Senator Bainbridge and make sure that you are the one to write the final draft of this commission's report. I assume you're okay with that."

"Are you serious?"

"Absolutely. I've already spoken to President Wade about your work here, and he agrees. Although he did point out that he and your fiancé have had a contentious history."

"Gideon's brother was scapegoated by a bunch of politicians after he sacrificed everything for this country, and when Gideon defended him, the president sold him out." Kate tried to keep her voice firm, but not strident. "He didn't have the backbone to stand up to the media and do the right thing."

"Your fiancé got caught in the crossfire. That's an occupational hazard if you work in Washington. But say what you will about President Wade: He's been consistent in his belief that we've punted on energy issues for a long time, and it's time to develop a sane, realistic long-term policy on energy. He had hoped that this commission would be a source of unifying ideas, rather than the squabble fest that it has turned out to be. You seem to be the only person in this room speaking the president's language."

Kate blinked. "That's . . . unexpected."

"The president believes that our national security policy has been defined by energy concerns for way too long. Energy *is* a national security issue."

"I agree."

Tom Fitzgerald slid into the seat next to her and leaned confidentially toward her. "I would imagine that some pretty harsh words have been passed back and forth in your household on the subject of Erik Wade. But I think you two are on the same page on this issue.

Could you put aside your fiancé's difficulties with the president and join this administration?"

"In what capacity?"

"Probably something at an undersecretary level. I have several unfilled positions that I need help with."

"I'm flattered." After spending a decade tromping around on oil rigs, Kate didn't feel particularly suited for normal work and was still sorting through her feelings about having a desk job. "I'd like to think about it for a few days."

"Of course. Terrific." Fitzgerald stood. "There were *two* things I wanted to ask you. The second is this—the president would like to put a face on this committee, so to speak. He'd like that face to be you."

"Meaning what?"

"Tomorrow at the State of the Union address, the president will be making a major energy policy announcement. He'd like to tip his hat to the commission as part of that announcement. He'd like you to be there representing the commission."

"Are you inviting me to the State of the Union address?"

"Unless you've got a previous engagement."

For a moment, all she could think was that she didn't have anything to wear. "Can I come in a pair of jeans and a hard hat?"

Tom Fitzgerald laughed, sincerely charmed. "Absolutely not."

Kate left the hearing room on a cloud of air. It felt good to be wanted, even if she was uncertain about whether the job was right for her. But her mood quickly changed when she passed a bank of televisions tuned to CNN. On the screen was a live report about a standoff between the FBI and a militia group in West Virginia. Several people were dead, and more wounded.

Gideon.

She looked down and saw that she had missed a telephone call from a number she didn't recognize. When she checked voice mail, there was a terse message from Gideon saying that he was okay, and whatever she might hear about him was not the truth. She tried calling him three more times, but he didn't answer.

Where was he? What had happened? It was no comfort to her to learn that he had been right. What good was being right if he was in danger?

24

POCATELLO, IDAHO

Collier pulled the Caterpillar D4 bulldozer to a halt and switched off the engine. He was still vibrating from the experience. Half a day ago, there had been seven living, breathing human beings in the building behind him—working, dreaming, going about their business. Now they were all buried three feet beneath the frozen ground.

And he was responsible.

A sensation of power unlike anything he'd ever felt before filled him like a rising tide.

He took a moment to luxuriate in the feeling. But then he forced himself to hop off the tractor and move on. He knew this was only a prelude. In a matter of days he would be responsible for what would probably go down in history as the most famous mass murder ever on American soil. But it wouldn't just be some aimless crazy act. It would be clean and beautiful, like the arrow of a Japanese archer, pure in its intent, just in its design, unspoiled in its execution.

The world was a mess, and if the politicians weren't responsible, they had certainly made it worse. What he and Wilmot were about to do would make the point that the American people were no longer willing to stand for a government infected with the multiple cancers of corruption and vote rigging and gerrymandering and media spin and corrupt lies. Would there be a spontaneous uprising that would sweep everything away on the heels of their attack? Maybe. Probably not, though. But thoughtful people might be inspired by their brave example to light their own fires. It would take time for their epic act of defiance to build into the wildfire of a true revolution, but he would be the one who had lit the fire and changed everything. Side by side with Dale Wilmot, he would make history.

What people would never appreciate, though, was how truly difficult, nearly impossible, it had been to pull off. So many details, so many tiny things to sort out, think through, nail down. Even a simple thing like burying a bunch of people in northern Idaho, when the temperature had been below freezing for five and a half weeks. The dirt was frozen six inches down into the ground. Even with a tractor, it took a long time to dig a large enough hole. And then he had to drag and push the bodies, now stiff with rigor mortis. And when he pushed the dirt over the bodies, the bodies rolled around and didn't want to settle beneath the earth.

As he climbed off the tractor he saw that he had messed up. A slim hand stuck up out of the ground. One of the bodies must have rolled over and gotten pushed up to the surface. He climbed back on the tractor, turned the key.

The tractor wouldn't start. There had been a loose wire in the tractor for weeks. Sometimes it started in seconds, sometimes it took twenty minutes. Right now he didn't have twenty minutes.

His phone rang.

"What's the holdup?" Mr. Wilmot said. "The plane is standing by. Wheels up in an hour."

"I'm on my way," Collier said.

He jumped off the tractor, walked over to the hand. He felt sure that it was Amalie's hand—slim, long-fingered, delicate. He was about to cover it with dirt when he was seized by an urge he couldn't overcome. For the umpteenth time he looked around to make sure no one was watching him. Then he got on his hands and knees and sniffed the hand. It had no distinct smell. He hesitated, then his tongue darted out and he licked one of the fingers. It had a mild earthy taste, like a lightly salted mushroom. He felt pleased and embarrassed at the same time. He did not want to be caught at this by Mr. Wilmot.

He stood, kicked a few clods of frozen black dirt around the hand. It would have been better to retrieve a shovel from the building and cover the hand completely with dirt. But the ground he had replaced was already frozen solid. Even if he got the shovel, it could take him half an hour to chop enough dirt free to cover the hand.

No, it wasn't worth the effort. Nobody would be out here for weeks. And by then it would be too late.

Evan rolled his wheelchair out into the yard as John Collier and his father loaded their bags into the Cadillac. The cold was bracing, and Evan watched the men huff with their effort. In addition to their suitcases, Collier had loaded in a sort of wheeled caddy containing two shiny canisters. The canisters resembled propane tanks but were slightly taller. Stenciled on the side of each one were red letters reading: R410A REFRIGERANT.

Wilmot spotted Evan and walked toward him. "Well, we're about to head off."

"So I see," Evan said. "You never really told me where you were going."

"DC," Wilmot said. "We're making a presentation to the DOE, meeting with Senator Elbert, Congressman Dade, a couple of other folks. Frankly we've reached a point where the ethanol project is just not going to make economic sense without some legislative help."

Evan nodded but said nothing.

"Margie will take care of you while we're gone," his father said.

"I'll be fine," said Evan.

"I've given her specific instructions."

His father didn't move but simply continued to look down at Evan. His face, usually so focused and guarded, seemed momentarily vulnerable and open.

Then he smiled, leaned over, and wrapped his arms around Evan. He squeezed Evan very hard, not letting go for a long time. When finally he did let go and straightened up, Evan was shocked to see tears in the old man's eyes.

"You're a good son and a fine man," Wilmot said. "And I want you to know, I love you very much."

Taken aback by his father's uncharacteristic display of affection, Evan asked, "You okay, Dad?"

"I'm fine. Better than I've been in a long time." Evan searched his father's face for clues, trying to connect this sudden emotion with whatever strange secret he and Collier were keeping. Wilmot continued: "For the longest time I felt so angry about what had been taken from you. I felt like it was my own damn legs that were gone, my own face . . ." He trailed off, a sudden swell of emotion threatening his composure. "But now I've made my peace with it. You and me— in our own ways we're all soldiers fighting for a better future. In our own ways, we all have been called to make our sacrifices."

"Green energy," Evan said, pointing at the canisters that Collier was still wrestling into the Cadillac. "Rock on, man."

His father's jaw clenched for a moment. "Just know that I love you, that's all." Then he turned and walked back to join John Collier at the Cadillac.

He said something roughly to Collier, who slammed the trunk shut. Collier glanced momentarily at Evan, a peevish, resentful expression on his face. Then the two men climbed in the car and drove away.

Evan watched until the car disappeared. Although he didn't quite know why, he felt a rising dread and fear.

"Everything's squared away, right?" Wilmot said. "The women are taken care of?"

"It's done," Collier said peevishly. He was tired of Wilmot hounding him all the time.

Wilmot stared impassively out the windshield, powering the big car just fast enough that Collier could feel it sliding a little in the snowy turns.

"I don't have to tell you what that shit will do if we crash into a tree," Collier said.

Wilmot said nothing. He flipped on the radio, tuned it to the news talk station in Coeur d'Alene.

"In today's top story," the man said. "The standoff in West Virginia appears to be over. Three FBI men are dead, and nine members of the so-called Seventh West Virginia (True) Militia are dead. According to FBI Deputy Director Raymond Dahlgren, two remaining suspects are wanted for questioning—the leader of the militia group, self-appointed Colonel James G. Verhoven, and his wife Lorene Taylor Verhoven."

"Jesus," Collier said. He could feel his breathing go shallow and rapid. "Oh, Jesus. What are we going to do?"

"Now's not the time to panic," Wilmot said calmly. "Call the emergency number, see if you can raise him."

Collier took a deep breath. Just the sound of Wilmot's voice calmed him.

"Right, right. Sorry. I'll call him on a burner."

He reached into his briefcase, pulled out one of the disposable cell phones they had reserved specifically for calling Verhoven, and punched in the number.

"No answer," he said, his voice going high and nervous. "What are we going to do if Verhoven can't execute?"

"Calm down," Wilmot said, his deep voice as serene and certain as if he were talking about the weather. "If the Feds had found out anything from them, there'd be guys in black fast-roping out of choppers onto our heads. We're fine."

"Yes, sir." Collier took a breath and closed his eyes, focusing on the thousands of details he'd committed to memory—air-flow calculations, duct schematics—until slowly his pulse returned to normal.

25

SOUTHERN WEST VIRGINIA

Tillman Davis wound through the mountains for twenty miles, heading south toward Virginia. He wasn't sure where Verhoven wanted to go, but he knew they needed to put some distance between themselves and the compound before showing their faces.

Finally he pulled into an old gas station, parking the truck near the tire pump in the back, far away from the pumps and the miserable-looking convenience store.

"How's she doing?" Tillman said.

Verhoven's face was grim. He shook his head.

"I was cross-trained as a medical corpsman," Tillman said. "We need to get her to a safe place. A hotel room would probably be best. I can do a few things for her, hopefully keep her stable."

Verhoven wiped his forehead. "I need to make a phone call," he said. "Keep her comfortable, okay?"

Tillman tried to help Lorene from the bed of the trailer into the truck. She was pale and shaking, too weak to walk, so he had to pick her up and set her inside the truck.

As he got her situated, he tried to listen to the conversation Verhoven was having on the phone. But Verhoven had walked out of earshot to a nearby Dumpster.

• • •

Verhoven thumbed the number he had committed to memory on one of the burners he was carrying. Wilmot answered after the first ring. Although he kept his voice even, it was pitched with tension.

"Where are you?"

"Twenty miles from my place," Verhoven said.

"It's all over the damn news. Did this have something to do with that snitch, Mixon?"

"Maybe," Verhoven said. "But like I told John, he didn't know any concrete details. And whatever little he did know, he never got to pass on to the Feds."

"Then we're fine."

"Not exactly. Lorene's been shot."

"How bad?"

"Bad enough that she may not be able to execute the operation."

There was a long silence. "Then you'll have to do it alone."

"Actually, there may be another way."

"Another way?"

Verhoven glanced over his shoulder. Lorene had been skeptical about Tillman at first. She said it had seemed awfully convenient for a guy who'd been as standoffish as Tillman suddenly to show up, all eager beaver at such a crucial time. But no FBI plant would have done what he'd done. According to Lorene, he'd killed two FBI men. Not to mention he'd saved her life.

"I have a man with me," Verhoven said. "A very special man."

"Absolutely not," Wilmot said harshly.

"He can get me the weapons and breaching charges I need for the operation. And he's trained to use them." Verhoven glanced toward the truck. Tillman Davis was eyeing him, so he quickly looked away. He didn't want the guy getting a read on his face.

"I said no," Mr. Wilmot said.

"Mr. Wilmot—"

"Jim, listen to me very carefully. This operation has been planned down to the last detail. There's no redo. Everybody involved has been vetted with extreme care. We can't just let some random person jump into the middle of this thing."

"Mr. Wilmot, with all due respect, he's not some random person—"

"Kill him, Jim."

"Mr. Wilmot."

"I said, kill him. And do it now."

Jim Verhoven respected Wilmot enormously. It had taken a man of extraordinary vision and courage to conceive an operation this bold and this complex. But Verhoven was a man who'd grown accustomed to giving orders, not taking them.

"Do it *now*, Jim."

The phone went dead in Verhoven's hand.

The moment Tillman saw Verhoven's face, he knew exactly what Verhoven had been told to do. He reached for his Glock just before Verhoven reached for his.

Verhoven feigned surprise. "What are you doing?" he asked as Tillman steadied the gun on him.

"I saw your face. Whoever you were talking to told you to kill me."

"I don't know what you're talking about."

Tillman measured Verhoven's expression. The man was clearly lying, but killing him or locking him down for the police would blow any chance of discovering his plans. But maybe there was another way to play this. It was a risky proposition—and if he miscalculated, he would pay for it with his life—but if he wanted to stop the attack from happening, it was his only real option. Tillman decided to take the chance.

He handed his Glock to Verhoven.

"If you're going to do it, do it now. Make it fast."

Verhoven's face tightened, but he said nothing.

Tillman found himself feeling strangely at peace. He didn't want to die, but if he did, he felt okay with it. He would be sacrificing his life for something larger than himself and go out in a blaze of private glory. Or maybe he just wanted to end it all—the relentless shame and boredom he carried around his neck like twin millstones. Whatever it was, he finally felt liberated from the previous two years of purgatory in which he'd been living, the neither-here-nor-there murkiness he'd been slogging through for so long.

"Come on, dammit," Tillman said. His pulse hammered in his ears, and a roaring sound echoed through his head. "Whatever you've got planned is bigger than either of us. I'm willing to die if it'll make this cesspool a little better." Tillman was surprised by how convincing he sounded.

Verhoven smiled fondly at him and pushed the gun back toward Tillman. "The reason this place is a cesspool is precisely because we don't have enough men like you." When Tillman made no move to take his gun back, Verhoven slid the Glock into the holster on Tillman's belt. "I was *never* going to kill you, Tillman. We need you. We need you more than you've ever been needed in your life."

Their eyes met. Verhoven seemed to be in the grip of powerful emotions.

"All right then," Tillman said. "Let's find someplace I can help your wife."

They got back in the truck. Lorene was still sleeping, oblivious to the drama that had just played out between Tillman and her husband.

They drove for another hour before reaching the town of Weston, not far from the Virginia border. Tillman withdrew four hundred dollars from an ATM machine. He then drove on to Buckhannon, where he rented a room in the Friendly Tyme Motel on US 33 under the name Doug Rogers, paying for one night in cash. After installing Lorene and Verhoven in the room, he drove to St. Joseph's Hospital, where he stole three bags of plasma, an IV setup, a tube of bacitracin, a bottle of rubbing alcohol, a box of large gauze pads, and a 1993 Honda Accord.

By noon, Lorene's wounds were cleaned and dressed and she had two pints of fluid in her. Her color had improved, and she had stopped shaking.

"Now," Tillman said as he threw the bloody gauze into the wastebasket, "it's time to stop playing footsie. What the hell are we doing here?"

Verhoven looked evasive. "I don't know the details of the main attack itself. We're not part of that. Our mission is a support operation."

"Okay, but what's our target? If I'm going to help you and maybe get myself killed in the process, I deserve to know what I'm getting into, don't you think?"

Verhoven met Tillman's gaze but didn't answer.

"For godsake, Jim!" Lorene said softly. "He saved my life. Yours, too, for that matter. Either we trust him or we don't."

Verhoven nodded but still hesitated for a moment. "It's the State of the Union address," he said finally. "We're going to decapitate the entire top tier of the US government. We're going to kill them all."

26

Gideon's encrypted cell phone rang as he was heading north on Interstate 79, cruise control set four miles above the speed limit.

"Do you have any clue just how deep in the shit you are right now?" It was Nancy on the line. "You're wanted for questioning as a person of interest in connection with the shoot-out at Verhoven's compound."

"'Person of interest'? What does that even mean?"

"It means Dahlgren's already spinning this to try to make it look like it's your fault. I suspect he's even trumping something up so that he can arrest you."

"He's the one who provoked the situation."

"Were you there?"

"I'm not sure I should answer that, given what you just said."

"You're not the only one who's in trouble. He tracked the equipment I gave you, which probably gives him some sort of unauthorized-use-of-federal-property charge if he feels like using it. After that, it's just a question of what other junk he wants to pile on."

"I'm sorry I got you into this," he said.

Gideon took Nancy's answering silence as confirmation of her own regret. The cell phone beeped again. Tillman's number popped up on the screen

"Can you hold on, Nancy?"

"Is it Tillman?"

"Yeah."

"Tell him to ditch his phone. Both of you need to do that as soon as we're done with this call. Our cells are encrypted so they can't listen to us, but they can still triangulate the signal to locate you."

"Okay. Hold on." Gideon put her on hold and took the other call. "Tillman?"

"We need to set up a delivery time and place for those items we talked about," said his brother. That was their cover. Gideon was Tillman's arms dealer.

From the way Tillman spoke it was clear to Gideon that Verhoven was in the room with him and might even be listening in on their conversation. "Where and when?" Gideon asked.

"There's a park on Sully Road in Centerville, just off twenty-eight. Be there in two hours."

"I'll need at least four to get together the whole package."

"Fine. Four hours then."

"But there's some options you need to specify on your shopping list."

He understood this was Gideon's cue for Tillman to communicate whatever he could about what he'd learned so far.

"Those last breaching charges you sold me were dog shit. I need the good stuff. Skip the Charlies, the Oscars, both of the things from Latvia, and none of that Irish stuff. I'd prefer the Eagles, but the Richards would also be okay."

"No to Charlie, Oscar, double Latvia or Ireland, yes to the Eagles and Richards."

"Write it down, man. I can't afford to have a problem."

Charlie, Oscar—that was radio letter code. He was pretty sure that's what Tillman was getting at. He wrote down the letters. C. O. L. L. I. E. R. Tillman continued: "While I've got you, I don't want you using that supplier you asked me about." He hoped Gideon would understand he was talking about Mixon. "It's a dead issue."

There was a brief pause. "Understood."

"Four hours."

"One last thing. I have an inside source says the Feds are upping their scanning game. You need to burn this phone and move on."

"Copy that. Thanks for the heads-up." Tillman hung up. He'd wanted to tell Gideon that he'd discovered the target was the State of the Union address, but that would have to wait for their face-to-face meeting four hours from now.

Gideon switched back to Nancy. "That was Tillman. Verhoven was listening, so he couldn't say anything directly, but he managed to tell me that Mixon is dead. And that the guy Mixon recorded talking to Verhoven: His name is Collier. Can you trace that?"

Nancy sighed. "Dahlgren grilled the hell out of me half an hour ago, and he's trying to get me to tell him where you are. I convinced him that I didn't know. And that's when he suspended me. He's in damage control mode right now. He won't listen to reason, he won't listen to me, and he especially won't listen to you. If he brings you in, it's just going to be so he can pin this whole disaster in West Virginia on you."

Gideon felt a rush of anger toward Dahlgren. Nancy had just been trying to do her job, and now she was being punished for it by a bureaucrat who was more concerned with covering his own ass than with protecting the public. Worse still, Nancy was his only ally inside the Bureau, whose resources he needed.

"Do you have any way to check out Collier? If we get some solid proof, Dahlgren won't have a choice except to listen."

He could hear Nancy breathing on the other end. He knew he was asking a lot of her, but without her help he would be operating blindly. Finally, after what seemed like minutes, she said softly, "I'll see what I can do."

Then the phone clicked dead.

Gideon was coming up on a rest stop, the welcome station for the state of Virginia. He pulled in, set his phone in a rack full of brochures detailing the state's many fine tourist destinations, and decided to forgo the cup of coffee he desperately needed so he could distance himself as quickly as possible from the traceable burner.

Nancy got off the phone and put her face in her hands. She was sitting at her desk on K Street, staring out the window. She knew

Gideon was right. Dahlgren wouldn't listen to reason, and without more evidence, they'd never be able to convince him. But what could she do? She'd been suspended. Someone from OPR was supposed to come in about five minutes and take her gun and her credentials.

She sighed and looked at her watch.

Dahlgren may have given the order for her suspension. But that didn't mean the word had reached the IT department yet. She logged into her account and started typing furiously.

It only took a moment for the computer to find a correlation between the names Collier and Verhoven.

Collier, John C. SS# 000-41-3797. DOB 4/16/85. Born Pocatello, Idaho.

She pulled his credit bureau report and found that his second most recent address was listed in Anderson, West Virginia. Six months ago, though, he had moved to an address in Idaho.

She pulled up the address, found it registered to Wilco Partners, LLC. A few more minutes of data drilling revealed that Wilco Partners consisted of only one partner, a man by the name of Dale Wilmot. A quick scan of Google revealed that *Forbes* magazine named him the 957th richest man in America, with business interests primarily in timber, but also in heating, air-conditioning, and trucking.

He was a big handsome guy in his late fifties who looked like the older brother of the star in a cowboy movie.

According to an article in *Forbes,* Wilmot's only son had been grievously injured in Iraq nearly two years ago, after which Wilmot had ceded daily operations of his companies to senior company management and, in the words of the article, "retreated to his majestic Idaho estate where he has devoted himself largely to philanthropic enterprises and to caring for his son."

The address of Wilmot's estate was unlisted, but Nancy managed to track it down through a federal tax assessment dated a year ago. But as the address came on screen, two tall men in dark suits walked into her office. "Special Agent Clement," one of them said, "I would request that you surrender your duty weapon and credentials, and then accompany me to—"

"Spare me the formalities. My gun and badge are already on the desk. Just let me grab my coat, okay?" As the two men turned toward the desk, she casually cleared her screen and pulled on her coat.

"Let's go, boys," she said.

The FBI team sent by Deputy Director Raymond Dahlgren to seize Gideon Davis surrounded the Virginia welcome station with more than thirty men. The signal on the secure phone that Nancy Clement had given him had not moved in twenty-four minutes.

Teams were dispatched to lock down the men's bathroom, the ladies' bathroom, both doors of the welcome station itself, as well as the candy station. In addition, a roving group accompanied by a canine "agent" patrolled rapidly down the line of cars. The canine had been given a shirt believed to have been worn by Gideon Davis in the hope it might pick up a scent trail.

The dog pounced on a van before the entry teams had gotten situated around the welcome station. The canine team was forced to breach the vehicle while the other teams raced for the welcome station.

After eleven El Salvadoran nationals emerged from the van, the nearly uncontrollable dog had invaded the vehicle where it discovered half a kilo of low-grade Mexican tar heroin concealed inside a hollowed-out stack of Brazilian pornographic magazines.

Meanwhile, women had begun to scream, children were running, tiny dogs were escaping from their owners—in short, all hell was breaking loose as the various teams attempted to raid the welcome center.

It took nearly thirty minutes to gain control of the situation, with the result that a great many perfectly innocent travelers, including one Japanese consular official, were held on their knees at gunpoint. The consular official, a former national judo champion who did not share the conciliatory nature of most of his countrymen, spent a good ten minutes screaming at the chief of the HRT unit in his excellent English that he was going to lodge a formal complaint with the State Department.

It was only then that Gideon Davis's cell phone was finally located, lodged behind a stack of brochures for Colonial Williamsburg.

27

WASHINGTON, DC

Special Agent Shanelle Greenfield Klotz liked to claim that she hated dog-and-pony shows. But the fact was, she was enormously talented at them, in large part because she enjoyed conducting them. She was a small, thin woman—as a matter of record, the smallest, lightest sworn agent in the entire Secret Service.

She was also—again, this was a matter of record—the smartest. At least as measured by the IQ test given to every prospective agent in the Secret Service. She was also the only biracial half-black, half-Jew in the Secret Service and generally recognized as the Service's leading expert in facilities security. She was, by any measure, an odd bird. Despite that, it was nearly impossible to find anyone who would bad-mouth her. Everybody in the Secret Service loved the shit out of her.

When she was eleven years old, Shanelle had come home crying one day from school. Her grandfather, Grandpa Joe Greenfield, asked her what was wrong, and she had said, "Grandpa Joe, everybody hates me!"

"Kiddo," Grandpa Joe said, "your problem is you're a smarty-pants. Nobody likes a smarty-pants. The secret, you want to be liked, you gotta be a *mensch*."

This was the first time Shanelle could recall having heard the word. "What's a *mensch*, Grandpa Joe?"

"Boiled down? He's your unpretentious guy who gives a shit about other people. He don't dress too snappy. He don't make people feel dumb. He don't make 'em feel funny-looking. He don't ever make 'em feel small. He asks 'em how they're doing. Then when they tell him, he *listens*. Just do that, and you can get away with murder." *Moidah,* that was the way Grandpa Joe pronounced it. He winked and pulled a silver dollar out of her ear. "See? I should know."

Shanelle had never forgotten the lesson.

As far as the world could see, she had become a mensch at age eleven. But, in her heart, she was still a smarty-pants. Which was why, although she would never admit it, she loved doing a dog-and-pony show. Because it was one of the few things in her life where she could just be a straight-up smarty-pants and people would thank her for it.

Her visitor was a spare, spiderlike man, Captain Fred Steele, the liaison for the District of Columbia Police Department. Steele was responsible for securing and monitoring the outermost perimeter, roughly five square miles, during the State of the Union address. Although there would be only limited coordination between his agency and the Secret Service, Shanelle had invited him here to get an overview of their protocols. She led the visitor through a full-body scanner, past two Secret Service agents, and through a pair of heavy oak doors into the House Chamber.

"The presidential security operation," Special Agent Klotz said, "provided by the United States Secret Service, is the largest, most thorough, most expensive, and most extensively trained executive protection detail anywhere. Other than the inauguration of a president, no single event consumes a greater share of the attention and resources of the Secret Service than the State of the Union address. Not only is the president in attendance, but so is the entire top layer of the United States government. Other than one so-called 'designated survivor'—a member of the president's cabinet, who is holed up in a secure location outside Washington, DC—all the rest of the top players in the government attend the speech, including virtually the entire House and Senate, the entire Supreme Court, and the cabinet."

They strolled up the aisle toward the podium where the president would deliver his speech to the nation in less than twenty-four hours.

"The president's speech, mandated by custom as well as by the Constitution, is given every year, except for the year of a president's inauguration, in the House chambers of the US Capitol."

Captain Steele eyed the large room. She sensed he was considering how a terrorist might use the terrain of the semicircular arrangement of the room to kill the president.

"To give you a sense of what we do to protect POTUS, I'll describe the various security rings. First of all, we surround the principal with a team whose job is to protect his person and the immediate space around him. That interior circle is manned exclusively by Secret Service personnel. Next we maintain a secondary ring to control and monitor the surrounding crowd, constantly scanning the venue for potential threats. Again, that's all Secret Service—although in this facility there's some assistance from the Capitol Police. Finally, we maintain a third security ring, which protects the grounds, the surrounding buildings, vehicles, perimeter entry and egress. Ideally, that ring is roughly half a mile in diameter. For the State of the Union address, it's even larger. Which is why we're enlisting the resources of your department along with FBI, Capitol Police—not to mention Air Force and FAA elements to monitor and control the airspace around the Capitol. Plus, while I can't get into specifics, one might presume there is a standby tactical force from, say, Delta or the SEALs or the FBI's HRT unit.

"Now, my modest little area of expertise is facilities. In a perfect world, I'd have torn this place down and built it from the ground up. Blast walls, air locks, filtration systems, cameras, sally ports. That's my little fantasy, you know, putting them all in a bunker. But unfortunately, I live in the real world. My job is made a little trickier because the US Capitol was designed in the late eighteenth century, without a shred of concern for security. It's been redesigned and rebuilt four or five times since. It's not commonly known, but there are secret passages, underground spaces that were bricked over a century ago, spaces behind walls, unused vents. From a security perspective, it's a complete nightmare.

"So we just have to grind it out. We work our way through every aspect of this building. Structural, mechanical, the electrical and plumbing and heating systems. Every bit of it has to be examined and reexamined. Visually inspected if possible. If not, then using a number of imaging technologies."

"What about sweeping for bombs?" the visitor asked. "What are the protocols for controlling access?"

This is a heavily trafficked public facility, so there are limits. That puts the pressure on us to conduct intense screenings and scans during the twenty-four hours prior to the speech. That's what we're doing now." She pointed to a man waving a wandlike device over the rear wall of the building. "We use all the standard technologies: nonlinear junction detectors, chemical sampling devices, Geiger counters, IR scanners. We use RF detectors to search for two-way comms, bugs, and so on. We also jam all cell phone traffic on the mall. No calls in or out during the speech as well as during the arrival and departure of POTUS and the other principals. And for identifying bombs and other explosive material, sniffer dogs are still our best tool."

"How do you control access?"

"Every person who passes through any door or checkpoint has been vetted and is on a master list. Plus, they all need to pass through full-body scans."

"Even dignitaries?"

"Everyone."

"What about mechanical failures, electrical problems, things of that nature?"

"There is a vetted list of federal employees who've been precleared to handle any infrastructure emergencies we might encounter. As a backup for more serious problems, contractors for all mechanical systems and subsystems maintain a list of on-call employees, all of them vetted and on standby. We have their pictures, fingerprints, and other pertinent information in the system so we can ID them if we need them. Electrical, plumbing, pipe fitters, heat and air, elevators, masonry, carpentry, roofing, even contractors for the subway system going from the Russell Senate Office Building to the Capitol. Same with fire and rescue personnel."

"How many agents total?"

"I'm afraid I can't tell you the exact number. But north of five hundred when you include all the duties involved, including comms, electronic countermeasures, transport, EPD, countersnipers, dog handlers, perimeter, tactical standby, logistics, civilian employees and so on. And when you add in Capitol Police, DC Metro, FBI, military . . ."

"Now I know what's causing the deficit," Captain Steele said.

Agent Klotz smiled. "Our counterparts in other countries think it's overkill. But I can tell you that even with all this, I won't sleep for twelve seconds tonight."

Her cell phone rang, and she excused herself. Her husband was defrosting one of the six meals Shanelle had cooked on Sunday night and left for him and their daughters in the freezer, but he didn't know how long to cook it.

"Men," she said after she hung up. But it was clear she took great pleasure in being needed. "If you'd like, we can go over the rest of tomorrow's protocols in my office."

28

PRIEST RIVER, IDAHO

Evan rolled aimlessly around the house. He felt full of an anxious, twitchy energy now that he was off the pills. His mind was a kaleidoscope of splintery questions about this whole ethanol thing with John Collier and his dad. Why had his father been so emotional? And what was up with the African woman who'd run out of the woods? None of the explanations quite made sense, but he hoped to find some answers in the woods. A few days earlier, he'd seen a pillar of smoke rising over the treetops a half mile away.

Outside the sky had gone leaden. A storm was gathering.

"I'm going outside for a while, Margie," he said.

Margie stood in the doorway with her arms crossed. "It's too cold."

"Just for a few minutes."

"No." She shook her head.

"What do you mean 'no'?"

"Mr. Wilmot won't allow it."

"I *am* Mr. Wilmot," he said with an edge in his voice that made her flinch. He felt the tiniest bit bad. It was kind of an asshole thing to say. But it was also true. He was not some kid who could be told what to do in his own house.

Other than a brief flash in her eyes, her big ham of a face did not move. "Your father would not allow it," she repeated.

Evan rolled toward her, stopping only just short of whacking her on the shins. "I served my country through one tour of Iraq and two tours of Afghanistan, and I'll be damned if you're going to stop me from going out in my own yard."

"Mr. Wilmot would not allow it."

Evan slammed the joystick forward on his wheelchair, but Margie grabbed the arms of the chair and held it like a nose tackle on a blocking sled. The electric motor whined loudly, and after a moment the chair began to emit a burned rubber smell. Finally Evan let go of the joystick. It wouldn't do him any good burning out the motor on his sled.

"All right, whatever," he said. He hit the reverse on his joystick, backed up, and rolled to the chairlift that took him up the stairs to his room.

When he got upstairs, he called down the stairs, "If you're going to be a pain in the ass, can you make me a sandwich? Ham and swiss on rye, okay? With a pickle."

He knew that there was no rye bread in the kitchen, that the only rye bread in the house was in the basement freezer. He waited until he heard Margie clumping down into the basement, then rolled his wheelchair out onto the side balcony of the house. The house was built on a hillside. His father had installed a wheelchair ramp, but he'd never really used it because the hillside was too steep to navigate in the chair.

Today, though, he figured he'd be okay because the remnants of the last snow still left on the ground would slow the wheels of the chair and keep him from accelerating down the hill too fast and turning over.

He figured wrong. The minute he came off the ramp, he could feel that his center of gravity was too high. He slammed the joystick forward, hoping to power down the hill without tipping, but the wheels caught, and the chair went end over end down the hill.

Next thing he knew he was lying in a heap about eight feet from his overturned chair.

"Son of a *bitch*," he said. Luckily he was unhurt. He had the wind knocked out of him, but that was about all. It was no worse than a good solid hit on the football field. He grinned and stared up at the ominous gray sky. It actually felt kind of good. "Pain is just the feeling of weakness leaving the body," he said out loud, recalling one of the many goading comments that Master Sergeant Finch used to yell at everybody during Ranger training down at Benning.

He wormed himself across the ice over to the chair. Getting back into the chair took nearly five minutes of struggle. But curiously he didn't feel daunted or angry or depressed the way he'd always felt doing therapy back at Walter Reed. In fact, he felt a steely determination, the same quality he thought had been blown away in the explosion.

Finally he settled back into the chair and moved down the walk, the nubby tires of the chair biting into the ice and snow with surprising efficiency.

Jesus but it was cold.

He'd put on a coat before leaving the house, but now his chest and hair and legs were wet from the snow he'd been lying on. And he should have worn a hat.

Nothing to do but keep moving.

He powered on down past the stables and onto the trail heading back into the forest. He was about five minutes down the trail when the first snow started falling. Within another ten minutes, the snow was coming down so hard that he kept having to knock the flakes off his eyelashes in order to see. Visibility was down to thirty or forty feet.

He didn't feel nervous, though. The wheelchair actually started riding better once half an inch of snow had accumulated. Soon, however, he was shivering.

But he was on a mission. He didn't have gloves, but he'd pulled his ruined hand back inside the sleeve of his coat.

The snow was beautiful, sifting down out of the sky in fat graywhite lumps. Every sensation felt bold, sharp, clear. Even the cold and the lump on his head where he'd whacked himself in the fall lifted his spirits, made him feel complete for the first time in a long time.

Why the hell had he been sitting around feeling sorry for himself all this time? Yes, it sucked having no legs. Yes, it sucked having to rely on Nurse Margie. Yes, it sucked having a face like Freddy

Krueger. But there were guys who didn't make it back, who would never again feel the clear, bracing cold of a day like this.

He hummed to himself as he bumped down the trail. He realized the place was farther than he'd thought. The chair was all charged up, so it would be able to make it there and back. But still, as he got deeper into the forest, he couldn't help feeling this was not the smartest thing he'd ever done in his life.

Finally, he came around a bend, and there it was: a large metal building that seemed unusually high. To the left was another structure, lower but longer than the first. Between them was some sort of massive air-conditioning unit, connected to the building by huge steel ducts. There seemed to be nothing going on, though. No African women, no vehicles, no steam coming from the chimneys, no lights. It was completely desolate.

He rolled to the taller building, found the door locked. There was a small window, but he couldn't see in. He rolled to the second building. The door to this one was open. He looked inside. In one corner lay a very large pile of what appeared to be sweet potatoes. The rest of the building contained a variety of industrial machines. Judging from the work flow, it looked like the potatoes were going into some sort of masher, which piped something to large stainless steel vats, which then led to a number of smaller vats or cookers. There was a lot of stainless steel piping.

Could he have been wrong about his suspicions? Sweet potatoes, he knew, yielded even more ethanol than corn. Was that all that was going on out here? How stupid he had been. A wave of shame crashed over him as he realized how susceptible he'd been to some imagined conspiracy between Collier and his father. He wished he could call his father now and apologize for his misguided fears.

Evan turned his wheelchair around and went back outside. The wind had picked up a little. He touched his hair, found it frozen solid. He was shivering pretty hard now.

This was not so good. He needed to get back to the house.

He rolled out behind the two buildings, using them to shield himself from the wind. By the edge of the second one he found his father's Cat D8 parked in the snow. Dale Wilmot had started in the business driving a Caterpillar, and he enjoyed using it around the property, knocking shit down or flattening ground. Like everything he did, the old man was a perfectionist with the Cat. Whether moving a pile of earth or digging a trench, his work was meticulous.

But here was a mess of broken earth, lumps and piles scattered here and there that hadn't been entirely covered with snow. Since his father couldn't have done this, he realized it must be Collier's handiwork. But what had he been doing here? It looked like he'd been burying something. Maybe some kind of industrial residue that his father didn't want dumped in the stream where he occasionally fished.

Evan rolled out over the lumpy ground, trying to get back onto the main path to the house. He pushed the chair sideways, spun it around, and then pushed it forward. For the first time since he'd left the house, the chair got stuck.

He backed up, then rolled forward, then backed up again. He cursed. The bottom of the chair had snagged on something. He rocked it back and forth, and felt a kindling fear in his belly.

If he got stuck out here, he was well and truly screwed. He leaned over and tried to look under the chair. But he couldn't lean too far without the danger of pitching over, which would only make a bad situation worse. Now that he'd stopped, he noticed this his entire body was trembling from the cold. It was a deep, biting, bone-deep cold that felt raw and burned.

He tried to spin the chair around, but the tires wouldn't grab the ground. The snow was coming down heavier, so hard that he could barely make out the Caterpillar, only five yards away.

Suddenly the chair broke free. He paused and turned to see what had caught him. It was a root, poking out of the ground.

Then his eyes widened. That was no root. It was a delicate black hand. A woman's hand, dusted with frost.

He moved closer and could see the fingers curled, as if the woman had been trying to dig herself out of her frozen grave. It was one of the African women who had been working with Collier. Now she—and maybe everyone—was dead, judging from the size of the frozen bed of earth that surrounded him. What he'd discovered was far worse than his initial suspicion would have led him to imagine. But he still lacked the context to understand why this had happened or what Collier and his father were up to.

He blasted forward, heading back toward the metal buildings—or what he *thought* were the metal buildings. But when he reached the vague dark shapes rising above him, he realized it was just the edge of the woods.

He looked around and realized he'd lost his bearings. All he could see was the trees and the snow. He pushed forward along the tree line while the snow absorbed all sound around him. It was almost as if he were enduring some diabolical sensory deprivation experiment. The tires of the wheelchair spun as they tried to grip on the slippery surface. He halted momentarily, then pressed on.

A minute later the tires spun again. He jiggled the joystick, waiting for them to catch, but they just kept spinning. He looked down and saw that the wheels had cut a trench. The initial friction had melted the snow—which then refroze into a solid glaze of ice.

His heart was pounding now. He jiggled and rocked and yanked on the wheel with his hand. But nothing worked. Nearing panic, he pressed the joystick to the forward limit. The tires made a soft buzzing sound on the ice. But the chair didn't move. And after another minute, he could hear the frequency of the wheels' buzzing begin to lower slightly. He was running down the batteries.

"Help!" he called. "Margie! Can you hear me?"

But the deep silence of the forest was his only answer.

A sudden resolve eclipsed his fear as he realized that there was only one thing left to do. He unstrapped the Velcro straps from his legs and slid to the ground.

The cold ground burned the stumps of his legs. Since coming home, he'd refused to do the therapy that would have prepared his stumps for prosthetics, and as a result, they were uncallused, thin-skinned, and sensitive.

He began to crawl.

Once he'd been a football star and soldier and a horseman, proud of his body and what it could do, the punishment it could endure without giving out on him. But now? It wasn't just that he'd been blown all to shit. It was also that he'd lain there feeling sorry for himself, letting his body weaken.

He still had the will, though. However different he and the old man were, Dale Wilmot had bequeathed him that one thing: will.

I'm not gonna die out here.

He crawled on and on, pushing himself, working through the fire that shot up through what remained of his limbs until they became completely numb.

I'm not gonna die out here.

After several hundred yards, he stopped in the middle of the trail to rest. Although the snow was still coming down, it had slackened a little, falling gently on his face and on his eye and on his outstretched tongue. It was peaceful, and the cold was like a blanket, and he closed his eyes so he could sleep.

29

WASHINGTON / IDAHO

A light dusting of snow covered the ground when the plane landed at Spokane International Airport in Washington State, just over the Idaho border. The airport was barely large enough for four gates, and Nancy Clement suspected its claim of "international" status was an exaggeration. Because of its size, however, she was able to purchase a last-minute ticket that she paid for at Dulles airport with her personal credit card, and to walk directly from landing to the Budget Rent A Car counter. The man at the counter was a morose-looking Indian guy who was missing all his upper teeth, giving his speech a lisping quality.

"Could be a vide out," he said, nodding his head as though in support of the notion that the worst possibilities are always the ones that actually come to pass.

"A what?"

"Vide. Out." He saw she was looking at him blankly. "A videout blizzard. So much snow you can't see your hand in front of your face, so please drive carefully."

"Thank you. I will."

He smiled a broad cheerless smile, showing off his gums. "Have a good day."

With that cheery send-off, she began driving north toward the address she'd found for Dale Wilmot's estate. The GPS showed the distance as only thirty-five miles, so she hoped she could get there before the roads became impassable.

The first part of the drive along US 90, wasn't bad. It was snowing hard, but the traffic kept the right lane relatively free of snow. The car felt stable and sure-footed, even at highway speeds. But then she swung off onto a rural route that wound upward into the higher elevations toward Priest Lake, and the conditions quickly deteriorated. Within minutes of turning off the highway, she began to feel a relentless tick of nervousness. Soon she was driving through four or five inches of virgin snow, not a single tire track on the road. She had rented a four-wheel-drive vehicle, a Toyota Land Cruiser, but still the car occasionally came unglued as she cornered, and once she even drove off the road far enough to worry about plunging down a hillside.

After that she drove with more caution.

To make matters worse, the map she carried was not very detailed, and the GPS in her car seemed to have no record of the road she was traveling on. She had finally switched it off after the condescending English-accented female voice had said "Turn around as soon as possible" for about the ninetieth time.

The wipers were going full speed, and the heater was blasting, but the windshield was getting clogged with snow. And even in the brief seconds when the wiper blades cleared it, she was unable to see more than a few feet in front of her. She found herself driving five miles an hour, more or less completely blind, up a mountain road. The notion that she might have to pull off the road and sit for a while started to seem entirely plausible, and the possibility made her hungry. She had eaten a nasty little ham and cheese sandwich in Las Vegas before changing planes. But that was six and a half hours ago.

And now the world had turned to an impenetrable gray mass. Finally, she gave in, stopped the car, got out, and stood in the snow. She had never seen anything like it before in her life. Raised in Tennessee, she had never even felt a snowflake on her cheek before she joined the FBI.

She would have thought that a whiteout blizzard would have been pretty and soft and white. But instead it had a grim grainy quality, like the soot from a crematorium.

She could more or less tell where the road was because the dim, black shapes of trees loomed over her, half visible through the snow. She glanced at her watch. A little after four o'clock. The sun would be going down pretty soon, which would only make matters worse. She'd probably be stuck there for the night.

For the first time she began to feel something that edged toward panic, when suddenly, mercifully, the snow let up. Perched on a hillside not more than a mile or two away, she saw a massive post-and-beam lodge, a house so big it almost could have been a hotel.

That was it. It had to be.

Five minutes later she was pulling up in front of the house. She climbed out and knocked on the door. But no one answered. Nancy looked around the house, trying to see inside, but there was no sign of life. Then, in the dimming light, she made out a dark figure trundling up a path, bundled in a heavy coat. It was a woman, a good four inches taller than Nancy, who outweighed her by at least a hundred pounds. She wore pale green scrubs beneath a huge parka. Nancy followed her inside. Framed by the furry hood, the woman's expression was tight with panic. Nancy showed the woman her identification.

"How did you know?"

"Know what?"

"That Evan is missing."

"Who's Evan?"

"Mr. Wilmot's son. I was just about to call the police."

"I didn't come for Evan. I came to talk to John Collier."

"He's not here. He's with Mr. Wilmot. They flew out together earlier today, but I need to find Evan. He's in a wheelchair, so he can't have gone far. My God, Mr. Wilmot will kill me."

"Slow down and tell me what happened so I can help you," Nancy said, trying to calm the frantic woman.

The nurse explained that she'd been given explicit instructions to keep Evan inside. He was not well, and might try to defy her, but for his own safety and health he needed to avoid the cold outdoors. Now she feared he might be dead from exposure. She was close to a nervous collapse. She had picked up the phone a dozen times to call Mr. Wilmot but had hung up every time.

"I told him not to go outside, but he did it anyway. You have to help me find him." The woman grabbed Nancy by the collar and yanked her though the doorway. She was immensely strong.

Nancy Clement thought for a moment. If Wilmot and Collier were gone, the son Evan might know something. Besides, she wasn't going anywhere in this weather.

"Have you got a heavy coat I can borrow?" Nancy asked. "Mine's kind of thin."

The nurse had searched for an hour by herself before she had come back and found Nancy at the door. The hapless caregiver had been looking in the wrong place, however. She assumed Evan would try to go down the driveway to the main road, but in fact he had gone off toward the woods.

It was Nancy who suggested they check the logging trail, and they soon found him. He had pulled himself into a ball inside his coat, protecting his head and face from frostbite. He was unconscious. The nurse picked him up and began staggering through the snow back to the house, carrying the young man like a baby.

Ten minutes later they had immersed him in a bath of warm water in a bathroom large enough to house an entire family. It took Nancy a moment to adjust to the young man's wrecked body—his truncated legs, his missing arm, the scar tissue that formed the topography of his face.

After a few minutes Evan began to shiver so hard that the women had to brace him.

"That's a good sign," the big nurse said. "It means he's warming up."

Soon the shivering stopped, and a few minutes later his eyes opened. He stared around dully, his eyes finally settling on Nancy.

"Who are you?" he asked

"My name is Nancy Clement," she said. "I'm with the Federal Bureau of Investigation."

The nurse said, "She came to help me find you."

The young man squinted at the nurse skeptically. "No, she didn't."

"Of course she did," the nurse said. Nancy had told her not to call the police, and now Margie felt indebted to the FBI agent, for saving not only Evan, but also her job.

"Margie, can you give me a minute alone with this nice FBI lady?"

"Why?" the nurse said.

"Please," he said. "Just once, can you just do what I ask?"

The nurse's slab of a face reddened. But finally she stood and stalked out of the bathroom.

Nancy felt awkward now, alone in the room with a naked man. But Evan Wilmot seemed unfazed. She supposed when you were disabled, you got used to people hauling you around, washing you, bathing you, seeing you naked.

"No," the young man said, as if reading her mind. "You never get used to it. It always sucks. But I have to stay in this water or I'll get sick."

Nancy cleared her throat.

"So," Evan said sadly, "my father has done something terrible, hasn't he?"

Nancy cocked her head. "*Has* he?"

Evan smiled sadly and looked off into the steamy distance. "Yes," he said. "Yes, he has."

30

MANASSAS, VIRGINIA

By all accounts, Gideon Davis was a gifted diplomat—engaged, charming, and direct. But because many of the qualities that make a diplomat effective are diametrically opposed to those that make a good soldier, the two professions often find themselves at odds. Gideon had often been sent places where only soldiers dared to go and had overcome the occupational bias against him. Over the years he had befriended a wide range of soldiers and CIA operatives and military contractors—some of them fairly shady characters.

So when he needed a mil spec weapons package, he knew just the man to call.

"Hi, Paulus," he said from a pay phone outside a 7-Eleven in Manassas. "It's Gideon Davis. Call me back on a secure line."

Three minutes later the phone rang. "Gideon," Paulus Lennart said, "it's been a long time."

"I'll make it quick," Gideon said. "I need breaching charges. Preferably ribbon-type-shaped charges. Plus some detonating cord and a trigger. Also a Barrett with ten rounds of armor-piercing incendiary."

"You're fucking joking," Lennart said.

"Not as long as you owe me for Cameroon." After a long pause, Gideon continued, "Plus, I guarantee that it won't blow back on you."

"How soon do you need this?"

"Two hours."

"Can't do a Barrett that fast," he said. "I've got an Accuracy International sitting around, though. Bolt action, .50 BMG, shoots a quarter minute of angle, nice Leupold glass, the whole thing."

"Fine."

"What do I get from this?"

"Besides my undying gratitude? Twenty thousand."

"I'll take the twenty, you can hold the gratitude." The phone went dead.

Two hours and ten minutes later Gideon was standing in the parking lot of a Super Target in Centerville when a battered blue van drove by. Gideon heard the door slide open behind him. But by then it was too late.

A bag had gone over his head and someone extremely quick and strong had lifted him off his feet. The door of the van slammed shut and then the van peeled away.

Gideon clawed for his Glock, but a massive hand closed over his fist, and the bag was pulled from his head. Holding him from behind was a young man with the physique of a battle tank, his arms looped around Gideon's chest like a band of steel. Paulus Lennart dug the tip of his gun barrel into the tender flesh of Gideon's temple.

"Don't ever do something like this to me again."

"Like what?" Gideon asked.

Lennart was a wiry South African with a short grizzled beard and longish graying hair. He had worked as a contractor for the State Department and was responsible for several killings in the small African nation of Cameroon, which—although committed in the interest of the United States of America—had nearly resulted in his beheading by an unfriendly local regime. Thanks to Gideon, however, Lennart was still alive.

"You didn't see fit to mention that you're wanted by the FBI?"

"Wanted for *questioning*," Gideon said. "Big difference."

"You think this is funny?"

Gideon pushed the pistol away from his head. "We have good

intelligence that there will be an attack against a target on US soil. If I don't have the weapons I asked you for, innocent people will die. Now are you going to help me or not?"

Paulus Lennart leaned forward and looked straight into Gideon's eyes. His jaw worked on a piece of chewing gum like he was trying to kill it. Gideon could smell the Juicy Fruit on his breath.

Finally Lennart leaned back and said, "I don't get you, man. You're supposed to be some diplomat, but you keep getting yourself into all this third-degree ninja shit. Who's the real Gideon, huh?"

"When you figure that out, let me know," Gideon said. "In the meantime, have you got my explosives?"

Lennart didn't move. "Am I going to be sorry I did this?"

"I have a great many talents," Gideon said. "But reading the future is not one of them."

"How did you ever become a diplomat, man?" Lennart said. "You suck in the reassurance department."

"Have you got the stuff or not? Because I'm on a tight schedule."

"You got my money?"

"You know I'm good for it."

"You're killing me." Paulus Lennart looked at the huge young man who was still holding Gideon around the chest, gave him a brief nod. "Go ahead," he said. "Get this guy his gear and get him the hell out of here."

31

CENTREVILLE, VIRGINIA

I've seen that man before," Verhoven said as he and Tillman crossed the parking lot of a sizable park in Centreville, and approached Gideon. Off in the distance a couple of joggers ran by, looking at their watches.

"He's been around, so it's possible," Tillman said evenly.

There had been a time a few years ago when Gideon had been on the news a lot. Gideon wore wraparound sunglasses that he'd purchased at a local CVS and a GLOCK SHOOTING SPORTS FOUNDATION hat. He hadn't shaved for two days and hoped that between the hat, the shades, and the scruff on his face that Verhoven wouldn't recognize him.

"You're late," Tillman said.

"You call at the last minute asking for very specialized items, you better plan on showing a little flexibility," Gideon said. He was making a strong effort to play the role of a professional soldier. "Where's my money?"

Tillman signaled to Verhoven, who threw a small gym bag on the ground. As Gideon took a quick inventory of its contents, Verhoven continued studying his face. His scrutiny wasn't lost on either Gideon or Tillman, though both men pretended not to notice.

"Couldn't track down a Barrett," Gideon said as he tossed the money in his car. "You're gonna have to make do with an Accuracy International bolt gun."

"It's still a .50 BMG, right?" Tillman said.

"Yeah."

Tillman looked at Verhoven, who shrugged.

"They make a hell of a good rifle," Gideon said. "SAS guys all use them."

"Scope?" Tillman asked.

"Leupold Mark IV. Mil-mil, ten power fixed. Just like the big boys."

"Good enough," Tillman said.

"It's all in the trunk," Gideon said.

As they all went to transfer the equipment, Verhoven kept stealing glances at Gideon, who decided it was time to call him on it.

"Is there a problem? Because you keep looking at me, and I don't like being looked at like that by anyone who's not a woman."

"I've met you before," Verhoven said.

"I don't think so."

Verhoven nodded, but he was clearly unsatisfied with Gideon's answer. A moaning sound from Verhoven's car interrupted the moment. It was Lorene.

"You should see how she's doing," Tillman said, hanging back with Gideon as Verhoven went to check on Lorene in the backseat of the car.

"They're hitting the State of the Union," Tillman whispered, waiting until he was sure Verhoven was out of earshot.

Gideon blinked. He'd been privately speculating on potential targets they might be hitting in the DC area, but this was far more serious than any scenario he'd imagined. In fact, because the State of the Union address was such a hard target, he had discounted it at the outset.

"Are you sure?"

"Pretty much. Although we're staging some support operation in Virginia. Not sure yet what it is."

Gideon felt the mounting pressure, as if sandbags were being piled on his shoulders. "We can't bring this to the FBI until we've got hard evidence."

"I know that," Tillman said. "Hang back and shadow me, and as soon as we've got something we can move on, we'll pull the trigger."

Gideon nodded as Verhoven rejoined them. "She's doing okay," he said to Tillman.

"Got a problem in the car?" asked Gideon.

"No problem. My wife isn't feeling well is all."

"You should take care of that."

"It's no concern of yours," said Verhoven.

Gideon nodded, then clapped Tillman on the shoulder. "I'll be seeing you," he said.

"Not if I see you first."

"Don't count on it."

Tillman laughed. "Asshole," he said. Then the two men climbed into the Honda and disappeared down the road.

As Tillman drove away, Verhoven said, "That man seemed very familiar to me."

"We go way back. Went through Ranger training together. Good man."

"He seemed quite disrespectful."

"He doesn't know you, that's all. Situation like this, a guy in his shoes has to be careful."

"I still recognize him from somewhere." Verhoven made a sucking sound through his teeth. "It'll come to me."

"Where to?"

"We need to find a quiet hotel, a place with no lobby so nobody watches us going in and out. We can drop Lorene off, then reconnoiter the target. That way we'll be ready first thing in the morning."

Tillman knew that Gideon was listening in on the radio that he'd left turned on in his pocket. "There's an Econo Lodge up there off of Lee-Jackson. How's that work for you?"

Verhoven shrugged. He seemed intent on his own thinking.

"There's always the Hampton Inn. Good breakfast buffet."

"Could we skip the travel review?" Verhoven said.

"Hey, you're the boss," Tillman said. "Econo Lodge it is."

32

POCATELLO, IDAHO

The Jeep started hard. Evan had given Nancy the keys to his father's vehicle. Outside it was dark, and the temperature had dropped to around ten degrees Fahrenheit. The snow was still coming down, but it wasn't the choking blizzard that it had been earlier. It took some careful driving to get to the clearing where the structures stood, but the big tires of the Jeep kept traction as long as Nancy went slowly.

Evan told her he had been investigating his father's suspicious behavior with John Collier when he came upon the woman's hand. Whatever his father was doing in the woods—and by now he was fairly certain that it did not involve producing ethanol—had resulted in the death of at least one woman. Evan explained that his father had become a stranger to him. Since Evan had come back from the war, his father had become harder and more reclusive. But nothing could rationalize the horrible truth of what Evan had discovered.

Evan gave Nancy directions back out along the logging trail where she had found him. He was too weak to go with her, and even if he weren't, he could not bear it. She took the keys to the Jeep and left Evan with his eyes closed, scarred hand extended up out of the blankets, as if he were a drowning man reaching for the surface of a pond.

Now Nancy parked the car, grabbed her flashlight, and climbed out, leaving the headlights on. Even with the mittens, the hat, and the coat she had borrowed, the air was bitterly cold. Behind the first building she found the bulldozer, the apron of broken earth spread out before it. She tromped through the snow that covered the rubble of frozen earth until her flashlight landed on a small lump about a foot high, toward the edge of the scar in the ground. She walked toward it, dusted off the snow with her mitten, and gasped—her sharp exhalation marked by a puff of condensation.

She was looking at a delicate hand reaching up through the frozen ground.

Unable to excavate with any efficiency, she pulled off her mittens to use her bare hands. Eventually, she uncovered the entire arm and the shallow form of a woman's chest.

Nancy pulled out the burner phone she had bought at the airport in Las Vegas and quickly discovered that there was no cellular signal. Then she put the phone away. Even if she *were* able to reach Gideon, what could she say except that someone—and maybe several people—had been killed here. But it still gave her nothing to take to Dahlgren. Dead people recovered from a pile of dirt was a state crime, something to alert the sheriff about. But there was no hard evidence of a plot against the government of the United States.

She got up and walked around to the first building. The door was locked, so she walked to the second building. Inside she found a tangle of complex stainless steel piping attached to various sizes of vats and pressure vessels. It looked similar to the larger pharmaceutical labs Nancy had raided during a joint task force she had served on with the DEA. But these vessels were far larger. And most importantly, it didn't smell like a meth lab. Small-scale meth labs could often be smelled by neighbors a mile away. But here the smell wasn't bad. Only a faint, bitter odor that reminded her of almonds.

She walked slowly around the deserted building, probing with her flashlight. On the far end of the room she found a pile of what appeared to be a root vegetable she didn't recognize, although it was similar to potatoes or yams.

She examined one, which was frozen to a rocklike consistency. She tossed it back in the pile and continued surveying the room.

It was clear as she followed the pipes that the roots were being ground up, the liquid residue piped into a large vat. That vat led to a series of increasingly small steel vessels. Something was being distilled from the roots, and perhaps chemically altered. She reviewed the various naturally derived drugs she was aware of: cocaine, heroin, khat, THC, psilocybin. None of them came from root vegetables.

At the far end of the room was the smallest of the vessels. It appeared to be refrigerated—though that seemed a little unnecessary today. At the bottom of the vessel was a small petcock. She turned the petcock. A single drop of a thin clear liquid ran from the petcock and fell to the concrete floor where it rapidly froze. She considered touching it, but then decided that might not be wise.

Was it possible, she wondered, to synthesize some kind of explosive compound, like nitroglycerin, from a vegetable? If so, she would be wise not to mess with it. She walked out of the shed and around to the other building. The door was reinforced with heavy steel. She drew her Glock and fired point-blank into the door bolt. Dahlgren had forced her to give up her service weapon, so this was a spare she kept on hand. It took half a magazine to finally blow a hole in the door so she could get in.

The room inside was spacious and appeared to be some sort of dormitory. Along one wall stood a row of bunk beds with personal items lying here and there—photographs, a Bible, several dog-eared magazines written in French, with pictures of people Nancy took to be Africans. It was clear that nobody was living here now. The room was nearly as cold as the ten-degree weather outside. On the far side of the wall was a small kitchen. She walked over and found several pots and pans on the stove, one of them full of scorched food. It was as if everyone had left the place in a hurry, before they could even remove their food off the stove.

Whoever had lived here was now probably buried beneath the snow.

Oddly, the rest of the room was empty. It seemed like an awful lot of space for the use it had been put to. Looking around some more, she noticed a foot-long smear of blood on the polished concrete floor. And now, having keyed in on this first blood, she noticed other jagged streaks of dried blood—like the brushwork of a desperate painter. Crusted in one of these was a clot of hair. Then, she felt her eyes begin to sting.

She became aware of the smell of almonds, and within a minute, Nancy's throat tickled uncomfortably, her nose burned, and she began to feel nauseated. She walked outside and took several deep breaths. The fresh, frigid air burned her nasal passages, even as it relieved the tickling sensation.

A survey of the perimeter revealed a huge air-conditioning unit that looked more suited to a far larger building. Still feeling woozy, she went and sat back down in the Jeep. She had left the vehicle running and was comfortable inside.

She considered heading back to the Wilmot house but decided to take one last circuit of the dormitory building. The wind was bitter cold, and although she understood that she had no choice, she was immediately sorry she hadn't stayed in the Jeep. Back inside the big room filled with beds, the almond smell seemed even more noxious—as if she were more sensitive to it now than she had been earlier. Suddenly her stomach cramped up. She ran outside and threw up in the snow.

And then, suddenly, she understood. It was like watching the fractured pieces of a puzzle knit themselves together into a unified picture.

Cyanide. Wilmot and Collier were manufacturing cyanide gas.

She ran to the Jeep, climbed in, and began driving quickly up the road. *Get to a phone.*

The Jeep bumped and slammed as she forced the aging four-wheel-drive vehicle down the slippery rutted road. She could see the house in front of her when she remembered Evan's wheelchair lying across the logging trail. Driving down here, she had steered carefully around the abandoned wheelchair. But her racing mind had forgotten that, and now the big lump in the snow rose up suddenly before her. She yanked the wheel to the right.

The Jeep pitched up onto its left wheels, hanging there for what seemed an interminable moment, before rolling over.

Once, twice, then a third time.

Nancy hadn't worn her seat belt. She felt herself slamming hard against the floor—or what seemed like the floor until she realized it was actually the roof.

The Jeep lay quietly, the noise of its impact muffled by the snow. From her inverted position Nancy could see the big house only a few hundred yards away, its windows lit up bright yellow against the whiteness of the snow.

She crawled out of the Jeep and felt something very wrong with her left leg. The pain was acute. Although she could barely put any weight on her leg, she began hobbling toward the house, which suddenly seemed very far away.

33

WASHINGTON, DC

Dale Wilmot and John Collier landed at Reagan National Airport, where they rented a gray Buick Enclave—an SUV guaranteed to attract no attention. They drove back to the hangar, loaded their luggage into the vehicle, then proceeded to downtown Washington, DC, where they checked into a suite at the Hay-Adams Hotel. The two men declined the assistance of a bellman and unloaded the vehicle themselves. Collier had managed to pack their equipment into several suitcases that fit neatly on the steel luggage cart.

Once they were in their suite, Collier turned on his laptop and began to review his notes on an encrypted file. But Wilmot found himself unable to concentrate and walked out onto the balcony overlooking the mall. Night had fallen, but the Washington Monument and the Capitol were brightly lit.

Despite its catastrophic government, this remained a great country. Even now, especially now, he felt a rush of patriotic pride when he saw the great dome of the Capitol building.

He wondered what Evan would think, knowing what he was about to do. In the breast pocket of his jacket, Wilmot carried the letter he hoped would explain his actions to his son. If not tomorrow, then someday, Wilmot hoped Evan would understand.

Wilmot recalled the first time he had looked down at Evan lying burned and broken in Walter Reed, his face slick with antibiotic ointment. He found himself wondering: if God himself offered to make his boy whole again in exchange for Wilmot aborting the mission he and Collier had planned, would he take the offer?

As he took in the majestic view, he decided that he wouldn't.

Fate had dealt him this hand precisely because of who he was: the only man capable of taking the harsh but necessary action of punishing those most responsible for ruining the state of the union.

"All set," Collier said as he joined Wilmot on the balcony. "Christ, it's cold out here."

"I didn't even notice," Wilmot said.

"Are you hungry?"

"I am," Wilmot said, not looking at the young man. He wished Evan were here. The truth was that whatever anger he had once felt toward his son had faded long ago. The young man had made a choice, a courageous choice, certainly not one that many people in his shoes would have made.

"Should I order room service?" Collier asked.

Wilmot realized that the last person he wanted to share his last meal with was Collier.

"If you don't mind, John, I think I'll dine alone," Wilmot said.

"Sure. Yeah. Okay." Collier's voice was etched with disappointment, but Wilmot didn't care a tinker's damn how John Collier felt. He was now, as he'd always been, an ugly, stunted person—angry, vicious, and weak.

Wilmot went down to the Lafayette Room. It was full of people he'd seen on television, even a few he'd met in person. But nobody approached him, nobody asked him how he was doing. Which was just as well. At the moment Wilmot preferred his own company.

Normally, he was a beer man, but tonight he was in the mood to celebrate. He called over the sommelier.

"Suppose this was your last meal," he said. "What would you drink?"

The sommelier didn't miss a beat, and suggested a Château d'Yquem '61.

"No. Something American."

"I *see*," the sommelier smiled conspiratorially. "Because of the State of the Union tomorrow. I have just the thing."

The sommelier brought out a big cabernet bottled in 1983 by a Napa Valley winery Wilmot had never heard of. He almost sent it back when he was told that it cost nearly six hundred dollars. But then he thought, what's the point of being rich if you were too cheap to blow a few hundred bucks on a bottle of wine on the most important day of your life?

Wilmot ate a steak, a bone-in filet, very rare, with a baked potato drenched in sour cream and butter, and declined the salad. Only a squirrel would eat a pile of leaves for a last meal. He smiled to himself. He had never enjoyed a meal so much in all his life.

The sommelier refilled his glass until the bottle was empty. He didn't feel drunk, but he noticed he had trouble holding his fork steady. He ate a slice of apple pie with vanilla ice cream for dessert, but the magic seemed to have drained out of the moment. He asked the waiter to scare him up an Opus X cigar, then paid his bill with a generous tip, and went for a walk along Pennsylvania Avenue.

Low, ragged clouds covered the moon as he walked past the White House and lit the Opus. Normally it was his favorite cigar, but today it tasted harsh and sour. Looking at the Capitol in the distance he felt suddenly impatient. He wanted to get the show on the road. He tossed the cigar onto the street, where it skittered across the asphalt with a shower of sparks. A pencil-necked geek in a Prius cursed at him as he slowed for a red light.

He felt the low flame of anger kindling inside him. When he was a young man he would have run up and given the little shithead a beat-down. Something in Wilmot's smile must have scared the driver, though, because he peeled out of there as soon as the light turned green.

Wilmot started back to the hotel, feeling ready. It was time to teach a lesson to the people who had taken everything from him. It was time to change the country. It was time to make history.

When he entered the lobby, he withdrew the letter he'd written to Evan, and reread the last paragraph.

As horrible as the events of this day have been, they were also necessary. The corrupt and cynical gang of thieves and madmen who call themselves our government have grown like a cancer that will kill its host unless it is removed. Today we, the people of the United States of America, have finally been given a chance to remove this cancer and to reclaim this great nation as our own. I hope that, in time, you will come to understand why I have done what I have done, and that you will be as proud of me as I have been of you.

With love,
Your father

He put the letter back in the envelope and addressed it to Evan. Then he handed it to the clerk.

"Would you mail this for me in the morning?" he asked.

"Certainly, sir."

"And I'll need a five AM wake-up call."

"Of course."

Then Dale Wilmot went upstairs to bed.

34

TYSONS CORNER, VIRGINIA

D r. Nathan Klotz slept soundly in the king-size bed next to his two daughters. With their mother working double shifts providing security for the State of the Union address, the girls insisted on a sleepover. He had not objected because it was easier to have them in the bed than to wake up every two hours when they called out for Mommy. He missed his wife, too, but the pride he took in her job made him miss her a little less.

Downstairs, the remains of the meal they had defrosted and cooked were still on the table. Dr. Klotz had been too tired to clean up after bathing and reading to the children, so he left the dishes and planned to deal with them in the morning. There was very little left over anyway; his wife was an excellent cook. Even the girls had polished off their plates.

Had he been awake and clicked on the real-time surveillance monitor his wife had installed on their desktop computer, he might have seen the old Honda that had passed before his house three times before finally stopping.

35

TYSONS CORNER, VIRGINIA

illman knew he'd have to make a decision sooner than later.

Until now, he had smiled and nodded at Verhoven's crazed political observations and had followed his orders without questioning them. But if he went much further, he'd be committing crimes that could get him sent to prison for the rest of his life.

Verhoven drove by the house slowly in the old Honda. It was like a dozen other houses on the same street in Tysons Corner: two-car garage, two stories, dormer windows, wood siding painted in one of the three colors of beige approved by the neighborhood association. They planned to invade it and hold its occupants hostage. Tillman's heart was thumping uncomfortably as he weighed whether to go through with the operation or turn his gun on Verhoven and Lorene.

The problem was that he had still not learned enough about how the principal attack would go down, and the part they were supposed to play in it. Would the plot fail or be aborted if Verhoven didn't execute his part of the plan? Or would the plan just have to be adjusted in some minor way? Could Tillman stop the killing of hundreds of people if he preempted whatever was about to go down in the home of Dr. Nathan Klotz?

"One more pass," Tillman said as Verhoven slowed the car. He was stalling for time.

"Why?"

"This is a normal-looking neighborhood, but the house has four pan-and-scan video surveillance cameras on the eaves. My guess is they're mounted on motion-activated servos. Whoever lives here is not some normal suburban Joe."

"That's immaterial to your role here."

"Dammit," Tillman said. "You're a drug dealer who runs around in the woods with a bunch of dumb kids playing war. I'm a professional. This is what I do. Looking at this place, I can tell you that if we mess up on one single aspect of the op, we will be royally and irrevocably fucked."

"This is a need-to-know—"

"I'm very familiar with what need-to-know means, Jim." Tillman was hauling out his most intimidating Special Forces NCO demeanor. "And right now I need to know what we're doing here. No offense, but you're in over your head."

"Oh, I am?" Verhoven glared icily at him.

Tillman met Verhoven's gaze and glared right back at him. After a moment Verhoven looked away.

"One more drive-by," Tillman said, "and this time you tell me every goddamn thing you know. Or I'm getting out of this car and hiking off into the wild blue yonder."

The car was quiet.

Lorene was lying prone in the backseat, and she propped herself up. "We need him," she said softly.

Verhoven grimaced, then continued around the block and said, "Look, I don't know any specifics about the individual who owns this home. All I know is that there is a state-of-the-art security system, top-notch surveillance, the windows and doors are bullet resistant, and there's a safe room on the upper floor."

"Are we here to kill these people?"

"No," Verhoven said. "Our mission is to capture the occupants and keep them alive. There are three people in the house—an adult male and two children, ages four and six. We are to capture and control these three individuals, hold the premises, and await further instructions."

"From who?"

"I've told you all you need to know," Verhoven said. "And more than I should have."

"Is there a wife? Girlfriend?"

"Wife. But she's not home."

"So what are the Barrett and the incendiary rounds for?"

"In case they make it to the safe room."

"I'm sorry, but that's the stupidest thing I've ever heard," Tillman said. "You'll burn down the house and everyone inside. Those .50s could blast through the rest of the house like tissue paper and burn down the next three houses on the block."

"I don't anticipate letting them reach the safe room." Verhoven stopped the car and stared stiffly straight ahead. Tillman heard the irritation in his voice.

"And the security system. A place like this, they'll have outcall through a buried cable and possibly even a radio backup."

"That's all been taken care of." He pointed to the side of the house. "The cable box there is a dummy. We've already planted a device that will cut the signal to the cable."

He reached into the pocket of a nylon gym bag sitting on the center console, pulled out a small black box with a button on the side. He pressed the button. "There. Done."

"What about cell phones?"

"It's all in the bag. There's a cell phone jammer. Now stop worrying and follow me," Verhoven said, pushing out of the car. Tillman had no choice except to follow him.

Tillman was prepared to abort the mission the moment it meant killing innocent civilians, even though he knew it would trash his ability to find out what was going on. Although he still felt okay about taking this operation to the next level, he suspected his brother might not be as willing to take that chance. He glanced around, half-expecting Gideon to pull up at any moment.

Verhoven walked up to the front door and pressed the doorbell on an industrial quality intercom system with a built-in keypad.

After a moment a sleepy and anxious-sounding man said, "Yes?"

Tillman knew that the man who answered was looking at them

through a camera. What he saw was a man wearing black tactical clothing and body armor. His first instinct would not be to open the door.

"Good morning, sir," Verhoven said, holding up to the camera some fake identification. Verhoven was banking on the camera's resolution to be insufficient for the man to make out anything other than an official-looking piece of plastic. "Greg Gillis, PW Emergency Services. I'm sure you heard the commotion. A chemical truck has overturned one block away. We need everyone to evacuate the area immediately."

"Uh . . . I need to confirm this with somebody."

"Sir, I am your confirmation. You need to exit this house *now.* There's no time to waste."

From the man's silence, it was clear that he had some kind of security protocol that he wanted to go through. Most likely he wanted to call the police department and verify that Verhoven was who he claimed to be.

"Now, sir!"

"Give me a second."

A few moments later an apprehensive-looking man, hair sticking up in all directions, opened the door about three inches. The door was still held in place by a security bar like the ones used in hotel rooms. Only this one looked much bigger and stronger.

"Please let me see your ID again, officer," the man said.

Knowing full well that his ID wouldn't pass scrutiny at this distance, Verhoven raised his shotgun. The man's eyes widened, but before he could slam the door closed or Verhoven could shoot, Tillman inserted the toe of his boot into the door. The man slammed his weight frantically against the door. Realizing that he was wasting his time battling over the door, the man retreated. Tillman could hear his footsteps pounding up the stairs.

Tillman hesitated for a fraction of a second. This was it: go or no-go. Point of no return.

He raised his boot and kicked the door just below the dead bolt, splintering the doorjamb as the steel security bar tore through the reinforced wood frame.

36

WASHINGTON, DC

T he front desk woke Wilmot at five o'clock. Collier was already busy at his computer.

Wilmot made himself some coffee, then sat down next to Collier and watched as he keyed in a series of commands.

"How long before the heat shuts down?" he asked.

"I was just about to do it," Collier said. "Do you want to hit the button?"

He knew Collier was trying to win him over after being snubbed last night. Wilmot leaned over and asked, "What do I do?"

Collier pointed at the keyboard and said, "Just hit enter."

Wilmot studied the screen. NATIONAL HEAT & AIR REMOTE DIAGNOSTIC SYSTEM appeared at the top of the screen. There was a bunch of gibberish code that meant nothing to him. Collier had explained that by remotely uploading a bug script into the air handler's controller, the fans would fail to come on when the gas next cycled on. With no air moving, the thermocouple in the temp sensor would eventually overheat, shutting off the gas. Then the whole system would shut down, and the Capitol would get very cold.

"All right then," said Wilmot. "Let's see if it works."

"It'll work," Collier said. "Trust me."

Wilmot stabbed the key. Nothing dramatic happened, but he imagined the signals sending their disruptive messages to the main circuit panel, finally putting in motion the plan they had spent so long preparing.

"I'm taking a shower," Wilmot said and walked toward the bathroom.

He came back out of the bathroom twenty minutes later, combing his wet hair, wearing white coveralls with a yellow patch on the left side of his chest that read DALE. A large printed logo on the back read: NATIONAL HEAT & AIR. WARMING HEARTS AND HEARTHS SINCE 1947. Below that, in tiny letters: A DIVISION OF WILMOT INDUSTRIES.

He sat down on the couch and put his feet up. Collier wore an identical pair of coveralls, with a patch on the chest that said JOHN.

Collier closed the computer and said, "Okay, then. Now we wait for them to call us."

At 5:33 AM, the phone connected through Collier's computer rang.

Collier let it ring once, twice, answering on the third ring. "Good morning, National Heat and Air, this is Ralph speaking. How may I help you?"

A voice on the other end said, "Hey, ah, yeah, this is Alfred Teasely, federal facilities manager at the Capitol. We've got a problem with the heating system at the Capitol."

National Heat & Air had bid for and won the contract to service the Capitol. And since Wilmot owned National Heat & Air, it had not been much of a problem for Collier to reroute their emergency phone system so that any calls coming in to the dispatch line from the 202 area code were automatically shunted to his computer.

"Do you have a contract number, sir?" Collier said.

"I'm at the United States Capitol. How many United States Capitols are there?"

"Yes, sir. I just need a contract number so that I can access your account."

The man groaned. "Hold on." There was some brief scrabbling around. "Okay. Eight oh one one five dash three."

"One moment, sir." Collier clattered randomly on the keys of the computer. "I show that that is a level-three secure facility. May I have your security code?"

"Nine six four dash Alpha Charlie Seven."

"Excellent. What seems to be the problem, sir?"

"Well, the whole damn HVAC system just locked up. It's shut down, and we can't access the controller. I'm just getting a blue screen."

"Have you installed the three-point-one-point-two update?" Collier was grinning at Wilmot. He loved all this techie mumbo jumbo.

"I'm checking the upgrade history now," the facilities manager said. "I'm not seeing anything. I've got the damn State of the Union address in twelve hours."

"Normally we update the software over the Internet. But it looks like . . . yes, sir . . . there seems to be something wrong with the broadband connection. What we'll need to do is dispatch a team to update that software and get you back online."

"I just need the damn thing to work."

"Not a problem, sir. We have two technicians on standby. Let me check the schedule . . . Okay, here we go. I've got two of our top guys on call. They've been precleared. I'll dispatch them right away."

"How fast can they get here?"

"Less than thirty minutes."

"Give me their names."

"Right. John Collier and Dale Wilmot. You have a great day now."

Three minutes later Collier and Wilmot were down in the lowest level parking deck, loading the steel cart containing two canisters of hydrogen cyanide into the back of a slightly battered white panel van that read NATIONAL HEAT & AIR on the side. He'd requisitioned it from the National Heat & Air motor pool, with legitimate plates, VIN number, and registration. Collier had seen to it all.

37

TYSONS CORNER, VIRGINIA

Gideon had lost them.

He didn't have a tracking device, only the small earpiece that fed him the static-filled audio from the radio Tillman had pocketed.

He still didn't know which house they were going to, or who was the target. He had followed Verhoven cautiously. Now it was five-thirty in the morning, and the greatest danger was that Verhoven would notice him following them. There were few other cars on the road in the suburban streets on which they were driving. By turning off his lights and trying to stay back at least a couple of city blocks, he seemed to have managed to escape detection. The price he'd paid was that at the last minute, he'd gotten separated. He knew that Verhoven had stopped, that the operation was a go, and that Tillman couldn't be more than a few blocks away.

But the neighborhood was a maze of winding roads lined by nearly identical houses. Now he was blundering around, hoping to stumble on the battered old Honda. He knew that by process of elimination, he'd eventually locate the car. But if Tillman ran into trouble before then, there was no guarantee he'd be able to reach him in time to help.

It had been a clear night when the sun went down, but an hour before dawn the moon was covered by low heavy clouds. The temperature hovered around thirty-five, rain threatened, and outside of the few puddles of light beneath the occasional street lamp, the world was painted slightly different shades of black. Gideon's mood, too, had gone dark. He hadn't slept in a very long time. And it seemed like they'd gone deeper and deeper into this thing without really learning anything new.

He stopped at a stop sign and let his engine idle. Left or right? He looked in each direction. There were cars parked on the street both ways, none of them clear enough to identify by make and model. He waited for audio from Tillman, but all he could hear was quiet breathing. *Dammit, Tillman, why didn't you say what street you'd turned onto?*

Gideon knew the answer, of course. Tillman had mentioned a few street names as they were driving. But he couldn't exactly carry on a constant monologue of directions without tipping his hand to Verhoven.

Gideon turned left, driving slowly because his headlights were extinguished, and in the darkness he risked running into something. Eventually he hit a dead end without seeing the Honda. He turned around, drove back until he came to the same stop sign, drove down the next street, hit a dead end, no Honda, came back and stopped at the stop sign again.

As he was idling at the stop sign, trying to figure out where he was, he saw headlights tearing rapidly down the street behind him.

He edged forward and eased into a space next to the curb, then slumped down in the car. His heart rate picked up, and he could feel himself sweating, despite the cold. He put his hand on the butt of his Glock. He could see the headlights slowing. He didn't move.

Suddenly blue lights began flashing.

He sat up and smoothed his coat, covering the pistol on his hip, and rolled down the window, only to see the car speed right past him.

This can't be good.

He took off in pursuit.

"Tillman, you need to answer me." He was practically shouting into the radio. "There's a cop coming down the street, and he may be headed right for you."

But the only response Gideon heard was static.

• • •

Tillman entered the house and sprinted for the stairs, bounding up them two at a time. Verhoven followed him inside, carrying the guns, while Lorene hobbled in and secured the door behind them.

By the time Tillman reached the second floor, he saw Dr. Klotz at the far end of the hallway, carrying two small children into another bedroom.

The handle was locked. Tillman calmly inserted the pry bar in the door. It was a high-quality wooden door, but nothing special. He pried it off its hinges in three hard strokes, jerked the door open, and charged inside.

He found himself in the master bedroom. The bedcovers were disheveled. On the far wall, another door slammed shut. He studied it carefully. There was no handle, only a very thin crack around the perimeter of the door, which was painted the same flat ecru as the rest of the room. If he hadn't seen the door slam shut, he would barely have noticed it.

It was a safe room, a panic room, whatever you wanted to call it.

Tillman looked at his watch. 5:34 AM. There was no reason to rush now. Verhoven had cut the phone and jammed the cell phone frequencies. There would be no 911 call.

He placed the radio back in his ear and heard Gideon's desperate voice.

"Tillman, do you copy?"

"Gideon?"

"Where the hell have you been?"

"I've been busy."

"There's a cop outside. He's walking up to the front door."

Tillman told Gideon to stand down. He hustled back downstairs, where Verhoven was tending to Lorene on the couch. She was wincing and holding her side.

"Where are they?" Verhoven said.

"They got into the safe room. But we've got a bigger problem."

• • •

Officer Leyland Millwood Jr., Prince William County Police badge number 3071, saw the aging black Honda parked on the street. It was the same car a neighbor had phoned in, complaining that it had been circling the block in the early morning hours. It looked out of place in a neighborhood where most of the cars were garaged, and most were new Audis, Volvos, and Acuras. Plus, there had been several break-ins reported over the last couple of months.

He parked his patrol car, climbed out, and put his hand on the hood of the Honda. It was warm. In this weather a car hood wouldn't stay warm two minutes after you turned it off.

He surveyed the area with his flashlight. There were no lights on in the street, no signs of anything odd going on.

He considered what to do. He didn't really want to scare some family by waking them up for nothing. But if a B and E was happening on his watch, he was damn well going to stop it. Leyland Millwood was a three-year veteran of the PW County force. He'd been driving around in the middle of the night rounding up drunks and giving speeding tickets to teenagers and stopping disabled veterans who'd forgotten to turn their lights on. He was ready to move on to something more exciting—possibly Special Investigations. A few good collars would get him noticed, and he would redeem them for a ticket out of this wilderness of boredom.

He approached the front door of the house and banged on it with the butt of his flashlight.

Verhoven's eyes widened when he heard the banging on the front door. He turned and strode toward the front of the house, his AR-15 at low ready. He looked a little panicky, like maybe he was itching to shoot somebody.

"Wait!" Tillman whispered sharply. "Just . . . wait. Don't do *any-thing.*"

Tillman bounded to the door, pulled out his utility knife, and stabbed the wall. Behind the Sheetrock he found the back of the intercom unit that faced the outside of the building. Beneath it was a piece of armored conduit running down through the wall.

He yanked the conduit free of the connector in the base of the intercom, then severed the wire inside it with one swift stroke of the knife. Then he looked through the window. A very young, pugnacious-looking cop stood on the front porch, looking warily at the front door.

"Another two seconds, that man up in the safe room would have been talking to the cop out there," Tillman whispered.

"Who is it?" Verhoven said softly. His gun was now pointed directly at the door.

Tillman ignored his question, instead whispering, "Get Lorene's clothes off. Everything but her bra and panties."

"Why? What are you doing?"

"Just do what I tell you to do."

Verhoven stood there, as if deciding what to do. He clearly didn't like taking orders.

"Focus on her clothes. Let me call this play, okay?" Tillman tried to compress all the urgency he felt into his whispered voice. He couldn't let Verhoven open the door. He'd have to stop him, effectively ending the operation he and Gideon had already put themselves on the line for.

Verhoven glared at him for a moment, before he finally relented. Verhoven was mostly bluff—and in his heart he probably knew it. They were deep into the weeds now, and Verhoven was smart enough to recognize that Tillman was better equipped to get them through this.

Tillman sprinted up the stairs two at a time, running to the bedroom, then dumping clothes from the chest of drawers onto the floor until he found a cotton nightgown. He bounded back down the stairs to find a drawn-looking and nearly naked Lorene Verhoven standing unsteadily in the middle of the room.

"Arms up," he said.

She put her arms in the air, wincing at the pain in her side. As though he were dressing a child, he slid the nightgown down her arms and over her head. There was a small amount of blood weeping from the dressing on her flank.

There was more banging at the door.

"Perfect," he said, mussing her hair so she looked as though she'd been roused from bed. "The guy out there is a cop. Go to the door, tell him you're fine. Whatever you do, don't let him in the house."

She nodded, walked stiffly to the door. Tillman motioned to Verhoven to hide out of sight in the dining room. Verhoven retreated, his AR-15 aimed at the door.

"Be cool," Tillman mouthed as Lorene neared the door.

She opened the door, looked out. "Yes?" she said.

"Officer Millwood, PW County, ma'am. Is everything okay?"

"Excuse me?"

"Is everything okay? A neighbor said there was a car circling the street, and now it's parked outside your house."

"Oh. Yeah." Lorene scratched her head. "My husband went out to get some coffee. He knows I can't be without it when I wake up."

"You're sure?"

"Look, I appreciate you're doing your job. But my shift at the hospital starts in an hour, and I'd really like to enjoy that coffee and get myself ready."

Officer Millwood stood there but made no move to leave. "I'm sorry if this sounds out of place, ma'am, but you don't look well."

"I'm just a little under the weather. But thank you for asking. Stay safe out there." She closed the door and sagged against the wall, breathing hard. There was a bloody spot on her side about the size of a tangerine, seeping into the white cotton fabric of the nightgown.

Verhoven dropped his weapon and propped her up. "You did great, baby," he said.

He kissed her forehead, but her eyes seemed to lose focus.

"Baby, I need to lie down now," she mumbled.

"Of course you do." He carried her across the living room, set her on the couch. Her face was misted with perspiration and her complexion had gone gray again.

"She needs fluids," Tillman said.

Verhoven looked down at her bleakly, his eyes unfocused. His body sagged, like a marionette with its strings cut. Tillman had seen it happen many times before. A soldier during combat would run on adrenaline for hours, performing just fine—and then suddenly they'd just fall off a mental cliff.

"Jim," Tillman said. "You with me? We're making history here. Nothing this big every comes easily. Operations like this always get bad before they get good again."

After a moment, Verhoven nodded.

The thing Tillman didn't say is that sometimes things got bad before they got worse. And then everything fell apart and people died for nothing. In combat you never knew which one it was going to be. And now it was up to him to make sure this wasn't the kind of op where the good guys ended up facedown in a ditch.

Tillman walked up the stairs, found the intercom on the wall next to the safe room, and pressed the button.

"Hi there, sir," he said. "My name is Bob and I'm here to make sure that you and your two beautiful daughters walk out of that room entirely safe and unharmed."

A man's voice came back immediately. "This is a fortified safe room, you son of a bitch," the man said. "I don't know if that means anything to you. But we've got food, water, Class III air filtration, weapons, and ammunition in here. The walls are made of solid reinforced concrete and the door is inch-thick steel plate. Take whatever you want from the house and leave. You'll never get us out of here."

"Sir, I apologize for the stress we're putting you through, but the fact is, we will get in there. And we'll do it in approximately five minutes."

"Not unless you have—" The man stopped himself abruptly.

"You were going to say 'Not unless you have plastic explosives.'" Tillman dangled the roll of ribbon charges in front of the camera. "This is a C4 breaching charge. You'll notice it has a curved anterior surface formed from a thin wafer of copper. This curve concentrates the blast wave into a one-centimeter-wide area, simultaneously converting the copper to a superheated plasma jet that will cut through one-inch plate like a knife through butter. In order to improve the blast strength, I'll hang about twenty Ziploc bags full of water on the back side of the ribbon charges. This will provide inertia, which will increase the energy of the blast tenfold. It will also dampen the noise of the blast so that your neighbors are none the wiser."

He began sticking the ribbon charge to the big steel door, running a band of it all the way around the outside of the door.

"Okay, now before I blow the door," Tillman said, "our legal department requires that we disclose to you the effect of the blast. Since you are in an enclosed room, the overpressure will have no way to dissipate, causing a fairly substantial shock wave to propagate through the safe room. This will burst your eardrums along with those of your lovely daughters. What I'm going to recommend that you do prior to detonation is open your mouths and stick your fingers in your ears. This will at least give your daughters a fighting chance to avoid becoming profoundly deaf for the rest of their lives. The downside, though, is that there's also a substantial chance of causing pulmonary hemorrhaging. That could cause you and your daughters to drown in blood produced by your own lungs. I've seen that happen and I can tell you, it's a fairly horrible way to die." He pressed a detonator into the end of the ribbon charge. Then he walked back and stood in front of the camera. "Or you could come out and we could have a civilized conversation."

There was a long pause. "You're using us to get to my wife."

Tillman didn't know what he was talking about. But there was no percentage in confessing his ignorance at this point, and he understood that the answer he was looking for involved the man's wife. "I'm sure your wife would not want you to sacrifice your children for her. And all I can do is give you my word that I'll do my level best to keep you and your girls alive. But unless you open the door, I'll have to blow it. And if that happens . . ." Tillman looked into the camera, allowing the unarticulated threat to linger for a moment. "One way or another, you and the girls are in this thing, and you're not holding any cards." He spread his hands. "Right now your only play is to open the door."

Tillman waited for a moment. Nothing happened.

"Oh, and before you come out with that gun in your hand and start shooting," Tillman said, "just understand that I shoot better than you do. And so do the people downstairs. Shooting your way out is not going to work either."

After a moment, there was a soft click. Then the door opened. A soft-looking man with thinning hair looked tentatively out into the room, squinting slightly.

Tillman nodded. "Smart move," he said. "Now bring the girls and sit on the bed."

The man emerged, his trembling hands draped protectively around the shoulders of his two little girls.

The older of the two girls was crying, and it was the younger one who said, "You're a bad man." She glared at him with coffee-brown eyes.

"I am," Tillman said, winking at her. "But not as bad as you think." He clapped his hands. "Okay, everybody on the bed. We're gonna play a game."

As the frightened family complied, Tillman felt his legs go weak, and his skin moisten with cold perspiration. Would he have breached the door? When he searched his heart, he wasn't sure. He might have. And if he had, God only knew what all that C4 would have done to those little girls.

Officer Millwood returned to his patrol car and drove down the street. But something about his encounter bothered him. The woman had not seemed right—the strange color of her eyes, the paleness of her face, her eagerness to get him out of there. He pulled over to the curb and called up dispatch on his radio. He had written down the Honda's plates and wanted to run a vehicle check.

He was waiting for dispatch to respond when he felt the distinctive metal end of a gun barrel against his neck.

"Tell her you were just checking in and put the radio down," said Gideon from the backseat. "Otherwise, I *will* shoot you."

Millwood did as he was told.

"Good. Now slide over on the seat, and keep your hands where I can see them."

The officer followed Gideon's directions.

"You may as well get comfortable," Gideon said. "You and I may be here for a while."

38

Dale Wilmot drove the white van to the service entrance of the Richard B. Russell Senate Office Building on the southern side of the mall, showed his ID to the Capitol Police officer, then waited for a second officer, who made a careful check of the vehicle's underside with a mirror fixed to a long pole.

When the check was finished, Wilmot pulled into the grim fluorescence of the lot and parked in the numbered space the officer had assigned him. Wilmot considered the irony of being assigned a spot in an otherwise empty parking lot, until he saw the three-man security detail waiting for him there. The team included a pair of Secret Service agents and a third man in tactical gear with a German shepherd on a leash.

There were no weapons in the van. Wilmot knew that to move forward, his and Collier's credentials needed to be clean. And they were. Their IDs came directly from the human resources department of the Arlington office of National Heat & Air, the company Wilmot controlled. It had been explained eight months earlier to the secretary that Mr. Wilmot might be doing a surprise inspection of some of his facilities, and so he and his executive assistant needed corporate IDs and the appropriate government clearances. Any calls to the company to check the validity of the information presented to the Secret Service would be verified.

Wilmot and Collier both carried Virginia driver's licenses, which led back to property owned in their names, all taxes and fees paid legitimately, credit card bills received and paid on time for a great many months. Every tool and manual and material in the truck was 100 percent legitimate, purchased by the company, serial numbers verifiable and matching and traceable.

Wilmot and Collier had both attended HVAC school in Coeur d'Alene almost a year ago so that if anybody asked them any questions about heating and air-conditioning systems, they would be able to talk just like pros. They had also studied at length the system they were about to sabotage and knew its workings inside and out.

"Sir, please step out of the vehicle," one of the Secret Service agents said. Both agents were intensely clean-cut and looked like they might have been scholarship athletes in college, and both wore blue rubber gloves. While the canine guy kept an eye on Collier, Wilmot was thoroughly frisked. Collier came next. There were no we're-just-doing-our-job pleasantries, no banter or discussions of the weather. The Secret Service didn't believe in that shit.

Wilmot appreciated the kind of commitment they displayed. Their job was to protect the president and Congress, not to make you feel good. Wilmot felt like he was floating above himself, looking down. He made no attempt to control his emotions.

Notwithstanding the fact that he appreciated the professionalism of the agents, they pissed him off. He didn't like being searched, didn't like being told what to do. And he saw no reason to pretend he did. You didn't want to arouse suspicions, but you didn't want to come off like you were pretending either.

Once the frisking was done, the K9 guy asked Collier to open the rear of the truck. Wilmot felt a pleasurable pressure in his temples. Now they'd see whether Collier was as smart as he said he was. He claimed that the cleaning process he'd used on the "refrigerant" tanks would make it entirely impossible for the dogs to smell the cyanide.

"Bring out whatever tool you'll need," the dog handler said.

Collier rolled the steel tool caddy to the rear of the van, and then together he and Wilmot lowered it to the pavement. Wilmot noticed that Collier's fingers were shaking a little. There was nothing that could be done about that. Collier was who he was.

"You're planning on taking that whole thing?" the dog handler said.

"Yep," Wilmot said.

The dog handler looked at the senior agent, who shook his head. "Then we've got a problem. Pressurized tanks aren't permitted."

Collier swallowed, face stiffening. Wilmot knew he needed to talk before Collier got all twitchy and said something stupid. What the Secret Service agents would be looking for right now was fear.

So Wilmot knew that he had to display a complete lack of fear.

"We've been asked to fix the heat," Wilmot said in a conversational tone, his eyes pinned on the Secret Service agent's face. "See that? In them two tanks there? That's R410A refrigerant. The HVAC unit at the Capitol is a combo heat exchanger and gas unit. What happens when the two-point-three-point-one controller software update has not been properly downloaded by the bureaucrats in the logistics office is the refrigerant overflow lines do an emergency bleed, the whole system loses priming, and you can't restart the system until they're reprimed." He gave the agent a broad smile. "How that's done, is you put fresh R410A in the fucking bleed lines. Now unless you plan to be the guy handing the earmuffs and the mittens to the president of the United States this evening, then I suggest you get on the phone to somebody capable of making a reasoned decision and get this sorted out, how we're gonna bring this stuff over to the Capitol. 'Cause I could give a shit. My grandson's got a wrestling match at his high school tonight, and I'd much rather be watching a bunch of sweaty teenage boys roll around on the floor than babysitting an HVAC unit. Which gives you a sense just how high my enthusiasm is riding for this job at this point in time. Sir."

The agent's face flushed and his jaw clenched. But Wilmot knew this kind of guy. You had to back his ass into a corner where he couldn't maneuver. Then he'd be sweet as milk. The agent exchanged glances with the dog handler and then spoke quietly into the microphone in his sleeve.

When he was done whispering into his sleeve, he turned to the

K9 handler and said, "Get the dog all over that cart. Then I will personally escort this gentleman to the X-ray machine at Bravo Checkpoint."

Wilmot was tempted to prod the guy with an I-told-you-so remark. But he knew that now was not the time. It was a delicate thing riding herd on a guy like this. You overplayed your hand, he'd go out of his way to wreck your day. But if you didn't stand up to him, they'd spend all day making phone calls to get clearance for the tanks.

Wilmot simply folded his hands over his chest and looked impassively into the distance while the dog sniffed at virtually every item on the cart.

Finally it was over.

"Gentlemen, come with me," the agent said.

"Get the cart, John," Wilmot said. Collier needed something to keep him busy right now or he was liable to pass out or throw up or do something stupid. "Come on, John, chop-chop."

Collier scrambled to get the cart in motion, pushing it toward a doorway on the far side of the parking lot indicated by the Secret Service agent.

"I will now be taking you to the credentialing checkpoint," the agent said. "You will be entering a highly secure perimeter. You will be issued access badges that you will need to carry with you at all times. Each and every room in the Capitol is designated as a separate zone. Your authorization will be time limited and zone specific. If you overstay your pass or attempt to enter a zone for which you are not credentialed, you will be subject to immediate arrest and imprisonment. Clear?"

"Absolutely," Wilmot said.

They passed through a doorway into a dim concrete passageway. One of the front wheels on the cart was improperly adjusted and the cart vibrated loudly. Wilmot knew that he had done about as much as he could do to keep the agent's attention off of Collier. Collier looked awful—sweating and pale. Instead of ignoring it, he knew he needed to take the bull by the horns.

"You look like shit, kid," he said. "You eat something bad this morning or something?"

Collier made a grimacing attempt at a smile. "I don't know . . . I—maybe I did. I feel a little under the weather."

"Son, we got a job to do, so get out your Vagisil and get your shit squared away."

"Yes, sir."

Wilmot had come to a realization early in life that you were always playing a role. If you wanted to be successful, though, you had to play a role that was close to your own character. Right now he was playing a role he knew well. He was pretending to be his own father. His old man had been a paratrooper in World War II, and when he wasn't drunk, he was one seriously tough son of a bitch. It was a role, Wilmot knew, that sucked the air out of a room, that kept attention focused on one person. And right now they couldn't afford for even half a shred of attention to be paid to Collier. The kid was a genius, but he'd blow away in a stiff puff of wind.

Wilmot clapped his hand on the Secret Service agent's shoulder. "Didn't mean to be hard on you, son. But I'm here to do a job. Just like you. The reason they send me to do stuff like this is because they know the job gets done when Wilmot shows up."

The Secret Service agent walked them through a second door into a large room. "The credentialing station is right there."

Wilmot surveyed the room. Everything was set up the way their intel had indicated that it would be. An X-ray machine and a metal detector, both of them similar to the ones used in airports, stood between two steel traffic barriers. On each side of the barrier stood an agent in tactical garb, each one holding an FN P90 on a tactical sling. Between them stood a Capitol police officer operating the X-ray machine.

The agent turned to the officer at the X-ray machine and said, "I know it's against regs to bring in pressurized canisters once final sweeps have been made, but I spoke to my supervisor, so you'll need to take this up with her."

The officer, a tall black woman, shook her head. "I am not admitting compressed gases through my checkpoint. You can forget that."

The Secret Service agent said, "Hey, I'm just bringing them here. You do what you gotta do. I'm going back to my post."

The Secret Service agent turned on his heel and walked out of the room.

Wilmot crossed his hands over his chest, looked at the police officer behind the X-ray machine, and said, "You want to be the one to explain to the president why it's twenty-four degrees in the House chamber? Hm? You got those kind of balls, young lady?"

"You did *not* just disrespect me," the officer said. "I *know* you did not."

Wilmot met her angry gaze and said, "See, I don't give a hoot in hell whether you feel all insulted or not. Either we're gonna fix the heat or we ain't. Your call."

The two tactical officers stood motionless, waiting to see how things developed before they did anything.

The officer continued to glare at him. Finally she picked up a walkie-talkie and said, "Sergeant Grandison requesting supervisory authority at Checkpoint Bravo."

"Do not move, sir," one of the tactical agents said.

"I'm not going anywhere," Wilmot said truculently. But he didn't move a single muscle.

The room seemed to vibrate with tension. Time crawled by. It might have been as few as two minutes, but it seemed to take forever. And yet, in a funny kind of way, Wilmot reflected, he was enjoying himself. He had never done anything more intense, more full of juice than this, not in his entire life. And he had lived a pretty full life. Some part of him understood why Evan had stayed in the military. Walking that line between life and death was an adrenaline rush without equal. The closer you got to dying, the more alive you felt.

Finally the far door opened and a short, wiry, coffee-skinned woman walked briskly up to the X-ray machine. She could have been African-American, Latina, or Middle Eastern. But Wilmot knew she was half-black, half-Jewish. In fact, he knew a great deal about Special Agent Shanelle Klotz. He had studied her file for nearly a year, and though he liked her on paper, he liked her even better in person. He smiled broadly. Here was somebody you could speak to like a grown-up, a rational being who could be counted on to make the right choices.

The compact woman surveyed the scene, her eyes immediately coming to rest on the two canisters in the cart.

"Gentlemen," she said. "I'd like you to explain in clear, simple language what those canisters contain and why you need them."

"Nothing would make me happier," said Dale Wilmot.

39

PRIEST RIVER, IDAHO

Nancy Clement left a trail in the snow as she dragged her bad leg toward the lights of the Wilmot house. She wasn't sure how seriously injured she was. All she could tell was that her leg threatened to buckle each time she put weight on it.

The snow was getting deep now and it would have been hard slogging even with two good legs. But now it was slow-motion agony.

Finally she reached the house. The door was locked. She pounded on the door with the flat of her hand. Nancy had cuffed Margie to the bed so she wouldn't cause any mischief while Nancy investigated, but now she worried that Evan had fallen asleep and she would freeze to death outside on the porch. Even if he were awake, she didn't know if he had the strength to help her.

She pounded again, and this time she heard the lock unlatching and then Evan unbolted the door.

Nancy staggered in and sank onto the nearest couch.

"What happened?" he asked.

"The car turned over," Nancy said. "I think I broke my leg." She pulled up her leg and examined the bruise that had already begun to swell. When she pressed on it, the pain was like something electric.

"Did you find the body?" Evan asked. He looked terrible. His lips were cracked and his skin had a splotchy look, as if it had been sandpapered, but his eyes were bright and troubled.

Nancy nodded. "You were right. They're making cyanide in the woods."

"Cyanide? Why?"

"I don't know yet," she said. Of course, she had begun to nurse some theories, but she saw no reason to trouble Evan with more worries than he already had.

"Whatever they're doing, you'll stop them, right?"

"I have to get in touch with my office."

"The phone lines are down. Cable's gone, too."

"Is there any other way to get an outside line?"

"Couer d'Alene is nearly thirty miles away. And the roads are impassable without a snowplow."

Nancy stood. "I'll have to risk it."

"You can barely walk."

It was three o'clock Eastern. The speech was at nine. That gave her just over three hours to reach a phone.

"I don't have a choice."

Evan thought for a minute. "My dad has a bulldozer," he said.

"Could I drive it with a broken leg?"

"It won't be easy. But, yeah, I think you could."

In the kitchen she splinted her leg as best she could with a pine plank, then Evan gave her instructions on how to start the big bulldozer.

"Good luck," he wished her.

"Thank you." She gave him the keys to her handcuffs. "Don't unlock Margie until nine o'clock. After that, it won't matter."

He nodded. "Part of me hopes we're wrong about all this, but the other part of me knows we're not. The crazy thing is I know he's doing this for me, *because of me*. But it's not patriotism, just insanity. You tell him that if you find him. When you find him."

She took his hand for a moment and was surprised by how firm it felt, no hesitation in his grip. But his face looked pained, and she turned away as the tears rolled down his cheeks.

Once Nancy got the dozer started, operating it was no big trick.

Instead of having an accelerator, the big Cat had a decelerator pedal, so that you only had to mess with it when you were stopping. Otherwise she was able to do most of the work with her hands. The steering was controlled by two handles in front of her, which controlled the relative speed of the treads. Another handle operated the blade. After a brief circuit of the area around the sheds, she felt competent enough to control the slow-moving machine.

Soon she was on her way with a full tank of diesel. The storm had abated, but the wind blew the flakes in swirling drifts, and the temperature had dropped. The cab was warm inside, and she had thrown on extra clothes. It would have been cozy if not for the searing pain in her leg and the desperate circumstances she was in.

The D8 had a blade that could be tilted to better funnel snow away from the Cat. She didn't have to completely clear the road; she just had to clear the top layer so that snow didn't start piling up in front of the undercarriage and force the Cat to grind to a halt. There was no great trick to it. Once she'd found the right height, she just let it sit there, and the dry, powdery snow peeled off and piled up steadily in a long mound to her right.

The first sign that the bulldozer wasn't a completely perfect solution to her problem was when she noticed that it didn't have a speedometer. When a motor vehicle barely goes faster than a brisk walk, she realized, it doesn't need one.

At five miles an hour, it would take nearly six hours to reach Coeur d'Alene. She only had about three hours to make contact with somebody in DC. She had to assume that somewhere between where she was and Coeur d'Alene there was a working cell tower or someone with a working phone or Internet connection. But for the time being, all she could see in front of her was snow.

The one thing that the absurdly slow progress afforded her was time to think about who she would call and what she would tell him. If she called Ray Dahlgren, there was a solid chance he would dismiss her out of hand. He was already heavily invested in the notion that she was a loose cannon, hell-bent on ruining his career and breaking every rule in the FBI personnel handbook. He was not the kind of guy to back up on something like that without a lot of evidence to the contrary.

At this point he would have nothing but her word. She had

found a hand sticking up out of a patch of frozen ground, and she had found a strange lab that made her feel ill and that smelled like burned almonds. And that was about it.

So Dahlgren was out.

That left the Secret Service and Gideon Davis.

If she called the Secret Service, they'd call Ray Dahlgren. Ray Dahlgren would tell them she was a suspended agent with a hare-brained theory and a grudge. He might even try to implicate her so the Secret Service would track her down. Crazy as that sounded, she couldn't rule it out as a possibility.

Which left Gideon.

But could Gideon and Tillman actually stop the threat by them-selves? It was her only hope.

In the meantime, there was the seemingly endless expanse of snow and the monotonous growl of the big Caterpillar diesel.

40

WASHINGTON, DC

The Richard B. Russell Senate Office Building is connected to the Capitol by a subway. This not only allows senators to pass from their offices to the Capitol without mixing with the hoi polloi, but it also allows deliveries to be made without backing unsightly, noisy, smoke-belching trucks up to the Capitol. It was through this tunnel that Wilmot and Collier needed to pass in order to reach their target. But first they had to get past Special Agent Shanelle Klotz, senior facilities specialist, responsible for security for the HVAC and related systems.

Wilmot patiently explained the likely source of the problem in the Capitol heating system in mind-numbing detail. Finally the Secret Service agent said, "Okay, that's far more detail than I'm capable of understanding. Officer Grandison is going to run those canisters through the X-ray machines, and we're going to take a very close look at them."

"Sure," Wilmot said.

Collier had assured him that the canisters would pass muster. But he couldn't help being apprehensive.

"Want me to load them on the—"

Special Agent Klotz shook her head. "Stay where you are, gentlemen." She motioned to one of the agents wearing tactical gear to load one of the canisters on the X-ray machine's conveyor belt.

Wilmot stood motionless, hands behind his back.

There was a soft whine as the conveyor fed into the central chamber of the X-ray machine. The whine stopped.

Special Agent Klotz approached and stood at Officer Grandison's shoulder. The two women stared intently at the screen.

After a moment, the police officer shook her head. "I don't like it," she said.

"What do you see?" the Secret Service agent said.

"The walls don't look right." Officer Grandison tapped the screen. "See? Too thick."

"If I may—" Collier said.

Wilmot cut him off. "Shut the hell up, John," he said smiling broadly. "Let the professionals do their jobs."

"Zoom it," the Secret Service agent said. She stared for a long time. "I don't like it either," she said finally. She turned to Collier and said, "You were going to say something."

Collier looked at Wilmot. Wilmot gave him the slightest nod. He wasn't opposed to Collier talking. He just wanted to make sure that Agent Klotz believed she was driving the train here.

"If I may . . ." Collier cleared his throat. "If you look at a propane tank or a compressed air tank, helium, argon, welding gases, things of that nature, they're always single-walled tanks. Refrigerant tanks used to be like that. But in recent years, now that we've transitioned away from Freon to R410A, the thermal characteristics of the compressed . . . well, I won't bore you. The point is that we've moved to double-walled tanks. Keeps the refrigerant temperature more stable. So, yeah, it probably does look funny if you're used to single-walled tanks."

Klotz held up one finger at Collier, then picked up a phone off the desk next to Officer Grandison and said, "Can you get me Ron?" She smiled blandly at Wilmot for a few moments. Then, "Ron, hey, Shanelle here. R410A refrigerant. Is it stored in double-walled tanks? Sometimes? Okay, thanks."

Collier gave her a weak smile. "I wouldn't lie to you."

Wilmot did his best to project a telepathic mental message to Collier to shut his mouth. Fortunately Agent Klotz spoke before Collier had a chance to say something he shouldn't. "Here's what

I'm going to do," she said. "I'm going to authorize entry with the refrigerant. But I'll need to accompany you personally to your destination. Once you reach your work space, I'll detail two agents to supervise you. At such time as you need to access the refrigerant, you will need clearance from me. Got it?"

"Fine," Wilmot said.

"But before we do all that, we're going to run one last test," she said.

Wilmot felt his pulse quicken.

"Refrigerant's nontoxic, isn't it? I mean, in small doses?"

"Wilmot swallowed. "Ah, correct, ma'am."

"Then show us. Let the gas out and take a small breath."

Wilmot hesitated, looked at Collier, who then reached toward one of the canisters.

"Not that one," Klotz said. "The other one."

Wilmot considered what to do. There really wasn't anything he could do. It would just play out however it played out. He inhaled, knowing he might not have a chance to breathe again for a while.

Then Collier turned the petcock, and the tank hissed angrily.

41

Verhoven was pacing back and forth in the living room. Tillman had given Lorene another pint of saline. He checked her belly, but it still wasn't rigid. And her breathing was okay.

So whatever was going on, she wasn't bleeding to death. But she wasn't doing well, either.

Tillman had brought the man and his two children downstairs. The two girls were watching a cartoon on the TV while their father sat on the couch rubbing his hands together and rocking back and forth. The older girl had stopped crying, but her face was streaked with tears, and she looked as if she might vomit at any second.

The man stopped rubbing his hands for a moment. "I'm an ER doc. This woman needs to be in a hospital."

"Shut up," Verhoven said.

"Maybe we should let him take a look," Tillman said.

Verhoven sighed, then nodded his okay. The doctor fetched his bag of medical equipment before Tillman's watchful eyes, then began a careful examination of Lorene's wound.

"How long since she got shot?" he said.

"A few hours," Verhoven said.

The doctor shook his head. "She's bleeding internally. It's not a gusher or she'd be dead. But she needs surgery."

"Her belly's not rigid," Tillman said, then explained, "I was a combat medic."

The doctor pointed to Lorene's lower abdomen. "Have you been peeing a lot?"

Lorene nodded feebly. Her eyes were dull now.

"Blood in the urine?"

"Yes."

The doctor turned to Tillman and said, "A bullet fragment probably punctured the bladder or one of the kidneys. Might have cut the vaginal artery or the inferior suprarenal. The blood's evacuating through the bladder. It's not good. If the bleeding isn't stopped— and I mean pretty soon—she's going to die."

Verhoven let out a groan, as though he'd been punched in the stomach. He pointed at the man with his trembling finger. "You save her! You save her, you little son of a bitch."

The doctor looked at Tillman as though appealing for help. It was obvious he could see that Tillman was the only seemingly calm, rational voice in the room right now.

"Let's just all calm down," Tillman said.

Verhoven sat down next to his wife and began stroking her hair. "It's okay, Lorene. You're going to be okay. The doctor's going to figure something out."

Verhoven was looking more unstable by the moment. And talking about Lorene's situation was not helping things. They were waiting for a phone call, presumably with further instructions. Verhoven wouldn't say exactly, and Tillman didn't want to press him. Instead he directed his questions to the doctor.

"Why does a normal suburban guy need so much security?" he asked.

"That's not my bailiwick," the man said. Then he looked as though he was sorry he'd spoken.

"Oh?" Tillman said. "Your wife's a security nut?"

The doctor squinted at him. "Are you making fun of me?"

Tillman studied the man for a moment. "Why do you say that?"

"Don't pretend you don't know what my wife does for a living," the doctor said. "The day of the State of the Union address?"

Tillman walked to the mantel and began picking up family photos. There were several pictures of the man with his two girls and a woman who was obviously his wife. She was a petite woman, very attractive, racially mixed. Then he saw an award certificate with a picture of the wife by herself, posed in front of a blue backdrop dominated by a large official seal.

Tillman studied the certificate. The wife wore a gun and had some kind of badge on her belt. Now the pieces were beginning to fall into place. "So this is your wife, huh?"

The doctor said nothing, but his silence answered Tillman's question.

At the bottom of the certificate was a label, which Tillman read out loud, hoping that Gideon was close enough to pick up audio from the earpiece he had stuffed in his pocket.

"United States Secret Service," Tillman said. "Your wife is Special Agent Shanelle Klotz."

The cop wasn't very talkative, but Gideon kept trying. At first Gideon had told him the truth: They were pursuing homegrown terrorists who had taken a family hostage. But when the cop pretended to believe him, and suggested they both drive down to the precinct to file a report, Gideon gave up. He could see things from the cop's perspective: a dirty, scruffy, ragged guy with a gun insists he's pursuing terrorists in the suburbs with his ex-con brother and needs the cop's help. Hell, he wouldn't help himself in that situation. So he stopped talking about Verhoven and started making small talk—if only to pass the time. But the cop was being uncooperative and grumpy.

Gideon could only hear snatches of what was going on in the house, but he gleaned that the woman who lived there was a Secret Service agent working the State of the Union detail, and her family was being held as some kind of leverage. But he still didn't know for what purpose.

Could it be something as simple as calling the agent up and saying: *Kill the president or we kill your family?* He didn't think so. Even if they could count on forcing a Secret Service agent to turn her gun on the president, the event would be over in seconds. Mixon had been very specific: This wasn't simply an assassination attempt but a "high-value, mass casualty" terrorist attack. And the State of the Union address was definitely the perfect setting for it. But without knowing the agent's role and assignment, without any word from Nancy, Gideon didn't think he had enough to take it to Dahlgren. Not if he wanted to convince the man and avoid being arrested.

Much as it pained him, he was going to have to sit tight and wait.

42

WASHINGTON, DC

Wilmot waited as the tank hissed, literally holding his breath. A pink stream shot out of the tank, vaporizing immediately in the air. Collier turned the tank back off again, leaned down, and breathed in the air near the tank. Wilmot expected him to claw at his throat and fall over, foaming at the mouth and screaming.

But he didn't.

Instead, Collier straightened and said, "See? Harmless." He grinned. "Doesn't smell so great . . . but totally harmless unless you suck in huge quantities of it."

Wilmot's pulse slowed. He tried not to look astonished. What the hell had just happened?

The tactical guy closest to Collier nodded to Special Agent Klotz. "Yeah, that's refrigerant. I can smell it. My brother-in-law tried to fix our heating until last year, busted the line, the stuff leaked into the basement." He wrinkled his nose. "I had to smell that crap every time me and my buddies played cards down there for two months."

Special Agent Klotz said, "Okay, gentlemen, I guess we're good. Let's go."

Wilmot followed Collier, Klotz a couple of strides behind him, her hand on her gun. Wilmot couldn't help being impressed. These Secret Service people didn't mess around.

The long concrete hallway led to the small subway station. A car stood motionless, doors open. Collier started pushing the cart toward the car. Two men immediately barred his way.

"We're going on foot," Agent Klotz said. "The subway was rebuilt in the 1960s on a bigger track. The old tunnel is over here. It's used as a service entrance for the Capitol building now."

Collier went through the entrance into the second tunnel, the front wheel on the cart wobbling and squeaking loudly. Wilmot followed.

The walk to the Capitol seemed endless. Along the way, Wilmot wondered why the gas had not killed Collier and deduced that Collier had consciously left out some critical details. Was there only gas in one of the tanks? Had Collier just held his breath and relied on the fact that cyanide gas was slightly heavier than air? If it was the latter, eventually the gas would disperse, and the people in the room would start to smell it and probably start keeling over. In which case he and Collier needed to move very fast. But Collier seemed unhurried.

Finally they reached the end of the tunnel, ending up in a small tiled room flanked by an elevator and a set of old iron stairs.

Everything was as he expected it, as laid out on the updated schematics they had reviewed when National Heat & Air got the HVAC contract for the building.

The Secret Service agent said, "Just keep moving, if you don't mind, gentlemen. We'll take the elevator." She spoke softly into her sleeve. "Send the South Capitol elevator to Location L."

Collier swallowed and started pushing the cart toward the elevator.

A few moments later, the doors opened with an ear-piercing squeak.

43

WASHINGTON, DC

Wilmot and Collier spent all morning in the HVAC Control Room, messing with the controls for the heating system. As planned, it had failed repeatedly. By noon, Wilmot told Shanelle Klotz, "Look, if you want this thing working during the State of the Union, you need us to stay here and babysit."

"You're not cleared to stay here."

"Up to you. Ten to one it breaks down again before evening."

Several phone calls later, Agent Klotz said, "Okay. You'll stay here. The door will be guarded. You do not open the door. Knock and the guard will enter. If you need to move to another location, I will have to personally authorize it and accompany you. Clear?"

"Not a problem," Wilmot said. He sat down and waited until the door closed. They were in a small dark closet of a room. The room had no direct access to the heating unit itself, only to the controller which ran it. There was nothing they could do from this location.

But for the first time, they were alone.

"Okay, so what the hell happened back there?" Wilmot said. "How come we didn't all die of cyanide poisoning?"

Collier gave Wilmot one of his sour, superior little smiles. "I suspected somebody might need to bleed a tank, so I built them both with double walls. In effect, each one is two entirely separate tanks. The outer chamber contains refrigerant. Turn the cock, you get R410A." He pointed at the tank. "See this little set screw? I tighten it three full turns and it breaks a seal between the inner and outer chambers. Then when you twist the petcock, instead of getting refrigerant . . ."

". . . you get cyanide."

"Exactly."

"Might have been nice to know that ahead of time," Wilmot said.

Collier stared at him intently. "I just want you to understand that you still need me. Right up to the end, you'll need me."

Wilmot put his hand on the boy's shoulder. "I've never had the slightest doubt about that, son," he said. "Not for one moment."

Collier's face glowed.

Wilmot sat back and put his feet up on the cart. "So you think the system's going to make it all day without breaking down again?"

Collier smiled broadly. "I strongly suspect it will not."

44

I-66, OUTSIDE WASHINGTON, DC

Kate Murphy finished putting on her makeup in the car, wishing she could talk to Gideon as the limo crawled through the DC traffic. In just a few hours she would be at the State of the Union address, yet all she really wanted to do was hear his voice.

She had been visited earlier in the day by a particularly unpleasant man—Ray Dahlgren, the FBI's deputy director—who claimed to want to know Gideon's whereabouts so he could "help" him. But Kate was no fool; she could spot a phony a mile away, and Dahlgren was as fake as a deposed Nigerian dictator with a bundle of cash. He soon dropped the pretense, and they had a nasty conversation where Dahlgren threw around words like "conspirator" and "obstruction of justice." Kate laughed off his bullying; but she was worried about Gideon. His voice mail said he was okay, but his investigation had clearly agitated Dahlgren. Now she feared his investigation pitted him against the deputy director and placed him in more danger.

She noted the increased security presence around the Capitol, which seemed intense even by DC standards. She knew the Secret Service left nothing to chance, but she wondered if they had really planned for everything. Threats came from everywhere, at any time, and even the most vigilant security officials could not be omniscient. Now, as the limo idled at a red light, she felt a flicker of concern over whether the State of the Union address could be a target, and whether she would be safe inside.

But she told herself she couldn't obsess about it. In the post 9/11 world, no one was entirely safe and no place entirely secure. That uncertainty was the new normal. She had to trust Gideon, and trust that if an attack were planned, he'd find a way of stopping it. The best thing for her to do was to focus on what was right in front of her.

An extremely junior member of the White House protocol staff, a young woman who looked as if she had graduated from Sweet Briar about ten minutes ago, had given Kate instructions on what to expect during the address. According to official protocol, guests were divided into three categories. There were invitees who were attending because they had given money to the president's campaign or because they fit into some visible and demographically attractive category—a Hispanic Medal of Honor winner, or a white female cop. Next up the ladder were people like Kate, who were staffers or members (present, former, and future) of the administration. Above that were members of Congress. And above them were the House and Senate leadership, a handful of important cabinet members, the Joint Chiefs, the Supreme Court, and finally the speaker of the house, the vice president, and then the president himself.

The lower on the list of importance you were, the earlier you had to get to the Capitol. Mere billionaires and war heroes and Olympic gold medalists had to reach the assembly point in the Russell Building four hours in advance. Kate, being one step up the ladder, was required to come three hours in advance.

But the limo barely moved in the DC traffic. She could see the dome of the Capitol in the distance. Was there an invisible bull's-eye painted on it? She felt her leg jiggling nervously.

She wished Gideon would call.

45

Doctor, I've found some medical supplies if you could take a look?" Tillman said, nodding toward the adjoining kitchen.

The man narrowed his eyes. "We don't keep medical supplies in the kitchen."

Verhoven looked up suspiciously. "What did you find?"

"There's bandages I think you overlooked." He pointed his gun toward the kitchen. "Let's go, Doctor."

"I'm not leaving the girls."

"Let's not get into a pissing contest," Tillman said softly. Then he gave Klotz a hard stare.

Klotz looked for a moment as though he was making a decision. Then he nodded curtly and walked quickly toward the kitchen.

Tillman hurried after him, but still he was unable to get there before Klotz disappeared behind the wall. When he entered the room, Klotz was leaning against the counter, his face blank, hands behind his back.

Tillman walked in and stood by the door for a moment. It was a nice modern kitchen—granite countertops, an island in the center of the room. Everything was spotless and neatly organized, pans hanging from the ceiling, knives stored in a wooden block. A pan for every hook on the ceiling, a knife for every slot in the block. Except one.

Tillman stood on the far side of the island, keeping his distance from Shanelle Klotz's husband. He leaned forward and spoke as softly as he could. "The man in the other room is very upset right now. He believes deeply in the cause that has brought him into your home. He wants very much to succeed. But he also loves his wife. He's in a very agitated state right now. It's important that we all stay calm."

Klotz glared at him.

Tillman walked around the island so that he was close enough to Klotz that he could speak without any chance of being heard by Verhoven.

"As you've probably figured out," he whispered, "an attack is planned on the State of the Union address today. I am here to make sure that doesn't happen."

Klotz closed his eyes, relief visibly flooding across his face. "Oh, thank God," he whispered. "You're a federal agent?"

"I wish it were that simple," Tillman said. "Suffice it to say, I'm working for the good guys."

"You're a cop?"

"Let's just stick to the important things here. First, we need you to play nice. Whatever I tell you to do, just do it. No smart remarks, no knives hidden up your sleeves." He reached out and clamped his fingers around Klotz's left arm. With the other hand he pulled a seven-inch boning knife out of the doctor's sleeve, slid it back into the empty spot on the knife block.

"Shit," Klotz said. "Sorry."

"Don't apologize for defending your family," Tillman said. "Second thing, we need to reach the people who are doing the operation. We don't know who they are, or where they are. But they're going to be in touch with us here. So whatever happens, just go along with it."

Klotz narrowed his eyes. "Do you have any proof of what you're saying? You could just be feeding me a line so I won't fight you."

Tillman looked at him directly and said, "Sir, to be blunt, you don't really have a choice. I'm your only chance of getting out of here. Now, I need to know what detail your wife is working."

"I don't know."

"She didn't tell you?"

"Look around. You see what kind of security my wife is into. That information is classified, and she doesn't tell anyone, especially her family."

Tillman looked closely at the doctor and realized he believed the man. "Okay. Then we're just going to have to sit tight. But we can't have Lorene dying on us here while we're waiting. You need to think of something to help her survive."

"I can't do surgery here! Even if I had good imaging so I knew where the fragments were, I'm not a renal specialist. I mean you're talking about very tricky vascular surgery."

"Then you need to think of something. The healthier that woman is, the safer your little girls are. I've got two used IV bags in the car, but I've already run two units of saline and two units of plasma through her. I'm out of fluids."

Klotz looked thoughtful. "I think I've got a few bottles of sterile saline up in the safe room. It's just for irrigating wounds, but . . ." Klotz rubbed his face. "I mean in theory we could mix in some sugar and put it in the IV bag, push the fluids, kick her energy up and get her stabilized temporarily. But we're likely to contaminate the saline. If we do that we could give her a systemic infection that might kill her."

"We need her alive today. Tomorrow will take care of itself."

"I take my oath as a physician seriously. First do no harm. I can't risk—"

Tillman whispered through clenched teeth. "Those pieces of shit in there are trying to kill a whole lot of people. Including your two daughters. To hell with her. If I have my way, that woman will be dead by the end of the day anyway."

Klotz's face went stiff. "All right," he said finally, "go get the IV bags out of your car. I'll see what I can jury-rig."

Tillman poked him with his gun. "Back in the living room."

Verhoven looked up expectantly when both men returned to the room.

"Nope, I was wrong about the bandages, Colonel," Tillman said. "But I think the good doctor and I have worked out a solution . . ."

• • •

Gideon asked the cop if he was hungry.

"I'm fine," Officer Millwood said.

"I've got a couple granola bars in my jacket."

"I'm fine," the cop repeated.

"Look, I know you're not happy waiting here with me, but I think things would go a lot better if you just trusted me and had something to eat."

"Why should I trust you?"

"You heard what's going on in that house. Do you think I made it up?"

"I haven't heard anything except a couple people holding an innocent family hostage."

Gideon sighed. He had been sitting with the cop for nearly six hours, and in that time very little had happened. Around him the neighborhood had come alive, as kids and parents came out for the school bus, and then, with the kids gone, moms and dogs came out for their walks, then the cleaning ladies arrived. Luckily, Officer Millwood still had another two hours left in his shift, and though the desk sergeant had called once, there were no emergencies that required his response.

He wished Tillman could radio him, but he understood there was no opportunity to place the transmitter in his ear. Instead he made do with bits of muffled conversation picked up from the mike in Tillman's pocket. It wasn't perfect, but at least it kept him updated. He learned they had hooked up Lorene to an IV. Gideon knew it would buy them another hour or two. But did they have that much time? The State of the Union address was just a few hours away, and every minute they waited was another minute closer to the attack. On the other hand, even if Tillman left the house now, they had little to go on except the name of the Secret Service agent. That might be enough in normal circumstances, but it wouldn't get them past security to do anything about it, and it certainly wouldn't convince Dahlgren. Time was ticking, but right now the balance favored waiting. Soon, however, Gideon knew, the balance would shift.

"What are we waiting for?" he asked no one in particular.

"That's what I'm wondering," said Officer Millwood.

Gideon turned to him. It was the first agreeable comment the cop had made. Maybe it meant the ice was melting.

But before he could respond, he was pulled from his reflections by a faint sound through his earpiece. A phone was ringing at the Klotz house. He heard Verhoven say, "Answer the phone. It's your wife."

46

WASHINGTON, DC

Ten minutes earlier, when the temperature in the House chamber had reached sixty-one, Collier opened the door, looked out at the Secret Service guard, and said, "I think you better call Special Agent Klotz. We've got a temperature control problem here."

The agent nodded, then summoned her on the mic in his sleeve.

When Shanelle Klotz entered the room, Wilmot explained that the heating problem was worse than expected, and that the chamber would be roughly the temperature of a meat locker within the hour.

"What do you need to do to fix it?" she asked.

"I'll need to check the panel in the hall while John feeds data into the controller. I figured you'd want to be here while I go out in the hall."

Agent Klotz nodded, then leaned out into the hallway. "Mr. Wilmot is going to come out here. I'll be inside."

"Yes, ma'am," the agent said.

Wilmot came out with the voltmeter, looked up and down the hallway, and waited for the door to close. Other than himself and the Secret Service agent, the hallway was empty.

"It's down this way, bud," he said, pointing to his left. "Did you need to come with me?"

"Yes, I do, sir," the agent said.

Wilmot started walking. "Oh, shoot, wrong panel," he said, turning abruptly.

This put him within arm's reach of the agent. Wilmot pretended to stumble, reaching out as though to keep the agent from bumping into him.

The device in his hand appeared to be a voltmeter. But it was not. In fact, it was a stun gun. A normal stun gun emits around 50,000 volts of electricity at a mere .01 milliamps. This stun gun, however, contained a very different capacitor and transformer than the normal commercial variety and produced roughly three amps.

Wilmot jammed the two nearly invisible spikes on the end of the voltmeter into the agent's chest and pressed the on button, dumping the entire contents of the capacitor into the agent's flesh. The amperage of the charge—enough to briefly power a toaster—was sufficient to stop the agent's heart in midbeat.

The agent spasmed so hard that his head smashed against the wall, making a sound like a machete cracking open a coconut. The agent was dead by the time his body hit the floor. Wilmot pulled the agent's SIG out of its holster, dragged him fifteen feet by one leg, then rapped smartly on the door.

When Shanelle Klotz opened the door, Wilmot grabbed her by the throat and propelled her back into the room, the SIG pressed into her face.

According to her records—which Wilmot had studied with great care—she had received the intense self-defense training given to all Secret Service agents. But he was more than a foot taller and outweighed her by 130 pounds.

She didn't have time to scream or grab her weapon before Collier had disarmed her and wrapped duct tape around her mouth. She struggled wildly with Collier as Wilmot quickly dragged the dead agent back into the control room, but by then it was too late. Wilmot closed the door and pointed his pistol at her face again.

"If our plan was to kill you," he said, "you'd already be dead. So you might as well calm down and find out what we have in mind."

She continued to struggle as Wilmot slipped flex cuffs over her arms and wrists. Soon she seemed to see the futility of further struggle so she stopped fighting. Wilmot could see she wasn't beaten, though—she was just conserving her energy and appraising her situation, looking for an opportunity to turn the tables. Her eyes still burned with controlled anger. The more he saw of her, the more he liked her.

"Phone," he said. "Unless you want your little girls hurt."

Her eyes widened, and Wilmot could tell he had gotten to her. Wilmot had spent a substantial amount on private investigators for this operation. He had read her psychological profile and chosen her because she was a mother of young children.

Collier pulled her cell phone off Shanelle Klotz's belt and plugged it into a thin cable that was already attached to the USB port in the HVAC system controller.

"We recognize," Collier said, "that the Secret Service jams all cell phone frequencies here during the State of the Union address. But the hard line to the diagnostic computer at National Heat & Air works just fine. It's part of the secure comm links that connect the Capitol to the government's secure backbone. So we're able to dial out on that line using the SIM card identifier on your phone. My friend John here could bore you to tears with the technical details. But the bottom line is that whoever picks up the phone on the other end will see your name on the caller ID."

Collier dialed her security password into the phone and then said, "According to my information, you've got your home number on speed dial number two."

He held down the two key. When it began to ring, he switched to speaker and held the phone out toward Special Agent Klotz's face.

After three rings, a man's voice, sounding terribly frightened, said, "Sweetheart? Is that you?"

"Hello, Dr. Klotz," Wilmot said. "At the moment, I have your wife standing right next to me. She has duct tape over her mouth and her legs and arms are cuffed. But she's listening very carefully. Right now I need you to give her an honest and clear assessment of your situation."

Wilmot could hear the Secret Service agent's husband breathing on the other end—a rapid, near-hysterical panting. "Sweetheart?

Are you there? There are . . . there are two men and a woman in our house. They're heavily armed. Not just guns. They have plastic explosives and stuff. They seem to have defeated the alarm, so there are no police here or anything. These are . . . I don't know, I mean, these are really—these are really serious people."

Shanelle Klotz looked furious. Her eyes were wide with anger and fear.

Wilmot put his finger over his lips. "Talk to him, Agent Klotz," he said. "But just understand that if you make a big fuss, your husband and your daughters will be killed."

Collier ripped the tape off her face.

"Nathan," she said, "You know I can't—" She couldn't finish her sentence.

"*Please*, sweetheart! Do what they say!" Her husband's voice was high and tremulous. "They have the girls."

Shanelle Klotz stared straight ahead, looking at the blank wall. Her face was hard, but tears were running out of her eyes.

"All we want you to do, Agent Klotz, is open a door for us," Wilmot said.

Shanelle Klotz didn't speak for several seconds. Then, finally, she said, "I can't, Nathan. I swore an oath."

Wilmot was astonished. Knowing how he felt about his own son, he couldn't believe a mother would be so callous with the life of her child. It had never once crossed his mind that a woman might make the decision that she had made. It was the reason he had chosen her. And now, President Wade was scheduled to make his speech in one hour and forty minutes.

In the living room of the Klotz home, Tillman was a little surprised to see Lorene Verhoven stand up suddenly from the couch where she had been lying. Although she looked half dead, the manic shine remained in her wild eyes.

She walked slowly to the phone, took it from her husband's grasp, switched off the speakerphone, and held the phone to her ear. Then she took the hand of Klotz's younger daughter.

"Hi, honey," she said, smiling at the little girl. "What's your name?"

"Wendy," the girl said.

"Wendy. That's a nice name." Lorene spoke in a feverish hush. "Just like the girl in Peter Pan, the one that always took care of everybody. Do you take care of your dollies?"

The girl nodded. "Yes."

"And does your mommy take care of you like you take care of your dollies?"

"Yes."

Lorene took the girl's hand and said, "Come with me for a minute, honey. You and me are going to have a little girl talk with your mommy, okay? Away from all these scary men with guns. Is that okay with you?"

The girl looked at her father. Her father looked at Tillman. Tillman nodded. Klotz nodded at the girl, who smiled, reassured by that simple nod that everything was okay.

Tillman couldn't remember ever having been that trusting. Maybe he had been. But he sure didn't remember it.

"Will you help me walk, honey?" Lorene said. "I don't walk so good right now."

"Yes."

"Thank you, honey."

Lorene and the little girl walked slowly, painfully, to the stairs, the little girl's tiny arm wrapped around Lorene's waist, then ascended toward the upstairs. After a moment they were gone.

Please, Tillman prayed, *don't let anything happen to that little girl.*

It took a while before the woman on the other end of the phone line began speaking again. "Hello, Agent Klotz," the woman said. Wilmot had never heard her voice before, but he knew it had to be Verhoven's wife.

Shanelle Klotz was looking at the phone in Collier's hand like you might look at a snake. "Hello," she said softly.

"My name is Lorene Verhoven," the woman said. "At least that's what I call myself now. The name my mother gave me was Alice. This little girl Wendy here—I can see in her trusting beautiful little face, that she believes in her mother."

Shanelle Klotz's hands were trembling, balled into fists. But she didn't speak.

"Me, I changed the name my mother gave me a long time ago. See, I never did trust my mother. My mother was a whore. I don't hold that against her, I'm just reporting that as a fact. She had a hard life. Men came to her and said terrible things to her, did terrible things to her . . . and she just took it. Never said boo to those men. But when the men were gone, when the doors were closed, when the locks were turned, when everything was safe . . . all that pain and anger would come out. The things she did to me when the doors were closed and we were alone—well, I could tell you about them . . . but I wouldn't want your little girl to have to hear those things."

Wilmot heard Lorene Verhoven draw a long, deep breath.

"Being a mother is a sacred trust," Lorene said. "I have frankly never trusted myself to take on that responsibility. I know the things I'm capable of. I do. Things with knives, things with sticks, things with cigarettes and hammers and pins and broken glasses. You'd be amazed the pain you can cause with things you can find in any old bedroom."

Lorene sighed.

"Oh, Wendy, you sweet little girl. Look at your pretty hair! I love your hair. It's so soft and wavy."

"Lady, why are you crying?" said a tiny little girlish voice.

"It's okay, sweetie," Lorene Verhoven said. "Don't you worry about me. I'm gonna be fine."

A choking animal noise escaped briefly from Shanelle Klotz's throat. "Don't!" she rasped. "Don't you—"

"Here's the thing," Lorene Verhoven said, her voice suddenly cracking like a whip. "I've told you my name. You understand what that means, Agent Klotz? I have made peace with my fate. My husband is a visionary, and he has brought me to this place as part of a great undertaking. On this day I have a chance to do something historic, something bigger than I could ever accomplish on my own. It's a culmination. It's a punctuation on the sentence of my insignificant life. So I don't care if your daughter can pick me out of a lineup. I don't care if she knows my name. Her silence is unnecessary. We're way past that. Nothing would please me more, when this is over, than if this sweet child were to walk out of this house as clean and pure and unspoiled and lively as she was when she walked in yesterday. But we all have our parts to play. Hers is not yet written. It could be very painful, very cruel, and very short. My fate is sealed. But her fate? Her fate is in *your* hands."

"You bitch," Shanelle Klotz hissed. "Don't you dare hurt my child."

Lorene said nothing, allowing the excruciating silence to speak for her.

Then there was a sharp, childish wail from the phone. "Ow!" the girl said. "You're hurting my arm!"

"No, sweetheart," Lorene said softly. "I haven't even *begun* to hurt you."

And in the blink of an eye, the fight went out of Special Agent Shanelle Klotz's face and her entire body sagged.

"Okay," Shanelle Klotz whispered. "Whatever you want. Just don't hurt my girls."

Tillman heard the cry of the little girl and raced toward the stairs. But by the time he'd reached the bottom of the stairs, Lorene and the little girl were walking back down the stairs, hand in hand. Lorene's eyeliner was dripping down the sides of her face.

"I'm sorry," Lorene whispered to the little girl. "I didn't mean to grab your arm so hard. I made a mistake."

"It's okay," Wendy said, wiping at the tears on Lorene's face. "I know you didn't mean to."

Lorene kissed the girl on the head. "You're so sweet."

Tillman lowered his shotgun and took a couple of steps backward.

When she got to the bottom of the stairs, Lorene held up the phone and smiled an odd empty smile.

"It's done," she said.

47

WASHINGTON, DC

The United States Secret Service is an organization in which paranoia is considered a virtue. The Secret Service has considered the possibility that assassins attending the State of the Union address might, among other things: wear clothes woven from explosive fabric; have plastic or ceramic guns concealed in their rectums; carry knives made entirely of glass or obsidian; and carry exploding pacemakers inside their chests, which would shower the room with Strontium 90, Cesium 137, Cobalt 60, or perhaps even Plutonium 239. If you have a pacemaker and plan to attend the next State of the Union address, expect to provide the Secret Service with the name of your doctor as well as the manufacturer, the model, and the serial number of your pacemaker at least two weeks prior to the event. They are *that* careful.

So it has not escaped the notice of the Secret Service that the heating system of the Capitol would be a fine device for pumping irritants, poison gas, or radioactive material into a room containing roughly six hundred of the most important people in America.

For each potential threat that might menace any major event, the Secret Service develops a written protocol. There is, for instance, a thirteen-page document filed away in the Secret Service headquarters that details the steps for foiling the deployment of an exploding radioactive pacemaker. The Secret Service has developed hundreds of protocols. To prevent airborne attacks through the HVAC system, there is a document that lists thirty-one so-called "Action Events," including specific team member assignments, seventeen on the "Prevent List" and fourteen on the "React List." Action Event number eleven on the "Prevent List" requires that before anyone enters the room with access to the gas furnace and blowers, authorization from the supervising agent of the protection detail be given. Furthermore, two armed guards are to accompany any technicians entering the HVAC Access Room. If any compressed gases are to be connected to the system, those gases are to undergo an additional and final inspection by a designated specialist and supervised by the senior facility specialist—who, in this instance, was Special Agent Shanelle Klotz.

"Before we go to into the Access Room," Wilmot said to Shanelle Klotz, "let's review our protocol. Here's how this is going to work . . ."

Three minutes later they arrived at the door where two agents waited for them.

Shanelle nodded curtly to them and said, "One of you come in, the other stay outside on the door."

The agent followed them into the room. Wilmot waited until the door was closed, then hit him in the head with a pipe wrench. As the agent felt to his knees, Collier looped tape around his mouth, then flex-cuffed him.

"You told me you weren't going to hurt him," Agent Klotz said.

"I lied," Wilmot said.

Collier looked at his watch. "Fifty-three minutes."

"Go outside and tell the guy on the door that everything's copacetic for now, so he can go back to his regular assignment."

Shanelle Klotz opened the door. "We're good here. You can go back to your post."

"Yes, ma'am." The agent, a large man in a gray suit, lumbered up the hallway and disappeared.

"Agent Klotz," Wilmot said, "I want you to understand that we have an extremely clear picture of how you do your job here. We know the emergency phrases, password sequences, authentication procedures, the chain of command—the whole bit. We know that today if you use the phrase 'par for the course' during a conversation with another agent, you have just signaled to him that an attack on the president is unfolding. So, unless you want Wendy to suffer whatever that maniac Lorene Verhoven has in store for her, I suggest you avoid saying 'par for the course' to anyone today."

Wilmot had a certain amount of information about the Secret Service protection detail, but there were distinct holes. The trick to managing Shanelle Klotz was to use the little details he did know to make it seem as though he knew everything there was to know. The more she *thought* he knew, the less likely she was to do something stupid.

As he was talking, Shanelle said, "Well, then you know we need to make one final check of these tanks full of, what, nerve gas? Ricin? Zyklon B?"

"Just for your own peace of mind," Wilmot said, "I want you to know that what we are doing is staging a massive protest. These tanks contain CS gas. I'm sure you know what it is."

"Tear gas."

"Yeah, well, they call it tear gas. But it makes you throw up is what it really does."

"So you're not trying to kill anybody?"

Wilmot shook his head. "This government is out of control. We believe that a massive shake-up is needed, and this action we're taking here is going to show how weak and silly and vulnerable our nation's government is. But we're not here to kill people. So you don't need to be wrestling with the question of whether or not to sacrifice your family to save all those fat cats out there. You'd just be throwing away your husband's and children's lives for nothing."

Wilmot wasn't sure whether the agent would swallow his lie or not. But it was worth a try. He knew getting someone to believe something—even if it was impossible—was often the difference between making him take action and succumbing to inertia. If his lie made her think for a fraction of a second longer about trying to stop them—well, that fraction of a second could be the difference between the success or failure of the operation."

"I'm not sure if I believe you," Shanelle Klotz said.

"I don't give a damn if you do or if you don't," he said. "Call the guy with the sniffer dog. Let's get this last thing over with."

Klotz talked into her sleeve.

"Fifty-one minutes," Collier said.

48

A s soon as she said "It's done," Lorene wobbled and clutched at the stair railing. The phone slipped from her hands, and she fell backward, sliding down the wall. She left a long smear of blood on the cream-colored paint.

Verhoven rushed to her side. "Lorene!" he shouted. "Lorene!"

Lorene's head lolled forward.

"Lorene!"

Lorene emitted a soft snoring sound. Tillman had heard that sound before. It was the sound of somebody who was not going to make it unless they got help damn quickly.

Whatever the doctor had done, it wasn't enough. The IV had given her a short burst of energy. But she'd burned through it fast, and now she was in bad shape.

Verhoven crouched over his wife, shaking her. She didn't respond. His face hardened, and Tillman saw something in his eyes that he knew meant things were about to end badly here.

"What did you do?" Verhoven shouted at Dr. Klotz. "What the hell did you do?"

"Hold on, hold on," Tillman said, grabbing Verhoven's shoulder. "We both watched him. He didn't do anything. Sugar and saline, that's all it was. She's just weak. She's going into shock. We need to lay her down and—"

Verhoven lifted his AR and pointed it at Dr. Klotz.

Tillman saw the fury and hopelessness on Verhoven's face and knew he was going to take out his rage on the doctor. Like an impotent thug, he would strike out at the closest object to his wrath.

Tillman still didn't know the exact location of the attack, or what its precise nature would be. But he knew that a Secret Service agent named Shanelle Klotz had been roped into doing something to further the plot. If he and Gideon could find out where she was stationed, they could stop the attack.

In short, it had to be enough. There was no time to mull over his options.

Tillman fired point-blank into Verhoven, racked the 870, fired again.

The shotgun tore huge pieces of meat out of Jim Verhoven's body, exposing blue loops of viscera. He pitched over backward, torso in one direction, legs in another.

The horrific banging of the guns must have revived Lorene. She sat up, looking around in puzzlement. It took her a moment to figure out what had happened—her husband on the floor, a wisp of smoke rising from the barrel of Tillman's shotgun.

She clawed at her Glock. "You motherfucker! You lying bastard!" she shouted. "You betrayed us!"

"I was never with you in the first place," Tillman said.

She continued to claw at her Glock. Because she was crunched up against the stair railing, however, she couldn't quite pull her gun from its holster.

"Don't do it," Tillman said, racking another round of buckshot into the 870. "Don't."

Her wide, crazed eyes stared straight into Tillman's as she finally freed the Glock. She was smiling now, a broad fierce feral grin. She knew what was coming. But in some way she must have welcomed it—this, the culmination of everything her sad life had been aiming toward.

"Don't," Tillman repeated.

She pushed herself slowly to her feet, laughed at him, and raised the Glock.

He fired, racked, fired, racked, fired again.

What was left of Lorene Verhoven fell slowly to the ground. Her shirt caught on the newel post at the bottom of the stair railing and tore free. She fell and hung there from the newel post, shirtless, her back bare and exposed. There were scars everywhere. Cuts, burns, thick ridges of pink skin—a topographical map of a stolen childhood.

"Come on," Tillman said to Klotz. "We need to get your girls out of here."

Klotz stood rooted to the floor until Tillman shoved him with the butt of his gun. Then he teetered forward, grabbed his daughters, and ran for the door.

Gideon heard the shots in his earphones and leaped from the seat of the car. He handcuffed Millwood to the steering wheel and sprinted across the front lawn. By the time he got to the door, Tillman, Klotz, and the two girls were coming out.

"Where's Verhoven?" Gideon asked.

"Dead," said Tillman. "Lorene, too."

"You okay? Klotz? The girls?"

"We're fine, but we need to get to the Capitol."

"After we call this in. We've got a witness. Klotz can verify everything we say." The doctor was eyeing him silently, the two girls clutching his trousers.

"We can't wait for the bureaucrats to wrap everything up. By the time they're finished taking our statements, the president, vice president, and most of the government will be dead."

"We can at least give them the information we have."

"You're still thinking like a negotiator, Gideon. That'll take hours. And then what? You think they'll believe us? You think Dahlgren will believe us? You think President Wade will believe us?" He spat out Wade's name as if it were a poisoned cherry pit.

Gideon knew his brother was right. Even if they had the time, they would be working against Dahlgren's natural antipathy and suspicion of their efforts. He wouldn't listen, and he would do everything in his power to stop them. They didn't have all the details of the attack, so there was only one thing for them to do.

Gideon turned to Klotz. "You need to give us time to get inside. Will you do that?"

Klotz pursed his lips, then nodded.

"Promise me, Doctor."

"I promise."

"The cops will be here before long. Tell them it was a home invasion and a private security guard fought them off. Tell them he went downtown to file a report."

Klotz agreed. "Please," he asked. "If you see my wife, tell her we're okay."

"I will."

Tillman shook his hand, then he and Gideon walked down to the car. Millwood was sitting quietly inside.

"Oh, this is interesting," said Tillman.

"Long story," said Gideon. He uncuffed the officer. "How do you feel about a little ride on the Metro?"

49

PRIEST RIVER, IDAHO

It was nearly five-fifteen when Nancy Clement saw the farmhouse in the distance. The bulldozer had been chugging steadily along the winding country road for two hours and she had not seen a house or a car the entire time, and still had no cell phone signal. The dozer's tank was nearly empty.

But now she had hope that whoever lived in the farmhouse might help her get through to somebody in DC. The Caterpillar was going so slow, it almost seemed to be going backward.

"Hello!" she shouted. "Hello!"

But nobody answered. She realized she was still a long way away.

She wound around a curve and the house was lost in the trees. Then it appeared again, then it was lost again, then it appeared again.

"Hello!" she shouted again.

She saw movement now, a man out in the yard, doing something. She chugged closer and closer. Chopping wood. The guy was chopping wood.

As he heard the engine of the bulldozer, the man set down his axe and walked toward her in a leisurely fashion.

When she'd almost reached him, she pressed the decelerator pedal, then switched off the dozer's engine so she could be heard.

"Taking the dozer out for a spin?" he said.

"Do you have a phone?"

"Lines are down."

"What about Internet?" she said.

The man looked at her like she had asked him if he was a space alien.

"Internet?" she said. "Have you got Internet access?"

The man continued to look at her with a puzzled expression. She took in the axe, the tiny house with its peeling paint and sagging porch, the battered pickup truck, the cockeyed chicken coop, and she felt a wave of despair. Internet, hell, she'd be lucky if this guy even knew what a computer was.

"Internet?" she repeated feebly.

"Of course I've got Internet," the man said, tossing his axe on a pile of split logs. "Who doesn't have Internet?"

It turned out he was not a redneck farmer but an IT guy from Boise who had bought the farm as a vacation place and then moved there as a temporary cost-saving measure after losing his job the previous year. His name was Hank Adams. He was a big fan of *The X-Files* and other conspiracy-themed TV shows and books and movies. He didn't have cable, but he had a big satellite dish that brought in all his favorite channels and the Internet. When she explained the nature of the fix she was in, he eventually came around and started to grow excited.

Soon she was sitting in front of a brand-new iMac with a massive screen logging into the man's Skype account. She typed in the number for the burner cell phone that Gideon had given her.

"Gideon?" she said, when he answered.

"I was wondering what the hell happened to you. Are you okay?"

"It's going to be a gas attack," she said breathlessly. "Hydrogen cyanide, I think. But I haven't figured out the target."

"It's the State of the Union address," Gideon said. "We're on our way to the Capitol right now. Tillman and me."

It took Nancy a moment to process this before she could respond. "A guy by the name of Dale Wilmot is behind this. He built a factory in Idaho to synthesize the stuff from some kind of root vegetable. It volatilizes at seventy degrees. They can smuggle the stuff into the Capitol in liquid form then spray it or spill it and it would vaporize."

"Assuming the ambient air was above seventy."

"Right."

"It's twenty-five degrees in Washington, DC, today."

Nancy felt a stab of irritation at herself. How had she missed a thing like that? There was some piece of the pie that she was missing.

"They must have figured out some way to atomize it," she said. "We need to call the Secret Service. We'll meet them at the Rayburn building."

"No. Dahlgren told them I'm nuts and you're a rogue agent under suspension who's fantasizing about some phantom attack on American soil. They'll never listen to me, or you. We're on our own. Here's what we know. Verhoven and Lorene were holding hostage the family of a Secret Service agent named Shanelle Klotz. They told her she had to open a door or her family would be killed. She must be with them now. If we can find out where she's posted at the State of the Union address, we'll have a chance to stop them."

"Give me a minute. There might be something I can do."

"Hurry up. We're on 66 right now. We'll hit Washington in about ten minutes. If the Secret Service won't do anything, we'll have to get in there ourselves."

"You'll need my help."

"I'll call you back, okay? Just work on where Wilmot and Collier are."

The phone clicked dead, leaving Nancy staring at the blue-and-white Skype logo.

"What about heating ducts?"

Nancy turned around. "What about them?"

Hank was hanging over her shoulder, looking at her expectantly. "I was listening in," he said. "Let's say hydrogen cyanide turns to a gas at seventy degrees. If you injected it into the firebox of the heating system, the air temp will be like one hundred degrees. It'll stay hot all the way through the ducts and blow right out into all the rooms in the building. You're guaranteed to deliver plenty of gas that way."

Nancy squinted thoughtfully at the blank computer screen. "Yeah, but how would those two guys get into the Capitol at all? How could they get access to the heating system?"

Hank reached over her shoulder and tapped the keys. She couldn't help noticing that he smelled like woodsmoke and after-shave. It wasn't an unpleasant smell at all.

"You ever heard of Google?" Hank said with a wry smile.

On the screen the first entry on the list of entries pulled up by the search engine read:

PRESS RELEASE: National Heat & Air Conditioning, a subsidiary of Wilmot Industries, was this year awarded the contract to refurbish the aging HVAC system of one of America's most famous buildings, the United States Capitol. The Capitol has been rebuilt several times since its inauguration on . . ."

"Wait a minute, wait a minute," Nancy said.

Suddenly she understood why the buildings in Wilmot's little manufacturing complex contained such massive heating and air-conditioning equipment . . . and why the room in which the workers lived had been so large. It was a test facility, probably an exact duplicate of the House chamber and the HVAC unit that served it. That's why the place smelled of cyanide. They'd tested it on the workers, injecting the hydrogen cyanide into the heating system, and then watched the workers die.

It made her sick to her stomach.

Nancy had been suspended and her FBI computer privileges revoked. But any security system was only as good as the people who used it. Dahlgren had given her his password when he was on the road and needed her to follow up on certain things. She was sure he wouldn't have thought about changing it.

She accessed the FBI Web site and intranet, then typed in the remote log-in sequence. When prompted, she entered Dahlgren's name and password. It worked perfectly. Then she logged into VORTEX, the huge database that drew on vast quantities of data resources throughout the government and the private sector.

Within minutes she had a track on Special Agent Shanelle Klotz.

Every single agent carried a GPS tracking device in his field radio. She superimposed a map of the Capitol on top of the GPS coordinates. Tiny glowing red dots indicated each of the agents. She tagged Agent Shanelle Klotz. One of the glowing dots turned from blue to red.

She zoomed in. Klotz appeared to be in the office of the speaker pro tempore of the House. Then something occurred to her. Maybe she was looking at the wrong floor. She switched to Basement 1. Now Special Agent Klotz was in the men's bathroom.

Nancy tried Basement 2.

And there it was: She was in the HVAC Access Room.

"That's it," she whispered.

"Now you just have to get them inside," Hank Adams said.

Her fingers flew over the keys. Ten minutes. She had ten minutes to come up with a plan.

50

The president of the United States, Erik Wade, nodded to the head of his security detail, Supervising Agent Karl Utrecht. "Ready," he said.

Utrecht nodded at his team. "Let's go."

The team barely needed instructions or commands. Every member had spent hundreds of hours in training, thousands of hours on the job, and was a veteran agent with at least a decade of experience in protecting high-value principals. They were a well-oiled machine.

As the president walked out of the Oval Office, his team moved around him—calling in whispered tones for elevators and cars and doors to be opened, checking hallways and windows for potential threats, cutting off angles, clearing hallways. The team acted so efficiently and seamlessly that President Wade was nearly unaware of their presence. Other than the twenty-three seconds it took for the elevator to descend to the first floor, he never had to break stride.

Doors simply opened, guards appeared and disappeared, and at the front door to the White House, his wife, Grace, joined him, slipping into place, like one of the Blue Angels sliding into formation at an air show.

It took one minute and forty-one seconds to get from the Oval Office to the door of the limo. The door to the armored Cadillac limousine opened, and the president entered. A second limo, the decoy, slid up behind it. The door opened and an agent of similar size and build to the president entered and sat down, and that door, too, closed.

With that, the motorcade took off down the curved driveway onto Pennsylvania Avenue, and the entire convoy was in motion.

At the precise moment when President Wade began his trip toward the Capitol, the sergeant at arms of the House was announcing the entry of the Honorable Christine Harris Minor, Supreme Court justice. The former attorney general of Missouri and an experienced politician, she paused to shake hands with every single member of Congress on the aisle leading to her seat.

The sergeant at arms whispered to his assistant, "How we doing?"

"Jesus Christ, if you put a talking dog on the aisle, that woman would have shaken its paw," his assistant said. "We're running four and a half minutes behind."

"Get outside and hurry these windbags along. I don't want the president out there sitting in the limousine picking his teeth, okay?"

"Madam Speaker!" the sergeant at arms called. "The chief justice of the Supreme Court of the United States, the Honorable Edison Lockhardt."

Edison Lockhardt had not only been a distinguished legal scholar, but he had also been the governor of New Jersey and as such he refused to be one-upped by the most liberal member of the court. As a result, he made a point to take even more time and to extend his arm even deeper into the thicket of legislators, leaving no hand ungrasped.

The sergeant at arms scowled. If his luck held, the show was going to run a good fifteen minutes late. God, he hated politicians. Sometimes he wondered if he hadn't gone into the wrong line of work.

"Madam Speaker!" he called. "The Honorable Francis X. Dugan, Junior . . ."

51

WASHINGTON, DC

They dropped officer Millwood at the Foggy Bottom Metro station. He promised he wouldn't turn them in, but even if he did, they would be at the Capitol before he could reach anyone. Getting inside, however, was a different matter.

"What now?" asked Tillman. "The mall's going to be completely sealed, and those Secret Service guys don't fool around."

As if in answer to his question, Gideon's newest burner began to ring. It was Nancy.

"What have you got for me?"

"Tunnels," she said.

"Which tunnels?"

"I've hacked into the Secret Service computer," she said. "You've got a pass waiting for you at the parking garage of the Russell Building. You both have clearance, but only for the perimeter. The Russell Building has a subway that goes to the Capitol. But there are two older tunnels. One is the old subway tunnel, which was replaced in the late 1960s with a bigger tunnel, and the other is a ventilation and mechanical tunnel that runs above it. Well, it's more like a duct than a tunnel, really. You'll kinda have to crawl."

"If you can get us into the parking garage, why not into the Capitol?"

"It doesn't work like that. All of the Capitol access is on a secure, nonnetworked computer that I can't get into."

"So, we'll have to find a way to get past the final security checkpoints?"

"Yes," said Nancy. "What I can tell you is Agent Klotz is in the HVAC Access Room, which is on the second subbasement level of the Capitol. I believe they will try to inject the cyanide in a liquid form into the heating system. The liquid will vaporize and spread through the building via the heating system, killing more or less everybody in the building. What I don't understand is how they're planning to get out."

"They're not," Gideon said. "They'll have to trigger it manually. All radio signals will be jammed."

It was a sobering thought. People who planned their own deaths were the hardest to stop. A man willing to give his life for something he believed in didn't offer much room for negotiation.

"Once you reach the Capitol, you won't be able to contact me," said Nancy. "I can get you to the Russell Building. But once you're inside, you'll be on your own."

"Got it," Gideon said.

"There's one more thing you should know." She hesitated, glancing at the TV that played C-SPAN behind her. "Your fiancée is inside."

"Kate?" Gideon was stunned. "What the hell is she doing there?"

"She's with the secretary of the interior."

He knew Kate had been working with Secretary Fitzgerald on the Deepwater commission, but he was momentarily stunned by the irony that she had accepted an invitation to attend the State of the Union address with him. That she was now at ground zero for the attack filled him with dread.

"Nancy, you have to get her out of there."

"I don't have any way to reach her."

"Figure something out. You must know someone inside. Give her this number. Tell her to call me."

"There is one agent I can trust . . ."

In her voice, Gideon heard her willingness to help and knew

that their own relationship had reached a new level of understanding. Nancy had set aside whatever lingering resentment remained in order to achieve their common goal.

"Thank you, Nancy," he said.

"Good luck."

Gideon disconnected and explained to Tillman what Nancy had told him.

"You okay?" Tillman asked.

"Yeah. But if we can't sneak or brazen our way through, we're going to have to mount an assault on the Capitol—something so over the top that it would force them to evacuate the building . . . or at least recheck all their security precautions."

"You're talking about some kind of suicide attack."

Gideon nodded. "Kate is in there. If I can't stop Wilmot and get her out. I won't have a choice. But you don't have to come with me."

"Are you kidding? Of course I'm coming with you. I'm your brother."

"I know how the government treated you. You don't owe those people a thing—especially not your life."

"Gideon, the truth is I would come with you even if you weren't my brother. I may not seem like much of a patriot anymore, but I still love this country, and I'm not going to let a pair of wackos kill a bunch of innocent people. But most of all, I'm not going to let them kill you or my future sister-in-law. Not if I can help it."

Gideon regarded Tillman's lined and tired face, so different from his own, and yet so familiar. "Thank you," he said, brimming with gratitude.

"Now let's go blow up some shit."

Gideon snaked around the bombproof barriers at the Russell Building parking garage entrance. When they pulled into the lot, a Capitol police officer checked their IDs wordlessly, punching them into the computer that held the list of people who were cleared to park there that evening.

Gideon's heart was pounding as the officer yawned and then stared at the screen. For all he knew the computer could be networked into whatever system listed them as wanted by the FBI.

But apparently the computer was just for parking clearances. The bored officer waved them through and went back to reading *The Washington Post*.

The parking garage was nearly full.

"Just leave it here," Tillman said once they'd wound down to the level of the tunnel connecting them to the Russell Building.

Gideon pulled up next to the elevators and climbed out of the car. He was still wearing his tactical gear.

According to Nancy, the entrance to the tunnel lay through a door near the elevator bank. Two heavily armed guards stood beside the door.

"Talk or shoot?" Tillman said.

"Talk," Gideon said. "If we start shooting right off the bat, everybody goes on high alert and we're screwed."

"Agreed," Tillman said.

"Follow my play."

As soon as Gideon got within earshot of the guards, he began talking loudly into his cell phone. "Yes, ma'am, I realize that. I realize . . . Yes, ma'am. I'll be there in less than three minutes, I promise." He ignored the two guards and walked straight toward the door.

"Whoa whoa whoa!" one of the guards yelled. "Stop right there."

Gideon waved irritably at the agent with the back of his hand, as though he were more concerned with whoever he was speaking to on the phone. But he stopped walking. "Yes, ma'am, I realize that. I'm already at the checkpoint in the Russell Building. If you could just . . . Right . . . right . . . right."

"Who the hell are you?" The guard raised his P90 and was pointing it at Gideon. "Stop right there!"

Gideon rolled his eyes. "Just a moment, ma'am." He put his hand over the phone. "Agents Dillard and Koons," he said to the guard. "State Department Security. I'm talking to the secretary of state."

"What?" the guard said incredulously.

"Some kind of SNAFU. The labor secretary's security is being held up at the door, and I have to get in there and straighten out the credential situation."

"Wait a minute, wait a minute, *who* are you?"

"Goddammit, I just told you! Are you deaf? Agents Dillard and Koons with the State Department."

"Where's your clearance? Where's your pass?"

"Here, look, talk to Secretary Bonifacio, okay?"

Gideon extended his phone to the guard, and the man regarded it as if it were radioactive. Secretary Bonifacio had a notorious temper, and Gideon could see the guard debating whether he wanted to risk her wrath. Then he said, "Go ahead. You'll have to surrender your weapons."

"Sure," Gideon said. "Of course. Mine is stowed in my vehicle already." He lifted his coat to show an empty holster.

Tillman unholstered his pistol and laid it on the table by the door.

The two guards then checked them with a metal detector and waved them on. Gideon and Tillman walked through the door, into the concrete tunnel, and began walking toward the Russell Building a few hundred yards away.

"I'm impressed," said Tillman. "You're very convincing."

"I've had a lot of practice," said Gideon.

They hadn't taken more than a few strides when one of the guards called, "Oh, gentlemen, I'll need to see your IDs."

Gideon and Tillman, of course, had only their real IDs, which would undoubtedly set off alarm bells.

"So much for talking," said Tillman.

"I'll take the one on the left," Gideon whispered.

They turned and walked back toward the two guards. When they got within two yards of the men, they both put their shoulders down and charged forward, smashing the two guards into the concrete wall. Tillman and Gideon were both sizable, fit men. But so were the Secret Service guards. Having spent his life training in the fighting arts, Tillman was better prepared than Gideon for what came next.

Tillman planted the heel of his hand under the Secret Service man's chin and slammed his helmet against the concrete wall. Even wearing a helmet the impact was enough to stun the man. Tillman then hit him with a short left hook to the jaw, and the man went down in a heap.

Meanwhile Gideon found himself grappling with a younger, stronger man. Within seconds, things were not going well. The

Secret Service agent had recovered after being momentarily caught by surprise and was now wrestling Gideon to the ground.

Tillman grabbed him from behind, hooking both heels around his hips and slipping his arms around the guard's head in what Brazilian jujitsu practitioners call a rear naked choke. It was the same move that police used to call a sleeper hold.

The guard attempted to scream for assistance. But his call for help amounted only to a spluttering, choking noise.

"Grab his arms!" Tillman hissed. "He's probably got a panic button somewhere."

Gideon immobilized the struggling officer's arms just as his fingers clawed for a small red button on the radio unit clipped to his belt. Within seconds the officer's entire body went limp, his brain succumbing to the sudden loss of blood.

"Get their clothes, IDs, and weapons," Tillman whispered, pulling a pair of flex cuffs off the unconscious agent's belt. "We have to move fast. He'll regain consciousness very quickly."

They undressed the guards and stashed them in the back of the car. Five minutes later they were crawling into the mouth of the ventilation duct above the old subway line.

Tillman crawled to the grate at the end of the tunnel and peered out. In front of him was the deserted platform of the older subway. There were no guards, no dogs, nothing. He pushed the iron grate out of the wall. It pivoted on rusty hinges with an ear-piercing shriek. On the opposite end of the platform a shadow moved across an open doorway.

"Hold on," he whispered, backing into the vent and pulling the grate shut.

The lights flickered on, bathing the entire room in bright fluorescence. A tall Secret Service agent entered, hand under his jacket on the butt of his gun. A second agent followed. The second agent shined a small but intense flashlight down the end of the platform to a larger tunnel.

"Clear," the agent with the flashlight said.

"I heard *something*," the tall agent with his hand on his pistol said. He signaled toward the tunnel. "Where does that lead?"

"To a ventilation shaft that connects to the bomb shelter."

Tillman had heard there was a bomb shelter underneath the Capitol. But this was his first confirmation of that rumor.

"Think we should check? That area is a rat's nest."

The agent with the flashlight shook his head. "There's a door at the end of the tunnel. It's been welded shut."

"Check it."

The agent disappeared, came back after a few minutes. "Like I said, welded shut."

"Well, goddammit, I heard something."

"So you said."

"What about that ventilation duct?" He nodded in Tillman's direction as he flicked on his flashlight.

Tillman froze. He knew that if they shined the light at the grate, he'd be spotted. But if he tried to back away from the grate, they'd spot his movement.

"Hold on," the agent with the flashlight said, cocking his head, as though hearing something in his earpiece. "POTUS will be arriving in four. We need to clear the corridor."

The tall agent frowned and shook his head grudgingly. A bead of perspiration ran down Tillman's face. Then the agent switched off his flashlight, turned, and both agents walked out of the room.

"*Go,*" Gideon whispered.

Tillman pushed the grate as slowly as possible. This time it only let out a soft, low groan.

The brothers climbed out from the ventilation tunnel.

"Where to?" Tillman said softly.

Gideon pointed at the tunnel the two agents had checked. "Let's try to pop the welds on that door. If we can get into an elevator shaft or a mechanical tunnel we should be able to get down into Basement two."

"Sounds good. We're way past bluffing our way through at this point."

They entered the tunnel. Tillman used the flashlight he'd lifted from the agent back in the Russell Building garage. When they reached the steel door, Gideon examined the three weld beads on the steel frame. All the welds were on the side of the door where the handle was. There was no welding on the side of the door where the hinges were located.

"Pull the hinge pins," Gideon said.

"Just what I was thinking."

Tillman pulled a folding knife off the belt he'd harvested from the agent. It was a good knife, a Benchmade automatic. The guy had good taste in knives.

"You take the top, I'll take the bottom," Tillman said, thumbing the button that triggered the blade to pop out with a satisfying click.

No further communication between the brothers was necessary. They knew exactly what to do. Tillman hunkered down and shoved the blade of his knife under the flange at the top of the hinge pin. Gideon stepped onto Tillman's back and got to work on the top pin.

Within seconds they had the pins out. Unlike those on the ventilation grate, these hinges had been recently lubricated with a heavy lithium grease.

Gideon hopped down, pried out the third hinge pin, and inserted his knife into the crack. Tillman did the same.

"One," Tillman said. "Two."

"Three," they said together. With a sharp twist of their knives, they were able to move the door about a quarter of an inch out of the frame.

"You brace, I'll go deeper," Gideon said.

Tillman applied steady pressure to the haft of his knife while Gideon drove his a little deeper into the crack.

"Go," Gideon said.

He braced this time, while Tillman moved his blade deeper still.

"One. Two. Three."

Another quarter of an inch. Now the welds were offering more resistance. So they were only able to move the door about an eighth of an inch.

They repeated the same process several times until finally the edge of the door cleared the frame. They stuck their knives in all the way, this time wrenching backward with all their strength. The welds popped and the door came free.

"Whatever happens," Gideon whispered, "I'm glad we did this. And I'm proud to be your brother."

"Don't be such a girl," Tillman said.

Gideon smiled and set the door against the wall. Tillman probed the other side with his flashlight. Beyond the door was a low tunnel made of crumbling red brick that looked like it might be 150 years old.

Gideon looked at his watch. He had eight minutes before the president began speaking. Eight minutes before he would either save Kate or die trying.

52

WASHINGTON, DC

At that moment Kate was enjoying the pomp and circumstance of the political pageant. Senators and representatives she had only seen from a distance or viewed on C-SPAN milled about her. Smart men and women in crisp suits shook hands or slapped each other on the back. Partisan differences were set aside as the anointed few hobnobbed and glad-handed, congratulating themselves and one another for their exalted positions and good fortune.

She was surprised when she felt a rough hand on her shoulder and turned to see a Secret Service agent with a wired earpiece summoning her as if she'd been a bad girl in school.

"Please come with me, ma'am."

Her first thought was that the Secret Service discovered she was just a low-level oil company executive who didn't belong among the movers and shakers. That thought was quickly followed by a fear that something had happened to Gideon. But as the Secret Service agent led her through the throng of politicians and government officials, it occurred to her that Gideon didn't even know she was at the Capitol, and there was no one here who would bother to tell her if he was injured or hurt.

By the entrance to the Russell Building, the agent handed her a device that looked like an old-fashioned transistor radio with a stubby rubber antenna. It wasn't a radio, however; it was a secure

VOIP wireless phone, operating on the NSA's proprietary network, as the agent was pleased to inform her. He told her there was a telephone call for her.

She could not have been more surprised if Gideon himself had appeared before her. But she was even more surprised when the voice on the other end was not Gideon's, but a woman's.

"Kate Murphy?" the voice asked. It had the slightest trace of a southern accent, and Kate immediately knew it was Nancy Clement. She recalled that Gideon said she grew up in Tennessee, the daughter of a tobacco farmer. A girl of privilege who had gone on to work a low-paying job as an FBI agent, which, despite herself, Kate admired.

"Is it Gideon?" she asked. "Is everything okay?"

"Gideon is fine," said Nancy. "But you're in danger. You have to get out of the Capitol building right away."

"Why?"

"I can't explain everything. The agent next to you is Ron Livingston. He's a good friend. He'll escort you out of the building."

"I can't just walk out of the State of the Union address. I'm a guest of Secretary Fitzgerald. What do I say to him?"

"Worry about that later. There's an attack planned in the House chamber, and there's no time. Gideon told me to get you out of there."

"Gideon?"

"He's there now. He's trying to stop it. But you have to get out."

She couldn't just abandon Gideon. "He might need my help," she said.

"Kate. Listen to me. These men who are planning the attack are fanatics. They won't stop unless they're successful, or dead."

"But Gideon—" She was interrupted by a large, gruff man whom she immediately recognized as Deputy Director Dahlgren, the same man who had visited her earlier looking for Gideon. He was accompanied by two other agents, and he signaled to Livingston to give him the phone. Livingston grimaced and reluctantly took the phone from Kate's hand and delivered it to Dahlgren.

"Now," said Dahlgren. "Let's talk."

53

WASHINGTON, DC

POTUS is arriving in sixty seconds," said the voice in Wilmot's ear. By now Wilmot recognized the calm, clipped tones of the communications specialist. He wasn't the detail commander but a sort of dispatcher who relayed orders throughout the security detail.

Dale Wilmot felt more alive than he had ever felt in his life. It was all coming together. Collier had screwed the first tank into the HVAC system. He was now working on the second one.

The voice of the comm specialist said, "Agent Busbee, Agent Weiner, radio check."

Every agent was supposed to check in every fifteen minutes with the command station. If they didn't, Command sent a radio check. They were supposed to respond immediately. If they didn't, it meant something was wrong.

"Agent Busbee, Agent Weiner, radio check."

Still no answer.

"Why aren't they responding?" Wilmot leaned closer when Agent Klotz didn't respond. "Tell me why they're not responding."

"They're in the parking garage of the Russell Building," she said. "Sometimes radios don't work right in these bomb-hardened concrete structures. The rebar in the concrete creates interference."

Wilmot studied her face.

"Agents Dennis and Roberts, Level Two station check, post nine," said the comm specialist.

"So those guys are going to check on the other two guys, right?"

"Right."

"Level Two, what's that mean?"

"Guns drawn, possible assault."

"How often does that happen?"

Agent Klotz cleared her throat nervously. "Not often."

"If there's a problem, will that affect us here?"

"Not unless there's a general alarm."

Collier nodded and straightened. "Then we're all set."

The Command voice came out of the speaker again. "POTUS arriving Station One. Two minutes to Station Two."

Station One, Wilmot knew, was the entrance to the Capitol. Station Two was the door of the House chamber. There were still a few minutes to go. The plan was to wait until the president had begun his speech to release the cyanide. They had considered doing it as soon as he entered. But they wanted the doors closed, and they wanted him in the center of the room where he would be harder to protect.

Until then they had to endure the political theater of the president's address. He had to shake hands all the way up the aisle, hand copies of his address text to the speaker and the vice president, and then stand there, grinning as he waited for the ridiculously long applause to wind down. Until he said "My fellow Americans," they would wait to release the gas.

Collier armed the tanks while Wilmot waited. He inserted a screwdriver into the set screws under the valve stems. He cranked hard, and the set screw moved. One, two, three turns and there was a tiny hiss within the tank. Then he pulled out a small box with a red switch on it. It was a triggering device that would override the HVAC's normal on/off switch. It worked remotely on a shortwave frequency as long as it was within twenty-five meters of the unit. Any distance greater than that and the jamming frequency would block the signal. When the red switch was flipped, the heat would come on. Then, ten seconds later, a solenoid inside the HVAC system would vent the two cyanide tanks directly into the hot air chamber, the squirrel cage blowers would kick on, and baffles in the system would direct all the air in the system directly into the House chamber.

Within another thirty seconds, the majority of the people in the room would be dead.

"POTUS is moving. Repeat, POTUS is moving."

Wilmot felt a steady thrumming that ran through his entire body, as if someone had pressed the lowest key on a very large and powerful pipe organ.

"Give it to me," Wilmot said.

Collier handed him the switch.

54

WASHINGTON, DC

President Erik Wade climbed out of the limousine in front of the Capitol, paused briefly to examine the facade of the great building as his wife joined him, and then began to walk up the stairs. At the top of the stairs he turned, waved to the small crowd assembled in front of the building, and then walked in.

Although this was his first State of the Union address, he wasn't nervous. He had given enough public speeches in his life to know that he was no Cicero, but he'd do fine. He had prepared thoroughly and wouldn't stumble over any words. His team on the House Majority side would make sure the applause was loud and plentiful. There were no major legislative issues at stake.

Yet he felt annoyed and apprehensive about the public reaction to the shootings at Priest River. He had been briefed on them by Deputy Director Dahlgren of the FBI just before heading over to the Rayburn building. It was that damned Gideon Davis again, causing problems where he had no business to be. Now Wade was going to have to address the disaster during what should have been a moment of glory, his place in a long parade of great men who had preceded him. He frowned as he reached the door of the building, and he went one way while his wife went the other. She would be seated in the gallery, nested among firefighters, hero cops, Medal of Honor winners, and guys in wheelchairs.

His cabinet was waiting. He shook each one's hand, shared a joke or an elbow squeeze or an inquiry after a wife or child. By the time he'd reached the secretary of health and human services, his wife was already ensconced in the gallery and the cabinet officials were beginning to file into the House chamber.

He took a deep breath. It was almost showtime.

55

Tillman and Gideon did a quick reconnoiter of the tunnels, which were full of steam pipes and fat electrical conduits. On any other day, it would have been an extraordinary tour of a secret American history—bricks dating back to the nineteenth century alongside heavy steel doors from the Cold War of the twentieth century next to optical fiber cables from the twenty-first. But today there was no time for reflection.

He glanced at his watch. A couple of minutes, that's all the time they had before the president began.

They followed the tunnel around a vertical shaft and then found themselves in front of another door. This one read: Basement 2. They were on the floor with access to the HVAC system but had no way to get through the locked door. Above it was a security camera that, no doubt, transmitted their images back to a command post. Gideon hoped that in their tactical gear and caps they wouldn't be recognizable.

"Agent Busbee, Agent Weiner, radio check," a voice said over the earpiece Gideon had picked up from one of the agents.

"I've got an idea," Gideon said.

He waved at the camera, then pointed at his microphone, and shook his head. Tillman, getting into the act, waved, too.

"Agent Busbee, we see two agents at an unauthorized location," the voice on the radio said. "Is that you?"

Gideon kept his head down and pointed at the door, as though discussing something with Tillman. But he gave a big thumbs-up to the camera.

"Agent Busbee, is that Agent Weiner accompanying you?"

Gideon gave another thumbs-up. "Just bang on the door," he said to Tillman. "They'll think our radios are messed up."

Tillman whacked on the door with the flat of his palms.

"Agents Busbee and Weiner, you are not authorized to be in your present location. Return to your post."

Tillman continued to whack on the steel door. "They may open the door," he said. "But when they do, there's liable to be about ten guys with MP5s pointed right at our heads."

"That's what I'm counting on," Gideon said.

Suddenly there was a scrabbling sound on the other side of the door. The door swung open, and four armed men stood around the door, P90s at low ready.

"Oh, my bad," Tillman said. "No MP5s. They've all got P90s."

After that came a chorus of *"Down on the ground! Down on the ground! Down on the ground!"*

Tillman and Gideon dropped slowly to one knee as a fifth man, the group leader, approached. He wore a weasly smile, his hair greased back and slick. It was Deputy Director Dahlgren.

"Gideon Davis," he said. "And this must be your brother, Tillman."

They were just inside a long concrete hallway. And there, about twenty yards down the hallway, was a large red door with a name stenciled on it in black paint: HVAC ACCESS ROOM.

"Dahlgren!" Gideon said. "There are two men in that room who are planning to inject hydrogen cyanide into the heating system. You need to get in there right now and stop them. If I were you, I'd do it quickly because if you don't, they're going to kill everybody in this building."

"You'll need to come up with a better story if you want to save yourself from an extended stay at Leavenworth."

"Listen to him, you shithead," said Tillman. "You're about to take your last breath."

"Language," clucked Dahlgren.

"Look," said Gideon. "Let me open the door. You have nothing to lose. If I'm wrong, it's just a few minutes of your time. But if I'm right, and you could have prevented the deaths of the president, vice president, and hundreds of senators and congressmen, you'll go down in history as the man that let it happen."

"You're not opening any door," said Dahlgren. But Gideon could see that his warning words had worked on Dahlgren as he signaled to two of the men. "Take them to the detention facility." Then he withdrew his pistol from his holster. "I'll open the goddamn door, and we'll end this bullshit once and for all."

Wilmot and Collier heard the commotion outside the HVAC Access Room.

"What the hell is going on out there?" Collier asked as he peered through the keyhole. "There are Secret Service guys arresting other Secret Service guys."

"Something's wrong," Wilmot said. "Initiate the sequence now."

"It'll take a minute thirty for the whole cycle." Collier pecked at his keyboard and began typing.

"I thought you had it ready to go," Wilmot said.

"I do. But the heat has to cycle on. First the gas, then the air handler heats up. The blowers don't come on until the air reaches—"

"Okay. Just get it going."

For the first time in a long while, Shanelle Klotz felt a flicker of hope. "You're not going to make it, you know," she said. "They'll be here in—" She looked at the door. "Never mind, they're already here."

The knob on the locked door jiggled, then someone kicked at it.

"Shit," said Wilmot.

Collier pecked away at the keys. "Just a few more seconds . . ."

Someone kicked at the door again.

Wilmot put down the small box with the red switch on it and

grabbed the gun he had taken from the agent. "We can't wait any longer. You finish up in here. I'll hold them off."

"No, sir." Collier stood. "Let me do it."

"But we need you to initiate the sequence."

"It's done. I've armed it." He retrieved the triggering device and handed it back to Wilmot. "All you have to do is flip that button."

Wilmot regarded Collier, then handed him the gun.

Collier didn't take it. "I've got something bigger in mind."

"Thank you, son, for everything."

Collier saluted. "I'm proud to have been your son."

Wilmot mustered a smile he hoped disguised his contempt for Collier. It surprised him that he felt that way, especially in the face of Collier's sacrifice.

President Erik Wade heard the sergeant at arms call out, "Madam Speaker, the President of the United States!" and he moved through the door into the House chamber.

Since Wade had been a governor before being elected president, he had only visited the House chamber a handful of times before. It was a little smaller, a little less grand than he'd remembered.

His security contingent was under instructions not to come on too strong. The room was full of people with long histories of service to the United States. At the moment this facility was probably as secure as Fort Knox. Wade wanted to press the flesh. He paused, shook hands with a California Democrat, a South Carolina Republican, a senator, a House member. Wade had a near-photographic memory and spoke to each person by name. The House member was a man he'd never met, but he managed to dredge up the congressman's daughter's name.

"How's Christine's leg, Ted?" he asked, referencing a soccer injury he'd read about in one of the many briefing books he'd absorbed since becoming president.

"Fine, Mr. President. Thank you for asking." The lowly congressman's face shone, surprised that the president even knew his name, much less the details of his daughter's broken third metatarsal.

"Thank *you* for helping me out on this energy bill," Wade said.

"I didn't know I was," the congressman said.

"Oh, I have confidence you will," Wade said with a wink.

Then he was moving along, shaking more hands.

When he finally reached the podium, the text of his speech clutched in his left hand, he noticed that the Secret Service agents were whispering intently into their microphones.

They looked stirred up about something. But that was their job. If it was something serious, they'd grab him and hustle him to safety. Meanwhile, he had other things to think about.

The president shook hands with his vice president and smiled broadly. Erik Wade disliked the vice president, and he was sure it was mutual. But this was politics.

He handed a copy of his speech to the vice president, then kissed the Speaker on the cheek. He not only despised the Speaker, but he also feared her a little. An onlooker gauging their smiles might have thought the two were long-lost cousins. "Good to see you, Madam Speaker. You're looking lovely as ever."

"Flattery will get you nowhere, Mr. President."

Erik Wade laughed loudly. "As demanded by protocol, Madam Speaker, I now present you the text of my address."

"As protocol demands, I cheerfully accept." She then moved toward the microphone and said, "I have the high privilege and distinct honor to present the president of the United States."

Erik Wade turned his back on the vice president and the Speaker and approached the dais.

"Thank you," he said, holding up his hands as the room burst into applause. "Thank you. Thank you, folks. I thank you from the bottom of my heart . . ."

The president noticed it felt unusually chilly in the room. He wondered if somebody would do something about the heat. But he had no more time to think about it because, just then, a tremendous explosion rocked the room, and he felt himself falling.

56

Hydrogen cyanide is an extremely volatile liquid at room temperature. It is highly flammable when mixed with air, and the smallest spark can cause an explosion.

When Dahlgren couldn't kick open the door, he withdrew his Glock and took aim. But just as he was about to fire several shots, the door burst open and Collier flew out, arms wrapped tightly around one of the canisters. Dahlgren got off one shot before Collier smashed into him, and the two men tumbled to the ground.

Although Collier intended to ignite the tank himself, he didn't need to. Dahlgren's bullet struck the metal wall, perforated the tank, combusted the liquid, and caused an explosion. The concussive force killed Collier instantly, and the flames seared Dahlgren's flesh, sending him into immediate cardiac arrest. Two other Secret Service agents, closer to Dahlgren, suffocated from the lack of oxygen, and a third agent would die later of cyanide poisoning.

Tillman was thrown against the wall while Gideon dived to the floor and just narrowly missed being hit by metal shrapnel. Fortunately, both men were far enough away from the fireball that the flames consumed nearly all the cyanide by the time it reached them. Their eyes stung and burned, and it would be weeks before Tillman could eat anything without the bitter taste of almonds in the back of his throat, but they both survived relatively unscathed.

Gideon stood and found his brother, who was on his knees and coughing into his hands. "You okay?" he asked. Tillman nodded but couldn't speak. The dead agents lay sprawled by Collier and Dahlgren, and the wounded agent was crawling toward his comrades whom he could no longer help. Gideon knew there were two men in the Access Room, and only one of them was dead, which meant one of them—he assumed it was Wilmot—was still inside. He reached out toward Tillman and pulled his brother to his feet. Then the two men picked their way through the rubble in the hall and headed for the room.

Inside the House chamber, when the blast occurred, Secret Service agents threw themselves against the doors.

Sealing the chamber was SOP, the smart play when there was a possible attack on POTUS. But it was also the worst thing anyone could do. Because the threat was not outside the chamber, but inside. Meanwhile, panicked people tried to rip the doors open. Senators grabbed congressmen, men grabbed women, women crawled over men, the strong pushed the weak, the weak trampled the unlucky. At every door, hundreds of people were smashed together, grunting, screaming, shouting—a serene, organized, and civil pageant reduced in seconds to a chaos of animals scrabbling for survival.

Kate had remained outside the chamber under guard after being questioned by Dahlgren. Now, in the chaos, all she could think about was finding Gideon. She hadn't given Dahlgren any information, not that she had any that would compromise Gideon. The explosion, she assumed, had something to do with the terrorists Gideon was chasing. It sounded as if it had come from a basement level. Kate shook free of her guard and sprinted for the stairs.

57

Gideon kicked open the unlocked door of the Access Room with the heel of his shoe. It burst open. He and Tillman rushed in, looking for targets.

But there were none.

On the floor lay two people, a man and a woman, both wearing the bland dark suits of Secret Service agents.

"Dead," Gideon said, checking the pulse of the man.

The other agent was sprawled out, a small trickle of blood running down the side of her face. Tillman recognized her as Shanelle Klotz, the agent from the family photos in the house out in Virginia.

"Is she dead, too?" Gideon asked.

As if in answer to his question, the agent groaned.

"No," Tillman said, his voice scratchy and raw.

"Where the hell did he go?" Gideon said. "There's no one here."

Shanelle Klotz sat up and put a hand to her head. "I know you," she said unsteadily.

"Gideon Davis," said Gideon.

"The FBI is looking for you."

Gideon didn't respond, all too aware of Dahlgren's trumped-up charges. "The guy who was here? Where did he go?"

It was only then he heard the WHUMMPPHH sound inside the big HVAC unit of the gas jets cycling on. Shanelle pointed silently across the room, and Gideon saw she was indicating an access panel or trapdoor built into the face of the unit. Gideon realized Wilmot must have crawled into the ducts, where he was controlling the HVAC remotely by shortwave.

"Stay right there!"

Gideon whirled. The agent was pointing a thin little auto pistol right at his head, the sort of pistol that people carried as backup. She must have hidden it on her body somewhere but been unable to get to it before now.

"Listen," said Gideon, "he's already turned on the gas. We have maybe sixty seconds before the cyanide kicks in."

"Cyanide?"

"He's going to atomize it and release it into the entire chamber."

"Oh my God." She pointed to the tank tied in to the condensation lines. "There's enough in there to kill everybody in the chamber."

"We have to move," said Gideon. "You have to trust me."

"They have my kids."

Gideon shook his head. "Your kids are fine. Tillman saved them."

The agent stared at them, eyes wide, not sure what to think.

"It's a long story," Gideon said. "But now we've got to go."

Shanelle Klotz continued to point the pistol at Gideon's face for several more seconds. Finally she lowered it.

"Go," she said.

58

Gideon began the climb up the dark shaft. In the distance he could hear shouts of alarm and caution.

The ducts thrummed with the vibration of the gas jets warming up. He knew that as soon as the air reached the proper temperature, the fans would kick in, blowing hot air laced with cyanide through the metal conduits and into the chamber. He and Tillman would be its first victims. Their only chance was to find Wilmot before that happened and shut down the system.

Gideon moved up the shaft as fast as he could. Tillman followed. The ducts were about three feet wide and four feet tall with indents for their toes every ten inches. They climbed like hunchbacks. After about fifteen feet, several lines branched off horizontally. Gideon tried to make out the footfalls of someone else in front of them, but the sound of screaming and of the HVAC system made it impossible. It crossed his mind for the briefest of moments that if he simply did nothing for the next fifteen or twenty seconds, he could close the chapter of a humiliating part of his life in a spectacular way. Given how President Wade had treated Tillman and him, it would be a righteous if perverse form of justice.

But it was only a brief thought. Gideon knew that what was about to happen was madness. This lunatic Wilmot was trying to pull down a temple that had stood for more than two hundred years.

True, it was flawed, but there was never going to be a perfect human institution. At least not until people became perfect. But America's was still the best system of government in the brief history of man.

He felt Tillman beside him. "You go this way," he whispered. "I'll go that way." Gideon agreed.

Tillman crawled into the duct. Then he paused and turned. "You see the bastard, don't hesitate even for a second," he whispered. "Just kill him."

Then he turned back and began to crawl.

59

WASHINGTON, DC

Dale Wilmot almost had to laugh. The security team had directed everyone to stay inside the chamber, which was exactly as he expected, and exactly the wrong thing to do.

Down on the floor of the House, the panicked herd was beginning to calm down, but people were still trying to get out of the exits, and Secret Service agents were swarming the president.

"Stay calm!" he heard. "Stay calm! You're safe inside!"

But they weren't, and only Wilmot knew it. Now that the moment had finally arrived, he couldn't help but want to prolong it. He felt as though his entire soul was cracking open, spreading out, becoming one with some great historical force. Had Lincoln felt this way at Gettysburg? Had the signers felt that way when they scrawled their names on the Declaration of Independence or the Constitution?

A vision of his son's face—not his ruined face, but the beautiful face he'd taken with him to Afghanistan—hovered briefly in his mind. Everything he had done, he had done for Evan, and someday, he was certain, his son would understand its importance. It was a great thing, a monumental thing, and history would judge him accordingly.

With the switch clenched in one hand, he raised his arms in triumph. In the darkness, the metal glinted like the flash of a silver bullet in the onrushing night.

60

Gideon shinnied around the corner and saw the big man with his hands outstretched inside the rectangular cordon, one hand on the switch that would kill everyone in the room. Gideon's only chance was to grab that switch out of his hands and override the HVAC system before the fans kicked in.

He settled his front sight on the big man's right hip and fired. There was no way to draw a bead on his head. He was just going to have to shoot him to pieces.

Dale Wilmot bellowed when the first shot hit him in the leg. Then he pushed forward with his good leg, his big hand still wrapped around the remote switch.

Gideon shot him again, this time in the lower back.

Wilmot grunted but didn't stop pushing forward. He still had the switch in his hand. If Gideon couldn't stop him, or get to the switch in the next thirty seconds, it would be too late for everyone.

He fired again.

Wilmot seemed unfazed by the terrible punishment he was taking. He crawled into the darkness, a shadowy figure in the gloom of the ventilation system. The shouting in the House chamber below had changed in intensity as the crowd heard the shooting and realized something was happening below them.

"America!" Wilmot shouted out. "It's your day of reckoning!" His words reverberated along the metal walls.

Then the back of his head exploded, and he slumped to the floor of the duct.

Gideon turned around just as his brother leapt past him. Tillman scampered ahead and grabbed the switch from the dead man's hand. He flipped the button, and with a SWOOSH the gas jets shut off and all was silent.

"Nice shot, brother," said Gideon.

"Looked like you needed a little help."

"He was going down. I had him."

"I just want it on record that *I* made the kill shot. I'm totally the guy who saved the day."

"One more shot, he was down."

"I'm just saying. *I* made the shot. The president thanks you, but *I* made the shot. Story of my life."

"I didn't have the angle."

"Yeah, whatever. I'm just saying."

They burst out laughing as they climbed back toward the hatch on the heating unit.

"I also want to put it on record that you're never going to make it as a college professor," Tillman said.

"Why do you say that?" Gideon said.

"I saw your face. You love this shit. You love it way too much."

Gideon sighed. Tillman could barely make out his teeth gleaming in the dim light, a broad smile breaking out on his face. "Yeah, you may be right."

They were still laughing as twenty armed men threw them to the floor and cuffed them. It took Kate, with the help of Shanelle Klotz, a good thirty minutes to get them free. But Gideon didn't mind; he was happy to sit peacefully with his brother by his side while someone else did the negotiating.

61

PRIEST RIVER, IDAHO

Nancy Clement sat on Hank Adams's couch and watched the television as President Erik Wade climbed back onto the podium and said, "My fellow Americans, we have all been witness today to an extraordinary event, an attempt to destroy the legally authorized and popularly mandated government of the United States of America. That attempt failed. Even if every soul in this room had died, it would still have failed. For all its flaws, our republic can't be destroyed by killing a handful of people. It's too strong, too resilient, too masterfully designed. We—all of us in this room— are simply instruments of the popular will. As much importance as we like to ascribe ourselves, the truth is, we're all replaceable."

The president scanned the crowd. Although it had thinned markedly, there were still hundreds of legislators who remained, ready to hear the entirety of Erik Wade's speech.

"That said," the president continued, "the Constitution mandates that I address this body with a report on the state of the union. And I have no intention of letting these would-be terrorists deflect me from fulfilling my duty."

This brought on a round of applause that threatened to go on for five minutes.

Hank Adams looked at Nancy and said, "Can I offer you a drink?"

Nancy looked up at Hank and smiled. She realized that there was something about him that she found intensely attractive. A little geeky, maybe. But then, she was a geek herself, wasn't she?

Erik Wade took a long deep breath and said, "So . . . before I was interrupted, I was making a point about American energy independence . . ."

"You know what?" Nancy said, putting her injured leg up on the couch. "Maybe you could turn that off while you're at it. I think I've had enough State of the Union for a lifetime."

EPILOGUE

Gideon Davis and his wife, Kate Murphy Davis, stood in the Oval Office and watched while President Erik Wade pinned the Presidential Medal of Freedom—America's highest civilian honor—on the chest of Tillman Davis. Beside them were Nancy Clement and her boyfriend, Hank Adams, and Evan Wilmot and his nurse, Margie Clete. The six of them were beaming.

President Wade walked back to his desk and said, "Usually I just sign these things and hand the pen to the guy who's getting the award and then I get them the hell out of my office as quick as I can. But today I have two documents to sign. I'm not going to read all this verbiage for the Medal of Freedom. You know what you did, Mr. Davis. But I do want to read this other thing."

He picked up a piece of heavy bond paper and read:

"Whereas Tillman Davis was convicted of several offenses related to the so-called Obelisk Incident, which occurred during his employment as a contractor for the Central Intelligence Agency;

"Whereas Tillman Davis was stripped of his rank and benefits as a serviceman in the United States military;

"Whereas Tillman Davis has given long and distinguished service to the United States of America;

"Whereas Tillman Davis has recently performed a unique act of courage and fortitude on behalf of the people of the United States;

"Therefore I pardon Tillman Davis of all Federal convictions and furthermore, by Executive Order, do restore to him his rank of Master Sergeant, United States Army (Retired) and to his pension and privileges thereto."

Erik Wade signed the paper, then walked to Tillman and shook his hand a second time. "You're a good soldier, Sergeant Davis," he said. "I'm sorry. I only hope this does a little to make up for what this government took from you."

"Thank you, Mr. President," Tillman said, looking straight ahead as tears slid down the sides of his nose.

After they left the office, Evan pulled Gideon aside and handed him the letter he had received from his father.

"I'm not sure what I should do with this," he said. "Turn it over to the FBI?"

Gideon read the letter. "He wanted you to have it."

"It doesn't really explain anything."

"He thought it did."

Evan considered this. "My father was a complicated man," he said finally. "But I don't think I'll ever understand what he did."

"Then maybe you should hold on to the letter."

Evan nodded. "Maybe I should."

Gideon handed the letter back to the young man. "Good luck to you, Evan."

"Thank you, Mr. Davis. Good luck to you, too."

Then Gideon took Kate's hand, and the two of them left Evan alone with his nurse. There was really nothing else to say, Gideon knew, and nothing else a man could do to make it right between a father and a son. Only time—or a brother—could heal all.

ACKNOWLEDGMENTS

After completing *The Obelisk*, I was humbled. Trying to write a novel is a sufficiently daunting endeavor, but doing it while trying to maintain a career as a television producer is pure folly. I will be forever grateful to my patient and beautiful wife, Cami, who continues to indulge my outsized ambitions even as she pursues her own. Both of us would agree, though, that we did our best work together, raising three great kids—Micah, Arlo, and Capp.

What started as a crash course in the publishing business has turned into a real education because of Richard Abate; I owe so much to you. To Rick Rosen, a super agent, but an even better friend, thank you for your wisdom and for believing in me. Since these books are about brothers, I am especially lucky to count among my best friends my own brothers, Lawrence and Richard.

To my assistant, my right hand, and my friend, Jose Cabrera, thank you for getting me through each day. To Carlos Bernard, thank you for giving a voice to Gideon and Tillman, and the entire cast of characters who populate these books.

To the entire team at Touchstone, thank you for your patience and professionalism. David Falk has been a master strategist in helping these books find an audience, and Stacy Creamer has been my greatest champion. Her enthusiasm is infectious and inspiring, eclipsed only by her intelligence and good taste.

Finally, I am grateful to the many authors whose work has not only provided me with hours of enjoyment, but has also inspired me to join their ranks. Among these, I owe special thanks to Walter Sorrells and Cameron Stracher. Without their generosity and talent, this book would still be an unfinished file on my laptop.

Go back to where it all started, as Gideon Davis battles the clock
to bring in a rogue agent – his own brother.

THE
OBELISK

Paperback: 978-1-84983-084-3
Ebook: 978-1-84737-905-4

Available now at your local bookshop and online.

Turn the page for a sneak preview.

PROLOGUE

COLE RANSOM WAS TIRED from the long flight, though not too tired to admire the functional design of the airport. Passing easily through customs, he followed the bilingual signs that led him outside to the area for ground transportation. He didn't lose a step as the glass doors slid open and he walked outside, where he was hit by a whoosh of blazing tropical air. Squinting against the impossibly bright sun, he could see the glass and steel spires of the capital city of the Sultanate of Mohan rising in the distance.

A man—unmistakably American—stood next to a black Suburban parked by the curb. He wore dark wraparound sunglasses, a camo baseball cap, and a heavy beard. An ID badge hung from his belt. The sign in his hand said dr. cole ransom. If not for the beard, he would have looked like a soldier or a cop.

"Dr. Ransom," the man said, lowering his sign and holding out his hand. Ransom reached out to shake it, but the man smiled. "I'll take your bags, sir," the man said.

"Right. Sorry," Ransom said, handing him his suitcase.

"I can take the other one if you want," the bearded man said, nodding toward Ransom's laptop.

"That's okay," Ransom said. "I'll hold on to it." He had come to Mohan on the biggest job of his career. The last thing he needed was his laptop getting smashed or stolen.

The driver put Ransom's suitcase into the back of the Suburban and closed the gate, then opened the rear passenger door for Ransom, who climbed inside.

The driver settled behind the wheel, then glanced at Ransom in the rearview. "Dr. Ransom, before we get going, you might want to double-check that you've got everything. Bags, passport, computer?"

Ransom took a quick inventory. "Yeah, that's everything. And you can call me Cole. I'm just a structural engineer."

The driver smiled as he started the ignition. "I know who you are, sir."

Ransom was, in fact, one of the finest structural engineers in the world. He was here in the Sultanate of Mohan to test the structural integrity of the Obelisk—a newly built deep-sea oil rig, the largest and most expensive in the history of man's quest for crude. There had been problems with the motion-damping system, and he was here to sort them out.

The Suburban exited the airport through a security gate, then turned onto a service road. To the right stretched a long swath of deserted beach and beyond it, the glittering blue surface of the South China Sea. Ransom would be spending the next few weeks somewhere out there. As the Obelisk was being phased into service, it had begun to exhibit some troubling sway characteristics in rough seas. Kate Murphy, the manager of the rig, suspected a design flaw. The rig's designers insisted that she was being paranoid, or at the very least, that she was trying to cover her ass to cover her production shortfall. Ransom had talked extensively with Kate before flying out, and she didn't sound even remotely like an alarmist. But you never really knew. Ransom had come here to run some tests and see who was right.

The Suburban suddenly lifted and fell on its suspension, pulling Ransom from his thoughts. The driver had turned off the service road onto a short gravel track that led down to the beach. He stopped the Suburban in what looked like an abandoned quarry. Ransom was puzzled.

"Why are we stopping here?"

"I need to make sure you've got your passport," the driver said.

Ransom gave the driver a curious look. That was the second time he'd asked about the passport.

"I told you before. I've got it."

"I should probably hold on to it up here."

"Why?"

"We've had some civil unrest these last few weeks. We'll be passing through some checkpoints the government's put up, and I'll need to show the soldiers your passport." The bearded man held out his hand, palm up.

Ransom wondered why the driver hadn't asked for it back at the airport as he dipped into his breast pocket for his passport and handed it to the driver. The bearded man scrutinized the little blue booklet. Ransom felt his heart rate speed up slightly, felt a tickle of concern in the back of his neck.

"This civil unrest . . . how serious is it?" Ransom asked.

The bearded man lowered the passport and looked up at Ransom. "Ever hear of the terrorist Abu Nasir?"

Ransom frowned and shook his head. "No, I haven't."

"Now you have."

Ransom saw the big black circle pointing at him before he realized the driver was holding a large automatic pistol in his hand. Then the driver shot him in the face.

CHAPTER ONE

UNTIL HE TRIED PUTTING on his tuxedo, Gideon Davis didn't realize how much weight he'd gained. The extra pounds were hardly noticeable on his muscular six-foot-one frame, but Gideon had felt the tug across his shoulders when he buttoned his jacket earlier that afternoon. Now, it felt even tighter, and he tried to keep himself from squirming in his chair as the president of the United States addressed the General Assembly of the United Nations.

". . . ten thousand lives have been lost in the bloody civil war between the Guaviare militia and the armed forces of the Colombian government, most of them innocent civilians. For years, both sides repeatedly rejected calls for a cease-fire, until the prospect of a peaceful resolution to the conflict seemed unattainable to everyone in the international community. Everyone . . . except for one man." President Alton Diggs nodded toward Gideon, who smiled a smile that felt as tight as his tuxedo. Being in the spotlight was something he still hadn't grown accustomed to.

Seventeen hours earlier, Gideon had been sitting in a jungle hut in Colombia, while armed men prowled around, waiting for an excuse to start shooting one another. The cease-fire he'd negotiated was the culmination of a three-month-long series of marathon sessions during which he'd spent day and night shuttling between government and rebel forces, usually eating the same meal twice—once with each faction—which accounted for the extra ten pounds he'd put on. In order to keep the warring sides at the table, he'd partaken of huge heaping portions of *ajiaco,* the traditional stew made of chicken, corn, potatoes, avocado, and *guascas,* a local herb, and *chunchullo*, fried cow intestines. As effective a diplomatic strategy as it was, Gideon knew that no amount of food would make the cease-fire hold. Chances were slim that it would last through the month. But the president had told him the best way to maintain the cease-fire was to get the international community invested, and the best way to get them invested was through a major media event. And the media loved Gideon Davis.

President Diggs continued reciting for the audience some high-lights of Gideon's career as a Special Presidential Envoy. He credited Gideon with defusing crises from the Balkans to Waziristan, and for being among the first public figures with the courage to argue that the United States needed to rethink its approach to the war on ter-ror. To his detractors, Gideon was dangerous—a pie-in-the-sky slave to political correctness who thought the enemies of Western civiliza-tion could be jawboned into holding hands and singing "Kumbaya." But anyone who'd ever spent any time with Gideon knew how far from the truth that was. They knew he was a straight talker with zero tolerance for bullshit. They knew he listened to people. Simple enough virtues, but ones rarely found in Washington—which was why some insiders had tagged Gideon as the fastest rising star in American politics. Before Gideon had left for Colombia, President Diggs had let slip that some party bigwigs were considering him for one of several upcoming races. One rumor even had Gideon on the president's short list of potential running mates. This caught Gideon by surprise, since he'd never had any real political ambitions. Expos-ing his private life to that kind of scrutiny, and having to make the inevitable compromises that come with holding public office, had no interest for him. But the prospect of wielding enough power to make a real difference in world affairs had caused Gideon to rethink his position. It was one of the reasons he'd agreed to squeeze into his tuxedo to accept this award from the president, who was now wind-ing up his introduction.

". . . more than simply building bridges, this man has dedicated himself to that ancient and most sacred cornerstone of our moral code: Thou Shalt Not Kill. And so, it is my great privilege to present the United Nations Medal of Peace to one of the great peacemakers of our time, Gideon Davis."

Gideon approached the podium to a generous stream of applause. He shook the president's hand, then bowed his head to allow him to place the ribboned medallion around his neck.

"Thank you, Mr. President," Gideon said, before acknow-ledging several other heads of state whom protocol deemed worthy of acknowledgment. "This is a great honor, and I accept it with gratitude and humility. All of us in this room know that peace is more than just the absence of war . . . it's also the absence of poverty and injustice. The real work still lies ahead of us, and its ultimate success depends on the diplomatic and economic support of every country represented in this room tonight." As Gideon continued to talk about the necessity of international solidarity, he saw a woman in a red dress stifle a yawn. He was losing them. But that didn't stop him from making the point he wanted to make—that the real heroes were the men and women in Colombia who had found the courage to compromise and to break the cycle of violence that had claimed the lives of so many of their countrymen. "With your support, their goodwill and hard work might actually make this a just and lasting peace. They're the ones we should be honoring tonight. And so I share this award with them." He took off the medal, held it in the air over his head.

But his gesture was met with silence.

I blew it, Gideon thought to himself. These people hadn't come here to be reminded of their moral and economic obligations. They'd come to feel good. They'd come expecting Gideon to shovel out the kind of self-congratulatory rhetoric that keeps the United Nations in business. Gideon scolded himself for ever thinking otherwise and wished he'd found an excuse to stay home and get some sleep.

But then the applause started. Sudden and decisive, like a thunderclap followed by a great rain that just kept going until it flooded the room with the collective approval of every person in the audience. Even the woman in the red dress was clapping. And for a moment, Gideon allowed himself to feel a flicker of hope that the cease-fire he'd worked so hard to make happen just might last. At least for a little while.

A few minutes later, Gideon was ushered into a large adjoining room. As successful as his speech had been, he had no illusions that it would have any real impact on the cease-fire. Making speeches was the easy part. Turning the enthusiasm of politicians and diplomats into real action was a much taller order. Most of the people here couldn't be counted on to follow through on any of the wine-inspired promises they'd made. Some of them were powerless; others were simply full of shit.

An embassy official from the Netherlands introduced himself to Gideon, who remembered that the man had been his country's foreign minister before being sidelined to an embassy post because of an ongoing relationship with a call girl. "You are a visionary," the embassy official said, his small hand clamping around Gideon's bicep.

Gideon did his best to smile. "I appreciate the compliment, but I just did what the president sent me to do."

"Your modesty is attractive, of course," the man said, "but you do yourself an injustice when—"

"Mr. Davis? I'm sorry to interrupt . . ."

Gideon turned toward the speaker. Unlike the people around him—all of them wearing tuxedos or evening gowns—the man who was addressing him wore a crisp military uniform. Dress blues with a white web belt. His hair was trimmed high and tight, with the side-walls rarely seen outside the United States Marine Corps.

"The president would like to see you."

"Excuse me," Gideon said to the embassy official, grateful for an excuse to end their conversation before it had a chance to start.

The embassy official glared at the marine, clearly unaccustomed to being interrupted by some lowly soldier, as he parted the crowd for Gideon.

The marine led Gideon to a door. Posted on either side was a pair of Secret Service agents. One of them opened the door for Gideon, who entered a large conference room, where President Diggs was talking quietly to a plain but pleasant-faced man in his sixties with the jowly, careworn expression of a hound dog. It was Earl Parker, Gideon's friend and mentor, and as close to a father as anyone in his life.

"Uncle Earl . . ."

"You were good in there," Parker said. "Truly inspiring."

"I didn't know you were here."

"I was standing in back," Parker said, smiling. "I'm proud of you, son."

Gideon returned Parker's smile, surprised at how eager he still was for the older man's approval.

He had known Earl Parker most of his life. Parker was not actually his uncle, but he had been a friend of his father's, and after Gideon's parents died twenty years ago, Earl Parker had stepped in, becoming almost a father figure to him—and to his older brother, Tillman. After their parents' deaths they had gone to live with a foster family. But Parker had come to visit them every weekend or two, playing football in the yard with them, checking on their progress in school, and generally acting as though they were related by blood. They had wondered enough about his constant attention to eventually ask him why he spent so much time with them. He explained simply that he had served in the Marines with their father and owed him a debt so great that caring for his sons would not even begin to repay it.

Beyond the fact that he'd never married, the boys knew precious little about Uncle Earl's personal life. Which didn't stop Gideon from trying to assemble some rough biography based on his observation of certain details. Like Parker's teeth. They weren't good, indicating an upbringing in the sort of family where dentistry was considered a great extravagance. When he spoke, his accent had the marble-swallowing quality found only in the highest, most desperate hills of east Tennessee.

But the public record had also yielded some choice facts, which is how Gideon first learned that beneath that modest exterior was an extraordinary man. Parker had been the first and only Rhodes scholar to come from East Tennessee State University. After his stint at Oxford, he enlisted in the Army, and served for eight years as a Marine, before going on to hold a string of increasingly powerful jobs in various departments and agencies of the United States government whose functions were rarely clear to the average American. His current job was deputy national security advisor, and his was generally considered to be one of the most important voices on foreign policy in the White House. Some said even more important than that of the secretary of state.

It was Uncle Earl who'd brought Gideon into the State Department, convincing him to leave his position at the United Nations. But after the Twin Towers fell, the apprentice found himself challenging his mentor. Gideon started supporting the position that the United States needed to engage more fully with the Islamic world, using the tools of soft power, like diplomacy and economic aid, while Parker argued that overwhelming military force was the only thing our enemies understood. Gideon and Parker had always engaged in good-natured debates over their political differences. There had been a time when the vigor of those debates had been part of the bond that connected them. But in recent years, their policy differences had begun to strain their personal relationship—especially as Gideon's influence with the president grew. Both men were pained by the widening rift between them, but neither knew quite what to do about it.

Gideon looked from Uncle Earl back to the president, who was now speaking. "How familiar are you with the Sultanate of Mohan?"

"Just what I've read in the State Department briefs." Gideon proceeded to tell them everything he knew about the small island nation—that it was equidistant between Malaysia and the Philippines, with a population of somewhere between five and six million people, 90 percent of them Malay-speaking Muslims, 5 percent ethnic Chinese and Indians, and a smattering of off-the-census tribes living in the uplands. Gideon also knew that Mohan was more or less the personal possession of the Sultan, who had ruthlessly put down an Islamist insurgency a few years earlier. With some back-channel military assistance from the United States, the Sultan's armed forces had managed to contain the jihadis to a few remote provinces.

The president nodded tightly. "Except it turns out the jihadis were down but not out. Once they realized how much oil was buried beneath those coastal waters, they started recruiting and rearming. And while you were in Colombia, they came out of hiding. They're moving against several of the inland provinces, and our friend the Sultan is in some serious trouble."

None of this had even been on Gideon's radar when he headed down to South America.

"I need you and Earl to get over there."

"When?"

"Right away."

Gideon ran his hands across his tuxedo. "In this monkey suit? I don't even have a toothbrush."

The president's eyes glittered with amusement. "I hear they have toothbrushes in Mohan."

"With respect, sir, I just got back a few hours ago. I haven't even been briefed on Mohan, I don't know the conflict points or the key players on either side—"

Uncle Earl interrupted, "This isn't about negotiating a truce."

"Then what's it about?"

"Your brother," he said.

Although Uncle Earl's face rarely betrayed emotion of any kind, it was as troubled as Gideon had ever seen him. "Tillman needs our help."

"Our help with what?"

Parker wrestled with the question before he finally answered. "We've got forty-eight hours to save his life." He glanced down at his watch. "I take that back. Make it forty-seven."

CHAPTER TWO

I T WAS AN AMBUSH, pure and simple. Kate Murphy had been told that she would be testifying at the Senate Subcommittee on Foreign Policy as a technical expert on offshore drilling. Deepwater fields had been discovered in the South China Sea, a few miles off the coast of Mohan. As manager of the Obelisk—the largest and most sophisticated rig in those waters—she had come prepared to talk about the trends and technology of offshore drilling.

But now that she was here, she saw the truth. She hadn't been subpoenaed to talk about horizontal drilling or steam injection or how she calculated the production of an underwater field. She had been brought here to get clobbered.

It had started pleasantly enough. The six men and one woman sitting at the horseshoe-shaped table facing her looked so much more human than they did on TV. Smaller, older, more rumpled, shoulders flecked with dandruff, teeth stained with coffee. They looked like a bunch of retirees, sitting around the old folks' home in their Sunday clothes.

The first questions had been disinterested softballs. What were the estimated reserves of oil and gas in the South China Sea? How many rigs were located there? How many oil tankers moved through the Strait of Malacca?

Then the questioning shifted to Senator McClatchy, the chairman of the subcommittee. He was a doddering-looking old fellow, with a thin comb-over and a slight tremor in his left hand. His watery eyes were magnified by his thick glasses, giving him a slightly idiotic look. He smiled uncertainly, as though not entirely sure where he was.

"Miz Murphy, it's so kind of you to fly all the way over from Mohan, just to talk to us."

"It's my pleasure, Senator," Kate Murphy said.

"We do appreciate it. I know you're a busy person, got all kinds of important things to tend to. I bet running an oil rig, a young gal like you, you must be a heck of a . . . a heck of a . . ." He seemed to lose his train of thought.

"Well, thank you, Senator," she said after the moment of silence had begun to stretch to an embarrassing length.

Then the senator's vapid smile faded and his eyes seemed to clear. "Now having gotten all the necessary formalities out of the way—could I prevail on you to tell me why you and the last four witnesses from Trojan Energy have all lied to me, to this subcommittee, and to the American people?"

She felt a flush rise to her cheeks. "Ex*cuse* me?"

"Let me rephrase the question. Isn't it true that your company, Trojan Energy, has on numerous occasions paid out ransom money to pirates over the past year?"

She stuttered, "Pirates?"

"Islamists. Jihadis. Insurgents. Call them whatever you want, but please answer my question."

"Honestly, I'm not all that sure what—"

"And isn't it true that these pirates are closely allied with Islamic terrorists in the Philippines, in Malaysia, and in the Sultanate of Mohan?"

"Sir, I was under the impression I was brought here to testify about oil drilling technology."

Senator McClatchy spread his hands widely and gave her a broad smile. "You were, were you?" Senator McClatchy's smile faded just the slightest bit. "See, and I was under the impression that you were here to truthfully and completely answer the questions I directed to you. *Whatever* questions I directed to you."

"I just—"

"You just what? You just wanted to avail yourself of your constitutional right to hold your tongue so as not to incriminate yourself?"

"I didn't say that."

"Then why don't you just tell this committee the truth? That Trojan Energy is funding terrorism."

Kate Murphy could feel the red spots forming on her high cheekbones, the ones that always popped up right before she said something she shouldn't. So she kept her mouth shut.

Senator McClatchy looked down at his notes. "How much do you know about a man named Abu Nasir?"

"Only that he's some sort of terrorist in Mohan. I mean, if the guy actually exists. Some people seem to think he's just a myth."

"Oh, he's not myth. I guarantee you that." McClatchy fixed his eyes on her for a long time. "Are you aware that Trojan Energy has paid over forty-seven million dollars in ransom to Abu Nasir in the past twelve months?"

She swallowed. "If that's true, I was not aware of it."

"Really?"

"Those decisions are above my pay grade." Kate Murphy had of course heard rumors that various ships owned by Trojan affiliates had been seized by pirates, and that substantial ransoms had been paid. But her bosses at Trojan had kept those details private.

"Above your pay grade. I see. Except it is a matter of the public record that Trojan Energy continues to receive U.S. government loans and loan guarantees to encourage its participation in the Obelisk project. Which means either you're ignorant or you're lying."

"You're free to draw whatever conclusions you like."

"So you refuse to comment on whether or not American taxpayer funds have been funneled into the coffers of Islamic terrorists and pirates."

Kate had an urge to stand up and shout that she knew nothing about any of this. But instead she kept her voice low and cool. "Refuse? No, Senator, I'm not refusing. I keep telling you, my job is to run a rig and make sure that when my bosses pull the handle, oil comes out. I just don't have the answers to your questions."

Senator McClatchy's eyes narrowed. "Don't you think that a bunch of ducking and dodging is out of place when our national security is being threatened by a bunch of fanatical terrorists?"

"I'm not dodging—"

The senator cut her off. "Don't you think it's time to start taking action? To stand shoulder to shoulder with our friends like the Sultan and fight our enemies instead of subsidizing them?"

Kate Murphy sighed. She knew none of this had anything to do with her personally, but it made her angry that she'd been brought here to get made a fool of on national television just so Senator McClatchy could rattle his saber and score some political points.

"Do you really think the United States of America should just sit around helplessly while these criminals and thugs take off with millions of dollars' worth of oil revenue *we* pulled from the ground with *our* technology and expertise?"

"I keep telling you, I don't know enough about the situation to answer that question." Then, without thinking, she added, "But if what you're saying is true, I damn sure hope we won't."

For a moment Senator McClatchy glared at her. Then a loud bleat of laughter escaped his lips. "Bless your heart," he said. "Young lady, you make me want to stand up and salute the flag."

When she was finally dismissed, Kate was still hot with anger. Her bosses at Trojan Energy had sent her to Washington because she knew enough about the Obelisk to be a credible witness but not enough to cause any real damage. She couldn't decide if she was angrier at them for making her their sacrificial goat, or at these smug politicians who spent their lives gaining and maintaining power by tearing down other people. So she decided to let it go and checked her BlackBerry. For some reason she couldn't access her email or her phone messages. Her display window read systems error. Being out of touch with her rig, even for a day, left her feeling uneasy and incomplete, the same way she imagined other women her age felt about being away from their husbands and children. Kate thought to herself that if Ben were still alive, she might have been one of those women. His face with the crooked smile appeared to her, then vanished just as quickly—along with the expectation of a life she knew would never be hers.

As she made her way down the corridor, she saw the subcommittee members emerging from the hearing room. They'd apparently adjourned after her testimony for a break. McClatchy was heading in her direction with another senator. She tried to avoid him, pretending to make a call on her broken BlackBerry. But he abruptly excused himself from his colleague and waited for her to disconnect from her imaginary call. "Sorry if I was a bit rough on you in there, Miss Murphy. Nothing personal, you understand."

"Right. Nothing personal," Kate said, trying to keep her voice flat.

Kate expected him to move past her, but instead he moved closer. Close enough that Kate could smell his sour breath. He lowered his voice to an intimate tone that made her skin crawl. "Listen, if you've got some time tonight, I was hoping you could join me for dinner. I'd like to show you around town, have a little fun."

Kate blinked, stunned. She felt like saying, *Are you out of your fucking mind, old man?* But instead she heard herself thanking the senator for the invitation, politely declining, and telling him she had to catch an early morning flight. Which was true. And once she brushed past the sour-smelling senator, the thought of getting back to the Obelisk eased her mind. The anger drained from her body, replaced by the comforting knowledge that tomorrow she'd be back on her rig, the only home she'd known in nearly two years.

A chopper was idling on the roof waiting to take Gideon and Earl Parker to McGuire Air Force Base. It was a white Sikorsky bearing unobtrusive air force markings. No sooner had they strapped in than the bird was aloft. It was a stunning view, the chopper sailing below the tops of the tallest buildings.

As they scudded over the massive construction site where the Twin Towers had once stood, Gideon had to restrain himself from asking Parker what the hell was going on. Back at the UN, President Diggs had preempted Gideon's questions, telling him it was a long and complicated story, and since they were working against time, Parker would brief him during their flight to Mohan.

Even if Gideon had tried to speak during the chopper flight, the noise inside the cabin would have made conversation impossible. So Gideon found himself thinking about his older brother. How they had fought for as long as he could remember—first over childhood treasures like candy and toys, later over sports and girls, and later still, over politics—and how all their years of fighting had come to a head one night seven years earlier. They'd exchanged some ugly words, too ugly for even the most sincere apology to erase. Not that either of them had even tried. But since then, they hadn't seen or even spoken to each other.

At Teterboro Municipal Airport in New Jersey, Gideon and Parker were escorted from the Sikorsky to a waiting Gulfstream G5. They boarded the jet and settled into a pair of leather seats that faced each other over a gleaming teak table. Before the engines had even spooled up, Gideon pressed Earl. "Okay, Uncle Earl. Tell me what this is about."

"You heard the president. There's not a simple answer—"

"Just tell me what's going on," Gideon insisted.

Earl Parker fixed Gideon with a look, then sighed. "I hate to do this to you, son, but you need some context to understand the trouble that Tillman's gotten himself into." From his briefcase, he pulled a thick, bound folder. "This briefing book has up-to-the-minute intel on Mohan. It'll help explain what's happened to your brother. Get through as much of it as you can, and I'll fill in the rest." Before Gideon could speak, Uncle Earl preempted him with an reassuring smile. "I promise."

"Twenty-four hours to save his life? That sounds a little melodramatic."

Parker regarded Gideon compassionately. "I'm not being coy, son, but I do need you to read the briefing. Especially the sections about Abu Nasir."

Gideon felt his body being pressed back into his seat as the Gulfstream accelerated down the runway. He looked out the window as they lifted into the air, climbing quickly before banking away from the Manhattan skyline. Then Gideon turned his attention to the heavy book Uncle Earl had handed him.

Abu Nasir? Gideon remembered seeing the name in the State Department briefs he'd read, but he couldn't recall anything more. *Who was Abu Nasir?*

CHAPTER THREE

GIDEON HAD LEFT BOGOTÁ on the redeye, so he'd only gotten a few hours of sleep. But Uncle Earl's cryptic words kept his fatigue at bay as he propped the briefing book on the table in front of him and tried to absorb as much as he could.

Mohan had been an independent state for nearly four hundred years. The State Department described the current Sultan as a decent and tolerant-enough leader who'd grown the economy tenfold by tapping the oil reserves beneath Mohan's coastal waters. The latest drilling project was a billion-dollar state-of-the-art rig owned by Trojan Energy and christened the Obelisk. If the geology was correct, it would be the most productive rig in history. Three other major energy companies had already closed agreements with the Sultan and were drawing up plans for a dozen more rigs just like the Obelisk.

But the Sultan's government also suffered from the typical problems found in most modern nations where one royal family runs the show: nepotism, corruption, and the lack of a broad power base. These weaknesses had created conditions that were now being exploited by the jihadis. No longer content to govern themselves under Sharia law within the boundaries the Sultan allowed them, they were agitating for another insurgency. The Sultan had requested military assistance from the United States to help suppress the jihadis, and a core congressional group, led by Senator McClatchy, wanted to comply. But President Diggs had refused, reluctant to get our troops stuck in the middle of another civil quagmire halfway across the world.

Of the several insurgent factions in Mohan, one was headed by the man Parker had mentioned, Abu Nasir. What Gideon found most interesting was that Nasir was not Mohanese. He was an unidentified Westerner wanted by the Sultan for smuggling drugs and dealing arms. He'd also developed a reputation for piracy and kidnapping, holding Western oil executives hostage for impossibly large ransoms, which he used to fund the insurgency.

Gideon spent another hour wading through the briefing book until the words started to blur. He read the same section over and over until he finally gave up, leaning back in his comfortable leather chair, and sinking into a fitful sleep.

By the time he woke up, the G5 was descending through a scattering of puffy clouds toward a large land mass in the distance.

Parker was drinking coffee from a mug with the presidential seal on the side and working on his laptop. He looked up over his reading glasses and said, "Sleeping Beauty awakes!"

Gideon took a moment to orient himself. According to the bulkhead monitor, their estimated time of arrival was in twenty minutes.

Parker glanced down at the briefing book, which was splayed open, spine up, on Gideon's lap. "I see you didn't get very far," he said, smiling with uncharacteristic affection. "You needed that sleep pretty bad."

"Yeah. But since we're landing soon, what I really need is for you to tell me what's going on."

"How much did you read about Abu Nasir?"

"No more questions, Uncle Earl. Just tell me what's happening with my brother."

"All right." Parker nodded but hesitated a good ten seconds before he spoke again. "We have good intelligence that Abu Nasir is your brother."

Gideon blinked. Unable to make sense of the words he'd just heard.

Parker dropped his shoulders, as if finally unburdening some great weight he'd been carrying. "He's dug himself into a hole, and now he needs you and me to pull him out before he gets himself killed."

Parker allowed Gideon to absorb this before continuing. "I know it sounds insane. I'm still trying to get my own head around it."

"How good is this intelligence?"

"Very," Parker said, then handed Gideon a photo from the pocket of his briefing book. Behind the CLASSIFIED stencil was a grainy surveillance photo of a bearded man who was clearly unaware that he was being photographed, focused instead on someone or something out of the frame. The features behind the beard resembled Tillman's, yet it was not him at all. The hot anger that had once animated his eyes was now extinguished, replaced by an icy and far more lethal indifference.

"This is Tillman?"

Parker nodded. "It was taken a little over a month ago."

Studying the face of the stranger reminded Gideon of why he'd decided not to follow Tillman into the army and had gone to college instead. Gideon knew that his brother's reasons were more pragmatic than patriotic. He'd enlisted in order to avoid serving time for a street brawl during which he'd almost killed a man five inches taller and a hundred pounds heavier than he was. The man was left in such rough shape that the D.A. tried to bump the charges from assault and battery to attempted murder. Because of Uncle Earl's well-connected intervention, Tillman managed to avoid prison, and found himself in the army. He thrived as a soldier and was quickly promoted to the most elite ranks of the Special Forces. He'd finally found a way to channel the anger and the violence that had always run through him like a live wire. As angry as Tillman had once been, though, Gideon couldn't bring himself to believe Parker's story.

"The last time you spoke to him, where was Tillman working?" Parker asked.

"Afghanistan."

"After that, he was sent to South America, then Indonesia. But Mohan was his first long-term assignment. Al Qaeda and its offshoots had been making inroads with the local population, and Tillman was sent to infiltrate their ranks. And he did. Posing as a Chechen arms dealer, he fed crucial information to the Sultan's intelligence service. With Tillman's help, the Sultan was able to beat back the insurgency." Parker sighed heavily. "But that's when things started going wrong." Parker tapped the seat beside him. "Come over here so I can show you."

Gideon switched seats, watching as Parker moved his blinking cursor and clicked one of his desktop icons. A map of the South China Sea appeared on-screen. Parker traced his finger along the southern edge. "See this skinny little strip of ocean here, from the Strait of Malacca just below Singapore, up to the coast off Vietnam? Sixty thousand ships, billions of tons of goods, over a trillion dollars' worth of commerce, pass through this corridor every year. It's one of the most heavily trafficked shipping lanes in the world, and the one most vulnerable to piracy.

"Last year, off the Somalia coast, we saw just how vulnerable. The jurisdictional issues are messy, the money is huge, and the shipping companies view piracy as a cost of doing business. A write-off. A ship gets seized, they don't call the navy, they reach for their checkbooks. Spending a few million bucks now and then is easier than jeopardizing the safety of their crews and cargoes."

Gideon held up his hand. "Hold on. What's this got to do with Tillman?"

"It was his cover story. Disaffected American soldier turned independent contractor. To prove himself, he seized an oil tanker bound for Mohan. It was all playacting, of course, with a local crew he'd put together and a cooperative vessel he'd hired to go along with the setup.

"Problem was, it worked too well. The jihadis wanted Tillman to do it again. He tried to stall, but they kept pushing. Next thing we knew, he and his men had seized a second ship. This time, it was a real one. Tillman claimed he had to do it in order to avoid blowing his cover. Said it was worth doing a few bad things to stop some much worse things from happening, and the Agency went along with it. Nobody gets hurt, a couple of big companies lose a negligible amount of money, all for the greater good. But after a couple more seizures, he broke off contact with his handler and started doing this stuff for real."

"What is that supposed to mean?"

"It means he started identifying with the people he was sent to destroy. He changed his name, became a Muslim. Or, I should say, a follower of the violent extremists who've perverted and co-opted that religion."

Gideon shook his head. "I don't believe you."

Earl blew out his breath. "That doesn't make it any less true."

"How long have you known about this?"

"Almost a year."

"*A year?* And you're only telling me now?"

Parker's eyes flashed. "Do not play the guilt card with me, son. The last time I asked you to reach out to Tillman, you told me to mind my own damn business." Parker was right. Gideon had traveled the world brokering peace between warring parties, but he'd been unwilling to reach out to his own brother. A dozen times he'd picked up the phone to call him. Each time, he'd hung up before the connection even went through.

Parker lowered his voice to a wistful register. "Besides, I knew there wasn't anything you could do about it. I tried contacting Tillman myself through an intermediary, begged him to come in. But he never even responded. For him to lose himself like that . . . I can't even begin to imagine the twisted logic that must have gotten into his head."

"Bullshit." It was the only word that fit. "Tillman may have changed, but he's not someone who changes sides. Not like this."

"You need to understand, he's not the same person anymore. Last year, in this shipping lane, over a hundred ships were seized. We've got multiple intelligence sources saying your brother was behind at least thirty of those."

Gideon kept shaking his head as Parker continued. "Problem was he got so good at it, he became a target himself. He pissed off the insurance and shipping companies. He pissed off some of the more radical jihadists in Mohan, who saw him as an outsider. Even worse, he pissed off the Sultan, the man he'd been sent over to help out in the first place. And now that the insurgency is gaining momentum—"

Gideon finished his sentence. "The Sultan wants him dead."

Parker nodded. "He ordered his top operatives to hunt down Tillman. They've been spreading around lots of money, squeezing some captured insurgents pretty hard. Two days ago, they located him."

"How did you find out about this?"

"From Tillman."

"You spoke to my brother?"

"Not directly, no. He contacted me through a man named Prang. He's a general in the Sultan's army who Tillman worked with. Apparently, your brother kept a back channel open with Prang, even after he went dark. Prang warned Tillman about the hit, and he's the one who's brokering this whole deal."

"What deal?"

"Tillman's agreed to surrender himself and provide intelligence about the insurgency if the Sultan calls off his hit. He's holding some big cards—safe houses, weapons caches, organizational structure, leadership, money flow, the whole nine yards."

"Then the Sultan agreed to call off the hit."

"Only temporarily. He's giving us until tomorrow to bring him in. After that, it's open season."

"And President Diggs signed off on this?"

"Absolutely. He's already getting pressure to send troops to Mohan. If this insurgency gets any bigger, he may not have a choice. He'd much rather let Tillman disappear into witness protection than be forced to put our troops in harm's way."

Gideon's head was spinning.

"All right. So bring him in. I don't understand why you need me."

"Because Tillman only agreed to come in under one condition. If he could choose who President Diggs sends."

"And Tillman chose *me?*"

"You're the only one he trusts."

Below the descending plane, the lush green canopy of the jungle was receding, giving way to the tar paper rooftops and steel containers of the sprawling shantytown adjacent to the airport. "How exactly is this supposed to happen?" Gideon asked.

"General Prang is still working out the operational details. He's meeting us at the airport."

Gideon sat motionless, turning over in his head what he'd just heard. As impossible as it sounded, he knew he had no choice but to see it through. At least until he'd heard more.

"Tillman's a grown man," Parker said. "He made his own bed, I realize that . . . but I still feel responsible for him. I feel that way about both of you." Parker's eyes welled, and his voice had more gravel in it than usual. He cleared his throat, as if trying to break through the delta of emotions that had collected there.

The plane hit the tarmac with a jolt and a screech of tires. As the aircraft decelerated, Gideon stared down at the photograph and realized that his brother, his only blood relative, had become a complete stranger to him.

"You need to bring him home," Parker said.

Despite the sick feeling rising from the deepest part of himself, Gideon found himself nodding his head.